PRAISE FOR NED KELLY'S SON

'A great cover and a great book.' Peter Watt, Australian author.

'Congratulations on the publication – well deserved after all your hard work. Enjoy the giddy life of being an author.' A J (Sandy) Mackinnon, Australian author

'I have spent the last few days reading your book; well done, I really enjoyed it and had trouble putting it down.' D Talbot, Australian historian and author. Wandiligong.

'Trevor, I bought your book today; have to go to bed early tonight and get stuck into it. Couldn't put the damn thing down. Enjoyed it greatly. Well worth the wait.'
R Brown. Sale.

'Ned Kelly's Son, indeed! Many thanks for your intriguing story of the Dungarvan lady!' W. Fraher, curator, Waterford County Museum. Ireland.

'In telling an action-packed journey through many lives, Trevor has painted the Australian landscape in words. So real is the picture, the unexpected raunchiness made me blush.' M. Edwards, Designer. Gippsland.

'Orla – her life of adventure and endeavour, her family, her friends, all in the right place at the right time. What if ??? A darn good read.' Jill T. Farmer. Stockdale.

'Bloody hell Tucks, this is really good! What a read—just brilliant. It's a fascinating story well told. It was especially interesting for me, knowing a lot of the people and places personally. I will treasure it— and I will promote and recommend it far and wide.' Ian Stewart. Surveyor, Launceston.

'Good on you Trev. I trust it will be a great success, and it might even be taken up as a film.' Catherine Lewis. Publisher at Wild Dingo Press. St.Kilda.

'Just finished reading your book. Fabulous! It's one of those books – you want to know how it ends, but you are enjoying it so much you never want it to end. Well done!' Viv B. Chirnside Park.

'It just goes to show that your dedication over the past few years is going to pay off. WELL DONE.' M & P Welch. Belgrave.

'Compelling! The story line is as good as anything I've ever read, written by an Australian author. I had trouble putting it down and was genuinely sad when it finished. Can't wait for your next book.' Rocky M. Farmer. Sale.

'I want to congratulate you on completing, and publishing, such a meaty and well thought out novel. It was a really interesting read, and I especially liked the focus on "original" characters that haven't appeared in any other Ned Kelly story. You displayed a skill at weaving an engaging narrative, and often approached situations from multiple angles without making the story feel overburdened. I enjoyed your descriptions of the environment, which really captured the sounds, smells and feel of the Australian bush. April Newton, Director at Newt & Co, publishing. Parkville.

'Hi Trevor, just thought I'd drop you a note to say I very much enjoyed "Ned Kelly's Son". It was a great read.' Belinda Ritchie. Adventurer & Barrister. Brisbane.

'A riveting yarn.' Eugenie Navarre. 'Kelly family' researcher, author, journalist and farmer. Queensland & NSW.

'You have a talent for writing; crisp prose, an intriguing plot and believable characters. Looking forward to your next oeuvre.' Peter Synan. Retired humanities teacher and researcher of local history. Sale.

ALSO BY TREVOR TUCKER

Aussie Anecdotes

The Stolen Maps

A Sense of Justice

God Only Knows When

NED KELLY'S SON

A SAGA OF AUSTRALIAN HERITAGE, ALMOST LOST IN HISTORY

TREVOR TUCKER

TREVOR TUCKER PUBLISHING

For Shelley, and for Callum

Embrace your greatest gift — this only life.

DRAMATIS PERSONAE

Orlagh (Orla) Aileen O'Meara:
Ned Kelly's unheralded lover; mother of Niall.

Thought to have been born in January 1861
Died: 9th March 1894

Niall Haydn Kelly:
son of Edward (Ned) Kelly.

Born: 19th December 1880
Died: 17th January 1961

PREFACE

Ned Kelly was pleased with the success of his plan although the entire funds from the bank barely filled one saddle bag. Not a shot had been fired. And forever, the good people of Jerilderie would have something to talk about.

As nightfall approached, Ned and his men were joined by the fifth man who had been guarding their horses. Their retreat was not challenged. But knowing that word of their escapade would soon reach the traps in Albury, Wangaratta, and Benalla, despite having cut down the telegraph lines, the five riders brutally urged their horses through the moonlit night. As if understanding the value of that freedom their Walers bravely kept to their tasks.

About an hour before daybreak they reached the Murray River. After two hours rest, they crossed the river then headed for their familiar sanctuary in the Warby Ranges. Their ultimate destination was still at least seventy miles distant but the final leg of that ride could wait for a few days.

Ned never engaged in such sport within the Buckland Valley Goldfields, which is at the foot of Mt. Buffalo in North-Eastern Victoria, although this valley had several goldmining communities at the time and was arguably within 'his' territory. This valley meant something much different to Ned: a place of refuge rather than easy pickings and probably the only place where he ever felt at peace and safe. Unsurprisingly, therefore, Ned's whereabouts and activities during his visits there produced very little recorded history. What has been recorded is not in dispute — however, it is incomplete.

Looking up the valley from the flats of the Buckland River, green takes on a blue-grey tone. The distant mountain peaks, when devoid of snow, become a hazy white mantle when set against an azure summer sky. And much of what Ned would have seen and smelt on each occasion he visited the Buckland Valley, during his last summer of 1879/80, remains to be experienced today.

* * *

On a summer's afternoon, shadows cast by the ancient red gums of the Oxley Flats near Glenrowan unfailingly creep across the parched earth: inevitably those shadows will diffuse into night. And as each year inexorably sheds its seasons, regrettably many worthy historical events will become vague and are thus fated to be lost forever.

But not always!

What then are the odds that a chance meeting of like souls in 1958 would result in the resurrection of hidden accounts of a mother and her son, whose amazing lives challenge the legend of Australia's most iconic bushranger?

PART I

ORLAGH

1

————

Clutching a bundle of native flowers she had picked in a nearby paddock, Orla skipped contentedly for home while thinking how she could best arrange those flowers to surprise and impress her mother.

About forty yards from the house, her much loved pup, Tuppy, raced ahead to greet a member of the Royal Irish Constabulary who was leaning his bicycle against the front fence of their house block. Suddenly, without either warning or any apparent provocation, the man proceeded to cruelly, viciously, stomp on her innocent and beautiful pet.

Orla skidded to a halt, and then froze, gawping in disbelief, dumbstruck. Her skin crawled. *That nasty man has just killed my Tuppy*, she thought. *But he's a policeman! Oh God! Will he try to kill me now?*

Though confused, she forced herself not to cry. 'You rotten bastard.' Despite her young girl innocence, she unashamedly whispered her first ever swear word. Then, consumed by anger, she wanted to hit back, to punish.

Not wanting to be seen, Orla jumped behind a large oak tree. Her flowers fell to the ground, forgotten; her fingers were now balled into fists. Peering from behind the trunk, she knew intuitively — and precisely — what had to be done.

Ducking low, behind some dense shrubs, she crept towards the house until she was within a few yards of the distracted policeman... and Tuppy. For just a few moments, Orla stared at the pup as its chest heaved for the last time and its tiny heart fluttered to a stop.

By sheer luck, there at her feet was exactly what she needed — a garden stake! She picked it up, positioning herself behind the constable. After taking a deep breath, she swung the stake, axe-like and with all her strength, squarely into the back of his legs. The man screamed and collapsed onto his hands and knees. His helmet fell off. Like the pup, he hadn't expected such an attack.

Orla stood beside the policeman's prone body, and without hesitation, delivered a vicious blow to the back of his unprotected head. On contact, his body went rigid; then it sagged and lay motionless on the pathway, unseeing eyes returning the pup's lifeless gaze.

'Bastard! Bastard!' she hissed, as she kept belting into him. At the peak of her rage, her father grabbed her arms and lifted her off the ground. Firmly restrained, the stake having been forcibly discarded, Orla thrashed about with surprising strength.

'I hate him, Da! I hate that bad policeman,' she bawled, tears trickling down her cheeks. 'He's just killed my Tuppy!' Orla suddenly stopped struggling. 'Da, why? Why was he so cruel?' she implored between sobs of grief and while trying to regain her breath. 'All Tuppy did was piddle on the man's silly bike,' she added, pleading her case while staring into her father's concerned face... begging his understanding. 'He made me really sad, and *so angry*! That's why I gave him such a good whack, Da.'

'Well I'll be buggered!' Dan was bewildered by the scene in front of him. 'You go inside, my girl. I'll take care of Tuppy and get rid of this lousy peeler.'

'No, Da, I'll look after Tuppy,' she replied dejectedly, but with unexpected force.

* * *

IN HER FAVOURITE place at the rear of their property, Orla buried her beloved pup. She then collected some glistening white stones from a small beach formed by the broad sweep of a nearby stream, and used them to lovingly cover the small mound. Back by the stream, occasionally tossing a stick onto its smooth gliding surface, Orla mourned her loss. Her anger flared again. *When I'm a big girl*, she fervently resolved, *nobody will push me about! And watch out if anybody ever again tries to hurt my animals... or my family or my friends!* But another thought persisted. *Why are the English people so damn cruel?*

Later that evening at dinner, Dan dispassionately discussed the day's event. 'What if she'd killed the swine of a man?' He continued before he received a reply. 'He'll live, but I'll bet he's still got one hell of a headache. And to be sure, he's got no idea what or who hit him. Mind you, I put him right. I told the cruel bastard 'it must 'av been Divine Intervention, or perhaps, t'was the Little People who taught him a lesson.' They all howled with laughter.

Orla quietly chuckled as she dropped off to sleep, feeling strangely content with her new found hatred of the English. Her parents slept little; they agonized over how to handle any official repercussions. However, her older brothers Sean, Colm, Clive, and Liam joyfully celebrated their sister's 'magnificent stick work' at the local Dungarvan pub.

APART FROM THAT HARROWING EVENT, Orla's childhood was typical. But her teenage years were, well... interesting.

Orla was trusting but not gullible. She was quick to learn and always willing to help others. Fundamentally, she was an outgoing child who carried mostly endearing traits into her teenage years and adulthood. But she refused to be controlled. Those who tried usually regretted it.

By thirteen, Orla could almost match her father's way with horses. She rode astride and as hard and skilfully as any man, and she could extract the absolute best from any reined team.

She was also a 'natural' with firearms. Not only was she incredibly accurate with a rifle, she could manage her father's six shot revolving-cylinder Colts equally well with either hand. Somehow she hit every target, even moving targets - a feat, neither her father nor any of her brothers could believe, let alone rival. Dan also saw to it that Orla understood the seriousness of pointing a gun at an assailant.

'Remember *always*, my girl,' he pleaded. 'There's no second chance if you're dead. So, be first, and shoot to kill. If an opponent means business... *they will*, to be sure.'

At sixteen, Orla was relatively tall and endowed with an eye-catching figure, which gave her the appearance of a grown woman. She was extremely agile and blessed with unexpected stamina: she could dance all the waltzes, reels, and jigs better than most and was in constant demand at the local pub on Saturday nights whenever the dancing started.

Orla's skin was pale; her russet hair cut unfashionably short, revealing perfectly formed childlike ears and giving prominence to her high forehead and cheekbones. Her square jaw-line, small but straight nose, and slightly pointed chin gave her face an elfin appearance.

But her eyes were the major attraction — large, viridescent and seductive — they turned the head of many an eager young man. (In fact, she was extremely lucky not to have fallen pregnant after mischievously 'losing her virginity' on several lustful occasions.) If anyone, child, woman or man engaged her in conversation, those eyes enchanted her listeners... however, they could also flash unmistakeable menace. No longer were those dark green eyes beguiling, but intimidating and fierce; indeed, fierce enough to guarantee her preparedness to kill.

Her lips were full and perfectly formed and her teeth flashed a brilliant white when she smiled. Normally, she spoke in her relaxed lilting Irish brogue, always friendly and enthusiastic. Her mouth, alas, was her potential downfall. To steal from her, to attempt to molest her, to generally cross her in any way, or if she witnessed the mistreatment of children or animals, then what shamelessly flowed from that mouth left little to the imagination. Offenders were thus 'warned', and if anyone then doubted her threats, they usually backed off once their eyes met.

And, out of habit, as Orla departed such situations, she would laugh hysterically. There was no denying it; Orla knew she was excited by challenge.

At first, Orla's mother, Kathleen, prayed desperately that her daughter's tempestuousness would be replaced by conduct more befitting a decent Irish woman. Instinctively, she knew Orla would forever struggle to keep her God-given 'boyo skills' — and her mouth — in check.

In her quiet times, however, Orla sometimes contemplated her short temper and worried that people might unfairly judge her family after having just witnessed one of her outbursts.

Orla yearned to travel. Her parents encouraged her dream and did their best to prepare her for the eventuality. When Orla formally announced she was 'off to see world', her brothers initially opposed her plans. But in her quiet way, Kathleen pointed out that Orla had well and truly proven her ability to look after herself. Eventually, her brothers were placated; when their sister settled they would be most welcome to visit. *But what if Orla never settles down,* Kathleen agonized silently on their behalf. And then, just faintly alarmed, she confronted her next thought. *Dear God, what if my little girl never returns to Ireland?*

Tragedy then struck; her father died just before Orla's seventeenth birthday. A horse kicked him in the chest as he was trying to free the terrified animal from a tangle of fencing wire. Understandably, Dan's death caused considerable grief for the entire O'Meara family. Orla's sorrow only temporarily tamed her rush into adulthood.

Soon after Dan's death, Orla confided in her mother. 'Ma, I've been thinking. I'm feeling uneasy about how I'll cope when I'm away, without you and my boyo brothers being around, I mean. And I know I'll miss you one and all. But ma, I have to admit, I'm convinced that I need to do this. I want to be free of all the English shite we have to put up with, and to do things in my own time and in my own way. Is that selfish?'

'My dear girl, you sound so grown up,' Kathleen reassured her. 'But no, not selfish. Perhaps a bit naïve, though. You'll cope, my love, of that I have no doubt. But mark my words, you'll find life difficult at times. Anyway, I'm through trying to talk you out of this.' After a thoughtful pause, Kathleen added. 'You've made a good decision, young lady. Now get a move on, you've got packing to do and people to call on before you leave.'

Packing was easy: one small case represented her entire belongings. Orla took particular care in concealing her father's treasured Colts and ammunition. Kathleen presented Orla with money saved for the occasion, not a fortune, but more than she'd ever seen before.

The cold and overcast weather surrounding the dock at Cork draped another layer of gloom over their feelings of loss. After a tearful farewell and promises to write regularly, Orla boarded a ferry to Swansea, in Wales. Her excitement swamped any last minute feelings of apprehension or regret.

2

———————

London's mix of opulence, art, industry, poverty, and misery were on a scale Orla never imagined. And the rank, ever pervasive smells disgusted her; in fact, after three weeks, the city's vast humanity appalled her. It also infuriated her that nobody seemed to have time for a chat. Reluctantly, she admitted to herself she badly missed the friendly folk of Dungarvan, not to mention the clear skies, familiar mountains, green pastures, and the sweet, clean waters of home.

But opportunity finally crossed her path, literally, quickly stripping away her mood of depression. As she was returning to her rented rooms one evening, a modern carriage swept around the corner in front of her. Mid-turn, the driver impatiently urged the horse on when two mongrel dogs darted from a doorway, barking on top note, both intent upon harassing the unsuspecting horse. The startled animal tripped and then crashed onto the cobblestone road among a tangle of shafts, reins and traces: the hapless driver was unceremoniously catapulted twenty yards down the road. As if congratulating each other upon their triumph, the dogs jumped about, still barking madly... then abruptly ended their lark and trotted away as if nothing had just happened.

Without a thought, Orla was beside the terrified, thrashing and heavily lathered horse. She methodically untangled the traces and somehow calmed the unfortunate beast. Exerting gentle authority, she then urged him to stand. Only when the horse stopped snorting and shaking, and she assured herself he had no major injury, did Orla's attention turn to the driver. It meant little to her that the man was barely conscious: she stood over him and told him *exactly* what she thought of putting the horse through such unnecessary suffering.

Suddenly, someone gently tapped her on the shoulder. Spinning, eyes still dark and brooding, she found herself gazing into the smiling, attractive face of a well-preserved middle-aged woman.

'Well said, young lady. It serves him right,' the woman whispered conspiratorially. 'Though why my husband thinks he needs to impress me is flattering. Incidentally, my name's Jean Stewart. But please, call me, Jeanie.'

Orla observed Jeanie as unobtrusively as possible. The woman was about the same height as she though slightly more rounded, and approaching fifty years, Orla guessed. She was also obviously well-to-do; her clothes fit perfectly and seemed fashionable without being pretentious. Her grey hair was loosely curled, shoulder length, and well groomed.

They both looked again to the unfortunate driver who was now moaning in pain and leaning against a shop front. He was obviously in shock and, judging by the ugly bruise on his forehead, probably concussed. Both of his elbows were bleeding. Regardless, the man's ruined clothes appealed to Orla's sense of justice. Jeanie attempted to introduce her husband, Frank, but he barely responded.

'Best we get him to an infirmary straight away,' suggested Orla, again easily taking control. With just a little charm, she seconded two male bystanders to lift Frank into the carriage. 'I'll take the reins,' Orla insisted as she climbed up to the driver's seat. 'But Jeanie, you'll have to navigate.'

To Orla's surprise Jeanie joined her. 'Incidentally, my dear, you haven't told me your name. And what brings you to this awful city?'

As Orla expertly guided the horse through the now darkening

streets, their exchange alternated between serious conversation and volleys of good-natured, albeit most unladylike, laughter.

* * *

IT WAS dark by the time Jeanie and Orla arrived 'home'. At the neighbouring mews, an attendant stabled, then fed and watered the horse. Certain that its injuries were superficial Orla groomed the horse as Jeanie looked on.

Thankfully it was only a short walk to the Stewarts' new, and rather grand, two-storey house, for the night air was cold and the fog, now flooding the streets, was heavily laced with the pungent smell of coal smoke from hundreds of household fires.

Jeanie immediately lit several lamps and then lowered the drapes. 'Servant's night off,' she said nonchalantly then proceeded to light the fire in the fireplace.

Orla studied the luxurious dining room surrounding them — everything screamed wealth. *They must be bloody well-heeled if this magnificent room is typical of the rest of their house,* thought Orla. The granite mantelpiece caught, and held, Orla's attention. Central upon it were impressive flower arrangements adorning the photographs of two young adults.

Following Orla's gaze, Jeanie enthusiastically declared, 'Our children, Anne and Owen. Anne's now twenty-one and happily married to James. He's a banker, but a real gentleman. They've been living in Adelaide for the past couple of years. That's in the Colony of South Australia. They've got a fifteen-month-old son, Michael, and he's our only grandchild so far. Anne's a good girl, she writes regularly. Anyway, we'll be visiting the colonies next year to hopefully catch up with *both* of our own kids,' Jeanie announced as she stood, having coaxed the fire to a cheery blaze. 'Yes, both of them, and our old colonial friends who we'd been farewelling earlier today... just before you, ah, rescued us.

'Our son is going on twenty-five. He left home four years ago after a terrible argument with Frank. Their differences arose over Frank's attitude towards guns; he despises them. But Owen maintained he needed them for protection when travelling after dark. I'll tell you all about it later.'

Gazing at her son's face, Jeanie added quietly, 'He hardly ever writes, but in his last letter he told us he's living in the northern part of the Colony of New South Wales. Apparently he's working in the business of buying and selling cattle and seems determined to make his fortune. And he was keen to tell us he already has several good horses and a small property of his own, though not much money.

'You know, Orla, Frank and I really miss them both very much,' Jeanie confided reflectively. 'We're just so glad they're both safe and happy and that they're earning an honest living.'

As the room warmed, Orla relaxed. But what she warmed to most was the calming aura of Jeanie's motherly persona: a warm smile never far away and a relaxed manner not dissimilar to her own mother.

A quick tour of the house confirmed Orla's notion of the Stewarts' wealth. She happily accepted Jeannie's offer to stay overnight and was assigned one of four splendidly furnished upstairs bedrooms.

The next day, Jeanie insisted Orla leave her rented rooms and stay with them. She was easily persuaded; her money was disappearing at an alarming rate. The arrangements for boarding were simple enough. Orla could stay as long as she wished, for free, in return for helping Jeanie with transport. Day servants would continue to attend to all housework, the preparation of meals, and to the upkeep of the garden.

Orla and Jeanie chatted affably for hours, revealing their respective upbringings and airing their future plans. Jeanie had a few surprises, the most astounding being how she treated leaving behind the comfort of her wealth as inconsequential.

'It's just a house after all, Orla. I'd swap it at any time to live in another country so long as it was warm for most of the year,' she announced. 'But my life is where Frank wants to be and London suits him for the moment.'

* * *

FRANK WAS BORED, sitting in a chair next to his hospital bed, impatient to get out. The door opened and two visitors stepped into his room. Jeanie he recognised immediately, but Orla made him feel decidedly uneasy, vaguely associating that beautiful, smiling face in front of him with excruciating personal abuse and ridicule. Jeanie, recognising Frank's confusion, good-naturedly explained the events leading to his hospitalisation. It also transpired during the subsequent conversation that Frank genuinely felt bad about laying into the horse. But he also felt equally obliged to explain that if he hadn't, his increasingly more urgent call of nature was going to do more than just blemish his reputation as a considerate handler! All three roared with laughter; he hadn't been trying to impress Jeanie.

As the women were about to leave, Frank playfully asked, 'Miss O'Meara, was it really you who gave me that dreadful earful? But listen, girl, I hold no grudges, so I hope we can be good friends.'

He felt enormous relief when Orla kissed him softly on his bruised forehead and replied cheekily, 'We'll see. But only if you call me, Orla.'

Frank was discharged from hospital the following week.

Orla already knew that Frank was fifty-six years old. He was tall-ish, about six feet, but rotund, thus giving him an imposing stature. She soon learnt that he took pride in his appearance. He shaved every day, kept his hair trimmed and wore elegant but not outlandish clothes. By necessity, he wore wire-framed spectacles to correct his short-sightedness.

Frank also had his moments of contemplation. 'Orla, please forgive me for appearing distracted,' he offered apologetically. 'It's a bad habit I know, but I worry about my son and I've got several business deals in the balance.'

Up to a point, Frank talked openly with Orla. 'I'm basically a hard working, down to earth family man. But I've been lucky. I've befriended some influential people and they've all helped my business prosper. But it's not my wealth that I want to be remembered for,

Orla. Besides, I don't like flaunting my wealth. I'm simply a 'doer',' he explained philosophically. After a reflective pause, he added, 'Some say I'm a visionary and an opportunist. That's also not far from the truth, I suspect.'

Unbeknownst to Orla, rumour persisted that not all of Frank's wealth could be attributed to legitimate enterprise. Even though he came from an upper middle-class background, as indeed had Jeanie, his success resulted from expertly cultivated 'friendships' with water-front stand-over men, immigration officers, bankers, parliamentari-ans, and mining executives... even with nobility. Of his clandestine dealings with such people, he confided in no one.

* * *

THE WOMEN'S daily routine put Orla in a new world. Jeanie seemed to have friends everywhere. Long and expensive lunches, music recitals, live theatre, and browsing through art exhibitions ensued. However, the number of women eager to debate the emerging, but very distant British colonies of New South Wales, Victoria, South Australia and Tasmania, surprised Orla.

Orla accepted that all of these experiences were broadening her perspective on life and stimulating her mind... even expanding her significant self-confidence; yet it cost her nothing.

'No need to be embarrassed girl, you're more than paying your way,' Frank responded, sweeping aside Orla's protests. 'How in hell's name would we get about safely without you driving us? Besides, hiring a good driver would cost me a fortune.'

Orla had indeed brought with her a most expert pair of hands with the reins. She quickly adjusted to the pace of life on London's roads and became adept at manoeuvring the carriage in the bustle and commotion of the heavy midday and evening traffic. Orla partic-ularly enjoyed this challenge, and even inclement weather failed to upset her. Confident in her handling — over confident some said — she refused to be bluffed by red-faced coachmen urging on their horses to the demands of their wealthy passengers. Unwittingly, she was steadily becoming a reckless bully and guilty of the very actions for which she had so vigorously criticised Frank. Nevertheless, she enjoyed letting other cabbies know when she had right of way by using either the most flagrantly crude hand gestures, or unladylike verbal abuse... or both.

But, when in the peace and quiet of her room after arriving home from her last outing, Orla began worrying. The horse had been in a heavy lather that night and uncooperative at the mews, clearly unsettled by Orla's earlier treatment. Orla felt a surge of guilt for her overzealous behaviour. She had also eavesdropped on the mew's overseer who was lecturing one of the stable boys.

'Remember, son, cabbie justice comes swiftly and in many guises,' he had said.

You'd better back off, Orla my girl, she concluded, *I don't fancy being done over in a stinking London alleyway.*

After five or six weeks, the social routine was losing its edge for Orla and she barely disguised her petulance and restlessness. Jeanie knew something was wrong.

'What is it my dear, what's bothering you? You've been acting like a bear with a sore head.'

'God almighty, is it that obvious? Please don't think I'm being ungrateful Jeanie, it's just that there's no real fun in my life. I haven't even got *one* lad trying to get into my bloomers!'

Jeanie interrupted and said mischievously. 'If you say so, but you've only got yourself to blame. You've been too damn standoffish.'

'Yes, you're right, of course. But listen, Jeanie, it's something else actually. You've both been wonderful to me. You've shown and taught me so many things in such a short time. It's funny, though, it's as if something's calling me. I can't explain it any better than that. It's the same feeling I had for years before leaving Ireland. And I've heard so much about the colonies of Victoria and New South Wales. It's where I'd love to visit. Please don't take offence, but I'll be leaving you soon, Jeanie.' Knowing that Frank's rehabilitation was complete, she quickly added. 'Besides, you don't really need me to cart you about anymore.'

Jeanie was not surprised. 'We'll both miss you very much and I hope you know that. But you live only once and this is the best time in your life to travel. And no offence is taken, my dearest Orla.' Jeanie then gave Orla a long hug, which was returned with equal affection. 'So when are you planning to leave?'

'Just as soon as I can secure passage I suppose.' Tears then flooded Orla's eyes at the realisation she was about to leave behind two wonderful people who she now thought of as her *other* mum and dad.

* * *

'ORLA, do you recall Jeanie and me telling you about our old colonial friends?' Frank quizzed Orla after dinner that night. 'We understand they've got a married daughter living in the colony of Victoria and, apparently, she and her husband need to spend more time looking after their stock and crops. But they don't have a suitable nanny to mind their kids. So, Orla, if you're interested in applying for that job, we'd be happy to provide you with a letter of introduction.'

In astonishment and obvious joy, Orla jumped at this suggestion. 'Yes, of course, but where do they live... and how do I get there?'

'Hold your horses, young lady. Jeanie and I have been aware of your impatience for some time. After all, 'you were off to see the world'. So when you continued to show so much interest in the colonies, I took it upon myself several weeks ago to write and alert our old friends of your possible plans. I'm confident they'll get our message to their daughter. But please understand, Orla, we can't *guarantee* the job with their daughter. However, we think our letter of introduction should give you a head start. Anyway, their daughter has two children and lives in a strange sounding country town called Wangaratta. I think it's about a hundred miles north of Melbourne, the colony's capital. I understand there's a train service to that town.'

Orla's passion to travel now acutely aroused, at least fifty additional questions followed in rapid order before they all eventually retired. Jeanie and Frank had done their best to answer Orla's questions, but sleep eluded her that night; her passion unquenched.

As promised, three days later, Frank presented Orla with the Stewarts' jointly signed and very complimentary letter of introduction. As Orla was about to express her gratitude, Frank handed her a second envelope before she could say anything.

'Well... don't take all night. Open it.'

'The bearer of this Right of Passage, Miss Orlagh Aileen O'Meara, a free British subject of sound character and with no financial or social encumbrances owing to any person, company, organisation or pleasure of the Queen, is hereby and forthwith granted lawful passage to the Colony of Victoria. Furthermore, Miss O'Meara is to be provided first class accommodation and be granted every consideration and assistance during the voyage since all costs associated therewith have been paid in full.'

A second sheet declared her to be an unaided emigrant.

'Those documents are authentic,' Jeanie added. Both carried a British Government letterhead emblazoned with the British Coat of Arms, an authorising signature, plus a Department of Emigration and Customs insignia seal.

Frank explained that the documents were not the usual ticketing procedure given the suddenness of Orla's decision, but were the result of him calling in a favour. What he did not explain, was that as official as the documents appeared, Orla's name would not be on the passenger list, that being the only way Frank could secure her passage — plus a hefty 'last minute commercial consideration'.

'Just show these papers to the captain of the ship when you board. Don't, under any circumstances, release them from your safe-keeping because they're also the basis of free colonial citizenship. The captain will ensure you're looked after and he's guaranteed me your voyage will be as enjoyable as possible. He understands well enough the consequences of not fulfilling our little arrangement.' Unknown to Orla, the captain had also been well paid to ensure the colonial immigration and customs officials processed her arrival without question.

Incredibly, the documents in her hand announced she would be sailing the next day!

Laughing excitedly, Orla hugged each of her amazing friends. 'How on earth am I ever going to repay such kindness?'

That night Orla wrote to her family, detailing her good fortune and forthcoming travel plans. She then set about packing. When checking her Colts, they still felt like natural extensions to her arms despite not having handled them for almost six weeks. She carefully concealed them amongst her belongings.

* * *

AFTER ANOTHER EMOTIONAL and tearful farewell, Orla boarded the steamer at noon and was shown to her cabin. It was depressingly tiny and provided only the most basic comforts, a far cry from the luxury of her bedroom at the Stewarts' home.

3

The steamer departed in early October 1879, and arrived in Melbourne during the fourth week in December of that year. Although considered a normal voyage, Orla never felt totally safe during the entire journey. And like most on board, she suffered from seasickness as they rounded The Cape of Good Hope. Later, when they confronted the massive swells of the Southern Ocean, the *mal de mer* returned with a vengeance. Two elderly passengers died from that dreaded curse and were buried at sea. There were also many cases of life threatening illness resulting from the appalling food and unheeded hygiene. Most passengers were friendly enough despite the conditions on board, and the men kept their hands off Orla (though certainly not their minds).

Worst, however, was the boredom. To relieve that state, Orla read stories to the children. All, and most of their mothers, hung on her every word as she elaborately embellished tales about the mythical leprechaun and legendary highwaymen of Ireland. However, they were disappointed to learn she knew no stories whatsoever about colonial highwaymen.

The Port of Melbourne was packed with merchant and passenger ships, in places berthed gunwale to gunwale, and three abreast. The sound of shrill whistles, the shouting and swearing of dockside work-ers, the dull rattle of chains being dragged across the wharf, the squeaking of overloaded luggage carts, and the excited chatter of impatient fellow passengers as they pushed by, filled the air to create an urgency typical of a country rushing into nationhood.

The breeze that had been coming in fresh off the bay was now blocked by the ship's hulls and huge dockside stacks of wool bales and bagged wheat waiting to be loaded. Consequently, whilst the lingering odours of humanity made Orla gag as she stepped onto the wharf, the prospect of soon being able to set foot on land almost overwhelmed her.

Nevertheless, it was disturbingly hot. As she gathered her belong-ings and headed for the immigration building, Orla was struck by a thought... *how on earth do people celebrate Christmas in such heat?*

The ritual of immigration and customs checks was over in minutes without so much as one officer raising even an eyebrow. She then found accommodation and arranged her journey to Wangaratta for the following day.

While reading a newspaper that night, Orla noticed the name Kelly for the first time. Apparently the man and his gang, who lived in the north of the colony, were keen on robbing banks and stealing horses and cattle. And, it seemed, they either divided their earnings amongst their families, or with poor neighbours. He sometimes returned horses previously stolen by others, indicating his fair-mind-edness to many. It also seemed he enjoyed eluding and then mocking the police despite their varied efforts to entrap him. Allegedly, he also killed three policemen though public opinion was divided about that being murder. *Interesting,* she thought, *but no business of mine.*

Next morning's train ride was initially cool. Orla was enthralled by the vastness and beauty of the surrounding grazing and bush lands, but searing heat soon imposed itself: she felt an immediate concern for the stock which appeared to have little or no water, and often only limited shade.

As the train slowly departed Benalla, sweat ran down between Orla's shoulder blades and her breasts. The seats made her backside ache. On impulse and without asking the other travellers their preference, she opened the carriage windows fully and propped the doors wide open — far better than sitting in that stifling, stagnant heat.

Soon the blue-grey humps of Mount Buffalo appeared in the east, stark against an azure sky. A north easterly breeze fanned the region, bringing with it the unique eucalypt and freshly mown hay fragrances. They washed over Orla's face and delighted her senses.

Upon arriving at Wangaratta, Orla sought refreshment and directions at the station kiosk. Engaging a cabbie proved easy — but *bloody expensive,* she reckoned.

Her driver, a middle-aged woman who seemed oblivious to the hundreds of flies either adorning the back of her shirt or buzzing around her head, proved to be a competent handler. The woman was friendly and relaxed in her manner, and interesting company. She happily outlined the exploits of a recently deceased bushranger, Mad Dan Morgan, who had operated to the north nearby, but mainly in the Colony of New South Wales. However, having no teeth, she tended to launch spittle everywhere when she laughed.

'I read in a Melbourne newspaper yesterday that there's another bushranger boyo up this way. Name of Ned Kelly, I think,' Orla said innocently. 'Do you ever see him?'

'Wher'd ya say yus was from, lassie? Ireland, eh?' the driver snapped, inexplicably changing the subject. 'An wut's ya business gonna be, eh? School teacha, mehbe? Govermet work, or wut?'

Orla was aware of a sudden tension, sensing she was also being interrogated and her allegiances tested. 'I hope to get a job as a nanny at the McIntyre farm. Do you know them?'

'Oh yeah, I knows 'em. You definitely not doin no govermet work then?'

Orla simply shook her head.

'Ned 'ates spies, ya know,' the driver's tone now an unmistakable warning. 'For that matta, he 'ates anyone as wut draws wages from them that govern this 'ere colony... or them as wut gets reward from that Queen of England.'

Realising she was probably in the company of one of the many loyal Kelly sympathisers she recalled reading about the previous evening, Orla wondered how quickly word of her arrival would get to the leader of the highly sought after gang of local bushrangers. *Couldn't give a damn,* she decided, dismissing the subject from her mind.

* * *

ORLA DID in fact soon become 'of special interest' to Ned via the cabbie — after all, Orla *could* have been an undercover police agent.

And, of late, Ned had cause to be wary given the increasing evidence his once good friend Aaron Sherritt had become a police informant. He was also disheartened that many recently arrived Irishmen — those he had previously assumed 'were of his own blood and therefore allies' — were now being persuaded by the police through the promise of regular wages, to either spy on him or take up arms against him.

4

The buggy conveying Orla rocked to a stop in front of the farmhouse. A couple, standing arm in arm in the shade of the front veranda, waved their greeting. After quickly unloading her luggage and bidding farewell to the driver, Orla turned her attention to the smiling couple. They were both about the same age, either in their late thirties or early forties, she guessed. The man stood over six feet tall, was square shouldered, but had a wiry build. His hair was receding and turning grey, cut short to match a closely trimmed beard, which did little to hide his deeply suntanned face and neck. He wore a long sleeved shirt tucked tidily into his trousers, but had bare feet. The woman, slightly taller than the man's shoulder, was slender and likewise had a deeply suntanned face, neck, and hands. Her hair was dark, streaked with grey and worn tucked up into a loose bun. She wore a long sleeved blouse and a full length skirt, despite the heat.

'I think colonial custom demands I say, g'day,' Orla said cheerfully in her gentle Irish brogue. 'Mr. and Mrs. McIntyre, I presume? Pleased to meet you both. My name's Orla, Orla O'Meara.' Turning her gaze upon the woman, she added, 'I understand your parent's friends in London, the Stewarts, have written to you on my behalf.'

Orla stepped forward to present her letter of introduction. 'I'm a long way from home, so I do hope you're aware of the likelihood of my arrival.'

'G'day to you, too, Orla O'Meara,' the man said welcomingly as he extended his hand in greeting. 'And yep, we've been expecting you, luv. But first things first, there'll be no more of that Mr. and Mrs. nonsense — my name's Alf, and yes, this is my wife, Joan.'

Joan gently hugged Orla. 'It's lovely to meet you, Orla. But let's get out of the sun and away from these damn flies before they cart us off.' As Joan ushered Orla to the house, Alf dutifully picked up Orla's luggage and followed the women.

The house was rustic, but inside it was airy and clean and obviously well lived in judging by the ordered chaos. Best of all, it was cool. Joan showed Orla to her room, explaining that regardless of the outcome of their talk later on she was expected to stay overnight.

After unpacking and changing into the lightest clothes she had, Orla returned to the kitchen where Joan offered her a fizzy brown drink.

'You can have tea if you wish, but we colonials prefer ginger beer at this time of day,' Joan gently mocked. In addition to a dry sense of humour, Orla sensed that Joan had the steeliness typical of Australia's pioneers, yet clearly she was still an attractive woman.

As Orla contentedly sipped the cool, sweet ginger beer, she took the opportunity to appraise Alf. His hazel eyes sparkled... a warm smile was never far away. But it was the man's measured relaxed voice, and his confident gaze, which appealed immediately to Orla; he was someone she felt she could trust.

After relating her chance meeting with the Stewarts, Orla then explained Frank's timely intervention in securing her passage.

'Joan's parents have often talked about Frank and Jeanie,' Alf responded. 'Frank seems like a nice old bugger, and shrewd. But he won't talk about his business deals, if I recall. By the way Orla, sometime in the New year, June or July we think, they'll be visiting us and have agreed to stay here for a while.'

'Oh, what a lovely surprise!' Orla responded enthusiastically. 'I do hope I'll be here to greet them. You'll really like them, I'm certain.'

'Sorry for interrupting but I have to collect the kids from school,' said Joan. 'Won't be too long. Alf will show you about I'm sure.'

'I thought most children walked or rode bikes or horses to school?' Orla asked innocently.

'Not likely, it's nearly a fourteen mile round trip,' Alf and Joan chorused their reply.

Alf escorted Orla outside. Just as he was about to introduce her to the family pet, a handsome sulphur-crested cockatoo, it launched into a deafening but surprisingly clear racket from its aviary. 'Aarrkkk. Aarrkkk. Siddown, yah yappin bastards.' Immediately followed by, 'Shudup Cocko, yah dopey shit.'

'Behave yourself Cocko, we have a guest,' berated Alf. 'No more of that language, right?' Eyes half-closed and contentedly marking time on his perch, Cocko quietly replied, 'Righto smart arse, righto.'

Orla had initially recoiled in fright, but was now laughing heartily, having thoroughly enjoyed the bird's colourful pantomime.

'You reckon that's funny,' Alf suggested. 'Wait till he starts on the stuff he learnt *before* we took him in!'

Both still chuckling, the tour continued. Orla easily matched Alf's stride. She listened with genuine interest as he outlined his future farming plans. As they walked, Alf pointed out his cattle and sheep in the distance. He then proudly introduced his three working dogs, each chained to its own kennel. In a nearby post and rail holding yard, two horses stood head to end, swishing their tails at the incessant flies. All of these fortunate animals shared the deep shade cast by a huge, towering peppercorn tree.

Orla knew instinctively that both horses were thoroughbreds: one a bay gelding of at least sixteen hands, the other a chestnut mare of fifteen hands.

'I understand that you like horses, Orla?' Alf asked, more as a statement than a question, and continued before Orla could respond. 'Joan loves riding and I know she's itching to go for a ride with you after dinner tonight.'

'Count me in. I haven't ridden for at least three months,' replied Orla, excited at the prospect of seeing what these magnificent beasts could do.

'I've got three other horses by the way – Walers. Do you know the breed, Orla? Actually, I prefer to ride them, they're my favourites. They do all the heavy work around here, too.'

'No, I've not heard of the Waler, and I've never considered riding working horses. Dad and I always reckoned they had it tough enough.'

'The name 'Waler' comes from 'New South Waler', a horse bred in the early days of that colony. Back then they were the preferred type used by the explorers, surveyors, and settlers. The Waler not only carried their loads but also worked their stock. Anyway, their agility, speed, and grace are legendary, but it's their endurance and courage that just amazes me. They've also been bred to handle extremes in weather conditions, just like this summer and the bleak winters we get here in the Northeast.

'They may be heavier than is fashionable, but they can handle all sorts of terrain,' Alf continued enthusiastically. 'They've got a quiet temperament, and they're never put off by hard work. When I put 'em to the plough, they'll go all day long and front up the next morning without any protest whatsoever.'

After a pause, Alf added, almost as if he was talking to himself. 'Indeed, there are some local lads who also swear by the Waler... and have them to thank for saving their necks on more than one occasion.'

They then refocused their conversation upon the thoroughbreds. Orla appreciated the quality of their lineage and chatted knowledge-ably about their conformation. Both belonged to Joan: wedding anniversary presents from Alf.

Eventually they strolled over to a large, rustic outbuilding. Inside were Alf's jinker, harness equipment, racks of hand-tools, a plough and a set of harrows, a small supply of hay and a few bags of grain. The resident cat quickly made itself scarce.

As the tour concluded, Orla threw a small handful of wheat to

Joan's twelve caged chooks and, finally, she met, Flo, the jersey house cow.

Strolling back to the house, Alf looked up. 'That'll be Joan with the kids,' he said confidently as he pointed to a small cloud of dust about half a mile away.

When the jinker stopped, two very excited children jumped to the ground and ran to Orla, eager to introduce themselves. The eldest, an uninhibited wisp of a girl about eight years old, was first to greet Orla.

'Hello, my name's Tylah and this is my brother, Jesse,' she said, thrusting out her tiny hand.

Jesse, about six years old, appeared a little shy, but nevertheless he swaggered forward, thrust out his equally little hand and said to everyone's surprise, 'G'day, Orla. Gosh you're pretty. Are you going to live with us?'

While pumping both their offered hands at the same time, Orla said, 'That'd be truly lovely. I'll be talking with your parents about that after dinner tonight.' Her bright, warm, lilting Irish voice immediately had the children captivated. Within a minute, the three of them were walking away hand in hand, chatting excitedly — the children determined to give Orla a *proper* tour of their farm.

After their first evening meal together, Orla helped the children with some schoolwork and when they eventually dashed outside to play, she broached the reason for being there with Joan and Alf.

Unbeknownst to Orla, Joan and Alf had already discussed the matter after their children had 'hijacked' her. In the short time they had known Orla, it was obvious she was an open, friendly, and energetic young woman blessed with an appealing, natural good sense of humour — and certainly 'no dill' according to Alf. It was equally obvious to them that Orla was an instant hit with their children. Joan was happy to share the news.

'Orla, the job's yours and you're welcome to stay as long as you wish.'

'And it'll be great to have your company,' Alf quickly added. 'But I don't want the four of you ganging up on me. And don't let the children trick you into believing I'm the only one who taught Cocko to swear.'

Orla was truly delighted, albeit, a bit relieved. They discussed the general terms of Orla's employment and easily reached an agreement. It was more a matter of fostering a happy family life than a job description. *Not really so different from life back in Dungarvan,* Orla thought, with pleasure.

As evening approached, Orla noticed that the neighbouring farmers were heading for their homes.

'Fancy a ride, Orla?' Joan asked eagerly, having quietly sidled up behind her.

'Oh, yes please! Let's get 'em saddled, eh?'

'No need to, luv. Alf's a jump ahead of us. He's already done that for us... and he'll keep an eye on the kids. Come on, let's get a move on.'

Just beyond the home paddock, Orla noticed Alf's three Walers. They shared a small grove of gum trees for shade and seemed at peace with the world except for the flies. *They wouldn't be my first choice,* Orla thought.

The two thoroughbreds were still in the shade of the huge peppercorn tree, swishing their tails in a vain attempt to keep the flies away. Both appeared drained of energy.

But when the women made it clear they were about to mount, both horses snorted petulantly and shuffled about. The bay gelding seemed determined to make it as difficult as possible for Orla. He turned his head away and downwards and attempted to circle away from her. But she was having none of that. Orla quickly and decisively shortened the nearside rein with her left hand, simultaneously grabbing a tuft of the bay's mane and held on tight to both. With equal assertiveness, she resolutely held her ground... but spoke calmly and quietly to the gelding.

To Joan's relief the gelding soon lifted his head and stood motionless, allowing Orla to swing effortlessly up into the saddle. With less grace but in a well-practiced manner, Joan followed suit, gathered her reins and walked the chestnut mare from the holding yard. The bay trailed obediently.

The light was still good although the sun was now below timber height and shadows were lengthening. And, to every person and every creature's relief, the temperature was falling rapidly.

The horses were quickly urged into a canter. As they felt their hearts starting to race with the rejuvenated blood now coursing through their bodies, both animals pulled hard on their reins, keen to be released from the boredom of the long hot day.

After another hundred yards or so, Orla gave a wild, excited yell and booted the gelding's ribs hard with her heels. Without breaking his stride he arched his neck downward, then, with a snort, lifted his now unrestrained head and lunged forward explosively, eager to settle into his work. Orla could feel the bay's strength through her legs and felt a primeval joy so intense that for a fleeting moment she thought that surely not even sex felt this good. Hunched over the bay's neck, horse and rider charged as one across the flat country, both exhilarated in the cool evening air as it washed over their faces.

Orla was leading by a considerable margin — and showing off. But the boundary fence was also looming very rapidly through the gathering nightfall. She needed to rein in sharply. The bay stopped just short of the fence. Orla's heart was pumping wildly and she released a most unladylike yell and punched the air in a vigorous display of gratification.

Yet incredibly, out of the corner of her eye, something caught and held her attention... and what she saw shocked her.

Beyond the fence, just within the timberline were four men, each sitting motionless upon their own grand looking Waler. The men all wore dark moleskin trousers that covered the tops of their riding boots, and wore either faded beige or green long sleeved shirts. One of them, the eldest man Orla guessed, was tall and thin and had a short, sandy coloured beard. Another man had a full, black beard and was also tallish, but much more strongly built. The other two were of slight build and looked quite young. *About my age,* she thought. They both had their broad-brimmed hats pushed to the back of their heads, with the strap under their noses. All of the men had revolvers either tucked into their trouser belts, or resting in holsters.

Nonchalantly Orla diverted her gaze to face Joan as she approached giving the impression — she hoped — that she'd seen nothing untoward. Neither woman spoke. Soon after, having regained her breath, Joan kicked up her mount into a slow canter and retraced their steps as darkness closed around them. Orla followed, perplexed by Joan's silence.

Back at the holding yards Joan was surprisingly withdrawn, still somewhat annoyed by Orla's earlier recklessness and waiting for the right moment to raise her concern with their guest.

As they finished grooming and watering their horses, Orla offhandedly asked, 'Did you recognise those four boyos watching us from the timber just beyond your boundary fence?'

As Orla's astonishing question registered, Alf, who until then had been idly watching the women performing their tasks, dropped the bucket of oats he'd been holding.

Simultaneously, a tortured look appeared on Joan's face and she yelled, 'What? No, *I* never saw anyone! Why didn't you *say* something? What did they look like? Were they armed, or what?'

'I didn't want to alarm you, Joan. I thought it best to let them think we hadn't seen them. They were in shadow, but I still got a pretty good look at them.' Quickly, but calmly, Orla then described what she saw.

'Bloody hell, that'll be Kelly and his boys for sure. You did right, luv,' said Alf. 'I'd better bring the horses in, just in case.'

Having settled all five horses into the house paddock, Orla suggested to Alf, 'I reckon it'd be a good idea to loose-chain your dogs nearer to the horses.'

'Good thinking, girl. C'mon, let's do it. They'll kick up a hell of a racket if Ned gets too close, and he won't want to confront any of *my* dogs if they do slip their collars.'

Afterwards, Alf made a well meaning but futile attempt to calm and comfort Joan. 'C'mon, let's all have a cuppa... and try not to worry too much, Joanie. Everything will be just fine.' In Joan's eyes, however, Orla already seemed aggravatingly calm.

While discussing their options, in the event that Ned and his gang did decide to rob them, Alf lamented, 'The facts are that it's futile to attempt anything heroic. We're outnumbered and all I've got is a single-barrelled shotgun and a few cartridges of duck shot. And it's too late now to send for help. Mind you, I'll give Ned a piece of my mind if he tries anything.'

Orla politely excused herself, but soon returned, casually brandishing her six-shot Colts. 'I'll gladly stay up and guard the horses if you'd like,' she offered casually while extending her arms in a fluid, well-practiced movement aiming at imaginary targets. 'If those boyos *do* turn up, they'll come a gutser... to be sure.'

Alf and Joan were bewildered by Orla's impulsive offer and shocked in equal measure by her unmistakable conviction. Alf recovered first and replied firmly. 'You're *not* going out there, my dear. You've had one hell of a first day here, so you'll get yourself off to bed. If anyone is going to sit outside and guard this place it'll be me. And if the dogs do start barking, stay inside. I won't ask now,' Alf added uneasily, vaguely sensing something lethal in his beautiful guest's persona. 'But it should be interesting to learn how you came by those pistols, young lady.'

'And two other things,' demanded Joan. 'Keep those damn guns out of sight, Orla, and we tell the children nothing about this, right?' Orla's nod seemed to placate Joan.

Reluctantly, Orla agreed with Alf's wishes, admitting to herself she was indeed nearly spent and, soon after, crawled into bed. But she could not immediately find sleep; she'd now twice unwittingly upset Joan.

* * *

DURING THE LATE afternoon of that particular day, Ned had indeed returned to the McIntyre property to cast a further well-practiced eye over the animals he had briefly sighted a few months earlier. *Those thoroughbreds will be fun at the Moyhu races, and those Walers are beauties that'll serve me well*, Ned had confidently thought.

As Ned watched the approaching horses, he was impressed by the confident style of the lead rider who was extracting every ounce of effort from the magnificent bay. He was sure the horse was about to crash into the boundary fence, when suddenly it skidded to a halt, almost squatting on its backside. The animal then reared while screaming, throwing his head about in protest at the rider's authority. The rider however whooped excitedly, an arm pumping the air.

Initially there was nothing to suggest this rider was a woman... until she removed her hat. Ned slowly elevated himself from the saddle and stared. His breathing stopped. His crotch tingled in unexpected lust as he slowly lowered himself back into the saddle and silently mouthed his thoughts: *God is she a looker, or what?*

But Ned was also annoyed. The untimely arrival of those two riders now frustrated his intention of stealing the McIntyre horses. *Those women wouldn't challenge me, but we don't need witnesses*, Ned reasoned wisely. *Bugger it, though! Now I'll have to find another time to lift those nags.* He turned his mount and rode leisurely back into the timber. His three gang members followed.

5

————————

At first light, Orla found Alf in the kitchen about to pour himself a cup of tea. 'Well, good morning sleepy head. I'll have yah know I've already done a day's work,' he teased. 'Join me for a brew?'

'Too right, thanks,' answered Orla. She yawned and stretched. 'Anything happen?'

'Heard nothing, saw nothing. Finish your heart-starter then let's ride down to where you saw your 'boyos,' as you called 'em. Hopefully they've moved on.'

In quiet companionship, they rode through an eerie morning ground mist to where the strangers were sighted the previous day. The fences were undamaged and no stock was missing.

During the return ride, Orla chatted, 'T'was my dear departed da who taught me how to use my pistols... and a rifle. But it was a real surprise when mum gave me Da's Colts as a going away gift. Her parting advice was that he would have expected me to use my God-given skills with those pistols... to protect myself and all those who I hold dear. And Alf, I can still hear his prophesy that one day I'll surely be 'put to the test'.

'"Remember, my love, he pleaded. In these unsettled times, you'll need to be able to recognise the difference between showing off and when it's time to kill. So don't hesitate if you ever sense that difference, because to be sure, someday, someone will want to either threaten or seriously harm you." And, he'd say every time... "When that happens, my dear girl, there's no point being the one that's dead when the dust settles."'

Alf never doubted her frank explanation; he simply nodded sagely and then chuckled uncomfortably to himself. But of her implied abilities, Alf thought, *she's certainly got spirit... perhaps, too much.*

After breakfast, Orla accompanied Joan and the children into Wangaratta.

At the small common school Orla met the teacher, a robust, single woman, and several parents. Tylah and Jesse were adamant that Orla meet their schoolmates, so it wasn't long before she found herself surrounded by a dozen children. They were all eager to know where Orla came from, to tell her about their pets, to enquire after Cocko and to have her come swimming with them after school in the nearby, Ovens River.

'All right, all right,' Orla begged, holding up her arms in surrender. 'Let me get settled in first, and then I'll be happy to join you.' This seemed to pacify them and the children raced away to complete some unfinished game.

The return trip gave both women the opportunity to learn more about each other and of their respective aspirations. But, Orla also wanted to clear the air with Joan.

'Joan, have I done something to upset you?'

Joan looked directly at Orla. 'Yes, as a matter of fact, you have. Charging off without knowing the lay of the land may have seemed like good fun to you, but one slip and both you and my valuable animal could've been killed. And second, I hate guns. Your display in the kitchen was unwarranted and will not happen again, right?'

Orla was taken aback by Joan's forthright speech. 'I'm really sorry,

Joan. It *was* a bit unnecessary I suppose. It won't happen again.' Nothing further was said, but Orla pondered the conflict surfacing in her mind... how to please Joan, but not shirk from her own ideals.

Christmas day of 1879 was hot; too hot to slavishly copy a traditional British Christmas menu. Instead, they celebrated simply with several glasses of cool ginger beer and fruitcake.

The hot conditions dragged on into the New Year, and as January 1880 drew to a close, the heat seemed only to intensify, and the flies' nuisance never abated. *Just as well Jeanie and Frank have planned their visit for later in the year*, Orla thought. *This isn't the sort of heat Jeanie would be expecting, or hoping for.*

By now, Orla's tasks had evolved into a smooth routine and her rapport with the McIntyre family had grown ever stronger. Her popularity with the school children escalated also, resulting in the teacher suggesting that Orla might like to read for them one afternoon. She agreed, but on her terms: that each child had to stand in front of the class and tell their own little story. They all confidently complied on the appointed day and, true to her word, she then accompanied them to the river. Orla had never learnt to swim, but happily splashed around in the shallows. That afternoon was fun and a huge success. It ended with Orla agreeing to read the children a new story every Friday afternoon... and to learn how to swim.

Orla's responsibilities, in and around the farmhouse, gave Joan and Alf their first real opportunity, since the birth of their children, to work together for extended periods outdoors. Orla often worked with them splitting and stacking firewood, improving fencing, and helping to yard and shear the sheep. And, as Alf and Joan heaved on crowbars, Orla expertly urged Alf's Walers to haul out unwanted tree stumps. Her previous hasty and dismissive views on Walers, particularly the one Alf called Boss Boy, changed considerably. *He's bloody good, this bloke,* thought Orla. *This boyo is strong and tireless and never complains... yet, he's so gentle and friendly. And he's so damned intelligent; he seems to anticipate my every command!*

So it was that Orla's unanticipated all-round farming abilities also created time for Joan and Alf to socialise and spend some quality time alone in nearby Benalla.

In the relative coolness of the evenings, Orla loved to sit on the back veranda and chat and sip ginger beer. She learnt much about the bitterness simmering between squatters and settlers in North Eastern Victoria and, inevitably, about the infamous Mr. Ned Kelly.

'Ned's already been judged guilty by the authorities for shooting three coppers at a place called Stringybark Creek. No trial, of course,' Alf explained cynically as he sipped on his drink. 'Somehow a fourth officer escaped and according to him, Ned and his gang murdered those other three in cold blood. But that's not Ned's telling of the story. That copper's name is also McIntyre, by the way. No relation, thank God.

'Yah see, Orla, Ned doesn't deny he ambushed the police, but he insists it was the copper's fault for the killings. According to Ned, it was self-defence when they refused to throw down their arms and a shootout erupted. Apparently the copper's packhorses were loaded with body bags and they were under orders to hunt down and kill him and his boys on sight, so perhaps Ned could plead a case. I'll wager that if Ned ever goes on trial he'll not receive a fair judgement. Pleading self-defence, without an independent reliable witness, isn't going to help him one iota. The authorities will see to it that the jury believe McIntyre. After all, he's a copper and therefore above reproach... of course.'

Orla believed she understood Ned's predicament, recalling her own frustration and anger early in her life when an English policeman brutally killed her pup — and who, of course, received *no official punishment*.

Alf finished his drink and continued. 'I admire Ned for protesting against our atrocious legal system and I've never ridiculed his political ambition. In fact, I'd probably help him if asked directly. But I am against him for relieving farmers of their stock to benefit his own wholesale and retail businesses. Anyway, those damn shootings have made the whole region uneasy... and that's why Joan's not keen on you having guns.'

On the other hand, Alf really enjoyed watching Orla practise with her Colts. They conspired to only have these practise sessions when Joan chose to collect the children from school. Orla explained to Alf that her father had meticulously reworked and maintained both Colts to eliminate the possibility of multiple firings, but even so, Alf was spellbound by the speed with which Orla handled both guns and was truly amazed by her accuracy — with either hand — even when a target was moving!

* * *

ORLA'S THOUGHTS frequently returned to her family, and to her 'other ma and da'. Although the light radiating from candles and the spirit lamp was not conducive to letter writing, Orla painstakingly composed lengthy letters to her mother and brothers, and then to the Stewarts.

On her initial visit alone to Wangaratta, she posted those letters. She then drove to the general store where she arranged for her list of goods to be loaded into the cart while she strolled the town. She attracted more attention than she expected, but being new to the area, she understood the curiosity and happily accepted the men's lustful, lingering interest. She eventually located the gunsmith's shop and purchased from a very curious owner, one hundred rounds of ammunition for her Colts. The salesman seemed gullible enough to accept Orla's word that these purchases were solely for her protection against snakes or to put down any seriously injured stock.

The gunsmith was quick to send word to Ned about the unusual purchase. *Why would a simple, though very attractive, Irish nanny really need so much ammo?*

* * *

ORLA VISITED town several more times over the following month and it wasn't long before people politely acknowledged her as she walked by, or waved to her as she drove past. Some even stopped and chatted for a few minutes. Most soon knew that she lived at the McIntyre farm. And, during this uneventful period, there were no further sightings either of Ned — or of any of his gang members — either near the McIntyre farm, or elsewhere.

6

One evening, mid-February, Joan declined Orla's invitation to go riding. 'You go, Orla. I haven't finished these repairs to Jesse's trousers.'

Not put off by this, Orla caught the handsome bay gelding, saddled him, and headed for a peak in the distant, low mountain range. That range, she knew, rose abruptly from the surrounding plains near the McIntyre's boundary line.

She allowed the bay to lope along at a leisurely canter for several miles. The shadows were lengthening and the temperature was falling... that magical time of day when the flies had finally had enough. The sky was cloudless and a light zephyr hopefully heralded a much stronger breeze that just might bring some much needed rain.

It became obvious to Orla that she would arrive at her destination after the sun set and would, therefore, not arrive back at the McIntyre farm until after dark. Cutting short her explorations, she turned for home but decided on the spur of the moment to climb the nearest ridge. The bay faltered in a few steep places, but completed the ascent with just a little coaxing from Orla. The faint track along the ridge was surprisingly clear of scrub, and in the even, but fading light, they made fast progress.

When Orla eventually reined in the bay, the McIntyre's farm was just visible in the distance. She also found herself overlooking Alf's boundary line... where four riders, each leading a horse, were heading towards a vandalized section of fence.

'Well bugger me... it's that bastard Kelly! The same four again, I'll bet,' she hissed, her heart suddenly pumping hard. 'You'll not be pinching Alf's horses, you shits!'

Without a second thought Orla urged the bay off the ridge and down the range, reining him in just inside the timberline. She now had a perfect view of the returning riders.

* * *

BREAKING open the fence presented little difficulty, and catching the horses proved much easier than Ned had expected.

The gang rode in close formation, urging the stolen horses into a canter in preparation for the climb onto the nearby ridge. The horse's hooves struck the hard ground in rhythmic volleys, sending ancient shale flying and dust billowing.

The men either had their heads down concentrating on the trail, or were looking back at their reluctant charges, when Orla and her bay suddenly charged onto the path in front of them.

'And what the bloody hell do you think you're doing, Mister Kelly?'

Horses and riders were startled in equal measure by her loud and assertive challenge, bringing them to a confused, but very abrupt stop only ten yards from her. The men reached for their revolvers.

Four gunshots coughed and shattered the tranquillity of the late evening: two shots fired close together, followed in quick succession by another two. The four men froze mid-movement. Four separate, lethal bullets had whistled by within an inch of each bushranger's face... despite the fidgeting and circling of their horses, and as Orla's bay skittered sideways across the trail. A nearby flock of cockatoos screeched their indignation in their panic to depart the scene.

'All right, Mister Kelly, you and your boyos can now drop all of your firearms. Be quick and don't try anything stupid.'

Ned suddenly found himself staring straight into two unwavering, smoking revolvers. He then raised his eyes and looked straight into the face of a stunningly beautiful young woman and gasped audibly in disbelief. He knew immediately who she was. But Ned also immediately recognised in that face a menace and a determination the likes of which he had never encountered before. What's more, he knew beyond any doubt that to attempt to either outsmart or overpower her was fraught with undeniable peril.

'Jeeezus! Ned, did you see that?' whimpered one of the younger men. 'She bloody well means it I reckon.' Without hesitation, he threw aside his revolvers.

Ned and the other younger man hurriedly followed suit.

In unison, Ned and the two younger men then turned to face the fourth member of their gang. He was by far the eldest man. But, unlike the others, he'd been gradually manoeuvring his horse towards the side of the trail. Clearly visible through his full sandy beard, his face was contorted in a menacing sneer. And his body language clearly foreshadowed readiness for action.

'And you sir, what are your intentions?' demanded Orla, angling one of her revolvers marginally. 'Do what I ask or my next shot won't miss that big boofhead of yours. Go on! Throw your guns away... now!'

'Golding! Don't be a bloody idiot, man. Do as she says,' Ned yelled.

Ignoring Ned's advice, Golding stupidly rose to Orla's taunt, whipping out one of his revolvers. But it was too late. Long before it was horizontal one of Orla's Colts coughed.

Ned watched in fascination. As if by magic a small neat hole suddenly appeared in the centre of Golding's forehead. Simultaneously, the back of his head exploded, spewing brain matter, bone and hair over the horse's rump as the bullet exited his skull. Golding's menacing expression instantly became one of surprise and then, as his eyes fluttered in bewilderment, his face took on a look of sorrow.

Gradually, the revolver slipped from his fingers. He leant sideways, slumped and slid from the saddle. With a muffled thud his lifeless body raised a cloud of dust as it hit the hard, dry ground.

'Right, get a grip of yourselves, my boyos. You've now got work to do,' she threatened, her manner portraying not the slightest concern for Golding. 'First, you'll return Alf McIntyre's horses. Then you'll make good the damage to our fencing. Come on. Stop gawping and get moving!'

Still dumbstruck and ill at ease, Ned took charge of Golding's horse and the one he'd been leading, and led his remaining gang members and the other stolen horses back to the damaged fence. The bushrangers then dismounted, tied their own horses to the outside of the fence, then walked the stolen horses back into Alf's paddock and released them. Orla then walked her bay through the opening and dismounted. Under her steely gaze, the fence was quickly repaired.

'Righto, my boyos, drop your ammunition belts. C'mon, be quick about it,' she commanded. 'I then want you back over the fence where you'll empty your revolvers and drop everything that's in your saddle bags, too... *if* you don't mind. Produce another handgun and believe me, you'll join Golding!'

All three men obeyed submissively.

'Now take your useless friend and be gone, *and don't return!* If you do, that's exactly how you'll all end up.

'Oh, and by the way, I was just thinking, Mister Kelly... your own fine horses should fetch a good price. Perhaps, I should keep them and make you all walk home. Would you like that?' she taunted. 'By the looks on your ashen faces, that wouldn't go down too well, eh? But then, if I tried to sell your horses, I dare say you couldn't produce proof of your initial payment for them. Right, Mister Kelly?'

In awe, and in fear of further bush justice, the three men emptied their revolvers and saddlebags. When the saddlebags produced nothing sinister, she let them be repacked.

Orla watched them carefully as they slung Golding's body over his horse.

'Now piss off and stay away,' she again ordered. 'And tell yourself that I'm an even better shot with my rifle, so don't go getting any fancy ideas as you leave.'

The three men remounted and headed off into the night.

* * *

NED NEVER FELT SO HUMILIATED — or intrigued. He hadn't gone far when, on impulse, he turned his horse and rode back to the scene of the shooting. Orla was still emptying their discarded ammunition belts.

At twenty yards, he called out cautiously but politely. 'Hey lassie, I've definitely seen you before, but I don't know your name? I know you're the McIntyre's new nanny, and somehow I don't think you're a trap. Mind you, times are definitely changing. So, who the hell *are* you?'

'Orla O'Meara's the name. Yes, we've seen each other before, and no, I'm not with the police, if that's what you mean. I'm just a simple Irish girl on holidays in this heathen country.'

'Then I'll not mention this ugly little business to anyone if you agree to keep it quiet,' Ned replied glibly.

'The damn cheek of you,' Orla snapped. 'I shot that idiot defending myself against outlaws hell bent on stealing my dear friend's animals, and you want *me* to keep quiet? Bloody hell, Ned, grow up!'

Ned soon learnt that she hadn't finished. 'And listen, Ned, if you really want top horses, then do the right thing and buy them legally for a change. Do Alf and Joan McIntyre a good turn and make them a true offer — and give them the right to decline. They're good folk, Ned. However, to do that you'd need to come and knock on their front door wouldn't you? But that's not your way is it?'

With that parting remark still hanging in the air, and before Ned could rally a reply, she effortlessly vaulted into the saddle and booted her bay into a gallop, heading for the dim lights of the farmhouse.

Sitting quietly on his horse, Ned watched her disappear into the darkness. No one had ever spoken to him like that before. About to turn his horse's head, out of the darkness floated Orla's uninhibited laughter. Yet another humiliation he would have to accept, but never forget. Her laughter faded as the distance between them grew.

Worse was to follow when he rejoined his men. Their laughter, the release of tension flowing from several tots of brandy, did nothing to diminish the humiliation he felt as their leader. However, Ned need not have worried; their respect for him had not diminished. And they certainly agreed with him to never again underestimate the gentler sex.

The ruthless, breathtaking suddenness of Golding's death had traumatized his younger brother, Dan, and his mate, Steve Hart — and genuinely shocked Ned. But he did not mourn Golding's passing: even in death, the man was a liability.

7

———————

It was quite dark when Orla approached the farmhouse. She recognised Alf leaving the holding yards.

'Over here,' she called. Alf immediately wheeled his horse in the direction of her voice.

'Do you know what time it is?' Alf asked, barely disguising his relief. 'We were getting a bit worried about you, young lady. Are you all right?'

'Yep, I'm fine. My friends the Webleys took great care of me,' she said, patting one of her holsters. 'But hey, isn't it a bit dark to be out shooting?' Orla teased as she leant over and patted Alf's old shotgun that was lying across his thighs.

'Yeah, right and... what exactly do you mean by that first remark?' quizzed Alf, now somewhat alarmed.

'I'll explain everything when the children are asleep.'

When they walked onto the veranda, the door flew open. Tylah and Jesse rushed to hug Orla and competed in asking her a barrage of questions. It was suddenly obvious to Orla that everyone was more than 'just a *bit* worried'.

Joan was holding the door open. 'You got time for dinner then, luv?' she mocked.

This seemed to break the tension and Orla started her infectious chuckle. They were all soon laughing in unabashed relief, particularly the children who had been allowed to stay up pending Orla's return.

'All right, all right,' Orla finally relented. 'Give me five minutes to clean up and I'll tell you what happened.'

The story Orla told the children was nothing like the truth, but it was a good yarn that held them intrigued for nearly an hour. After giving Orla one last hug, both children happily went off to bed.

Orla finished her meal with several cups of sweetened black tea, and then asked Joan to check that the children were asleep. When Joan confirmed they were 'unlikely to surface', Orla related the events of her evening, leaving nothing out.

Joan frequently shook her head from side to side, grimaced and ground her teeth, but said nothing. She was clearly having difficulty accepting Orla's encounter.

'So what now do you reckon?' Alf asked. 'Will Ned honour your wishes and keep away? Or will he disregard your threats and try again? And I'll bet the bloody police will soon be onto this.'

'Ned's no dill,' Orla replied in a measured manner. 'He knows I'm serious and he'll think long and hard about today's happenings. Oh, he'll be pissed off, no doubt. My gut feeling, though, is that Ned will keep his part of the strange bargain he was so keen for me to accept.'

'And I bet there were no witnesses,' Alf interjected.

'The only witnesses were Ned's men and I don't think there's any way they'd be stupid enough to cross him,' Orla responded evenly.

'But what about the police?' asked Joan, now undeniably anxious. 'What on earth are we going to say?'

'Nothing. We should say absolutely nothing about this... to anyone. I don't think the cops will be calling on us. But if they do, we simply deny having ever known the bloke I shot.'

'But what if the police do somehow get wind of your involvement?' Alf asked quietly.

'So help me, I'll hunt Ned down and kill the bastard if he can't explain how the hell the cops learnt of that man's death. And as far as pinching your stock in the future goes, I doubt that, also. I gave Ned the ground rules for our peaceful coexistence. If he chooses to ignore them, again, I'll happily save the hangman a job.'

Alf whistled. 'Yes, girl, I think you would. We don't doubt your threats for a second. And you may well be right, young lady,' he added. 'But while you're living under our roof you've got to keep your temper in check, or whatever it was that compelled you to act so violently. There'll be no more killing, regardless of the circumstances. Is that understood?'

In recognition of Alf's genuine concern, Orla nodded her acceptance and felt suitably chastised.

'Well, let's call it quits for the night,' said Joan. 'And thanks luv, for not saying anything about this to the children. Let's keep it that way.'

Orla knew she was not going to sit idly by and see anyone take advantage of her dear friends, even if it meant disobeying the McIntyre's wishes — and killing again if her principles were challenged.

Despite the conflict this created for her, it dawned on Orla that her actions had indeed been rash. *Alf's right. From tomorrow, I've got to try harder to curb my impulsiveness.*

Satisfied with her earlier rationale of events, Orla slept contentedly. However, Joan and Alf got very little sleep that night.

8

By the end of February 1880, the McIntyre's supply of horse feed was running low. None of the usual local suppliers had any for sale. Happily, however, their luck changed. When Orla collected the children from school, she overheard one of the parents boasting that she knew of a farmer selling hay at reasonable prices from his Wahgunyah run, up north, on the Murray River.

Although it would involve a round trip of approximately one hundred and twenty miles, Alf had no option but to buy some of that hay. Since the children had to attend school and Joan had no desire to sleep rough, Orla successfully pleaded her case to accompany and assist Alf.

The next morning, Orla collected Alf's three Walers and led them to where he was preparing his four-wheeled dray.

'Hold Boss Boy, luv, while I hitch these two in place. After the dray's clear of the shed, tie him to the back.' Alf directed. 'There's no point knocking him about before we collect our load. We'll need all his strength for the run home.'

After securing their swags, clothing, food, waterbags and cooking utensils, they said their farewells and set off into a rapidly dispersing mist.

Along the way they stopped regularly to rest the horses where there was plenty of shade. When they found drinkable water and a pick for the horses, they camped overnight. Mid-afternoon on the third day they rolled into Wahgunyah. After introducing themselves to the property owner and a friendly yarn, a fair price was negotiated for the hay.

For the next three hours Orla worked non-stop, side-by-side with Alf, binding the recently cut hay into manageable sheaves.

'Come noon tomorrow, we should have all this loaded,' said Alf, his tone clearly indicating he was happy with their progress. 'Take a break, luv, or go for a swim. But whatever you do, keep a sharp lookout for snakes. I'll be over there with the horses,' he continued, wearily pointing towards the trees lining the river. 'I think I'll have a snooze.'

'I'll be all right. But pass me your shotgun and three or four cartridges, please. I'll see if I can bag a few ducks for dinner, eh?'

The day was at its hottest. Orla felt at peace with the world as she strolled through the dappled shade of the massive and ancient red gums surrounding her. Some of the giants which once lined the river had been undermined and now lay partly submerged. To her delight she noticed several tortoises sun-baking on the trunks of those trees, just above the water line. But whenever she approached them, they'd suddenly dive back into the river, their rapid decent following the shafts of golden sunlight that also sought the river's depths.

Orla gazed in awe upon the river. *It must be at least one hundred yards wide here,* she estimated. At first glance it was just a flat, shimmering expanse that disappeared in both directions. But as Orla stared, she could almost feel its might as it relentlessly shouldered its way to some far off destination. She was intrigued by the many powerful upsurges and whirlpools, the offspring of continuous conflict between hidden obstructions daring to challenge the river's might.

The dry air carried a strong eucalypt fragrance and was filled with the monotonous buzzing of insects. The bird life was prolific: sulphur crested cockatoos, grey and pink Major Mitchell parrots, and many gaudy, smaller parrots — either 'talking' to one another or screeching in mock alarm at Orla's approach.

And there was no shortage of ducks. Her meanderings sent many of them whirring into the air. On the next rise a pair scarpered towards a billabong on her left. In one smooth motion Orla brought the shotgun to her shoulder. She tracked their line of flight... and fired. Feathers flew. With soft thuds, both ducks crashed onto the hard-baked earth.

Orla expertly broke the breech of the shotgun, removed the spent cartridge shell then casually set off to collect her kill.

A familiar voice shattered her reverie. 'Damn good shot, that.'

She spun around and stared in disbelief as Ned stepped from behind a nearby red gum. Instinctively, Orla raised the shotgun and pointed it at him. He made no attempt to reach for his revolvers: undaunted he walked straight up to her. He wore a squat, wide brimmed leather hat, a green, sun-bleached, long sleeved shirt which had large wet patches under the armpits, dark brown moleskin trousers, dusty riding boots — and a broad, friendly smile which his beard could not disguise.

'Well, well, if it isn't Orla Aileen O'Meara,' he teased, obviously savouring her disadvantage. 'You can give me the shotgun and then tell me what you're doing here. C'mon, hand it over. And don't even think about reloading.'

'Yeah well, all right, you can have the gun for the moment, but I want it back. It's not mine.'

Ned seemed happy with her response and stepped forward to take the shotgun. But as he reached out, Orla suddenly jabbed the end of its barrel hard into his midriff, just below his trouser belt. The unexpected impact forced Ned to involuntarily drop his eyes and move both of his hands to protect his manhood.

'Bloody Hell! Why'd ya do that? I wasn't going to do anyth...' Ned instantly realised his mistake. He was again staring straight down the barrel of one of Orla's Colts which appeared, as if by magic, from the folds of her dress.

'Well, well, that was bloody stupid of you, eh Ned? You knew the shotgun was empty. Perhaps, I should do the traps a big favour... right here and now. But it must be you've got the luck of the Irish with you today. I'd much rather talk than dump you in the river,' Orla mocked. She lowered the hammer on the Colt and returned it to its secret holster. 'So where are your boyos?'

'I'm alone,' replied a very relieved Ned. 'The other lads are cutting timber to build a new hut. And, I suspect, doing a bit of prospecting in their spare time.'

'So why are you here, and how did you know it was me?'

'Actually, I was about to move a few cattle across the river. I left 'em about three hundred yards, downstream. I don't think they'll go far in this heat, but still, I can't leave 'em alone too long.'

'Why's that Ned, worried someone might nick 'em? They all carry your own brand, I suppose?' Orla goaded. She then turned and sat, dangling her legs over the high bank of the river.

Ned followed suit, about two yards away. From the corner of his eye he studied her profile. His heart jumped. She then turned her head to face him, her expression friendly, entrancing. Ned almost stopped breathing. His mouth was unexpectedly dry, but neverthe-less, he chose to ignore Orla's earlier jibes and pressed on.

'I was about to tell you that I was taking a break when I noticed the birds carrying on as if someone else was in the area. So I scouted about and caught a glimpse of someone upstream carrying a gun. Being the curious lad that I am, I thought it wise to investigate. Got around behind you easy enough but didn't realise it was a woman, let alone *you*. That unbelievable shot was the clincher. Yah don't often see that; two for one I mean.'

'Yeah, right,' Orla replied dismissively and changed the subject. 'I've recently learnt how to swim. Want to join me, Ned? Oh, it's all right, I've got my swimming costume on underneath!'

'I'd love to, but I really need to get a move on. My client will be getting impatient. But hang on, Orla. Why are *you* here? It's a bloody long way from Wang just to go for a swim.'

'I'm not following *you* about if that's what you're thinking, boyo. Actually, I've been helping Alf McIntyre load hay. It was getting too bloody hot, so we decided to take a breather. This is such a magnifi-cent place. I thought it'd be nice to have a look about... and bag a few ducks, maybe. Actually that shot was a bit of a fluke, I only intended to down one bird. Anyway, we'll be heading home tomorrow.'

'Well, I'll bid you good day, Orla O'Meara.' Ned stood and walked away. Suddenly he turned, waved and yelled, 'Don't forget to pick up your ducks.'

Orla smiled jovially and demurely returned his wave. She then got to her feet, picked up the shotgun, collected the ducks and without looking back, set off to find Alf. The screeching of indignant cockatoos overhead masked her laughter.

Alf was bemused as Orla chattered happily about the tortoises, the bird life, and her observations of the river. They both enjoyed the tender, though 'gamey' flesh of the roasted ducks, but it was not until well after the moon had risen, that Orla casually mentioned her unexpected encounter.

Alf was genuinely surprised, but refrained from probing too much. He also realised he was smiling just before he fell asleep.

But Orla felt confused. That handsome bloody bushranger was actually a friendly, nice bloke. Orla lay on her back watching the stars for some time, her confusion giving way to a wonderful warm feeling in her chest before she finally nodded off.

* * *

WITH THE HAY loaded and secured, they turned for home. This time Boss Boy was in harness and soon leaning into his work. Progress was slow but steady. Extended rest breaks were taken to avoid the worst of the afternoon heat. On the morning of the fourth day, Boss Boy picked up his pace perhaps sensing the end of their journey. Although the other Walers stuck gamely to their job, Alf rotated them out regularly. However, Boss Boy remained in harness.

They arrived home at noon on the fifth day, tired but content. Joan and Alf hugged in a long embrace and then Joan kissed Orla on her cheek. As the three of them walked back to the house, with Joan in the middle and their arms looped around one another's waists, Joan added her cheeky good humour.

'Right, when you've got that lot unloaded, you can sweep the verandas, bring up four loads of wood, whip into town and bring back two bags of flour... then I want you both tubbed up... before you even think about dinner!'

'That'll be no problem whatsoever, Joan, my love. Ginger beer first, though. What do you reckon, Orla?'

'Sounds good,' Orla replied unconvincingly, for she was distracted and finding it increasingly more difficult to rid Ned from her mind.

9

———————

Shortly after nightfall about two weeks later, they heard the unmistakable sound of a horse approaching the McIntyre farmhouse. Such late visits were uncommon and generally meant either a neighbour needed help, or police were alerting farmers to sightings of bushrangers and reminding them of the consequences of harbouring. Strangely, Alf's dogs weren't barking.

Whoever it was dismounted and purposefully strode up the pathway. Footsteps crossed the veranda. Firm but cheerful raps on the front door followed.

Accepting it as his duty, Alf rose from his chair, picked up a night lamp and opened the door.

The man standing before Alf was not quite six feet tall, wide shouldered and had the powerful athletic appearance of a man in his prime. His bearing was confident but non-threatening and his eyes sparkled in the lamplight as he returned Alf's gaze. His beard and moustache were dark and full, and his hair combed straight back. Though his clothes and boots appeared clean, they showed their age.

The visitor then smiled and thrust out his hand. 'Mr. McIntyre? My name's Kelly, Ned Kelly. I mean you no harm and conceal no grudges or firearms, despite your unsettling surname. May we talk?'

Alf immediately recognised Ned's strength, not just by his warm but strong handshake, but more so by his directness.

'Call me, Alf, and do come in, Ned.' He held the door open for his guest.

From the sitting room, Joan heard the men's introductions and stood in nervous anticipation of Ned's entrance. Her considerable unease quickly evaporated when Ned politely offered his hand.

'It's nice to meet you, Mrs. McIntyre. Your home reminds me of my own dwellings... for its family atmosphere, I mean. Though mine usually lack these comforts,' he said with a grin while looking about.

Orla however, remained seated. She'd been giving Ned 'the once over'. *Bloody hell, he's a handsome boyo... even in this light.*

When Alf turned to introduce Orla, she raised her hand to interrupt. 'It's all right Alf, we've already met, remember?' she said nonchalantly. 'Though initially under far less friendly conditions as I recall. So what business brings you here, Ned? Horses again, perchance?'

Looking straight into Orla's beguiling eyes, he replied quietly, 'No, you do.' He then casually turned away to face Joan and Alf.

Orla's heart leapt... and strangely, she actually blushed.

Cups of tea and fruitcake soon appeared on the sitting room table. Ned remained courteous and seemed relaxed. At every possible opportunity he tried to include Orla in the conversation. He also listened with genuine interest when Alf and Joan spoke about their children's future and of Orla's much appreciated help around the farm.

But, at the mention of stock, Ned raised both hands as if surrendering. 'You've got my word, Alf,' he said submissively. 'Orla's already convinced me not to remove any of your livestock while I'm attempting to eke out my living.'

Orla thought Ned's little speech was hilarious and chuckled good-naturedly at his discomfort, convinced he would indeed keep his word.

'However Alf, I have to admit, I've been admiring your Walers.

Would you be interested in me separating two of them from you?' Turning to squint at Orla, he added, 'At the right price, of course.'

'Well frankly, not right now, no,' Alf replied. 'At last there's some prospect of a summer crop to get in and I'll need all three of my boys for that work.'

'I don't need them for at least another four months,' Ned persisted. 'Besides, I'll only want them for a week or so if everything goes to plan.'

'May and June usually aren't too busy, so that should be all right,' Alf replied. 'But give me your word you'll not flog 'em to death — and that you'll return them!'

'Done deal, and thanks,' said Ned, risking a quick look at Orla as he leaned across the table to shake hands with Alf.

Orla added sarcastically, 'Don't worry, Alf. I'll guarantee it.'

Most of the evening's conversation concerned Ned's views on the oppressive and unfair harassing tactics which the local police and magistrates repeatedly inflicted upon his family, in particular, the injustices imposed upon his dear mother and sisters. He also expressed remorse over his actions at Stringybark Creek, but maintained it was not murder he either sought or inflicted, but rather, self defence followed by an act of kindness to end one man's suffering. Ned's anguish was genuine. He insisted he only intended to warn the police to get off his back, but admitted his plan of a simple ambush and robbery had unexpectedly gone horribly wrong.

Ned was also passionate about the future for the people of North Eastern Victoria. Interestingly, he hinted that he was already hatching a plan to benefit everyone, but conceded his success called for continued unwavering support from all local people.

Orla was impressed by Ned's convincing, yet never egotistic manner. It was easy to see his leadership qualities. To her, it seemed such a pity that his actions left him with no legitimate means of returning from living outside the law.

'I've already suggested that the other lads should leave this colony,' Ned confided to his guests. 'But to a man they've stayed put and agreed to back me and my plans, no matter what.'

Not wanting to lose the mood created by Ned's frankness, Orla popped the question that had been massaging her curiosity and inflaming Alf's and Joan's deepest concerns. 'So, Ned, who was the bloke I shot? And where's his body?'

'He wasn't from around here,' Ned replied in a down-to-earth tone. 'Reckon he'd learnt the ropes, up north... from a fellow named Captain Thunderbolt. Horses were the captain's specialty, too. Apparently, when Thunderbolt was shot in cold blood by the traps, your man headed south. When my friend, Joe Byrne, found an article in the Melbourne Herald confirming the Thunderbolt story, I took that bloke on. Begged he was stone motherless broke.

'Anyway, he went by the name, Rupert Golding, but it probably wasn't his real name. Then again, some people confuse me with a chap called Mr. J. Thompson. I can't imagine why.' Ned chuckled. 'To be fair, he was quite handy with horses. But he was continually on the grog, unreliable, always irritable and always hostile towards my younger brother, Dan. He also picked a fight with Steve, another cherished and loyal friend. I know Steve can be a bit cranky and strange at times, but he's only a lad. Had to break it up in short order and advised him that if he didn't change his ways immediately, then he could piss off. Oops, sorry, Joan... I mean, clear off. It's a fair bet that Rupert's temper over-stepped the line with the captain, too. Anyway, he was simply trying to survive with us while keeping as much distance as possible between himself and the police up north.'

'Well go on, get on with your story,' Orla interrupted impatiently.

'Should have booted him out right there and then, but he begged me to let him prove himself by lifting some horses. Because I had Joe organising some scrap metal for one of my construction jobs, I gave him one last chance. That's when I first saw you, Orla... and you, Joan. Remember the day you raced each other to your boundary fence?'

Ned paused. He thirstily drained his cup, then looked up and spoke directly to Orla.

'Orla, no one's likely to find Rupert's body. He's a hundred or more feet down an abandoned gold mine and some considerable distance from here. If anyone ever discovers him, it won't be in our lifetime. And, I imagine, it'll look as if he was accidentally killed by a rock fall... rather than by your handiwork. I say good riddance. He was a nasty bastard.'

Shortly after midnight, they called it a night. Ned warmly expressed his pleasure at having met the McIntyres. Joan and Alf reciprocated.

As Ned walked to his horse, he chuckled. 'You'll find a nice sized roo hanging in your shed, Alf. You'll not be needing food for your dogs for at least another week.'

Just then, Joan rushed from the house and handed him a bundle. 'Don't eat it now, or you'll not eat your breakfast,' she suggested in good humour.

Ned laughed and thanked Joan, guessing correctly that he now had the remnants of one hell of a tasty fruitcake all to himself.

As the front door closed behind Joan and Alf, Orla stood rubbing the muzzle of Ned's elegant grey mare. 'She's truly gorgeous, eh?' she said quietly then turned to face Ned. 'You got far to go, boyo?'

Ned gently brushed the back of his warm hand across Orla's cheek. 'Her name's Music, and yep, she's a lovely animal all right. But no, we don't have far to go. Fifteen or so miles, I'd guess. Orla, listen... if you ever need me, I can be back here in no time.'

Orla was about to chastise him for his last presumptuous remark but without warning Ned stepped forward, wrapped his muscular arms around her, leant forward slightly and then urgently, but tenderly, kissed her full on the lips. She surrendered to a wild, sensual rush, allowing herself to be kissed, savouring its unexpected-ness and the thrill that came with the soft, gentle pressure of his lips. But then she became aware that his whiskers were tickling her and pushed him away.

'So, is this how you treat every girl on only their third meeting with you, Mr. Kelly?'

'No, it's not,' Ned whispered huskily, his breath playing across her cheek. 'But good God, Orla, for just a simple Irish girl on holidays in this heathen country, you're... you're different, like me, I reckon.

You're bloody good on the eye and smart, too, to be sure. And I've seen you do some amazing things. If only we'd met years ago, things might be very different now.'

Again leaning against him, this time savouring his strong manly scent and the faint hint of smoke on his clothes — and very aware of the pressure and spread of her breasts upon his chest — Orla quietly teased him. 'Steady now, boyo, we've only just officially met, remember. But that was nice of you to say. I'm flattered... really. Come to think of it, though, if I *could* find a reason for you to visit me again, how do I contact you?'

'Do you remember the old girl who first brought you here?' he said as he reluctantly disengaged his arms and swung up into the saddle. 'Contact her in Wang and leave the rest up to her.'

He then swept Orla a kiss with his hand, swung Music around and headed off at an easy canter down the driveway. *To God only knows where,* thought Orla.

And again, the dogs never raised so much as a whimper.

As Joan and Alf lay in bed in the early hours of the morning just before sleep overtook them, Joan whispered, 'It's upsetting to see how such a positive fellow could be in so much strife. He'll probably never again have any real peace of mind or receive justice. But what worries me most... did you see the sparks between those two? Damn it, Alf, I really like the man.'

10

———————

It hadn't exactly been love at first sight, but close to it. Orla spent the next week as if in a daze.

Joan recognised the not so subtle change, but chose to say nothing for several days, suspecting Orla needed time to rationalise her feelings. Eventually, Joan broke her silence.

'A really nice fellow and quite handsome don't you think?'

'Ooohh yes,' Orla whispered, realising Joan was reading her thoughts. 'His eyes; did you notice how they seemed to glow? He certainly looks strong, but he's sort of, well, gentle, too. Knows what he wants, even if the law's against him at every turn. He's got a really serious side to him, I know, but he makes me laugh, too.

'You know what, Joan? The real scary thing is that despite our dreadful first couple of meetings, and his unfortunate reputation, I'm, well... sort of buzzing inside. It's as if I just *have* to be with him.' After a thoughtful pause Orla continued. 'I wonder if that's just our Irish heritage, or if I've fallen for the big monkey. Is that wrong, Joan?'

'No, that's just the nature of things, my dear girl. However, listen. Alf and I are both thrilled for you, but have you thought carefully about the position it puts you in should you choose to get involved with the man?'

'Yes, I could be either killed or put in prison for simply being in his company. I understand that well enough.'

'Being in love with a man is never a crime in God's eyes, and neither is being in love with Ned Kelly. But you're only nineteen and you haven't lived with a man. You've only just met him and you don't know how he'll treat you once he gets you out in the bush. Your life will change dramatically if you run with him. Will your love endure? Have you thought about these things, Orla?'

'Yes, constantly.'

'We both know he's on some kind of personal mission, right? Has he confided in you about that? I bet not. Are you sure he's not leading you on, just to satisfy his physical desires? Whatever his motives are, he stands a bloody good chance of ending up in prison and dragging you along with him. You've already acknowledged that. And well, he's a lot older than you, Orla. He could be set in the ways of an old man and lose interest in you within a few short years — then what?'

Orla reacted to Joan's blunt questioning. In frustration she clenched her teeth, tightened her lips and half closed her eyes. But after a few seconds she grasped the underlying good intent in Joan's words and relaxed. Nevertheless, tears began welling in her eyes.

But Joan hadn't finished. 'It's those bloody guns I worry about, Orla. You both have a predisposition to resort to violence and that's bound to get you into trouble eventually. Or killed!'

'Ooohh, why Ned? Why couldn't he be someone else?' Orla sobbed. 'You just don't want me getting involved with him, do you? Damn it, Joan, you're probably right. But I think it's too late. What on earth shall I do?'

Joan bent forward and looked Orla squarely in the eye. 'Regrettably, I think you already know the answer, my love. But life's too short and true happiness can often be such a fleeting thing. So grab those moments, Orla. Perhaps you can show Ned that he can't change the world on his own. You might even be able to convince him to return to Ireland with you and escape the persecution he's imposed upon himself. Go with Ned, but never allow him to dent your spirit or your beliefs.'

Orla threw her arms around Joan, hugging her tightly. 'Oh... thank you, Joanie; that's exactly what my mum would have told me.'

The scene Alf witnessed after returning from visiting a neighbour was of the two women embracing and sobbing quietly, confirming what he guessed was ailing his guest. 'So when are you leaving us, Orla?'

The women released each other. Though surprised in equal measure by Alf's unexpected return and his astute words, they quickly regained their composure.

Without hesitation, Orla replied. 'Soon, I think, Alf.' But then in alarm, she quickly added. 'But what if Ned doesn't feel the same and doesn't want me tagging along?'

'Oh, but he does,' Alf butted in.

'How can you possibly know that, Alf McIntyre?' scoffed Joan.

'Why not ask him?' Alf replied jubilantly. 'He's right here.'

As if on cue in the gathering darkness, Ned appeared from the side of the house. 'I couldn't wait for your message, Orla. I just had to see you again. And it's good to see you too, Joan.'

Orla flew from her chair, sprinted across the veranda and launched herself into Ned's arms. As the passion in their embrace grew, Alf gently took Joan's arm and led her into the house.

'I'd barely got onto the main track when Ned just cantered up beside me and said, 'Evenin' Alf.' Frightened the begeezus out of me, I hadn't heard him approaching. Anyway, we had a real good talk. His feelings for Orla are genuine enough, I'm certain. He wants to marry the girl. In fact... he even asked me for *my* permission. Can you believe that?'

Just then, Ned and Orla entered the kitchen, hand in hand.

'Well, you two, what are your plans? But first, Joan and I want you both to know that whatever you've decided is all right with us. But naturally, given Ned's current circumstances, we'll worry about your safety, Orla.'

'I'm leaving with Ned... tonight,' replied Orla, tears suddenly racing each other down her cheeks. 'I realise it's terribly short notice. I know I'll miss you both very much — and your wonderful children.

But this just feels so right. I hope you understand and can forgive me for bailing out on you.'

'Nonsense,' replied Joan. 'Alfs' just got through telling you that you're a free agent. You can choose to do whatever you wish. You have our blessings, although your decision *is* a bit sudden... and you know my reservations.'

'And also remember, girl,' Alf added before Orla could reply. 'This will always be your home for as long and whenever you want. You're both always welcome. Be sure though, Ned, to look after this wonderful young woman. If you don't, you'll have more than the police to contend with.'

Alf's threat surprised Ned. 'I've already given you my word on that, Alf, just as I've given it to Orla. But hang on. I reckon it'll be more like Orla looking after me. You've seen what she can do with her revolvers!'

Orla and the men chuckled. Joan frowned: Ned's blasé acceptance of the need for violence had strangled her humour.

Chatting amiably, Alf guided Ned outside.

Donating two blankets, Joan set about helping Orla pack her meagre belongings. Orla packed her revolvers, her still considerable amount of ammunition and other personal items into one blanket, while Joan wrapped her clothes in the other. Using leather swag-straps, they secured the blankets into tight bundles.

When the women carried the bundles outside, Orla noticed that the men were still chatting, obviously relaxed in each other's company. Ned had his arm draped affectionately over Music's neck, while Alf held the reins for the saddled thoroughbred bay and the halter on his favourite Waler.

'Come on, Ned, let's get Boss Boy loaded before it's time for breakfast,' Alf joked.

Orla stood in awe at what was unfolding. Joan and Alf, people who only a few short months ago never laid eyes on her, were about to give up two of their most prized animals so that she might pursue love. Their unexpected generosity and sacrifice made her feel extremely honoured... and special.

'Come on, girl,' Joan begged. 'You haven't got all night.' Any protest or possible change to Orla's mind was swept aside by Joan's impatience.

After again warmly hugging Joan and Alf, Orla swung up into the saddle, her tears and excitement hidden by the darkness. The bay fidgeted as if wanting to be away, but Orla quickly exerted her control.

Music whinnied softly as Ned eased himself into the saddle, leather creaking as he made himself comfortable.

'Please return the bay in a few months' time, luv, but keep Boss Boy,' said Alf, his voice catching as he gave the Waler a parting pat and ear rub. 'He'll serve you well, mark my words.'

Alf then turned to Ned. Raising his arm, he firmly shook Ned's hand and said quietly, 'Good on you, son, you've won the girl's heart. Now Godspeed and look after yourselves.'

'You're a damn good man and a good friend, Alf McIntyre,' Ned replied. He then took Boss Boy's halter rope from Alf, and at an easy canter led Boss Boy into the night. When Orla caught up, they leant from their saddles and briefly kissed.

* * *

DESPITE THE HEAD spinning speed with which the evening's events unfolded, Orla's emotions were in check. For a moment, she reflected upon stories Alf had told her... about tame and docile working mares who had crashed through fences to be with a brumby stallion, to run free with his herd — and of their loyal bitch who had slipped her collar to run off with the first dingo that called by. Orla knew that Alf's stories had not influenced her, but she suspected there was probably a similar force at work with her. Regardless, she felt exhilarated and rejoiced in her decision.

They chatted happily in the bright moonlight, travelling at a steady canter through well grassed, lightly timbered grazing country. Five miles slipped by, then Ned called a halt and signalled for Orla to stop talking. He then stood up in his stirrups and looked about, listening and taking in deep breaths through his nose.

'Sound travels a long way on still nights like this,' he whispered. 'But Music will hear any horses approaching long before we do. She'll snort and shake her head to let me know. Sniff the air, Orla. Smoke also travels a long way on just the slightest breeze. And look through the timber. Campfires are a dead giveaway; their light travels for miles provided there's no fog or ground mist. If you see, hear or get a whiff of anything tell me straight away and then use hand signals only. Right?'

Orla obediently stood up in her stirrups, sniffed exaggeratedly and strained to peer into the darkness. She then sat and shrugged her shoulders. 'Clear as a bell, I'd reckon.'

'Agreed... c'mon, let's press on.' Both were to repeat that precaution many times during the night, and many more times during their life together.

At the first hint of dawn, Ned called another halt near the bank of a fast flowing river. They dismounted and allowed the horses a well-earned but short drink before tethering them to a nearby tree. Ned then filled his battered pannikin and handed it to Orla. The crystal clear water was so cold it almost took her breath away. Ned waited patiently for her to finish and, he too, drank thirstily.

Ned then led Orla to an elevated clearing where they sat and admired their unrestricted view of the river as it tumbled towards them.

'This's the Ovens River. And that mountain to the east is Mount Buffalo,' Ned explained. 'I've been told the views from up there are spectacular.'

'Yes, I knew it was Mount Buffalo. You can't mistake its distinctive outline, even from as far away as the McIntyre's farm. But as lovely as the river is, I don't think I'd like to swim in it. Too bloody cold for me.'

'During the next really hot day you might have second thoughts about that.'

Ned shifted to sit shoulder to shoulder with Orla and, awkwardly, placed his arm around her waist. Orla leaned her head on his shoulder and draped her arm around him.

'Ned, please tell me you love me. I only ever want to hear you say it once. I know that I'm in love with you because I feel so helpless and cosy inside when we're close like this.'

'Ooohh, Orla,' Ned groaned. 'May God be my witness; I love you as I've never loved anyone or anything in my life. Since the day I first saw you at that boundary fence you've been constantly on my mind. But be patient with me, I'll never tire of telling you how I feel.'

Ned then turned and kissed her softly on slightly parted lips. As he encouraged Orla to lie on his oilskin coat, she passionately returned his kiss, vigorously thrusting her tongue into his mouth. Released of any inhibitions she then alternately kissed his neck and gently nibbled his ears... while desperately trying to remove his moleskin trousers. Ned hardly needed further encouragement: they were soon both naked and eagerly exploring one another's bodies.

Neither of them felt the cold morning air nor the discomfort of partly hidden rocks as they lay in an intimate tangle. Their souls were also as one in the relief and euphoria following their sexual release.

'Don't ever leave me, Orla,' Ned whispered. 'Please... will you marry me?'

'Yes, of course, I'll marry you. But that bit about leaving goes both ways, boyo.'

For moments they blissfully watched the pastel shades of dawn declare the new day. Then Ned broke their embrace and gathered their scattered clothes. After a quick wash and a few mischievous splashes of the near freezing water sent in Orla's direction, both were dressed and urging their horses into a comfortable, now familiar canter.

'So, my boyo, exactly where *are* we going?'

'The Buckland Valley.'

* * *

ORLA REFLECTED upon her short life as they rode in contented silence. Not yet nineteen years of age, she had taken leave of her beloved Ireland. And now, she was not only in a heathen country on the far side of the world, but in the middle of the bush in the care of her lover, soul mate and, hopefully, soon to be husband. With an emotional jolt of reality, Orla suddenly thought, *bloody hell, what would Ma and Da, and my brothers think?*

However, her immediate euphoria remained unscathed despite the fact that her man was also the most sought after outlaw in the colonies of Victoria and New South Wales — which, by her association with him, automatically made her an accomplice, and, therefore, *now also an outlaw!*

11

'You're going to meet two special Chinamen, Charlie and Ong. They're brothers and in their late sixties, I'd say,' Ned explained. 'They live beside the Buckland River, about two miles upstream from a small goldmining settlement known as 'The Junction'. Hopefully, we can share a decent breakfast with 'em.'

As they skirted the settlement of Porepunkah, Ned continued with his explanation. 'They're cunning and knowledgeable old bastards, but good friends, indeed. They insist that I'm welcome back any time. 'Their home is always mine' they keep telling me. Anyway, from here, we've still got about twelve miles to go. How's that lovely backside feeling?'

'A bit sore, but is it any wonder! Let's press on, lover boy.'

As they navigated their way along a deeply rutted bush track, Ned happily recounted for Orla his first meeting with the Chinamen.

'It was a really hot day in early '77 — not far from Wang. One of the wheels from Ong's cart had fallen off. Poor bugger was fighting a losing battle trying to keep his herd of about sixteen pigs from eating all the corncobs that spewed from his cart when it collapsed. So I rode up and gave him a hand. While Ong kept his pigs at bay, I refitted the wheel, improvised a locking pin, then helped reload what remained of his spilled cobs.

'He was friendly, but had no idea who I was... I introduced myself as Edward. Anyway, we shared some water and I learnt that Ong was returning to the Buckland Valley to continue working his gold mine with his younger brother, Charlie. After I'd explained I was also going his way — to look over a bank at The Junction actually, but I didn't tell him that — out of the blue, the little old bloke invited me to dinner. That sounded pretty good, so I tied my horse to the rear of his cart and joined him on the driving platform.

'Our progress was slow — to protect the wheel — but I enjoyed his company. It was comical, though frustrating at times, how Ong attempted to explain things or ask questions in his jumbled Chinese-English. Anyway, we persevered and with hand signs and by repeating things, we eventually understood each other.

'But what really fascinated me was the way Ong kept his pigs together. None of them were tethered and he had no dogs, you know. Anyway, about every half of a mile or so, he'd throw a single corncob onto the track behind us. The pigs trotting in the shade under the cart would then dash out, squealing and grunting in a mad frenzy to be first to the cob. Usually a fight broke out. The winner would happily eat its prize and then run back to the refuge of the cart's shade and rejoin the disgruntled losers. They'd all trot along, patiently waiting for Ong to throw out the next corncob. Ong very proudly explained that he'd used this trick many times over the years — all the way from Wang where he'd bought them, to the holding pens at their mine. That's a round trip of about one hundred and ten miles. And mind you, he boasted he'd never lost a single bloody pig! Yah know what, Orla? I believe him.

'When we eventually arrived at his mine site, the brothers insisted on a grand tour. Thank God Charlie's English is easier to understand. Anyway, they've got amazing vegetable and herb gardens and they keep their pigs about fifty yards from their house. I swear, those pigs had no smell whatsoever!

'And, another thing. They've built a network of sluice races for watering their gardens and to supply the pigs. Like I said, they're clever little buggers.'

Ned then lapsed into a thoughtful silence

* * *

AFTER TOURING the Chinamen's mine site, Ned strolled with them to a nearby bend in the river where a stand of gums provided solid shade beside the river. To Ned's surprise, Charlie squatted and started pulling hand-over-hand on one of several strings that disappeared into the deep, dark pool swirling at the river's bend. A brown bottle quickly surfaced. Charlie deftly removed its lid and passed it to Ned, indicating he should sample the bottle's contents. Ned raised it to his mouth and closed his eyes. The bittersweet liquid was unmistakably beer, the best he'd ever tasted — and delectably cold, thanks to the permanent chill on the bed of that deep pool.

When Ned lowered the bottle, intending to pass it on, he saw two more strings now lying on the grass and that both brothers were eagerly draining a bottle of their own. Ned effusively congratulated the brothers on producing such a marvellous brew.

Before long, six strings lay in a tangle at their feet. At sunset, a very unsteady Ned rose to bid his hosts farewell, also telling them that it was his intention to seek accommodation at The Junction.

Both brothers now knew exactly who Ned was, but insisted he stay with them for the night. And when Charlie alerted Ned that he'd seen a police constable the previous day at The Junction, Ned had gladly accepted their kind offer.

Moreover, at least eight strings then lay on the grass and Ned doubted if he could mount, let alone find his way back to the settlement. Besides, he recalled being *very* hungry.

The meal that night was better than anything Ned could ever remember tasting. After devouring several servings of tender, delicious pork and mountains of oriental spiced rice, they all retired to canvas chairs on the veranda. Ned had again thanked the brothers, but they'd insisted it was their simple way of thanking him for helping Ong earlier that day.

They talked well into the balmy night. Ned learnt that when the brothers lived in China, both served their Emperor, Charlie as a sword maker and Ong as a furnace maker. Charlie had also studied art, had a passion for steel sculpture and claimed to have been taught by masters in the ancient oriental art of woodcarving. Ong's skills ranged from firing of porcelain artefacts to the heat treatment of iron tools and weaponry.

A rumour had swept their part of China. Gold nuggets were literally waiting to be picked up from the gin clear waters of the many creeks and rivers on the east coast of a large country to China's south. That had been more than enough incentive for the brothers to give up their respective poorly paid jobs and strike out on their own... and, hopefully, amass personal fortunes.

The brothers arrived in Sydney Town in 1851 and made their way to Bingara. But, after three years of hard work, they barely managed to stay alive. Word then reached them of a new series of gold strikes in the Colony of Victoria. On their way south, they worked the Araluen gold fields near Braidwood for about a year with considerably more luck, but then, because of the atrocious treatment inflicted upon Chinese miners, they decided to risk everything and move on. In 1856, they established themselves on their Buckland River claim and stoically refused to give it up regardless of how many of their countrymen were murdered, during that, and the following years.

Despite the next day's hang over, Ned took considerably more interest in the structure of their *most* unusual dwelling. It had, the brothers lamented, evolved out of necessity; they needed to be able to defend their home while continuing their mining operations.

The brothers had stumbled upon a rich seam of gold-bearing quartz, which retreated into the mountain. The planned tunnel opening was far enough above the normal river level to be flood-proof. However, prior to penetrating the mountain, they enlarged the tunnel opening and built around it, a façade that imitated a normal post and slab house front, complete with windows and veranda.

But it differed significantly from a normal bush shack. The façade windows were made to be quickly converted into firing slots. The door was of slab timber, reinforced internally with heavy wooden beams, designed to slide quickly into locking positions.

But to Ned, the final feature was ingenious. Above the roof line, resting on the steep slope immediately above the façade, were several huge logs and skilfully restrained heaps of rocks, all concealed by carefully planted undergrowth. The Chinamen explained how they had strategically placed explosives at the base of the logs and rock piles, the idea being that if their lives were in danger, they would light the explosives fuses and then retreat into the sanctuary of their mine. The resultant avalanche would hopefully kill their attackers and simultaneously entomb their mine. And Ned recalled being shown their small, secret escape tunnel, which the brothers intended to use when it was safe to venture outside.

* * *

NED SUDDENLY SNAPPED out of his reverie. 'Sorry, Orla, I was remembering how capable my old friends are. You'll soon see for yourself. C'mon, let's get a move on.'

12

Ned made his way through the bush, avoiding the main road. By the time they approached a small settlement nestled in a picturesque valley, Orla was hungry.

'Much further, Ned? My stomach thinks my throat's been cut.'

'Roughly two miles, I reckon. And I'd walk to China for a good cuppa right now.'

Orla now knew The Junction was so named because it was located where two small creeks joined the Buckland River. Mournful, yet mellow calls from a 'happy family' of choughs filled the air. She noticed that a thin veil of smoke enveloped the settlement, permeating the surrounding trees and drifting down the valley. It wafted from the chimney of every established building, but the principle source was the open fireplaces belonging to the crude shacks and tents that littered the settlement approaches and side tracks.

'This way, Orla,' said Ned as he pointed to a partially overgrown track and quickly urged Music forward. It served them well, bypassing the main thoroughfare of the settlement.

The valley floor rose gradually. Twenty minutes later, Ned turned Music abruptly down another small, but well used side track.

'This takes us down to the river. It's steep in places so don't push your horse too hard. And hang on.'

'Yes, Ned,' Orla replied sarcastically, causing Ned to pivot in his saddle and return her cheeky smile.

Without stopping, Orla followed Ned across the gin-clear river. It glided evenly over their crossing point where it was obvious all of the larger riverbed rocks were removed. On the eastern bank they turned north and continued for a half mile along a well-used track surrounded by massive stands of eucalyptus. Abruptly, they entered a clearing and Orla saw a small house which seemed to disappear into the side of the mountain. Well-kept vegetable gardens flourished near the building and she heard the distinct squeal of pigs coming from low-slung shanties located downstream.

Orla was about to speak when a clear, high-pitched voice sang out from the house. 'That you, Ned?'

'It is indeed,' Ned called back happily as he dismounted. 'G'day, Charlie. Are you there, too, Ong?'

Orla watched as the front door suddenly flew open. Two small and quite old oriental men jostled through the opening. One of them almost threw himself down the steps and then ran on short bandy legs to greet Ned. Both men were smiling broadly as they enthusiastically shook hands.

'Bloody good see you, Ned, bloody good,' chortled one of the Chinaman.

'And you too, Charlie,' Ned replied with genuine pleasure.

Orla noticed an unmistakable look of disbelief on Ned's face as the second old man shuffled over to Ned, but that expression quickly evaporated into a sincere, happy smile.

Ned grasped the old man's offered hand in both of his. 'My dear Ong, it's not like you to let Charlie beat you so easily.'

Ong chuckled then replied in a thin piping voice. 'Glad see you, too, Ned. Charlie, he not that flash. He just show off in front this buteful lady.'

By now the brothers had turned their full attention upon Orla.

'She not sister, eh, Ned?' Ong teased. 'She very much too good looking to be any sister of you.'

Ned laughed loudly. So did Ong, ducking, but failing to avoid Ned's playful flip to one of his ears.

'Listen you, two,' Ned continued. 'I'd like you to meet, Orla. And no, she's not my sister.'

Orla was intrigued how small the Chinamen were. And their effervescent, uninhibited and forthright manner was not what she had expected. Her brother had told her Chinese people were diminutive, but extremely polite and shy!

Ong wore a small pointed beard and both men were almost bald though Charlie had the remnants of his hair pulled back into a ponytail. Their clothes appeared very clean, were loose fitting and their three quarter length trousers exposed bare feet. But the most striking thing about them was their light brown skin.

'I've heard so much about you boys,' Orla said cheerfully. 'Ned reckons you're his best and most loyal friends, so any friend of Ned will always be my friend. Oh, and by the way, he reckons you two are the best damn cooks in the colony.'

Her genuine well-chosen words and soft lilting Irish voice had both brothers spellbound. They looked from Orla to each other, and then, smiling happily and nodding, muttered something in Chinese. The brothers took it in turn to gently shake her hand, explaining it was their deepest honour to be so worthily considered.

Ong then shuffled back to the house, calling over his shoulder as he went, 'Ong can take hint. I get something you for blekfast.'

While Charlie and Ned fitted hobbles to the horses, Orla removed the saddles. Ned then unloaded Boss Boy. As he slung his saddlebag over his shoulder, he placed one arm around Orla's waist. He draped his other arm around Charlie's shoulder and together they walked towards the house.

'What's wrong with your brother, Charlie?' Ned asked, knowing they were still out of earshot of the house. 'He's changed so bloody much in only a few months. Has Ong been mistreated by any of the

European miners? Mark my word, Charlie; I'll happily square the ledger if he has been.'

'No, no Ned, nothing like that, we all time keep away from them. I know long time that Ong been slowing down, not that he admit to it. I frightened it be much worse. He drinking and he smoke the poppy most every day now and has much pain most times. And he even sometimes is not eating my cooking! I think his time coming soon, Ned,' replied a disconsolate Charlie. 'Confucius agree, I think.'

'Listen Charlie, if there's anything I can do, you must let me know. Right?'

'Thanks, Ned. But not much you can do.'

Ned nodded to convey his understanding, though, not his acceptance.

True to his word, Ong soon arrived with their breakfast. Ned and Orla ate ravenously: bacon, tomatoes, and a rice dish mixed with finely chopped vegetables, followed by mugs of green tea. Ned and Orla enthusiastically thanked their hosts for the generous, much-anticipated meal.

Once they were all seated in the shade on the veranda, Orla watched as Ned nonchalantly picked up his saddlebag. With an exaggerated flourish he first withdrew a bottle of brandy, and then with equal display, produced a brown paper package. He simultaneously handed the brandy to Charlie and the paper package to Ong.

Charlie's delight was immediate. He clapped his hands and smiled a broad, gap-toothed smile. 'Ahhh, just what needed for new recipe, not for drinking eh Ned? Blandy not like Ong too much; make Ong go silly in head.' They all laughed at Charlie's veiled threat for Ong to keep his hands off Ned's gift.

Their attention was now upon Ong, who was tearing the paper from his gift.

'You bute, Ned! This be best barley sugar! You know my sweet tooth, eh?' he said in obvious delight, but quickly added. 'Need teeth to eat this. No good for Charlie, his teeth long gone.' Again they all laughed at Ong's barbed but good humour.

As the afternoon unfolded, punctuated by either Ong or

Charlie producing cups of perfumed tea and a variety of biscuits and rice-cakes, it was agreed that Ned and Orla would stay overnight.

Whilst the brothers had no idea of the purpose for Ned's visit, it was clear to them that a very sober Ned had something important on his mind.

'Ong, do you remember the tricks of your trade from your days of building furnaces?'

'Of course,' Ong replied. 'All still in this old Chinaman's head and will go with me forever. Why you ask me that, Ned?'

Orla quickly excused herself, anticipating the men were about to discuss something of little interest to her. As she descended the veranda steps, Ong caught up to her.

'You come with me, only be gone little time. Ong show you interesting thing. But first we put on something keep off bloody flies and mossies. Works good.'

Orla took the small bottle offered by Ong, then, following his example rubbed some of its brown liquid contents onto her bare arms and then onto the back of her neck.

'From herb garden. You like smell, Orla?'

Ong then turned and shuffled away. Intrigued, Orla happily followed the little man. In single file they followed a narrow track, which accompanied the river upstream. Having walked about three quarters of a mile they then waded across the river and ascended a gentle but heavily overgrown slope. The terrain soon levelled out revealing several rocky craters: abandoned goldmines. Ong carefully led Orla to the opening of one of them, then picked up a fist-sized rock and handed it to her.

'You drop now and listen it finish falling.'

Orla did so and waited for what seemed like an eternity before she finally heard a muffled thump. She quickly scrambled back, sending loose rocks cascading over the edge of the mineshaft.

'Bad place to fall and land on head,' said Ong with a knowing grin. 'What you think, Orla?'

Immediately understanding the significance of this site, Orla placed a hand on Ong's shoulder. 'You advised Ned well, to be sure. No one will ever find that man. Thanks, Ong.'

Orla allowed herself a few moments to reflect upon her previous indifferent, blasé attitude towards Rupert Golding's death. Her justified sense of virtue gave way to a twinge of discomfort as the reality dawned that the poor bugger really didn't have a chance, and his wasted life would be forever upon her conscience.

Orla and Ong ambled back towards the house, relaxed in each other's company. They stopped once for Ong to rest where he casually pointed out a large red-bellied black snake sunbathing on a tangle of logs.

'Not poisonous, but make sick if he bite you.'

'Well, *I* don't intend to find out! Let's go.'

A little further on, Ong showed Orla how to catch the noisy but colourful alpine grasshoppers. Despite Ong's age, illness and lack of agility, he shuffled to the location where he anticipated a descending grasshopper would land after its whirring, clacking flight... then pounced just as it landed. His technique was almost flawless.

Orla tried to copy Ong's tactics, but inevitably the grasshoppers would escape. Ong was delighted. He hopped from leg to leg, chuckling to himself as Orla's frustration mounted.

'They good to eat, Orla, but need catch many. Ong too old for that now. Good, too, for catching fish.'

'No thanks Ong; I'd rather stick to bacon and eggs. Though, it'd be nice to stay and do some fishing. But Ned seems restless. I think he wants to get moving. I've got no idea yet what he has in mind, but I'm sure he'll let me know soon enough.'

When they arrived back at the house, an exhausted Ong sat beside Orla on the opposite side of the table from Ned and Charlie. He briefly explained where he had just taken Orla, and how she had mastered the art of catching grasshoppers: they all laughed as Ong animatedly described Orla's catching style... but no one commented further about the unorthodox gravesite.

After the laughter died down, Orla again excused herself and rose from the table. She walked behind Ned, wrapped her arms lovingly around his neck, gently kissed his ear and then strolled down to the river. She removed her boots and waded about in the crystal-clear water for a minute or so then sat on a large rock in the shade, her feet dangling in the cool water.

She watched a bright, iridescent blue male dragonfly hovering over a slow stretch of water. Whenever another dragonfly approached, the male immediately challenged it. If the intruder was another male, combat ensued. Their high speed aerial jousting produced noisy flashes of electric blue as the resident dragonfly fought to defend his territory. If the intruder was a receptive female, mating invariably took place.

As the afternoon turned to early evening, Orla felt strangely tired. Her deepening tiredness was a most unusual experience, even allowing for her lovemaking and riding nearly fifty miles within the past fourteen hours. She was accustomed to busy, long, and productive working days when living with the McIntyre's without ever feeling like this. Nevertheless, she wandered back to the men, yawning. Ned suggested she get some sleep.

Orla awoke with a fright, not immediately recognising her new surroundings. She was relieved to hear Ned's laughter. Feeling drowsy, though refreshed and again quite hungry, she joined the men. It would soon be dark; however, three oil lamps already provided an insipid yellow light, casting weird shadows of the men against the veranda wall. The air was laced with a tangy aroma Orla immediately recognised as Ong's insect repellent. The mosquitoes had obviously arrived; their attention divided between dancing their lives away against the glass of the lamps, or savouring the men's exposed skin. It was also obvious the men had abstained from drinking — indeed, there was an air of seriousness and anticipation surrounding them.

Orla suggested she should start preparing their dinner.

'You come sit here, Orla,' Charlie insisted. 'It no problem, I get you dinner. We already eat few hours ago.'

Shortly after in the rapidly gathering darkness, the brothers wandered off to feed their visitors' horses. Orla continued watching them as they adjusted water flows in the channels serving the pigsties and their vegetable and herb gardens. *Ned wasn't joking*, she thought. *They really are clever little buggers.*

Ned moved and sat close to Orla. In a matter-of-fact, methodical manner he explained their earlier discussion; his plans for the future of North Eastern Victoria and how he hoped his actions would deliver peace and fair justice to the region. He then outlined events he would soon instigate at a small town called Glenrowan exuding an extreme confidence that his actions there would be decisive, his plan infallible.

'Bloody hell, boyo, are you sure you haven't bitten off more than you can chew? I mean it. It sounds grand, but what *if* something goes wrong? What about us? Wouldn't we be better off — and a damn site safer — to just leave this colony... or this country, and start over?'

'I never said it was going to be easy or safe,' replied Ned. 'But someone needs to challenge those bullying bastards... our so-called authorities. I've had a gut-full... I'm also convinced that if I make a positive move, the good people of the Northeast, like the McIntyres, will support me.

'I'll explain my special plan for Glenrowan in more detail later, but you should know it includes making protective body armour for me and the boys. I'm convinced our armour will be a major surprise to any traps, and give us certain protection against close-up small arms fire... if it eventuates.'

'I dunno, Ned. You've obviously thought about this a lot, but the armour thing sounds a bit fanciful to me. Where on earth are you going to get it from?'

'Actually, it's not as fanciful as you might think. In the morning when we leave, Charlie and Ong are coming with us. Their backgrounds are in fashioning steel. And, well, when I mentioned my plan, they convinced me that their ancient know-how will slash the armour's manufacturing time, and that they would be honoured to assist. Joe's already organising the steel. I told you about that, remember?

'I know it seems unfair to subject Ong to the rough travelling and the living conditions that'll be involved, but he wouldn't accept his ill health as a reason for not helping. It's me who should be honoured,' Ned confided.

'You're one determined boyo,' replied Orla. 'I'll tag along with you, Ned. But you must promise me you'll be careful, and be man enough to bail out if you reckon things look like getting on top of you. And, I'll gladly help keep an eye on Ong's condition, but you must insist Charlie tells you when Ong isn't up to anything you ask of him. By the way, when will you be taking my measurements for this glorious armour? You'll be needing my help too, boyo.'

Ned said nothing but simply slid his arm around her shoulder, drew her closer and kissed her gently on her temple.

But a shadow of doubt crept into Orla's psyche. She found sleep difficult, continually revisiting Ned's words in her mind. Something unstoppable was building, but everything about it seemed to anticipate violence. Ned was determined and committed, that was palpably obvious. She also felt strangely maternal. She wanted to support him and his dreams, but she wanted him alive.

Eventually Orla drifted off to sleep — this time with Joan's words ringing in her mind — determined that she would further discuss with Ned how to achieve his outcome but with less potential for bloodshed.

An hour before dawn, a small breakfast was shared in relative silence. The horses were relieved of their hobbles and Ned and Orla went about brushing, saddling, and distributing the load for Boss Boy so that Charlie and Ong could ride two up. Both brothers were to carry small packs containing food, blankets, and clothing... and Ong's supply of opium.

Charlie secured the house: he had no idea when, or if, he would ever return to his beloved home. Not wanting his pigs to starve, he released them, then threw open the gates to his vegetable gardens.

Orla felt sympathy and respect for Ong and Charlie as they stood shoulder to shoulder facing their home while silently bowing their heads, presumably, in prayer. After a few minutes the brothers turned as one and strode to Boss Boy. Ned gave each of them a leg up; Charlie up front to command Boss Boy, and Ong behind, with his brother for support when needed.

13

Unnoticed, the four riders skirted The Junction just after daybreak. By mid-day they had passed Porepunkah and were headed for Greta, Ned's hometown. They travelled at a steady pace avoiding well-used tracks, fence lines, and any outbuildings. It was obvious to Orla that Ned knew the country well, keeping them within cover of heavy timber and following barely visible trails... and always moving below the ridgelines.

A halt was called every half hour for Ong to rest, and to spare the horses. Late afternoon, Ned led them through thick scrub up onto a high ridge. Surprisingly, at the peak, there was a natural clearing that provided a restricted, but adequate view of Greta in the distance. Ned called a halt.

While they ate a meagre meal of salted pork, Charlie noticed that Ong was more than just tired. Ong needed his pipe. Through a pain-easing opiate fog, Ong reflected upon his upcoming duty. Silent prayers sought help from Confucius... that he should be granted time to fulfil his promise to his dear friend, Ned. But Ong was also a practical man. He knew the devil tormenting his body was rapidly stripping him of life. And when the uninvited thought of also possibly failing Charlie suddenly surfaced, tears of abject frustration rolled slowly down his shiny brown cheeks.

'We camp here tonight?' Charlie asked Ned.

'Maybe, maybe not,' Ned replied. 'Actually, I'm expecting company soon. We agreed to meet here, today, if the coast was clear. That's *if* the traps haven't been up to their usual games and arrested my friend, Tom.'

For the next hour they rested in the shade, chatting occasionally. Insects buzzed. Flies tormented. A walk into the bush to answer the call of nature provided relief from the hard ground and the opportunity to stretch tired muscles.

Suddenly Music threw up her head and whinnied softly.

'That'll be Tom, I reckon,' Ned announced excitedly.

A few minutes passed, then suddenly, two riders ghosted into view in a gully far below. Ned pointed them out to Orla and Charlie and they all watched as their visitors steadily made their way up through the timber. When the riders eventually drew rein in the clearing, Orla looked on with interest.

The lead rider was well built and loose limbed, and dressed in the fashion of the working bushman. She guessed he was about Ned's age, though not quite as tall. He also wore a three-quarter beard and a warm smile. He was not wearing pistols, but a rifle was tied to the large pack straddling his horse's rump.

The second rider, Orla soon realised, was a young woman about seventeen or eighteen. A sizeable pack also hung down over the flanks of her mount. Despite wearing a long brown skirt, she rode astride. She also wore a light green shirt with button-down long sleeves and puffed shoulders, good quality riding boots and a wide brimmed hat with a trailing plume of feathers. And she was very attractive — a detail not overlooked by Orla.

'How's things, cuz?' shouted the man as he swung from the saddle and strode over to Ned.

'Wouldn't be dead for quids, Tom,' Ned replied as they enthusiastically shook hands and slapped one another's shoulder.

Ned then ran to the young woman, helped her from the horse and embraced her in an unabashed fashion, lifting her off the ground and spinning her about. Both laughed in obvious delight.

'Kate, you look beautiful and so grown-up,' Ned whispered into her ear, and then took her by the hand. 'Come on, meet my friends.' Ned called for everyone to gather around. 'Righto. I'd like you to meet my cousins. First, this is the lovely Catherine Lloyd — but she calls herself Kate — and this is Tom Lloyd, my mentor and great friend.' Ned then introduced Orla, Charlie and, finally, a very comatose Ong.

After handshakes all round, the men sat and talked and drank some of the rum Tom brought with him... leaving Kate and Orla to get better acquainted.

Orla was bristling. 'So, for cousins, you seem to be on rather good terms with Ned.'

Kate spun to face Orla. She glared, but her expression immediately vanished when she recognised a deadly menace in Orla's return gaze.

'Let's go for a walk,' replied Kate. 'We need to clear the air.'

When the girls were out of earshot, Orla said in a very brusque fashion, 'Well, Kate, what do I need to know?'

'I think I've always been in love with Ned. But he's changed so much in the past year... I hardly know him anymore. What's really frustrating is that he always makes me feel special, but treats me like I'm a ten year old. And now it appears you've taken him from me.' After a thoughtful pause Kate continued. 'I'll not contest his affections, Orla. I've already seen how he looks at you. But he'll always be my dearest friend; you can't take that from me.

'And all he talks to me about is how he intends to rid this region of the biased and antagonistic judicial system. That's what's eating at Ned you know, and it's diluting my feelings for him because he never includes me in his future. I don't hate you, Orla.' Kate was now in tears. 'It's the damn police I hate.'

Looking directly at Kate, a now more relaxed and sympathetic Orla replied, quietly. 'It's just the same in Ireland, you know. I hoped when I came to this country I'd escape that shite for a while, but look what I've landed in. I've agreed to marry Ned and I accept his aspirations, so mark my words, no one dare try and take him from me. And, Kate believe me, I'll never interfere with the special friendship you'll obviously always share with Ned.'

'I accept that, Orla. But don't think you can boss me about. I won't put up with that. Otherwise, I think we can easily be good friends. What do you reckon?'

A bit taken aback by Kate's forthrightness, Orla replied, 'As I've already said to Charlie and Ong, any friend of Ned will always be a friend of mine.' The two young women embraced and then, chatting amiably, rejoined the men.

* * *

ORLA LIKED TOM. He was alert but relaxed in his manner, never averted his gaze and seemed genuinely interested in what anyone said.

'Hey, Ned, the traps rode through Greta yesterday,' Tom announced at the first opportunity.

'Bastards! That makes things decidedly unhealthy,' Ned hissed angrily. 'We'll have to give Greta a miss for the time being.'

Tom obviously shared a close relationship with Ned. Orla was intrigued that they sat privately, shoulder-to-shoulder, chatting quietly for nearly half an hour. However, during that time she overheard Tom marvelling at Ned's uncanny luck in recruiting the skills of the Chinese brothers.

Tom also struck an instant rapport with Charlie and Ong, encouraging them to explain how they'd go about making the armour Ned had in mind.

Orla listened attentively as the Chinamen pointed out that the forging operations were bound to generate uninvited interest if either too much noise was heard repeatedly coming from one site, or if abnormal comings and goings was noticed on the approaches. Unanimously they agreed upon multiple manufacturing locations: all would not be lost if the police discovered a *single* forge.

As the sun set, Orla and Kate prepared an evening meal. After the meal, Ong was again made as comfortable as possible while he purposefully surrounded himself with clouds of pipe smoke, a now familiar sight.

Charlie retreated to his own swag, his head reeling from the effects of his brother's excesses. Orla and Ned spread their swags well away from the others.

However, Tom and Kate positioned their respective swags in close company to the tethered horses. As usual, Tom employed the gang's time proven alarm system, loosely wrapping one end of Music's halter rope around his wrist, the purpose being that if the ever alert mare suddenly raised her head in recognition of approaching riders, he would be instantly woken and able to quickly warn the others.

Despite the night's chill, hordes of bloodthirsty mosquitoes, and the discomfort of the hard ground, deep sleep soon engulfed everyone beneath a brilliant starlit sky.

14

Before daybreak Orla and Ned led the horses to another nearby ridge clearing where subalpine grasses were plentiful. Each tuft was adorned with multiple dew-laced cobwebs. All five horses grazed contentedly as Ned and Orla swept their hands over each horse's back to remove any grit. The animals also cooperated as Orla methodically checked each horse for leg or hoof injuries.

It took little time to get ready to ride out, but Ned waited patiently while Charlie helped Ong swallow his opiates. When they set off, Kate handed out their breakfast — four small sweet biscuits and a handful of dried grapes.

The air was cool as Ned led them down off the ridge. Fine shreds of high cloud fought to subdue any tentative warmth from the early morning sun. The calls of the choughs and the cockatoos, the sight of unconcerned wallabies eating nearby, the trickle of a creek, and the fresh clean smell of the peppermint gums gave a special feel to the new day. A heavy mist slowly gliding up the surrounding valleys would soon burn off as the sun continued its ascent.

Even though they stopped occasionally to allow Ong to rest, by mid-morning they'd travelled at least eighteen miles according to

Ned. At that time, he again changed direction. The others followed in single file. Wattle scrub soon gave way to steeply rising terrain where eucalypts towered overhead and unusually tall bracken surrounded them. They scrambled onto a ridge that was devoid of undergrowth which provided an incredible view of the surrounding ranges and of the valley flats they had left far behind. Everyone had felt the strain of the last ascent... except, Boss Boy, who appeared barely winded. The other horses were now lathered and blowing hard.

'We should be there in another half hour,' Ned advised. 'But first, let's have a drink while the horses take a breather. How's Ong coping, Charlie?' Ned interpreted Charlie's silence to mean Ong was fine. But while Ong lustily drew on his opium pipe the opportunity arose for Ned, to confront Charlie. 'Look at the poor bugger, Charlie. He won't be able to put up with much more of this. It's not fair on him and it's not fair on us if we need to give the traps the slip.'

'I know you not happy, Ned,' Charlie replied sadly. 'But he much want to teach you his craft before he die. Ong say he owe you that. Leave him rest for ten more minutes... then we go.' After a thoughtful pause Charlie asked, 'We go now to place you choose to make armour suits?'

'Yes, but Ong must be taken home as soon as possible,' said a genuinely concerned Ned. 'We can't care for him properly when we have so much to do. And Charlie, there'll be a lot more of this bush bashing before we're finished. You must think about that.'

'I understand, Ned. I get Ong home as soon as we finish number one furnace firing. One week from now, no later I think,' Charlie pleaded.

'All right, old friend,' replied Ned, now impatient to leave. 'A week it is, and then home he goes. Come on you lot, let's get moving.'

The descent from that ridge was extremely difficult. There were loose rocks, hidden logs, overgrown abandoned wombat burrows, and the relentless downhill gradient. Boss Boy handled the rough going with amazing self-assurance. In places where the other horses slid on their rumps, Boss Boy would gradually ease himself forward and step confidently before again easing himself forward to place his next step. It was as if he sensed his balance was vital for the old men on his back. At least Ong never complained. In fact, he never complained, no matter how dreadful he felt... or how little he felt.

Ned's estimate was good. It took them slightly less than thirty minutes of taxing riding to arrive at a natural clearing in a heavily timbered gully. Ned immediately called a halt. At the opposite end of the clearing, Orla noticed a makeshift hut, its bark roof held down with rocks. A wisp of smoke rose from an equally makeshift overlapping bark chimney... but there was no sign of life.

Suddenly, Boss Boy whinnied in alarm. In the distance, on the far side of the hut, three riders appeared. In single file, their horses loped along a track leading to the hut.

'At em girl!' Ned yelled without warning while simultaneously booting Music into a full gallop, obviously intent on charging across the clearing.

It took only a few seconds for the three distant riders to react. Revolvers quickly appeared. But they gently drew rein and casually re-holstered their weapons when they recognised Ned.

As Ned drew level with them, he growled angrily, 'Bloody hell, you lot! We could've all been coppers, and you could've all been dead by now! What are you playing at? You should've known better, Joe, for not having someone posted.'

'And it's great to see you, too, brother dear,' said Dan, who cheekily added before Ned could reply. 'Ah, take it easy, Ned. Steve saw you coming ages ago when he *was* on lookout. We just thought we'd get up your nose for a bit of fun. You know, to make it look like we're an easy target — just to stir you up like.'

'Yeah, righto,' replied Ned, secretly enjoying their prank. 'I'll believe you this time, but...'

'Hey, just a fuckin' minute, Ned,' Dan interrupted, pointing animatedly as he suddenly recognised Orla. 'Isn't she the sheila that damn near killed us?'

'All will be revealed in good time. Just relax, Dan,' said Ned with light hearted authority.

'Yeah, right, but she snuffed Golding... remember? What the bloody hell's she doin' here?'

Ignoring his brother, and his anxiety, Ned turned to face Joe. 'And how's things with you, mate? Just as well I can still rely on someone.'

'Maybe, but the lads have been unusually well behaved,' replied Joe in an offhanded manner. 'But Dan's right. If this *is* that tart who put the fear of Christ in you lot, what do you expect? Mind you, she is a looker.'

Ned slapped Joe on the shoulder. 'No tart, mate. Just hang on and I'll explain everything, shortly. And, Steve, me boy. Fancy you... keeping out of trouble; that's a first,' said Ned in a mock father-like voice.

'Anyhow, it's a good thing you're all still alive. And hey, the new hut looks real good. Well done, lads,' Ned continued, clearly impressed by their handiwork.

As the other riders approached and reined in, Ned added. 'Now, before you three do or say anything else, I want you to meet some friends of mine. Dan and Steve, you already know Orla so you know what to expect if you step out of line.'

'G'day Orla,' replied Dan tentatively. 'I've no axe to grind if Ned reckons you're with us. But, where the hell did you learn to shoot like that?'

'From my da,' Orla replied good naturedly. 'And his name was Dan, too, and every bit as good looking as you.' Fully taken in by Orla's words of conciliation, Dan puffed out his chest as if he had just won a prize.

Steve mumbled something incomprehensible, barely acknowledging her.

'Now, Joe, this is Orla, my wife soon to be. Yes, my wife.'

'God Almighty!' Joe responded somewhat sarcastically. 'I turn my back on you for five minutes and look what happens? However, any bride of Ned must be a friend of mine.' He offered his hand, and nodded respectfully to Orla. 'Pleased to meet you Orla.'

With an expansive wave of his arm in their direction, Ned announced, 'And these gentlemen are my trusted and dear friends,

Charlie and Ong. They're going to show us something about making armour, so look after them and listen carefully to what they have to say.

'First though, you three, help Ong and Charlie down, then get Ong into the shade... and see if he wants a drink,' Ned instructed, easily resuming his complete and natural authority. 'Then give Tom and Kate a hand with their gear and get this Waler unloaded. And after that, would you be kind enough to take our horses down to the creek... and see if you can rustle up some decent feed for them while you're at it.'

After more handshakes and hugs reserved only for Kate, Orla was amused by the furtive sideways looks from Dan and Steve, whom she realised, were probably taken by her good looks but still understandably edgy given the experience of their previous meeting.

'Rest easy, boyos, we're all on the same side now,' she said, trying to placate them in her genial Irish brogue. But she knew instinctively Dan would need more than that to win him over, and Steve seemed annoyingly aloof. Joe on the other hand was polite, yet behaved somewhat indifferently. *Perhaps he's preoccupied*, she thought.

During this meeting, Orla discreetly studied Joe, Dan, and Steve. Joe Byrne stood about two inches shorter than Ned and was not as well muscled. She guessed he was probably the same age as Ned. His hair was medium length and swept to one side across his head. He also had a straggly beard growing below his chin and along his jaw line, and he wore a droopy moustache. On closer inspection, Orla realized the moustache was concealing either a harelip or some disfiguring facial wound. He was soberly dressed in typical bushman clothes and wore his long sleeved shirt buttoned down. He appeared quite relaxed. It also intrigued Orla, and obviously pleased Charlie and Ong, that Joe had greeted the Chinamen in their tongue.

Dan Kelly, she guessed, was about the same age as she. He looked like a slim youth when standing beside his brother, and Dan's sallow face belied his age and outdoor lifestyle. His hair was jet black but he had little or no facial hair. Well-worn and ill fitting clothing indicated to Orla that Dan was probably wearing cast-offs. He appeared to have a quiet, yet morose, temperament... and was clearly devoted to Ned.

Steve Hart also appeared to be about the same age as Dan, though not as tall, but marginally heavier in build. His hair was brown, medium length and centrally parted. He was by far the best dressed, though, what he wore had also seen better days. Apart from his aloofness towards Orla, his otherwise youthful face had a vindictive expression. Orla experienced a brief unsettling moment when she tried to hold his gaze. *He's trouble, this one*, she thought.

Above all else, they all seemed healthy, strong and athletic, and all of them according to Ned, were exceptional horsemen. Orla felt a rush of youthful excitement at the prospect of taking them on.

It seemed to Orla that morale between these three had held up, despite a disturbing lack of food. The side of bacon, which Tom had somehow managed to 'pick up' in Greta, brought loud cheers from the boys. The other provisions brought in by Tom and Kate would also be most welcome, particularly the old newspapers, since toilet paper was always at a premium, even if not living it rough.

With the unloading finished, Orla watched Steve ride off to resume lookout duty. Tom offered to relieve him in about three hours, which would give Ned and Tom time to quiz Joe.

* * *

NED WAS PLEASED. The hut was finished and Joe had already stripped nine broad steel blades from the ploughs of unsuspecting Greta and Oxley farmers. These mouldboards would be used to fashion Ned's armoured suits.

Mid-afternoon, Tom took over as lookout. He would return just after dark since the police were unlikely to attempt any heroics after sundown. Joe led the others to his chosen forge site. While Charlie inspected the close-by creek, Ong shuffled about looking at the ground, occasionally making clucking sounds.

'Good spot, velly good,' Ong said encouragingly to Joe. Ong then called the others together and with help from Charlie set about explaining what needed to be done. Orla listened intently. Ong was happy with the size of the clearing and its level location, but now needed three materials — the right kind of wood, flat rocks, and a special type of clay. He then emphasized that he only wanted dry hardwood; wood that would burn hot and evenly for hours. Such timber was abundant.

The second item was easy. There was an unlimited quantity of flat rocks, of all sizes, both in the creek and along its banks. But the third item had Orla perplexed. Now obviously tired, Ong sank to his haunches in the shade but indicated they should all follow Charlie downstream. Where the creek's bank presented little resistance to flooding, Charlie dropped onto his knees. From a depression, he then scooped up some dark yellow mud.

'This clay we need much of.' He then pointed out several other promising collection sites.

Using simple dirt sketches, a near exhausted Ong then illustrated how the forge was to be constructed. The sides, front and back would be made from the flat rocks and laid to progressively form an overarching hood. That meant the rocks in any course had to marginally overhang those in the course below. The rocks would essentially be held in place by their own weight, but all gaps had to be liberally packed with the special clay to reinforce the structure and trap the heat. A level stone foundation was important: it, too, had to be packed with the clay.

'No gaps,' stressed Charlie. 'Forge it then work good. You all savvy?'

The main opening in the forge would face the creek and be large enough to allow the steel armour segments to be easily inserted and retrieved. A piece of flat steel placed over this opening would provide basic airflow regulation and temperature control. Ong was adamant their forge would ensure that each steel segment would uniformly and rapidly rise to its required working temperature... and thus slash the time needed to fashion the armour.

A small opening was to be left at the top of the forge. It, too, would be covered with a flat piece of steel to regulate the release of combustion gases and any smoke. Finally, three small openings were to be crafted at the base of the forge to allow a draught to force its way up through the fire pit and to also provide the means of removing ash.

You clever little buggers, Orla realised. *It won't need a bellows!*

Ong and Charlie were confident that if everyone pitched in, the forge could be built within a week.

Sadly however, Ong was now trembling and on the verge of collapsing. Ned quickly placed his arm around the old man's waist and supported him as Charlie took over.

'Location velly good,' Charlie said enthusiastically. 'All smoke go up this valley. But if heat be good quality inside, there be velly little smoke anyway. No one see that I think. But must keep fire going. If you let fire go out, or heat it be lost, forge soon blake up.

'Shaping armour it be noisy business,' Charlie continued. 'I know we in much hidden place, but noise it travel long way. What we need do is make only little noise.'

'And how pray tell do we do that?' Dan asked impatiently.

'Easy I think,' replied Charlie. 'We cut tree on this side of creek and let fall across that side. You jam it in bank on both sides and have it half in water, half out. I show you how, no problem. It then be anvil for shaping steel. Much noise stay in trunk, and water it take away much sound, too. Creek it also be quench — to make steel tough.'

Genuinely astounded, Ned commented, 'Bloody hell you two, you've thought of everything.'

'But how big does the tree need to be for this anvil of yours?' Steve asked.

Charlie pointed to a nearby stringy-bark gum. Orla watched as Ned and his gang exchanged looks of disbelief.

Ned broke the silence. 'Well, what do yah say? It's only a forty-footer. Are you blokes up to it, or not? We'll get started first thing tomorrow, right?' He didn't wait for a reply, but turned to Charlie who was tapping him on his shoulder.

'Perhaps after this one built, Ned, it be much more easy next place,' he suggested good-naturedly. The prospect of repeating this exercise failed to spawn any enthusiasm. But then again, the China-men's plans made sense.

Orla looked about while she helped Charlie and Kate prepare the evening meal; they'd agreed to eat outside that night. Joe was rebuilding the outdoor campfire. Dan and Steve were hauling buckets of water from the creek for brewing tea and washing up: the boys had already split enough wood to keep the campfire blazing for hours and the indoor fire going well into the next morning. She also noticed Ned chatting with Ong, and twice saw him refill the old man's opium pipe.

As the meal was about to be served, Tom appeared from the dark and reined in. 'How's that for perfect timing?' he jested. 'Don't wait for me, tuck in. It sure smells a bit of all right! I'll join you after I've washed up.'

Well-chewed chop bones were the only evidence of that meal. The first of many cups of tea was poured. Everyone then relaxed in quiet companionship, alternating their gaze between the spectacle of the rising moon and the licks of flame pirouetting from their almost smokeless campfire.

An hour lapsed. Orla then gently ordered Dan and Steve to collect everyone's plates and cutlery. Both ignored her. So she raised her voice. 'Move your lazy arses you two or you can do the washing up on your own.' Ned's glare further motivated them: both boys rose and sauntered off to the hut.

Ned and Joe lit two night lanterns, one for Orla and the boys, the other to light the path for anyone who needed to visit the long drop. Not long after as the other gang members settled in around the campfire, chuckling sounds were heard coming from the hut. Dan was soon laughing uncontrollably. When he paused to catch his breath, another hesitant, but then full belly laugh erupted — some-thing Ned, Joe, Tom, and Kate had not heard for a long time. To get Steve laughing like that, Orla had obviously found a way of pene-trating his moody demeanour. And when Orla joined in, their merri-ment — with all three of them on top note — even made the older men and Kate chuckle.

Dan was still giggling intermittently when Orla left the hut to join the others around the campfire. Struggling to contain her own giggles, Orla happily explained the cause of the boy's outbursts.

'I simply told them about my brothers back home in Ireland. Whenever they'd wade into fisticuffs to protect their little sister, it was usually *me* who finished the fight. But what really tickled those two boys was how I would question the parentage of each moron in the fight — and then point out how useless they all were. They had a good laugh, eh?'

Ned again chuckled to himself. He knew only too well what she was capable of, and Dan and Steve certainly had no reason to doubt the truth underscoring her story. Joe was smiling. The serious tinge to this outbreak of mirth was not lost on him, either, because Ned had previously confided in him about their second demoralizing meeting with Orla.

After helping Ong settle into his swag with his opium pipe, Charlie rejoined the others at the campfire. 'Much we need do tomorrow. No stay up when moon go past this high,' he said with authority, signalling with his raised arm that he meant no later than ten o'clock. Charlie bowed slightly then walked purposefully away into the night.

'Righto, Charlie, you're the boss,' replied Ned. 'We won't be far behind you.'

And to Ned's surprise Dan and Steve yelled out 'good night'. More loud laughter erupted, but soon, their night lamp was extinguished and the laughter faded... and then stopped.

Ned, Orla, Tom, Joe, and Kate sat around the campfire for another hour or so, quietly chatting and drinking tea. Joe was obviously relaxed in Ned's company and freely spoke his mind. It was during this time Orla first learnt of *his* misgivings about Ned's plans.

'I'm still a bit uneasy about this armour lark,' Joe confessed. 'I think it's a waste of bloody time and not worth the effort. But if you reckon it'll work, Ned, then I'll go along with it. I must say though, they're smart old fella's, those two. Where'd you say you met 'em, Ned?'

Ned patiently reminded Joe of how and where he had met the

Chinamen, how their friendship had grown and how their collective advice and their respective backgrounds convinced him the armour suits were viable. Ned insistently added, 'Our future plans depend upon it, Joe. When we strike, we'll need an unexpected and telling advantage over any coppers.'

Joe said nothing but nodded slowly to himself as if still weighing up the outcome. For Tom's benefit, Ned and Joe explained the forge construction plans. They agreed unanimously that the building of any subsequent forges would only proceed if their first attempt was a success.

It has to be a success, Ned thought. *Time's running out and I don't really have an alternative plan.*

15

Tom woke before dawn the next morning, saddled his horse and quietly left the camp. From a vantage point about half a mile from and overlooking the valley, which contained the forge site, he could clearly see the surrounding ridge lines and all approach routes. If two or more approaching riders were spotted, he was to immediately ride back to the hut to notify the gang. Depending upon the time, the actual number of riders sighted and their location, Ned would then decide to either stay put and post defensive guard positions until after dark, or leave immediately, taking with them only essential belongings.

Tom also knew that after a month of having initiated this lookout system, and given that not a single sighting had been made, the gang could feel reasonably confident of remaining undiscovered. However, he realised with every passing day it theoretically increased the possibility of detection. On balance, he trusted Ned's judgment that their seclusion and lookout system would provide ample time to complete their task.

Only Ong and Charlie were exempt from the watch roster agreed the previous night.

* * *

AND SO CONSTRUCTION of the first forge began. Dan and Steve attacked the chosen stringy-bark gum with youthful energy, their axes ringing steadily. The tree soon crashed to the ground, easily spanning the creek, but unfortunately, not landing precisely where they believed it would. By mid-morning all of the branches had been removed from the tree.

Ong and Charlie seemed pleased with the progress in preparing what they called, the 'water anvil'. They took measurements then marked where they wanted the tree trunk shortened at both ends. Next they explained how the remaining middle section needed to be manoeuvred: it *had* to be at right angles to the run of the creek.

All agreed it seemed possible, but realised they were in for one hell of a physical challenge. Orla watched as Charlie clambered down to the creek. With Ong's guidance and sightings, Charlie gouged some markings into both of the almost vertical banks of the creek.

Ong explained that he wanted a recess dug into each bank to secure the ends of the log in the correct position; the recesses had to be a specific depth and only just wider than the tree's diameter. If Ong's calculations were correct, approximately half the diameter of the log would remain above water, thereby creating the water anvil.

'Bloody hell,' moaned Joe. 'He doesn't want much, does he?'

While Ned and Joe dug the recesses, Orla and Kate collected an impressive quantity of rocks.

At noon, Charlie called a halt. They all retired to the shade where a small meal of stale bread and hard cheese was washed down with cold creek water. Without any prompting from Ned, as soon as Joe finished his meal he mounted his horse and headed off to relieve Tom as lookout. Not long after, Tom returned to the work site.

'So why haven't you finished?' he cheekily taunted, then ducked for cover as he was pelted with small stones and sticks.

They resumed work an hour later but by mid-afternoon Ned called a halt. 'Righto, that's enough for today, it's too bloody hot to keep this up.' Released from their toil, everyone again sought shade and rested until the sun nearly set.

Later, in the light of a lantern, Orla and Kate gently massaged one of Charlie's mysterious green pastes into the men's tired and blistered hands. They all acknowledged its immediate relief. Everybody retired early; there was to be no laughter or chatting that night.

Ong, however, was restless. He was acutely fatigued, twisted in pain, and frustrated at the prospect he would surely die soon. And all the while seeing in his mind's eye, the fleeting visions of his life — hoping he could stall those images long enough to revisit some of the happy, wonderful times shared with his talented and loving brother.

The next morning was refreshingly cool, however, a warming northerly breeze soon picked up. Orla saw Tom leave to take up lookout duties; she had already been awake for over an hour, curled up in Ned's arms. She felt tired and was angry she had overeaten the previous evening, the reason she suspected for her two visits to the long drop during the night. She dared not say anything to Charlie in case his cooking was to blame. And though she wouldn't admit it to Ned, she secretly missed a comfortable warm bed.

Aching bodies soon loosened, as work got under way. The collective mood was surprisingly bright and cheerful. However, there were two exceptions. Ong was clearly in pain despite having just swallowed the last of his supply of liquid opiate. Orla, too, still felt decidedly unwell and struggled to raise a smile.

After some minor adjustments, Charlie was soon satisfied with the excavations. On the far side of the creek, Dan and Steve were arguing how to use the horses to manoeuvre the log into position. They'd unsuccessfully tried human muscle power aided by improvised levers, and now faced the problem of how to harness the horses without injuring them.

'I'll see if I can sort them out,' Orla called out to Ned. 'You keep going with your mud pies.' Ned smiled sand waved her on, inviting her to cross the creek.

She soon understood the young men's frustration and immediately adopted an appeasing tone of voice which held the boys attention — a ruse she'd always adopted to win over her brothers when she wanted something done. Orla detailed her idea of making a collar by lashing together two opposite-facing forked branches, padded with blankets and canvas. Despite a minor spat and initial resistance from Steve, it took only two hours to complete the collar.

Co-incidentally another milestone was reached at that time: the forge's foundation was completed.

Not long afterwards, a hilarious, but ill-timed stroke of bad luck befell Joe. He innocently sat by the creek and removed his boots and socks. Extracting a troublesome stone from one of his boots, he decided to wash his feet. When he'd finished, he pulled on one of his socks. Suddenly, Joe screamed. He charged up the creek's bank and proceeded to put on an incredible performance. He hopped and ran about, jumped up and down, and stamped his feet — all the time whimpering and howling in pain.

'Christ all mighty,' Ned yelled as he rushed to assist his mate. 'He's been bitten by a bloody snake!'

When Ned reached Joe and grappled him to the ground, the real reason for Joe's performance was obvious. With Ned's help, Joe finally, desperately, ripped off his sock. And there, marching or jumping from the sock's opening was at least twenty highly agitated bull ants, all eagerly seeking further retribution. Each ant had a shiny black body about half an inch long and a yellow head. The ants had simply responded to having a sock thrown onto their nest. They'd seen fit to explore its interior, but weren't expecting to have Joe's inconsiderate foot thrust upon them!

The others gathered around to see what had happened. Stifled chuckles were soon replaced by howls of laughter, which rang through the nearby gullies. Joe was unimpressed: the pain was unbearable. Most of the gang had, at one time or another, been the recipient of at least one bite from the infamous *jack-jumper* of North Eastern Victoria. But Joe had copped at least twenty bites! They weren't laughing so much at his misfortune, but rather, the fantastic footwork and language accompanying his departure from the creek. Together, Steve and Dan comically gave their versions of that footwork, which in turn brought even more howls of laughter at Joe's expense.

Charlie retrieved what remained of his green ointment and rubbed it into Joe's tortured, and now very swollen, foot. Some of his immediate pain abated, but as they all knew, worse was to follow... the powerful, incessant itch from just one bite could send its victim crazy for a week. In Joe's case, that itch was guaranteed to plague him for months.

Ong had another solution – he shared his pipe with Joe. Soon after, Joe collapsed into a comatose sleep that rendered him useless until well after sunup the next day. Though obviously in severe discomfort, Joe stoically hobbled around, helping out where he could.

Despite its weight and bulk, Boss Boy settled into the makeshift collar without apparent discomfort. Dan and Steve did not share Orla's confidence that Boss Boy alone could move the log into position, but agreed that if he couldn't, they'd simply make a second collar and try again using two horses. A separate rope was attached to each side of the collar. The other end of each rope was tied to the end of the log, which was furthermost skewed from the required line.

Orla took Boss Boy's halter and talked to him quietly, gently massaging his muzzle. Ned positioned himself behind Boss Boy, making certain the horse knew he was there, while Dan and Steve positioned their levers on the far side of the log. With growing anticipation, the men awaited further instruction from Orla.

Orla walked the Waler slowly forward until all slack in the ropes was taken up. She then turned. Now facing Boss Boy she continued to urge him forward until the hauling-ropes came up tight. Orla pulled hard on Boss Boy's halter. He tried to follow but seemed distressed as he felt the load. Then, with no further encouragement, he suddenly threw down his head and lunged forward. Neck and shoulders arched, Boss Boy strained hard into the collar, snorting and screaming defiantly. His powerful rear legs shuddered. His entire body quivered.

Orla then yelled, 'C'mon you lot! Get stuck into it.'

With Ned's urging from behind and the two boys enthusiastically working their levers, the log moved slightly. Boss Boy continued to strain... his mighty effort was being rewarded. He took his first step. And then another. Man and beast intensified their efforts.

Excitedly, Orla yelled. 'Stop!' Both ends of the log were now only inches from their respective recesses. Breathing heavily, lathered in sweat and still trembling slightly as his muscles relaxed, Boss Boy stopped and stood quietly. Orla patted his neck gently and talked soothingly into his ear. The men rushed forward and fussed over him, marvelling at what they'd just seen. Though nearly exhausted, Boss Boy had sustained no obvious injuries... and the makeshift collar had held.

The log was now positioned at right angles to the creek, but... it still needed to be manoeuvred into the recesses. After a fifteen minute rest, Boss Boy was led into the creek facing downstream and away from the log. However, this time the ropes were positioned around the log's centre. Dan and Steve positioned themselves on the far bank with their levers in place behind the narrowest end of the log. Ned and Joe positioned their levers behind the heavier butt end, on the bank nearest to the forge.

Slowly Orla led the Waler forward, taking up the slack in the ropes. Again she urged him forward. Orla yelled her command for maximum effort. Again Boss Boy lunged, scrambling for purchase on the slippery rocks while the men worked feverishly on their levers. Gradually the log rotated. Then, with a loud thump, the log landed neatly into position. Sheets of water went flying.

Excited whoops echoed through their valley. There was much backslapping and Ong even managed to perform a little jig. Charlie clapped and shouted, 'Bloody good, bloody good!' Only Boss Boy seemed unmoved by their antics.

While Orla disconnected the hauling ropes, Steve and Dan removed the collar. Satisfied no harm had befallen Boss Boy, Orla led him into the nearby clearing, removed his halter and released him. Boss Boy was not without company that afternoon as he either dozed in the shade or grazed at his leisure: Charlie sat and watched him, producing several elegant charcoal sketches.

By the end of the day the forge, too, was complete. Charlie and Ong were elated with the result and proudly announced that firing could start the day after next. All seemed in readiness for that eagerly anticipated event. A small mountain of wood lay stacked beside the forge.

Their meal that evening was by necessity frugal. Copious cups of tea failed to stop rumbling bellies. Though their chatter extracted an occasional smile from Ong, eventually his eyelids fluttered and he fell into a trancelike sleep.

Orla was the only one who had no desire for food; her thoughts were elsewhere. A realisation struck. It was now the end of March... and she had missed her period.

16

———————

Ned declared the following day a rest day. Kate generously volunteered to perform lookout duties for the entire day. When she returned to the camp, Ned addressed his gang.

'Listen, you've all done an impressive job, but there's bugger-all to eat. We have to do something about that and soon. And I need to get Culphie up here quick smart to start on the armour. I've also promised to get Charlie and Ong back to their place up the Buckland.'

Tom immediately volunteered to return to Greta the next day with Kate, and all being well, bring back sufficient supplies for another week. A list of essentials was drawn up.

'Why not get Tom to call on Culphie *and* the Deveneys? They could all return with Tom, with their bits and pieces. And surely they could fetch in even more food? In the meantime, Dan and me can pay a quick visit to Moyhu and pick up a bottle or two of rum. While we're there, we'll find out if there are any upcoming races,' Steve suggested.

'You're not just here for your good looks, young fella,' Ned replied. 'But no opium, do you hear me. We all need clear minds from now on. Is that idea of Steve's all right with you, Tom?'

'No problems,' replied Tom. 'But won't Culphie and Patrick and his boys have a lot of heavy tools and such with 'em?'

'Only tools they need be tongs, shifter, and smithy hammers,' Charlie interrupted. 'And two sizes chisels, bolts and rivets. All not too heavy. You tell them that, Tom. Then you load up horses with plenty food and other things much needed here.'

'Right, we'll all now try and get a good night's sleep so we can make an early start in the morning,' insisted Ned. Then, in a considered, businesslike fashion he continued. 'Joe, you go with the boys and keep an eye on them. It'll give you a chance to get off that crook foot. And by the way, I'll be going with you initially. Someone needs to tee up some more smithies and pick up the additional mould-boards we'll need at the other forge sites. And Joe, you'll need to find Aaron. He might have some up to date news about police movements. But whatever you say to him, *don't* tell him where we are now or where we intend to set up the next two forges. Aaron's playing a deadly game and the less he knows the better. Right?' Almost as an afterthought, Ned continued, 'Oh, and Orla, would you stay here and keep an eye on Ong?' It was more like an order, which Ned didn't intend... and immediately regretted his ill-chosen words.

Orla was instantly furious, but bit her tongue. She glared at Ned. She watched him relax when she replied in a cynical but otherwise good-natured way. 'Yes, of course, but keep your hands off any strange women you come across. And see if you can get more opium... for Ong. While you're out and about, boyo, you'd better give Alf McIntyre some idea of when you expect to return his bay, and don't forget to tell him how proud he should be of Boss Boy. And, while you're at it, please give my love to Joan and the children.'

Ned wisely nodded in acceptance of Orla's reasonable demands.

The truth was, however, Orla sensed a gathering momentum compelling Ned to progress his plans and she knew intuitively if she continued feeling so dreadfully unwell every morning, her condition would disrupt and delay those plans if she insisted upon tagging along.

About half an hour after the last night lamp was extinguished and the sounds of men sleeping could be heard over the chirping of crickets, Orla nudged Ned.

'You asleep, lover?'

'Not yet. Why?'

'Well, it seems we're going to have a baby. How does that grab you?'

Ned instantly sat bolt upright in their swag. In the light cast by the remnants of the campfire, his initial expression was that of total disbelief. But a broad, happy smile quickly filled his bearded face.

'Jeeesus, Orla! That's fantastic bloody news.' An excited Ned took both of her hands in his and squeezed them firmly. 'How long have you known? When are you due? Why didn't you tell me earlier? There's no way I would've let you do the things you've been doing. You could've done yourself... and *our child*... an injury. Good God, Orla, is this really true? I'm gunna wake the others and give 'em the news.'

'Whoa, whoa, boyo.' Orla gently pulled Ned down to her. 'First things first, as Alf McIntyre would say. Yes, it's true all right,' Orla whispered as she held his head between her hands and looked directly into his strange glowing eyes. 'Let's just you and me share this moment. We can tell the others in the morning. Besides, they all need their beauty sleep, remember?'

Ned nodded but said nothing. As they lay on their swag Ned entwined her in a loving cuddle, savouring her clean, sweet musky woman scent, which wafted from her neck and her hair. He had never felt like this in his life — and did nothing to remove a self-satisfied, if not stupid, smile from his face. At that moment, Ned's worries slipped from his shoulders as he embraced the gift of fatherhood.

After a few minutes, Orla gently pushed Ned away, intent upon continuing their conversation. 'I guessed about a week ago. I've missed my period and I can remember Ma telling me about the 'morning blight' when she had my brothers and me. You've no idea how crook I've felt every morning... during the last week, in particular. That's why I agreed so quickly to stay behind while you go gallivanting all over the countryside. Charlie could've looked after Ong well enough, mind you.'

'Fair enough. But who would've been lookout while Charlie tended to Ong?'

'True, smart arse,' said Orla, as she playfully jabbed Ned with her elbow. 'But Ong needs serious help, so I really don't mind staying behind. He's been wonderful to you and he deserves good care. Anyway, if I went with you and kept feeling this dreadful in the mornings I'd only slow you down. Right?'

'Yes, I guess so,' Ned replied honestly, but again asked the question he most wanted her to answer. 'So when are you due?'

'End December, I reckon.'

17

————

If there had ever been any uncertainty amongst the gang about the relationship between Ned and Orla, Ned's announcement the next morning removed any doubt. Tom and Dan were ecstatic. Charlie and Ong exchanged knowing looks.

Charley shook Ned's hand. 'You know Ned, you blind sometimes. We see this woman, her skin not right. And she be up sick early most days. But still you no see?'

Ned was shocked by the perceptiveness of the old Chinaman, but upon reflection he recalled, and had to admit to himself, she had indeed made a few hurried retreats to the privacy of the communal long drop.

'Is there anything else I need to know, old friend?' Ned asked sarcastically.

'No, but Ong and Charlie think you make best father,' Charlie replied. 'We already know she make best mother. We much happy be godfathers your child.'

Again, Ned and Orla felt humbled by their sentiments and gracious offer. 'Of course, you can be godfathers,' Orla replied. 'But we're the ones who must honour you both for all that you've done and shown us.'

'That settled then,' Charlie replied. 'But work not done yet. Must show how all things work and how must keep heat so steel it can be shaped and later make tough. But I reckon that job best wait till smithy's they all arrive.'

Joe was happy for them both, but asked in his typical pragmatic, though cynical fashion, 'Does this mean Orla won't be riding with us then, Ned? I was looking forward to seeing her form with those pistols you've told me about.'

'You can count me in, boyo,' Orla retaliated before Ned could say anything. 'I'm pregnant, not disabled!'

For some reason Steve seemed the least interested. He still congratulated Ned and Orla but did not give Orla a hug, as had the other men.

Kate was last to congratulate Ned. 'You'll know you're alive now, cuz,' she said. 'Does this mean I don't get to marry you?' Ned and Kate laughed happily as they hugged, both gladly sharing an unmistakable end to some misunderstanding that went back several years.

Finally, Kate embraced Orla. 'Oh, my God, Orla,' Kate said, with tears now in her eyes. 'This is just the nicest surprise. I know you'll be happy and make Ned toe the line. But remember, if ever you need help of any kind, please ask me. You know I'll support and defend what Ned is trying to achieve and that includes helping you and your child, at any time — no matter what.'

Orla warmly thanked Kate for her unsolicited generosity and commitment. She gently broke from her hug, and yelled theatrically.

'Be gone you heathen lot, you've got work to do and very little time to do it in. Be sure you all return safely, but don't come back unless you're armed with some good food for a change. You know, like eggs, peaches, tomatoes and maybe even some sweets. And for heaven's sake, we need a stack of newspapers. We're damn near out of toilet paper again and I'll be buggered if I'll use both sides of what's left!'

They all laughed and continued with their preparations for departure.

Ned once again wrapped Orla in his arms and planted a lingering kiss full on her lips. After reluctantly unravelling Orla's arms from around his body, he swung up onto Music, the saddle creaking as he positioned his feet in the stirrup irons. Ned led the gang across the clearing and, just as they were about to disappear into the scrub, they all turned in their saddles and either raised their hat or waved an arm in farewell.

18

The next day, despite feeling 'off colour' as Charlie put it, Orla took lookout duty from dawn until mid-afternoon. This gave Charlie and Ong plenty of secure time to fire up the forge. Over the next ten hours, Charlie gradually fed wood into it, creating a substantial bed of red-hot glowing charcoal. The 'trick', as Charlie had previously explained, was to maintain that condition for the next week.

When Orla returned, she announced enthusiastically she had not seen any smoke above the treetops, nor smelt it. Despite that good news, Ong would not touch his meagre evening meal or drink anything. And regrettably, throughout the night he became progressively feebler as his pipe lost its battle.

At daybreak Charlie was distraught. 'I think Ong he soon die, Orla. Have told him we soon go home, but he not happy. He know I still must show Ned how all things be looked after. Can only wait for Ned... see what happen with Ong then. You very kind girl, helping look after Ong. We not forget.'

Mid-morning two days later, Dan and Steve returned to the campsite with several bottles of rum and brandy. Tom arrived at noon the day after that, accompanied by blacksmiths Bill Culph and Patrick

Delaney and his sons, John and William. All of their horses were laden with bedding, food, an assortment of blacksmiths' tools... and three additional mouldboards.

Ned rode into camp late that afternoon. Orla ran to meet him, but then stopped and simply stared at him. She was unable to disguise the sadness she felt. Ong had passed away... alas, not more than an hour before. No words were exchanged. Their eyes locked, and Orla nodded. The impact upon Ned was immediate, his expression a mix of disbelief and grief. Her heart went out to Ned as he obviously fought to hold back tears.

Ned dismounted and walked purposefully to Charlie. 'Mate, we'll all miss your brother. He was such a good man and so damn clever.' Then, holding Charlie by the shoulders and looking directly into his eyes, Ned continued. 'I'm so proud to have been his friend. But listen, your work here is finished, Charlie. I'll take you and Ong home tomorrow, if that's all right with you?'

'Thank you, Ned,' Charlie replied. 'Ong he say special words for you as he die. He wanted you to always think our place as belong you — at any time and always. And he say, next time you visit, if I not be there, you not just take our blessings when you leave. He insist you also take something to remind you of what Charlie and Ong achieve in this land — something to add to good memories our short time together. He also say, he sorry he unable become godfather.'

Charlie's words touched Ned. Although he could not possibly have fully understood the true meaning behind Ong's message, he nevertheless reached out and hugged the old man.

'Whatever the future brings, you can be proud of your achievements here. You and Ong might bloody well have shaped the future you know. So thanks for your help, my dear friend. I've always valued our friendship and I'll never forget either of you.'

Orla listened intently as Ned later retold that private conversation. She was intrigued and suspected she, too, would always remember and never dismiss the old Chinaman's insistent last wishes. That night, Orla said her own words over Ong's childlike figure. The sentiments of her Christian sympathy had to suffice, but regardless, tears flowed and sadness hung heavily over the small bush gathering. After the service, Charlie returned his brother's body to his swag... then carried him into the night.

As the campfire blazed, Ned announced what he and Orla were to do in the next day or two, and what he expected of his gang members while he was away. By the time the campfire died down, Orla had no doubt Ned's instructions would be followed to the letter.

Steve, however, appeared disconnected with the passing of Ong and when Orla challenged him, he replied, 'Means nothing to me, just another Chinaman. What's he ever done for me?'

'You miserable piece of shit,' Orla replied angrily as she spun to face him, her eyes fierce with menace. 'He's done all he could to keep you alive, that's what! Why don't you just piss off, Hart. You've overstayed your welcome in my book.'

'I'll talk to you in the morning if you're still here, Steve,' Ned quickly intervened, and then added, threateningly, 'In the meantime, I suggest you pull your head in and apologise.'

Steve said nothing as he walked away in a huff. Those uncaring remarks hurt Orla; she wondered how dreadful Charlie was feeling over the loss of his brother, let alone how lonely his life would become. She remained angry with Steve. But before dozing off, Orla resolved that after Ned's imminent plans were fulfilled, they would regularly visit their child's remaining godfather.

* * *

NEITHER JOE nor Kate had returned with the others. Kate returned to her home, near Greta, to resume a customary existence. Joe, however, secretly visited his mother in the Woolshed Valley near Beechworth. He did that at great personal risk since the police had set up twenty-four hour surveillance of his mother's home in the hope they would trap him there sooner or later. That they never did was testimony to his cunning and knowledge of the local terrain.

Both Joe and Kate were devastated when they eventually learnt of Ong's death, in particular, Joe, for he greatly respected Ong and his fellow countrymen. Despite a few minor differences, Joe always shared an amicable relationship with the region's Chinese population. Indeed, many held him in high regard. He enjoyed their food, respected their customs, and even made the effort to speak basic Cantonese. They were reliable friends who supplied him with opium and willingly provided him with safe hideouts from the police.

When Joe rejoined the gang, Ned was encouraged to learn how convincing his loyal sympathisers were, readily and regularly reporting bogus sightings of his gang. The police seemed preoccupied in conducting sporadic searches in the distant Warby ranges — and were, therefore, currently of no concern.

But it continued to worry Ned, Tom — and Joe — that Joe's close friend, Aaron Sherritt, was spending so much time with the police, even though Aaron steadfastly insisted his actions were intent upon side-tracking and misleading the authorities about the gang's hideouts and their activities.

At first light the next day, Charlie woke Ned, and then the blacksmiths. After their protests had abated at being snatched into consciousness, Charlie wasted no time in again explaining the forge's operating features and its all-important fuel requirements.

Culphie was genuinely impressed with the water anvil, Patrick even more so with the construction of the forge. Both blacksmiths spent considerable time debating with Charlie the desired colour of the fire bed for tempering the steel. Charlie also ensured that his instructions regarding the final size and shape of each steel section of the armour suits were understood. Quenching the finished armour was also discussed, but Culphie was now in charge.

'Ah c'mon, Charlie, stop telling us how to suck eggs.'

'Both damn good smithies,' Charlie confided to Ned, content now that his brother's transfer of knowledge was complete. 'Both know design that you want for armour and know what they doing. Just need some measurements, your boys. We get moving now, Ned?' Charlie then asked — his tone impatient — more like a command than a question.

Ned, Orla, and Charlie packed their swags and some provisions, and secured them, together with Ong's body, onto Boss Boy. Ned would ride Music, Orla and Charlie the bay thoroughbred. Taking Boss Boy's halter, Ned led the way from the camp for the second time that week.

Although Steve surfaced to meekly wave farewell, he looked extremely sheepish and avoided looking directly at Orla.

'The little bugger. Don't know what gets into him sometimes,' Ned said in exasperation. 'I've given him a few things to think about, mind you. But listen, Orla, if he doesn't come good with an apology when we get back, let me know.'

* * *

THEY ARRIVED at the Chinamen's fortress-home late the following day, tired, but confident they hadn't been sighted. They carried Ong into the house and laid him out on a bed in front of, and facing, an ornate wooden temple. Charlie then began murmuring a prayer; his chants, accompanied by tendrils of fragrant incense wafting steadily upwards, soon permeated the entire house.

'Charlie, we both feel your grief,' Orla interrupted quietly. 'But we need to keep moving. Much has yet to be done, as you know. You'll be right, you're still strong. And we'll try to visit you soon, we promise.'

Charlie walked with his friends to their horses. When they'd mounted, Orla watched as Charlie extended his hand and peered into Ned's face. Ned responded, holding the old Chinaman's hand in both of his. But neither spoke... they simply nodded to each other.

Charlie then patted Orla on her thigh. 'He good bloke, Orla. You look after Ned and yourself — for sake of child. Charlie pray you have much riches and good times. But now be gone... unless you want see old man cry.' Charlie then stepped back and watched, as his friends wheeled their mounts and disappeared into the setting darkness.

Orla found it difficult to shrug off a strong sense of foreboding and she doubted she would ever see Charlie again. And, despite the darkness, she saw tears glistening on Ned's cheeks.

19

———————

The armour's design was to provide protection when on foot, for close up action. But it could, if necessary, be worn on horseback. Several adjustments were made to the prototype armour before it was finally completed to Ned's satisfaction. To test it, Ned fired a bullet from a stolen police Martini-Henry rifle into the inside of the breastplate from about ten yards away. Only a small dent resulted; the test was considered a success. Following completion of a second suit of armour, Ned ordered the hut and the forge to be destroyed.

'Can't see the point in wrecking everything,' said Tom, somewhat bewildered. 'The hut could be useful later. And, Dan and Steve found some colour in the creek when they were building the hut. I thought I told you that. Who knows how much gold might be here, Ned? This could be our luckiest find yet.'

'All right, Tom. Leave the hut, but get rid of the forge. I don't want the coppers drawing any conclusions if they stumble on this spot in the next few weeks.'

As Culphie and Patrick Delaney and his sons were preparing to leave, Ned approached them.

'Thanks for what you've done, lads. But from today, until I say otherwise, you're all sworn to secrecy about the armour. If the traps somehow get wind about it, I'll come looking for the culprit and so help me, I'll throttle the bastard.' The men pledged their compliance; Ned's threat was to hang over their heads long after the farewell handshakes.

* * *

MOMENTUM WAS GATHERING in Ned's grand plan. In equally remote locations, two additional bush forges were hastily prepared, though not in the fashion of Ong's forge. Time was weighing heavily upon Ned so he opted for a more basic type of forge, open to the elements and requiring a bellows to reach and then maintain the required temperature to shape steel. They worked well enough but generated a constant plume of smoke, thus elevating the risk of being discovered by patrolling police.

Charles Knight and Tom Straughair were also recruited to help complete the other suits of armour. The only impediment to completing them had been obtaining sufficient mouldboards, but before long, Ned and Dan 'sourced' five additional pieces from properties near Myrrhee. To save time, despite the risk of discovery, some segments of the armour were brazenly fabricated by those blacksmiths in their hometowns of Beechworth and the Woolshed Valley. With some helpful advice from Culphie, the remaining suits were completed during the next five weeks.

Ned's luck held; the police remained unaware of the gang's activities. But, as soon as the last suit was finished, he ordered both of these bush forges be destroyed. Nevertheless, Ned knew he could not totally prevent gossip; he left those who had participated in the final round of manufacture with no doubt he was deadly serious about them avoiding idle chatter.

Several times, Joe argued that moving fast and shooting straight were better protection than armour. This annoyed Ned, but Joe's accommodating friendship was never in doubt.

Despite frenetic comings and goings, the gang's mood remained buoyant. Very few arguments surfaced. When things did become tense, Ned would typically say, 'Keep that up and I'll bang your heads together so bloody hard you'll both end up cross-eyed.' If normality failed to return, the antagonists were given an unmistakeable glare. A glance into Ned's blazing eyes soon convinced them his patience was wearing thin... and guaranteed an immediate truce.

On occasion, Orla would attempt to defuse potential arguments by challenging everyone to a point-to-point race. Despite knowing her condition, these challenges were always enthusiastically accepted. But somehow, Orla seemed to get the better of them on Boss Boy, who, although not the fastest horse on the flat was by far the most daring in the bush and on steep slopes. This did not mean the men pulled those races, they all proved to be exceptional horsemen and fearless in their own ways, but they had undoubtedly met their match. Orla and Boss Boy possessed an unwavering determination to win and clearly had total confidence in each other.

'Your light weight gives you the edge every time, Orla,' Joe complained. 'You should be weight penalised, I reckon.'

'You're wrong, Joe. I'm getting heavier all the time, surely that's penalty enough,' Orla responded, and then taunted. 'Perhaps, I should have twins? Anyway, I'd still beat you; you're putting on a bit of flab yourself, boyo.'

At the end of each race they teased each other about their respective misadventures, and bragged heartily about their own daring, or tactical manoeuvres. Forgotten were any earlier arguments.

But not always...

Steve occasionally sulked and vowed not to race again. He, too, in his own way was highly competitive, but he was also a poor loser.

'Oh, come on, Steve. I cheated,' Orla joked on one occasion, trying to placate him. Steve walked away, still in a huff over some previous disagreement. This annoyed Orla but she was sure that at the next suggestion of a contest, he'd be in it.

Orla always insisted they check the legs and hooves of their mounts for injuries. However, after their last race, these simple grooming requests sent Steve into a rage, emphatically telling Orla to mind her own business. Annoyed by that riposte, Ned abruptly grabbed Steve by the arm, marched him into the bush and once out of earshot, delivered a final ultimatum.

Orla thought hard about her situation... and Steve's antagonism. It suddenly dawned on her that her assertive nature was unwittingly undermining Ned's authority in Steve's eyes. Steve did not return to their camp with Ned, but when he did, he confronted Orla and spoke his mind. When she apologised for unintentionally overstepping her position, he offered his hand. *I should've been a wake-up to that. The poor bugger probably didn't deserve that grief,* she thought to herself, now feeling sorry for Steve, and slightly embarrassed.

But Orla persisted in making her feelings known in relation to hygiene — or rather, the lack of it; her annoyance initially surfaced during the building of the forges. None of the men, including Ned, seemed to care about their body odour and none of them were happy with her personal attacks.

Hands on hips and glaring, she would typically berate them. 'God Almighty, you blokes. You all stink worse than the long-drop. Don't any of you come to dinner unless you've tubbed-up first! Right?'

Even Ned received his share of ultimatums. 'Ned bloody Kelly! You stink like a vulture's crotch,' Orla shouted at him on one occasion. 'Don't even consider coming to bed unless you've had a damn good wash first.'

A withering glare followed, but that soon turned into a resigned grin as he trudged off to the creek. He knew he was being blackmailed, but not sharing his swag with Orla was unthinkable.

* * *

SOON THE MILD, gentle days of another benign North East autumn retreated. Word then reached the gang — via Aaron Sherritt — that aboriginal police trackers intended concentrating their resources in and around the Oxley, Greta, and Winton regions. That news seemed suspiciously out of date and therefore, unreliable, so Ned took decisive action. He instinctively knew the black trackers would be ineffective in the cold, so with winter now closing in, he led his gang into the high country. They had to move quickly, the late autumn rains would soon soften the earth and make it difficult to conceal their tracks.

When possible, their temporary campsites exploited stands of heavy timber and natural rock formations to deflect most of the wind. They were further protected by sheets of canvas, which doubled as windbreaks and crude tents. During the bone-numbingly cold evenings, the gang draped their swags and a blanket or two over their backs, and then sat around a smokeless open fire for hours, chatting and drinking bottomless cups of steaming black tea. Regardless, they were isolated fugitives, the gallows their destiny if they could not handle these conditions: a necessary discomfort if they were to remain free.

Their conversations were wide ranging, but invariably led to name suggestions for Orla's and Ned's child. Dan, and Steve in partic-ular, enjoyed listening to Orla's tales about her beloved Ireland and both said they would like to meet her brothers. However, with just a mix of wishful thinking and sarcasm, Joe suggested it would help their cause no end if those four boyos — all apparently handy with guns — could turn up out-of-the-blue next month and join their gang.

This pause in their activities gave Ned the opportunity to privately discuss many things with Orla. On one occasion, while gazing into her beautiful eyes and reaching out a hand to pat her bulge, he commented matter-of-factly. 'I'll not pretend that I've led a blameless life or that one fault justifies any other. As a young bloke I took up with a bushranger whose name was Harry Power. He was a nice old bugger and we robbed a few mail coaches together, but he was a boozer and the traps eventually nailed him. My mother remar-ried and my stepfather taught me a lot about stealing horses and how to sell 'em.'

'Obviously not well enough,' Orla quipped, clearly referring to their second meeting.

'Anyway – I, too, ended up in Beechworth jail for a few years, on a false charge I couldn't defend. I'd met a bloke who said he'd lost his horse. I stupidly loaned him one of mine, which he promised to return... but never did. I eventually found his horse wandering through the bush and I claimed it as mine. When I rode the damn thing into town, the owner recognised it. I got arrested and charged with receiving stolen property. Would you believe that? I had no idea it'd been stolen and, of course, I couldn't prove that I hadn't stolen it.

'To make ends meet we built a distillery or two and illegally sold our whiskey. And as you already know, the boys and I have robbed the banks at Euroa, Benalla, and Jerilderie.'

'And you've got nothing to show for it but a bloody great reward on your head,' said Orla. '*And* they don't mind if they nail you alive... or dead.'

Ned looked at her in surprise, annoyed by her flippant remark. After a few minutes, Ned continued. 'Oh, by the way, I've asked Joan McIntyre to write to your mother to explain our situation. And Alf says your friends, the Stewarts, will be visiting them sometime in July.'

'Oh Ned, you must meet them,' Orla said, hugging him while recalling the Stewarts' plans. 'They're just the nicest people.'

'Yes, I'd like that,' Ned replied as he pulled his blankets around her and quietly added. 'God willing we can do that soon, but first things first, my love.'

* * *

THE HORSE RACES at Moyhu were a welcome relief from their harsh living conditions. They attended the meeting and good fun was had by all, although the gang arrived late and departed early to ensure they did not stand out, the crowd as their cover. Had anyone noticed them, they would probably have believed they saw Ned with Kate Lloyd and, if pressed, would have said she was wearing a fashionable long dress and one of her plumed hats. But they'd be mistaken, of course.

Over the following weeks, observers reported seeing Ned and

Kate on their horses, 'racing here and there' over the Oxley Flats, but again they were mistaken.

Orla also accompanied Ned on most occasions when he left their hideouts to visit family and close friends. Those chosen friends were sworn to secrecy about Orla having effectively adopted Kate's identity. Orla's name was never to be used by those people in casual town talk. Instead, they were all encouraged to perpetuate a Ned and Kate relationship; that they were 'a bit more than cousins'. Such visits were usually at night and they departed before daybreak. Accordingly, they generally went unnoticed. Any chance sightings of them were fleeting, thus making clear recognition of Ned's true partner highly unlikely.

Ned also saw to it that individual home visits were staggered. Four figures seen riding at any time in the region meant to most observers that the Kelly Gang was 'out and about' and such sightings, if reported, were bound to interest the police.

Ned arranged for Tom to discreetly accompany each gang member when it was their turn for some relief from their prolonged stays in the bush. Wisely, Ned also insisted that commonly visited places were to be approached from different directions and their arrivals and departures be conducted only after darkness. Ned also trusted Tom to ensure the boys kept off the opium. However, Joe tended to ignore Tom's counsel. This annoyed Ned, but while he tolerated Joe's occasional indulgences when it came to grog and women, heroin usage met with Ned's full fury.

During the months leading into June 1880, Orla, although now showing signs of her pregnancy, was blissfully happy. She spent most of her time with Ned, either sharing routine day-to-day jobs, or attending to the horse's needs. She had grown to love the broad grassy plains of Oxley, Greta, and Moyhu, and the ancient red gums that graced the country. But with Mount Buffalo as a constant, imposing backdrop, she also felt as if her life was somehow being cradled and nurtured by the surrounding ranges. She was growing to understand and respect her mountain sanctuary and thoroughly enjoyed her treks along the high ridges even though it often meant carrying bulky and heavy loads... and, occasionally, in great haste.

Nevertheless, Orla was feeling a lack of intimate privacy and became increasingly annoyed with their frugal existence, the most irritating aspect being the overhanging threat of capture that dictated their every decision and action. Orla helped Ned stash the armour, but wondered why it was built with such urgency. She realised soon enough. He needed time to solicit support for his ambitions for the North East. He was also accumulating ammunition and, he explained, he needed time to further test Aaron Sherritt.

In their favourite hideout in the Warby Ranges — an open-air cave concealed by surrounding boulders — Orla pondered their good fortune that Ned and Joe had found such an ideal place; hidden from the prying eyes of police, close to their sympathisers, with easy access to good pickings and water for their horses... and close to Glenrowan.

At night Orla cuddled up to Ned, and often during these times, he expanded upon and reviewed his forthcoming intentions until sleep overwhelmed them. She knew Ned's love for her was undeniably genuine. She, too, was deeply in love and now strongly believed in the likely success of Ned's plans. She also admired Ned's supreme confidence.

'Nothing will derail my plans,' he emphatically told her. 'After the police surrender at Glenrowan, we'll ride into Benalla, rob the bank again and demand our region be proclaimed free! And I'll only release our prisoners, and return the money, when the authorities formally agree.

'Actually, I'm not against the need for authority and a police force. But I'm dead against how that authority is being applied now. The coppers and judges have continually ill-treated and even jailed my mother and many good people for unjust reasons,' Ned angrily but patiently explained. 'People who live in large towns have no idea of the cruel and overbearing way the local police carry on and abuse their powers. It's going to stop!

'My God, Orla, we never wanted to kill those coppers at Stringybark. I demanded they bail up and throw down their arms. If I'd wanted to murder 'em I could've done that before they knew what hit them. They needed to be taught a lesson to stop hounding us. We wanted more guns for sure, but so help me God, it wasn't revenge for our families, or anything like that. None of us have ever gone out of our way to ill-treat anyone and I've always refrained from cowardly acts. I've tried every reasonable means I know to get them to listen. I've written to the authorities to explain myself, but they just dismiss my pleas and choose to ignore me.

'My mind's made up, Orla. I'll not continually put up with their shite behaviour. It's time for action and I intend to carry it through. Besides, I've got the highest regard for those aboriginal trackers... they're damn good. I'm worried that if I don't act soon, they'll nail us before long, despite them hating this cold weather.'

Orla never doubted Ned's determination. However, there was a changing mood developing between Ned and Joe that would dramatically change their initial plans. Aaron Sherritt, although he'd been a close mate of Joe, and had privately declared himself a Kelly sympathiser, was also now being put into more and more lookout roles by the police and was seen daily in the company of the police. This inevitably resulted in Joe concluding Aaron would soon, perhaps unwittingly, compromise the gang. Joe had heard that an increasing amount of money was being offered by the police to convince Aaron that he should 'dob in Ned' — and indeed police parties had, on a few recent occasions, come very close to one of Ned's hideouts. Aaron's continued association with the police was therefore seen by Joe and Ned as too great a risk. Too much was at stake, and besides, Aaron had lately made it clear he still did not want to ride with Ned.

Orla and Tom were horrified to learn of Joe's plan to kill Aaron. They repeatedly attempted to quash Joe's treacherous intent, but he had already convinced Ned that Aaron's murder would be significant to the police, and that his elimination would therefore play into Ned's hands.

So an unsuspecting Aaron was soon to become a sacrificial figure in their plans. His murder, Joe and Ned concluded would trigger the police into an action they would forever regret. If everything went to plan, the unexpected, albeit deliberate derailment of the special police train as it sped past Glenrowan on its way to Beechworth to investigate Aaron's murder, was surely guaranteed to kill the maximum number of police.

That Joe and Ned were prepared to kill Aaron for what they believed was for the good of their country, their murderous plan was not only a measure of their desperate situation, but proof of their commitment to a free Republic for North Eastern Victoria.

Orla listened carefully to Ned's revised plans. She fully supported him attempting to get the world to take notice of his family's plight, typical of so many Irish men and women just like her own family who had suffered a similar fate under the unjust and merciless rule of the British. She also realised the local folk, including many released felons, were the backbone of the future development of North Eastern Victoria and that they only wanted to live a peaceful and productive life.

But Orla would not condone murder. It was her contention, if somewhat naively, that Ned should continue to win over honest local people with political aspirations in guiding the colony's future. Then, surely, he'd be pardoned for his prior actions. After all, she'd been told that an increasing number of fair-minded people viewed Ned's actions as a legitimate response to unwarranted police provocation.

Tom strongly believed it was simply too late, that the forces of injustice were so far out of control that Ned, Joe, Dan, and Steve should all abandon the colony and start a new life in either New Zealand or America... or even in Ireland.

Both Orla and Tom begged that Aaron be given fair warning of the gang's concerns and allow him to leave the colony for a few years. Their pleas fell on deaf ears. They could not sway Ned. Time was up. Aaron would, sooner or later, become a police informer and must be eliminated.

Orla and Tom were united in their contrary beliefs, but so, too, was their loyalty sworn to Ned... an awful irony. Only the most tightly knit mateship would have enabled such a plan to be hatched, its intended execution now inescapable.

Such was life as the winter winds howled across the Oxley Plains.

* * *

'WHAT DO you mean I'm not going with you?' Orla's voice was raised.

'I'll not subject you to this, Orla. Not in your condition,' replied Ned, baffled by Orla's vehemence, but becoming angry himself. 'Believe me, Orla, the first thing I'll do after this business at Glenrowan is over will be to collect you so you can ride with me into Benalla. Be reasonable, Orla.'

Her fury quickly abated. 'All right, all right,' she conceded. 'I'll admit that lately I've been finding it difficult to do things, but I don't like being left out.' Secretly however, she was surprised how easily she capitulated; the baby's safety having mysteriously overridden her need for involvement.

And so, during the afternoon on the 26th of June 1880, Orla made her way to an agreed hideaway and set up camp.

Joe and Dan departed at the same time, but they rode into Woolshed, near Beechworth, on a separate mission. That night, they neither gave Aaron Sherritt an opportunity to escape, nor did they ask him to leave the Colony of Victoria and never return. In cold blood, with no explanation or hint of compassion, Joe shot Aaron dead with his double-barrelled shotgun. The two outlaws then rode off for Glenrowan, certain that news of their deed would travel fast... or so they hoped.

As that evening closed in around them, Ned and Steve then headed for Glenrowan with four Walers in tow, all heavily loaded with the gang's armour — and explosives to blow up the rail lines.

20

Increasingly annoyed with waiting for Ned — now nearly a full day overdue according to his predictions — Orla impatiently mounted her bay just before dawn on the 28th of June, intending to head straight for Glenrowan.

With Boss Boy fully laden in tow, she set off through a cold, heavy ground mist. Soon, after travelling only a mile or so, she heard the faint sound of sporadic gunfire, followed by an occasional fusillade.

Just as she was about to kick the bay into a canter, she was shocked to see a horse — a familiar grey — staggering sideways, crashing clumsily through the undergrowth on her left.

'Oh, God! Music...' she murmured as horror grabbed her. 'There's no way Ned or Joe would ever abandon her in that condition!'

Orla easily captured Music, but the mare was shivering and obviously traumatised. With soothing voice, Orla quickly examined the mare's legs. Clearly, Music had recently taken a heavy fall, but there was no obvious sign of bone breakage. Orla moved to Music's far side... then froze. A cold shiver raced down Orla's spine... Music had been shot! Blood oozed from two bullet holes, coating the mare's side and underbelly. Both wounds were the result of the deflection of a bullet that penetrated under her midsection skin, ran along her ribs and then exited in the heavily muscled tissue on her withers. A third bullet wound on her rump was a superficial graze, but hurtful to Orla's touch.

Orla quickly applied pressure to the bleeding wounds and after fifteen minutes, the flows stopped to a trickle. There was nothing else she could do except offer up a quick prayer in the belief she would soon have ample time to help this brave, beautiful mare.

Orla remounted her bay, took both Music and Boss Boy in tow and headed off slowly in the direction of the gunfire. Gamely, Music kept up.

Cresting the slope of a wooded gully, Orla quickly drew reign. Boss Boy and Music instinctively stopped. Beyond the timber line there was a clearing, which sloped down towards the settlement of Glenrowan where the railway line ran through.

In the near distance she could see several people, all peering towards, but standing well back from a small building. She followed their gaze. Gunmen, most in police uniforms, suddenly released a volley of heavy calibre rifle shots into the building. Orla gasped in shock. Strangely, there was no return gunfire... and she could see the building was in the process of being torched.

Towards the railway line, and off to Orla's left, another distressing scene played out. Wheeled towards the railway station on a handcart was a large, bearded, and bloodied figure with six well-armed escorts.

'No! Oh, Jesus, no! That's Ned,' Orla gasped, her panic rising. 'They've got my Ned.' Despite feeling as if she'd just been brutally punched in her gut, she instinctively reached for her pistols. *She needed to do something! But what?*

Uncharacteristically Orla froze... it struck her that Ned was probably already dead. Her anger flared again. For a second time she all but committed herself to storming down into the clearing.

Her bravery was something she had always taken for granted, its roots never known or questioned. It was just inbred, but so, too, was her mother's advice. 'Look before you leap, Orla, my love'. Perhaps impending motherhood also challenged Orla's rage. Regardless, despair now had her in its grip. She could only sit and watch. The compulsion she felt to throw herself into the action suddenly, totally evaporated, leaving her feeling utterly deflated and sick — and frightened, for the first time in her life.

* * *

POLICE WITNESSES CLAIMED that when Ned was finally looking down the barrel of a still smoking rifle, he was heard mumbling, 'Water, water, please let me have water.'

But in fact, if the gallant police officers who arrested Ned had listened more carefully to the words coming from within his steel helmet, they'd have recognised his more poignant cry of, 'Orla, Orla, please let me see, Orla.'

* * *

AS NED and his guards arrived at the station, Orla gazed pitifully upon the scene through tears of abject grief and frustration. A small movement suddenly caught her eye. Ned had somehow managed to raise one of his bloody forearms as if trying to wave farewell to her. *Had he seen her?* Probably — her silhouette was certainly obvious had anybody cared to look in her direction.

Without delay, Ned's unsuspecting captors wheeled him into the station building — and forever out of Orla's life.

21

———————

Senior Constable John Kelly should have paid closer attention to the gullies to the southwest of the historic battleground immediately after he captured Ned. But he didn't. Another arrest could have followed; his success would then have been complete. He plainly failed to see a bay thoroughbred ridden by a lightly framed individual who was leading a fully laden packhorse and a grey... urging them to maintain a canter while retreating through the scrub.

Suddenly, Orla stopped. She pivoted in her saddle and gazed back, as if debating her next move. It had flashed into her mind's eye that she had seen four horses in the distance standing forlornly in the cold, on the opposite side of the Glenrowan railway line. Five or six uniformed black trackers were guarding them.

Orla hissed quietly to herself, 'Shite! They were Ned's back-up horses and two of them were Alf McIntyre's Walers.'

Again she felt useless and powerless to act. Against such odds, *how could she possibly retrieve Alf's Walers without either being shot or arrested?* A modicum of calm returned to her when she remembered Ned's words.

'If anything ever happens to me I'll not have a Bill of Sale for those Walers. So, Alf can front the police at any time and claim that someone stole them. Both carry his brand plain enough.'

She desperately needed time to think. Her life, which had been so full of happiness and promise until thirty minutes ago, dramatically imploded. She was now without her *alter ego*, her beloved Ned. Orla slumped in anguish, feeling cheated that her contentment had been ripped from her. That she had no money and was more than three months pregnant somehow seemed the least of her problems.

Instinctively, she returned to the relative safety and seclusion of the hideaway where she had waited in vain for Ned. Her heartbreak intermittently sent her into convulsions. She vomited until she could only dry retch. Tears flowed and she cried hysterically, not caring whether she would ever control her grief. Only dehydration and exhaustion finally sent her into a deep but fitful sleep.

* * *

NED'S GLENROWAN strategies had failed disastrously, despite the gang's months of planning and toil: his regional aspirations had also come to nothing.

The 'bait' to lure the police had worked brilliantly, although it had been of inexcusable savagery. But unforeseeable delays conspired against Ned's plans. The witnesses to Aaron's murder were tardy in reporting the crime and the special train, loaded with police, anticipated to be rushing to Beechworth to investigate that murder, was delayed due to police ineptitude in organising their numbers. Those unexpected delays thus created for Ned and his gang, a heightened level of anxiety, which had never been contemplated. And, most of Ned's sympathisers — hand-picked locals, his reinforcements, if needed — abandoned the scene, either bored by lack of action or because vital farm jobs required their attention.

Consequently, too much grog flowed to quench that 'delay anxiety', whereupon Ned's thinking became addled as tiredness set in.

Making hostages of town folk was a sound strategy; gambling chips in a deadly game, redeemable if things went wrong. But unintentionally, innocent people died and several others were hurt because Ned underestimated the ruthlessness of the police in their relentless pursuit to either apprehend or kill him and his gang.

Betrayal of trust by a local schoolteacher, masquerading as a sympathiser, also played its part. Ned had not anticipated the train stopping at Glenrowan; the police having been forewarned by the school teacher of Ned's location and of his plans to kill as many unsuspecting policemen as possible when their special train was derailed after it sped past Glenrowan.

The siege could have been averted. Ned could have called the whole thing off and easily made good his escape as soon as he saw the armed police pouring from their train. He must have realised quickly enough he was seriously outnumbered but still chose to challenge them.

The armour was an unmitigated failure. Ned's gang could not get close enough to inflict police casualties, a disadvantage realised very early in the gun battle. The armour's much-vaunted invincibility was somehow breached: stray bullets unexpectedly found gaps, fatally wounding Joe, and probably so, both Dan and Steve.

Ned's meticulous escape plans were essentially ignored, or arguably, the gang's retreat was simply forgotten; overridden by their determination and raw bravery to turn the gun-battle to their advantage.

These revelations were, of course, essentially unknown to Orla at the time. Fortuitously, she had not witnessed the events at Glenrowan as they unfolded: given her shattered state of mind, suicide may well have been the preferred end to her agony.

Hindsight is an amazing thing. Ned should have taken Joe's advice to abandon the armoured suit strategy. Their derailment plan would still have failed, but on horseback, in all likelihood they would have averted capture and thus extended their freedom... though, for how much longer, nobody would ever know.

Furthermore, had Ned not been so protective, Orla's ability to provide lethal handgun support and equally deadly rifle fire cover would have afforded Ned and the gang unquestionable escape opportunities, or even sufficient bluff to overwhelm the police entirely. Ned may well have rued leaving Orla out of his intended plan at Glenrowan. But that had been his firm decision; protection of his unborn child was paramount in his thinking.

* * *

At dawn, Orla still had a crushing feeling of separation: the space where hope once filled her soul was now a great emptiness.

The beauty of the morning did little to deflect her thoughts from the reality of the prior day's horror. But, with her thirst quenched, she at last started to think. Her tears and shaking were now under control, but she struggled to accept her circumstances. The memory of her mother's words when her father died so suddenly and tragically returned to her. 'As heart breaking as things may be, Orla, you'll soon accept that your life must go on. You might not want to hear this, but it's true — time cures all things, my love.'

How soon, Orla dared not imagine — her love and reliance upon Ned had become so complete. With a jolt, she wondered if the events of the past twenty-four hours would have hurt their child and reached down to protectively cover the swelling in her belly. Inexplicably, her feelings of insecurity vanished. Her self-confidence surged. Orla then realised she was hungry – very hungry.

After devouring a sizeable meal and drinking several mugs of hot black tea, a compelling thought surfaced. *Kate! I must find Kate.* Orla was not overly concerned about being seen. She was confident she'd never been recognised in Ned's company. However, she decided to stay put and fully gather her wits before moving. Besides, Music needed her attention and also required more time to recover.

It was during this stay that Orla accepted the power of nature: her unborn child was demanding her commitment to life.

There were no flies to torment Music; however, she was in pain and weak from blood loss. Despite it all, Orla concluded the brave mare would live. After cleaning the bullet wounds several times with water, Orla managed to insert a few simple stitches to close both wounds. Not once did the mare shy away when the needle penetrated her inflamed and torn flesh.

On the third day after Ned's arrest, Orla finally left her hiding place.

She arrived at the Lloyd farmhouse after dark, not caring about the barking dogs. To her astonishment, Tom stood at the front door with a night-lamp held at shoulder height. Orla flew out of her saddle and ran to him. They embraced in a frantic hug of affection.

'Oh God, Tom, I'm so glad to see you,' she sobbed. Unrestrained tears stung her still red and puffy eyes, and then rolled down her cheeks. 'I thought you were inside that building, too. I reckoned you'd all be burnt to death, for sure.'

Kate then ran from the house, recognising Orla's voice. All three embraced and wept, sharing a terrible loss... and the enormous relief they were alive and still free.

'I *was* inside. For a short time,' Tom quietly announced. 'The coppers were concentrating on Ned when he stepped outside for the last time. I went after him when he fell, but I couldn't get the bugger to give up. Eventually, I took my chances and bolted. I was unbelievably lucky. Bullets were still flying everywhere. Anyway, I mixed with the town folk then slipped away. Went bush for a few days. If the coppers ever caught up with me, I'd say that I'd been looking for stray cattle for the past week.' Tom took a deep breath, and then whispered emotionally, 'Joe and the boys are dead, Orla... but we think Ned's still alive.'

Kate gently disengaged herself from their shared embrace. 'Would you take care of Orla's horses please, Tom? While you're doing that, I'll put the kettle on and rustle up something for Orla to eat.'

'Be careful, Tom. Music's been shot,' Orla said quickly. 'Have you got anything you can put on her wounds? Her shoulder's the worst.'

'I'll see what I can do. She's a beautiful mare, all right. Ned and Joe really loved her, eh?' Tom replied. 'By the look of 'em, they could all do with something decent to eat, even Boss Boy. How yah doing, fella?'

As Orla ate, she described what little she had witnessed at Glenrowan. Tom explained how things had gone so horribly wrong, what Ned had put himself through to make sure his remaining sympathisers were removed from harm's way, and how Ned had so valiantly tried to save Joe, Dan, and Steve while under merciless personal attack.

No attempt was made by Tom to embellish Ned's bravery. But he did lament that if Ned had taken his and Orla's advice, Ned might still have lived a long and happy life. Tom again explained how, during the height of the battle, he had tried to convince Ned to either give up, or get away. While relating Ned's frustration and fierce determination to fight on, Tom suddenly started crying. 'He insisted I reload his pistols, yah know. At that stage the poor bugger couldn't do it himself.'

Alas, all had been in vain. Ned was now in the Melbourne Gaol, clinging to life, with little prospect of a fair trial and facing an outlaw's death.

Tom's descriptions of how the lives of the gang had ended distressed Orla and left her feeling hollow. She knew she could handle the reality of their deaths, but no more would she hear their cheeky jibes, race them across the Oxley flats or regale them about her beloved Ireland.

THE FOLLOWING AFTERNOON, Orla and Kate wandered down to a nearby creek. They sat listening to its soothing babble for several minutes before Kate broke the silence.

'What do you intend to do, Orla? I've got some money and...'

'No Kate, it's not your money I want,' Orla interrupted gently. 'But

I would cherish your word on something for which I'll forever be in your debt.

'I've been thinking hard, Kate. Our lives were going to be tough enough, even with Ned free. But in the future, life for me and, our child, in particular, is bound to be one of humiliation and persecution. I'm not ashamed to have conceived Ned's child but I don't want the world knowing. So would you be prepared to continue our little deception, that you were Ned's woman? It'll require that you never, under any circumstance, let it be known that Ned and I were lovers and that I'm having his child. It's not the child's fault the father chose a life outside the law, regardless of his intentions. If the truth becomes known, there's nothing I might say that'll alter public perceptions. The badgering will just carry on, and that's a legacy no child should be burdened with. Can you maintain that deception for us, Kate?'

'Yes, I reckon I can do that, Orla,' replied Kate. 'No point creating more unnecessary misery. All I ask in return is your friendship. And Orla, you must know there'll never be a debt to discharge.'

There was no embrace, Orla simply nodded, overwhelmed by Kate's generosity and spirit.

Kate then took Orla's hands and firmly squeezed them in hers. 'Orla, we have to get Tom to make that same commitment,' she quietly announced. 'The police are already showing a lot of interest in him. Oh, and by the way, I've been given permission to visit Ned in the Melbourne Goal soon. Perhaps, our little plan is already working. The police still think we're going steady. But look, it's equally important that Ned also understands and commits to this oath, don't you think?'

'Yep, you're right once again. But he's so damn full of himself about this child that it'll be hard for him not to say something. I just desperately wish it were me going to visit him, Kate. You will tell him that I lov… '

'Leave it to me, Orla,' Kate interrupted. 'I know what you want me to say and it *will* get said.'

'Thanks, Kate. You're a darlin', that's for sure.'

That night the girls confronted Tom and explained Orla's wishes. He never hesitated and wholeheartedly gave his pledge.

* * *

ORLA'S MISSION at the Lloyd farm was now complete. Mainstream life was set to continue — and be recorded — as if Orla had never existed.

22

———————

Orla deliberately avoided human contact over the next few weeks, concentrating upon taking care of Music. The mare's recovery was astounding and her condition improved so rapidly that Tom suggested she could soon be ridden. However, Orla was also acutely aware that Music's continued presence could become a source of interest to the police.

But she need not have worried because Tom was a step ahead; Music would soon be discreetly accommodated well out of the area.

Kate made her fleeting visit to Melbourne to see Ned. Upon her return she patiently repeated their conversation to Orla, tactfully playing down the seriousness of Ned's wounds and his physical agony, and the mental anguish he was experiencing. Orla took some relief in knowing he was alive, but grieved nonetheless as much for his state of mind, as her premonition that he was assuredly lost to her and their child.

Two nights later, Orla said her farewell to Music. Faces touching, she spoke gently into the mare's ear, the grassy, musky odour of the mare evoking bittersweet memories. Music whinnied softly; just as Orla imagined she had done countless times when in Ned's care.

'Good luck, Music,' Orla whispered abruptly, then turned and walked away. They never met again.

Orla spent the next morning checking her meagre possessions and ensuring Boss Boy and the bay were well fed and watered. Her pistols and the rifle Ned gave her were still in good condition and her ammunition plentiful. Money, or rather lack of it, was still not her most immediate problem. Her health was not in jeopardy, either. She was young and fit and kept reminding herself that she was pregnant, not sick or injured. Instinctively, she knew that safer refuge was her primary need, and she knew without question where to find it.

And so early afternoon, Orla said an emotional farewell to her good friends; then, assisted by Tom, she swung into the saddle of her bay. With Boss Boy in tow, and without looking back, she kicked the bay into a familiar, steady canter and headed eastward.

* * *

When Orla arrived at her destination, she was shocked to find that a considerable chunk of the mountain had recently collapsed and come to rest just short of the river. Huge logs, tons of rocks, and masses of scrub were lying about in a massive tangle... but there was no sign of life!

Apart from remnants of the pigsties and a few sections of the vegetable garden water races, everything was demolished... including her hope of sanctuary. *But why on earth had Charlie set off the charges to destroy his home and in all likelihood killed himself in the process? Orla wondered. To be sure, a few months ago he'd been alive, although mourning his dead brother. But otherwise, he was lively and mentally active... and in no apparent danger from either the police or disgruntled miners.*

Orla pondered this further gut wrenching loss, but the reason would always elude her. Regardless, in her mind, this site would always be a monument to those two lovable, heroic, and clever Chinamen.

She suddenly noticed, about twenty yards from the wreckage, the

Chinamen's partially concealed two-wheel cart. It had been pushed back into the nearby scrub, and to her surprise, she found it intact and usable. Without hesitation and despite her condition, she removed the bay's saddle and slung it, together with Boss Boy's load, into the cart. Then, with Boss Boy's cooperation, she harnessed him into position. She then tethered the bay to the rear of the cart.

Taking a deep breath before heading back to the main Buckland River road, Orla thought she detected just the faintest whiff of incense on the late afternoon breeze.

23

Tired, but with bright moonlight to assist her, Orla set up camp where Devil's Creek flowed into the Buckland River. The combination of a crisp clear starlit winter's night, a full stomach, and a warm fire caused her to drift into a dreamy, reflective state. Although her discovery earlier that day tormented her, eventually her thoughts shifted to her unborn child and how she might handle their future life.

She could return to Ireland, but probably didn't have sufficient money for her passage even if she sold both of her horses and the cart. She needed a place of her own; somewhere to raise her child and, hopefully, find work... teaching, perhaps.

The answer hit her with a jolt. 'Of course; Joan and Alf,' she whispered excitedly. 'Why in God's name didn't I think of them before? Orla, you're an idiot.'

She quickly suppressed feelings of guilt for losing touch with her friends, but she knew they'd understand. *Hadn't they reassured her that falling in love wasn't a crime?* Living with the McIntyres, she'd be out of the public's eye, and since Joan and Alf had understood and liked Ned, she was certain they'd never intentionally reveal the identity of her child's father.

Having found inner comfort for the first time since Ned's capture, she lay back in her swag and relaxed. For no apparent reason Orla suddenly remembered Ned's news that the Stewarts would be visiting the McIntyres sometime in June or July. She allowed herself a contented smile as sleep claimed her.

Her campsite proved to be a pleasant location where she idled away a few days before heading for Wangaratta. She surprised herself at the ease with which she oriented herself, a natural legacy from having spent the past four months living rough... and on the run.

* * *

COCKO WAS first to announce Orla's unexpected arrival. He screeched on top note, bobbed his head, and performed fancy rotations on his perch. The dogs soon chimed in but were immediately told to, 'Shut up, yah dopey bastards.' Cocko had lost none of his eloquence or any of his desire to be both the centre of attention and in control. Alas, the McIntyre dogs seemed destined to a life of domination.

Alf bolted from the house, followed closely by Joan. He ran up the driveway a short distance. Turning in excitement as he ran, he called to Joan, 'It's Orla. See, I told yah. I told yah it'd be her. Get the kids, quick!'

Orla reined in Boss Boy, and then slowly stepped from the cart.

Alf raced up to her. 'Thank God, it's you. Are you all right, luv?' They flew into a hug and Alf easily lifted her from the ground and spun her around. Orla now breathless and with tears pouring down her cheeks, wailed in relief as much as happiness.

'Yep, I'm fine. Can you forgive me for not keeping in touch?'

'Rubbish, girl, you did right,' Alf replied, as he gently pushed her away. Holding Orla at arm's length, he quickly added. 'Ned needed you more than you can imagine. Besides, it's your life to live as you choose, you know that. But whoa, hang on a minute, what's this?' Alf asked in mock astonishment as he pointed to her prominent bulge. 'If that's what I suspect, young lady, when are you due?'

'Mid-December as best as I can figure it,' Orla replied a little sheepishly. 'So, what do you fancy, Alf... a godson or a goddaughter?' They both laughed and hugged again.

'Bloody hell, Orla, either will do, I don't care. This is just terrific news. Look, here come the others. Say g'day to them while I take care of the horses. And thanks for bringing back the bay in one piece. In fact, they both look to be in pretty good shape to me, love. Ned told me about Boss Boy and the water anvil. I'd expect nothing less from this bloke. Anyway, I bet you've seen a thing or to, eh? Tell me all about it later when everything settles down a bit. But hey, welcome home!'

Meeting Joan was something Orla would also never forget. Joan's face was strangely expressionless given the circumstances. With hands on her hips she looked straight at Orla and sternly remarked, 'Well, I suppose that 'lump' puts paid to us going for a ride tonight?' In a few steps, they were in an affectionate hug. But then, just as quickly they broke their embrace, stared at each other, and started laughing hysterically.

Then the children were all over her. Orla felt their hearts beating against her chest as they hugged her.

'Where have you been all this time,' Tylah giggled as she cheekily patted Orla's belly. 'And just what have *you been up to*?'

There were obviously many things the children wanted to tell her, but before anyone could intervene to stop any further questions, Tylah innocently asked, 'Orla, did you know the police have captured that Ned Kelly bloke, and people are saying he's going to be hanged?'

Silence struck.

'So I believe,' Orla replied calmly, showing neither distress nor surprise; at least, none the children recognised. 'That sounds really interesting. You can tell me everything after dinner tonight, and then I'll tell you what I've been up to, all right? How about helping your dad unload my things?'

Standing quietly arm-in-arm in the background, Jeanie and Frank Stewart watched this joyous homecoming.

Released from the attention of the children, Orla looked up and stared. It was her turn to be surprised, her hands flying to her face.

'Good God, you made it!' she yelled jubilantly, then raced to her old friends and wrapped her arms around them.

'Fancy you being here at this time,' Orla said excitedly. 'I've missed you so much, and I've thought about you both nearly every day. But I bet you didn't expect this... me being with child and not married, eh?'

'Well yes, it's all a bit of a surprise,' Jeanie replied, sounding just like her mother. 'Alf's filled us in and we're both truly very, very sad knowing what's befallen Ned. But just look at *you*! You're positively radiant and it seems you've lost none of your confidence or sense of humour. The main thing is, Orla, you're not on your own. If there's anything you want or need to talk about, please feel free to approach either of us at any time. Anyway you knew that, eh?'

'Thanks, Jeanie. Yeah, I knew that,' was all that Orla could say.

As they all walked into the house, Frank, as imposing and mischievous as ever, slipped his arm around Orla and whispered. 'Pray tell me, girl, have you learnt how to drive that cart... *politely*?'

24

———————

They talked beyond midnight. To an almost disbelieving, but nevertheless enthralled audience, Orla's story laid bare her frustrations and fears of the past few months: the denial of everyday freedom, the deprivations of food and basic comfort, and the ever-present threat of betrayal and capture.

Orla implored her friends to never discuss Tom Lloyd's involvement with the gang. Given his courageous support of Ned, she argued he deserved a break; that he would not be remembered as an outlaw.

'He may have ridden with Ned on some of his hold-ups but he never actually took part in any of them, and he definitely never shot anybody,' Orla explained emphatically. 'Besides, Tom constantly argued against Joe's idea to murder Aaron. He wanted Ned to clear out and return with me to Ireland.'

'Don't trouble yourself, Orla. We understand Tom's tricky position... we'll not say anything,' replied Alf. The others nodded their agreement.

'Anyway, the worst thing for me was abandoning Ned at Glenrowan. I can't explain it, something made me hang back,' Orla continued, now crying. 'I'm ashamed to say this now, but at the time, I could have killed any number of those traps and not cared less. If I hadn't stumbled upon Music, I'd have arrived at Glenrowan before the bastards captured Ned, and God only knows what I might have done then.' Orla wiped tears from her eyes and then took a deep breath. 'I couldn't risk throwing away our child's life. I think Ned understood that well enough; he didn't want me getting involved. But still, if the life of someone you love is on the line, you should do something. Anyway, that's what my da always said.'

'Maybe you could've intervened, but you did the sensible thing, girl. To have charged in guns blazing makes no sense to me whatsoever,' Joan immediately responded. 'You'd have died, Orla. They wouldn't have stopped shooting just because you're a woman.'

Orla found some comfort in those words, but her frustration remained. After a lull in the conversation, she continued. 'I can't present myself in Melbourne in my condition claiming to be the mother of Ned's child. That won't help him. But it'll implicate me and they'd probably throw the book at me. The world would then know, and my life and the life of our child wouldn't be worth living anyway. Ned has vowed *his* silence and that's why I need your oath to do likewise.'

She need not have worried. Her wonderful friends gave their unconditional agreement: future peace of mind was at stake for everyone in that room.

'If Ned's given his word, nothing will sway him,' said Alf. 'So, Orla, you must try and relax. The other lads can't say anything, sadly, they're dead. And anyone else who knows the truth will surely pledge their silence... if they know what's good for them.'

Orla then explained the deception that Kate was Ned's lover. She then retold the conversation Kate recently had with Ned when she visited him in prison in Melbourne. Ned had stoically lamented just before the guards led him away. 'So for all of us then, such is life.'

* * *

BEFORE CLIMBING into bed that night, Orla prayed her frustration and bitterness would pass, but she secretly doubted if her love and loss of Ned would ever diminish. She did, however, realise her very existence was now guaranteed to diffuse like a shadow into the night.

Still, there had been another unusual message Ned insisted Kate relay to Orla, one Orla did not discuss that night. 'To always remember what Charlie and Ong repeatedly told you — to treat their home as yours; to take whatever you want to remind you of their friendship.'

A well-intended gesture, to be sure, but surely their plea now amounts to nowt. Or does it? She pondered the offer, before finally falling asleep.

* * *

Drought continued to dictate life at the McIntyre farm.

Orla assisted around the farm where she could, but Joan soon put a stop to that. By the end of October, helping with the dishes and tutoring the children after dinner was her limit. She had never expected that 'this pregnancy lark' as she put it, would ever necessitate taking a nap in the afternoon!

The newspapers were full of the courtroom developments regarding Ned's involvement in the murder of the three policemen at Stringybark Creek. So when the children were out of earshot, the adults all offered their opinions on the charges and dubious trial proceedings, and openly castigated the Crown's evidence.

Whilst Orla remained in control of her feelings, she did not hesitate to loudly berate the government and judiciary for ignoring the massive swell of support Ned had somehow managed to gather around him in Melbourne; tens of thousands of people wanted to see him released.

Arguably, the majority of those people recognised him as a true leader of men, not befitting the outlaw tag that a bewilderingly arrogant, intimidating, corrupt, and uncaring British legal system had foisted upon him. But not one of those sympathetic folk learnt that Ned was about to become a father. And, sadly, to the regret of many, on the 11th of November 1880, the hangman dropped Ned into immortality.

Orla received the news later that afternoon. She had prepared herself. The inevitability held no shock, just sorrow. She wondered how Ned must have felt the previous night. *Did he sleep? Had he been thinking about her and their child? Had he awoken feeling sick with fear?* Orla doubted that. She had convinced herself that his mind would have been clear and his spirit unbroken.

At the McIntyre farm thirty eight days later, Orla went into labour shortly after noon. She gave birth to a beautiful, robust, nine pound baby boy — and named him Niall Haydn Kelly.

* * *

IT WAS Frank who quietly suggested to Orla she shouldn't be too hasty in having the boy christened. He explained that this meant records needed to be established and the well-intentioned people of the church were then duty-bound to verify parental details. And besides, there was no law that dictated when your child had to be christened, if indeed, that was what you wished for your child.

Sound advice indeed, thought Orla. *Niall's christening can wait.*

25

Late December threw an unrelenting blast of hot weather at the south eastern corner of the continent. Despite this, Frank and Jeanie were insistent that a memorable Christmas be had by all. Anticipation of the celebrations was infectious, and more so as Christmas party invitation acceptances started rolling in.

Everyone pitched in, working long and hard setting up shade, positioning tables, borrowing and placing chairs, and generally, tidying up the house and its immediate surrounds.

The traditional tasks of making Christmas cakes, puddings and all kinds of sweets were shared by Jeanie, Joan, Orla, and young Tylah. Alf and Jesse began cultivating several large batches of ginger beer, and bottles with intact seals were begged, borrowed and, in some cases, stolen.

The cooking ingredients, cured meats, alcoholic beer and spirits for the men, fancy drinks for the women, and all of the party paraphernalia such as coloured streamers and Christmas tree decorations were ordered a month before and paid for by Frank. Upon Frank's insistence, Jesse helped him collect these items from town. But there was a problem — the Christmas tree still hadn't arrived.

At dawn on Christmas Eve, Orla rose early to feed Niall. She was surprised to hear a horse cantering away from the house. Upon opening the back door she was further surprised... and elated. Leaning against the house wall was a ten foot tall pine tree. The attached note read, 'Merry Christmas, Orla and Niall. See you in the New Year. Love, Tom and Kate'.

Alf then came to the back door. 'I thought I heard someone riding off. Were you expecting anyone?' he said offhandedly, but quickly added when he noticed that Orla was sobbing quietly, 'Hey, girl, what's up?'

As Alf stepped outside he placed a fatherly hand on her shoulder. 'Wow! What a beaut tree. Bugger me, what a surprise! So who dropped it off? Did you get to talk with them?'

Orla said nothing but handed him the note.

'It was Tom. He'd gone before I got outside. It's a beaut tree, to be sure, but as you can see, they won't be coming to our party, damn it.'

'They're more than welcome should they change their minds,' Alf said cheerfully, and then passed the note back to Orla, as he stepped inside.

The real pity was that by missing the party, Tom and Kate unwittingly were denied the opportunity of ever seeing Orla again.

* * *

FOR MOST OF THE MORNING, Orla and the children decorated the tree, but by midday Alf and Frank were close to exasperation. Cocko for some reason seemed offended by all the attention being given to the tree and persistently screeched his annoyance.

'Hey, Alf, do you reckon the bird could do with a drink?' Frank asked roguishly. 'I believe such birds like the odd drop of whisky. Shall we give him a slug?'

'Let's try it,' Alf replied eagerly, chuckling at the idea.

The pantomime that played out was amazing. Cocko eyed the strong smelling liquor as if with disdain, but whenever the men appeared to be preoccupied, he'd quickly sample the offering, then throw back his head and simultaneously raise his brilliant yellow crest. His annoying shrieks soon abated, replaced by the continuous movement of his strange tongue. An hour later Cocko was making soft cooing sounds. Then his head drooped. By late afternoon, he was unconscious on the bottom of his cage. Peace reigned.

'Well mate, it definitely works,' Frank whispered to Alf. 'But I think we'd better dilute it a bit tomorrow.'

'He'll probably have such a terrible bloody hangover he'll stay off the stuff for ever,' replied Alf. Both men roared with laughter.

The children and Joan, in particular, were not impressed.

* * *

By noon on Christmas Day, twenty or so party guests arrived. Acquaintances were eagerly renewed. Drinks were offered and gladly received. Children excitedly exchanged gifts.

In the afternoon heat, the children's initial boisterous energy was quickly blunted. Orla then entertained them with board games and told far-fetched Irish stories. Some of the children laughed so much their faces ached; unable to control their laughter they had to walk away.

Orla hoped that the following year Niall, too, might start to laugh at some of her stories. Secretly, Orla grieved that Ned had forfeited all of it.

Everyone ate enormous amounts of food, drank with gusto, and laughed happily at one another's tall stories. At an appropriate time, Joan called for everyone's attention and offered up brief prayers for the sumptuous meal and for the privilege of everyone sharing Christmas together.

As Joan sat down, Alf rose unsteadily and proposed a toast. 'To dear friends here, one and all... and to those recently departed,' he said, while looking directly at Orla. 'We're thinking of you and thank you for the happiness you brought into our lives.'

There were a few seconds of reflection, and then Orla quietly murmured, 'You bet. Thanks, Alf.'

By late afternoon, the adults lay about in the shade either quietly yarning over a beer or whisky or trying to sleep off their excesses. The singing had stopped. It was far too hot for dancing. Regardless, a wonderful day was had by all.

Cocko remained quiet all day. Not once did he respond when the dogs announced either the arrival or departure of guests, for he was again upside down on the bottom of his cage, fast asleep.

The last guests departed at sundown. Orla collected Niall from his crib then went outside and sat in her favourite quiet place away from the house. Mercifully, Niall had also slept most of the day, but Orla, Joan, and Jeanie had taken it in turns to check on him. That Niall hadn't cried once was a godsend: their much rehearsed explanations as to whom he belonged were not required.

However, a few people had enquired why they hadn't seen Orla for months. Anticipating this, Orla explained she'd been visiting friends who lived near Bright. The McItyres and the Stewarts saw no reason to contradict Orla's story.

Without warning, Frank sat companionably beside her. 'Here, let me hold him for a while.' Expertly he positioned Niall into the crook of his arm. They said nothing for a few minutes, enjoying a cooling breeze, but eventually Frank asked, 'Orla, can we talk privately? Is now a good time with you?'

She looked at him, smiled, and gently nodded... so he continued.

'Orla, there are going to be a few changes happening over the next few months and I thought it best you know what Jeanie and I have in mind. Joan and Alf know of our plans, so you can talk openly with them about this.' After a pause to sip his beer he went on. 'We'll be leaving here soon. Don't look so shocked, luv. We don't want to overstay our welcome, and we're running up one hell of a bill at our hotel in Wang.

'We plan to return to Melbourne next week, and then catch a steamer to Adelaide. We've written to our daughter Anne and her husband, James, and they've invited us to stay with them. We've accepted, of course. It'll be nice to finally meet our grandson, Michael. He'll be two years old by then.'

Frank took another mouthful of beer and collected his thoughts. 'After that, we're going to the colony of Queensland... for two reasons. The first is we want to try and locate our son, Owen. We haven't heard from him for such a long time and well, you know, we both worry about him a lot.

'But, there's another good reason for going to Queensland. You remember my good friends in London who were able to organise your voyage to Australia at such short notice?'

Orla was intrigued; she nodded but remained silent.

'Well, some of those friends are in positions of, shall I suggest, 'unique privilege'. So, from time to time I hear of certain *opportunities* long before anyone else. It seems that back in 1867 in a place called Nashville — but which the local people now call Gympie, by the way — alluvial gold was everywhere and that started a rush to the small town. However, the easy pickings only lasted a year or so. Then the individual miners formed themselves into teams and set about what was called 'shallow reef mining' where they sank shafts into the gold bearing quartz reefs. Up until the mid 1870s that proved profitable, but eventually the miners hit a layer of extremely hard rock, called 'greenstone'. That curtailed their operations quick-smart, and in most cases, permanently.'

Frank continued in a more conspiratorial voice. 'But you see, Orla, a geologist who is undoubtedly also an opportunist of the first order, had previously seen similar rock formations in highly successful gold fields in South Africa. He was convinced that anyone prepared to risk it, could win gold in quantities undreamed of... *if* that greenstone could be penetrated.

'That's when I got involved. Back in London, it was suggested to me that I approach that man. I had him checked out by some other friends, and then I engaged him to oversee my own mining venture until we either struck it rich, or made bloody fools of ourselves.

Regardless, he's confident of his prediction and is a compelling, very likeable and trustworthy chap.'

'And at the same time,' Orla interrupted, as Frank drained his glass. 'Being located at Gympie, you'd hopefully be a lot closer to your son. And Joanie, I bet, is looking forward to some decent weather.'

'Exactly! But what I want you to know, Orla, is should you want to join us there, after we get settled in, then you're most welcome. I'm certain we can find work for you, and locate a place for you to live where it'll be safe for young Niall.

'Well, what do you reckon, girl? Will you join us or stay here? This is a magnificent region, but I remember you telling us you wanted to see the world. No more freezing winters, eh?'

Orla was dumbstruck by Frank's proposal, but never doubted his sincerity. She thought about it for a few minutes and then replied, almost breathless. 'It sounds like too good an opportunity to let slip by, Frank. So when do you reckon you'll know if you've been successful?'

'My mine manager, Mr. Robert D'Angelese, the geologist bloke I talked about... well, he's already in Gympie finalising the purchase of the site he's selected for me. He's installing some of the specialist machinery I had shipped out from England. So, you can see, things are already moving at a fair pace. I'd say that in six or seven months from now, we'll know our fate... and, hopefully, be expecting you both.'

'You sure don't mess about,' Orla replied with a laugh. 'Frank, your offer is astonishing and I again thank you for your kindness. But hang on. I'd better consult Niall to see if *he's* up to it.' Chuckling, they both shook the baby's tiny hands to cement the deal.

When they stood up, Frank, still holding Niall, put his other arm around Orla's waist and together they walked back to the house.

Just before they went inside he asked, 'Did you wonder how Tom learnt we needed a Christmas tree?' Frank continued before Orla could reply. 'Remember that old lady who first brought you out to the McIntyre's farm? Well, she's driven Jeanie and me to and from Wang on many occasions and she volunteered to get in touch with someone she thought could lay their hands on just about anything. Said his name was Tom Lloyd, a real good bloke to some, and that he would take care of it. I didn't say anything to you because I wanted it to be a surprise. I hoped he would deliver the tree and stay for a while. Nearly worked, eh? Cut it a bit fine with his delivery though.'

PART II

THE JOURNEY

26

───────

On New Year's Day, Orla posted another letter to her mother, devoting a whole page to Niall. She was honest about her adventures and tried to convey her relief since returning to live with the McIntyre family. She also attempted to convince her brothers to consider a trip to the colonies, suggesting that if they were interested, they could meet in Gympie: Frank would surely find jobs for them in the gold mines.

By June of 1881, Niall was a typical curious child and crawling everywhere. Innocent mischief was no stranger, however, he delighted in playing with the McIntyre children whose tolerance he only occasionally taxed. And he never ceased to delight Orla. *God, those eyes,* she often thought to herself. *And Ned's skin colour, too. What a handsome little boyo you are.*

Niall had a strange effect upon Cocko; it seemed the bird enjoyed entertaining the tiny child. Typically, he'd suddenly raise and lower his brilliant yellow crest a few times, or comically waddle about the cage floor, rocking his head from side to side. Niall always cackled in delight at these exhibitions.

If Niall's fingers ever strayed into the cage, Cocko gently nibbled on them. This, too, made Niall giggle... but made Alf feel sick.

'Quick!' he'd beg of whoever was nearest. 'Get the boy out of harm's way.' Alf knew only too well just how powerful Cocko's beak was; having nearly lost his index finger on the day the McIntyre family took ownership of the bird.

* * *

FRANK AND JEANIE'S letters from Gympie eventually arrived at the beginning of September, one for Joan and Alf, and one for Orla.

Jeanie's letter proudly announced that their daughter, Anne, was pregnant again. And, that James was about to be promoted to manager of the bank where he worked. Apparently, they'd saved enough money to afford an extended leave of absence before James took on the new role in about eight or nine months' time, perhaps, even a visit to Gympie was on the cards.

If only they could locate their son in the meantime, thought Orla.

The letter also informed Orla that Frank's mining upgrades were progressing beyond expectations. Clearly, Frank and Jeanie both loved Gympie and felt certain Orla would, too. They'd already purchased a small cottage for her just out of town, about a mile from their own property. Jeanie was supervising its renovation, including installation of a modern walk-in 'Coolgardie safe', which stored perishable foods – kept cool by its novel evaporative system — and repelled blowflies.

'True friends indeed, my little man,' Orla whispered to Niall. 'And, boyo, what an *incredible* opportunity?'

The timing was exquisite, and time, she admitted to herself, was indeed blurring her sorrow at losing Ned. A new life beckoned: an inexplicable freedom teased her senses and lifted her spirits.

'What do you think about the Stewarts' amazing offer?' Orla asked Joan and Alf, knowing that Jeanie and Frank had previously outlined their offer to them.

'We were wondering how soon you might raise the subject,' Joan replied.

'I can't imagine ever getting such an opportunity again... so... I'll be moving on — yes, again,' said Orla, while fidgeting and wringing her hands. 'And soon. I'd like to be away next month. I know I'll miss you both very much, and the kids, too. And I'll wonder forever how I can possibly repay your amazing support.

'I need to leave behind some horrible memories, too. My life's been enriched by Ned but I can't just stand still. It's what I need; something fresh, a new start. And I still have an urge to see more of this great land... and I want to share that with Niall. Maybe one day you can visit us in Gympie. You'll never need an invitation, you know.'

'Orla, listen,' Alf replied. 'We think of you as one of our family. Your decision to keep moving *is* just what you need. And be sure of one thing, you owe us nothing, except perhaps a letter from time to time.

'But, Orla, you must know that when you leave here, you do so with our blessings. And your past love of Ned shouldn't spoil your chances in the life before you. We'll both pray that you and the boy find true happiness. But enough of this, we need to sit down and write a list of what you'll need. First though, how do you propose to get to Gympie?'

Joan interrupted in her typical pragmatic fashion. 'Orla, are you sure the young bloke's old enough to travel so far?'

'Yep, he'll be fine. Just look at him, he'll be walking in no time. We could return to Melbourne and catch a steamer to Brisbane, but staring at nothing but ocean and coastline for weeks would be boring. I'd much rather be in the bush, I feel at ease there. Ned taught me so much. We'll be all right, Joan.'

Alf removed his hat and scratched his head. 'Then that's settled, you'll take Charlie's cart. It's in reasonable condition now, but it'll be just like new after I've done it up. And, my girl, you'll need Boss Boy again.'

'Thanks Alf, you're the best,' said Orla, giving him a hug. 'I know Joanie's bay is a damn good horse, but Boss Boy has it all over any other horse I've ever known. You know, at times it's as if he *even thinks for me*. So I reckon it'll be more a case of him looking after me, rather than the other way round.' No greater praise could any person have bestowed upon Alf's beloved, Boss Boy.

And so, throughout October, Alf threw himself into repairing the cart. With the help of a local blacksmith he replaced both wheel rims, adjusted and tightened spokes, replaced wheel-bearing blocks and greased both axle hubs. Next, he fabricated a three-sided frame over the cart's tray. This he covered, top and sides with canvas; the canvas sides could be raised and lowered to suit the conditions of the day, and easily secured for protection against inclement weather. Three water bags were then fitted to the outside walls of the cart's tray.

All harness was either repaired where necessary, or replaced, and then meticulously treated with conditioning oil. Boss Boy's saddle received the same preservation treatment. Neither Boss Boy, nor any of Ned's Walers, had ever been shod: Alf was not about to change that.

Orla's sense of anticipation grew, heightened one day by a lengthy visit to Wangaratta, with Joan. Fortunately, Orla's extended intervals between town visits no longer raised comment from the townsfolk, though they were surprised that Orla was leaving the district. 'To see the world' became her stock reply to satisfy their curiosity as she bustled about purchasing essential food items, bedding, clothing, footwear, cooking and eating utensils, needles and thread, old newspapers for toilet paper, canvas, hub grease, and bags of chaff and oats.

During the week before Orla's departure, Alf visited a friend — a retired wagon master — and obtained important route details leading to Sydney Town. However, it would be up to Orla's common sense and resourcefulness from Sydney Town to Brisbane, and onwards to Gympie.

Some folk said that Orla had lost her mind to think she could travel such a distance without a man; but then they didn't know Orla. *Why should she care what people thought anyway?* She reasoned that her determination alone would suffice. Besides, she'd been soundly tutored in bush survival by some of the colony's most capable bushmen. And unbeknownst to those doubters, she *would* have a man with her, though only a year old.

Initially, Alf concealed his concerns, for he had never travelled further north than the Murray River. Nevertheless, he gallantly counselled Orla on likely conditions and potential pitfalls.

'All things considered, if anyone can do this, you can, Orla. But you'll be on the road for at least eight to ten months; you do realise?'

Joan's concerns were more maternalistic. 'Orla, I know you'll look after Niall. But I worry about you, luv. Don't encourage strangers — particularly men.'

As Orla listened to Joan, she thought, *that's exactly what Ma would say.* But she was equally certain her mother would have encouraged this audacious journey. Nevertheless, Orla felt a tickle of self-doubt.

As they finished packing the cart on the day before departure, Alf continued offering practical advice, and even taught Orla a few bawdy songs when Joan was out of earshot.

Orla intended keeping her rifle and handguns loaded and within easy reach under the driver's platform. However, she decided to wear her Colts when approaching civilisation: comfort came from knowing her colts would always be nearby, even if God wasn't.

Well pleased with their effort, they retired inside. For dinner that night, Joan served roast lamb; Orla's favourite. When Tylah and Jesse were in bed, Orla retold them a few of her now famous stories about her beloved Ireland. She finally said her farewell to them, insisting they promise to write to her. In the meantime, Joan and Alf entertained Niall; it would probably be a long time before seeing him again... if ever.

After a quick breakfast the following morning, Alf fed and watered Boss Boy then gave him a final grooming before harnessing him into Orla's cart. Alf took the reins back to the driver's platform, talking as if giving Boss Boy some last minute advice... but Alf knew his fearless Waler would never let Orla down.

Joan and Orla walked from the house, Joan carrying Niall. Alf gently took the sleeping boy, kissed him on his soft warm cheek and then, without waking him, tucked him into his new bed in the cart.

After lingering hugs and farewell kisses, Orla climbed up onto the driver's platform. As she was about to sit down, she noticed an envelope on the seat. 'And what pray tell is this?' she asked looking back at her friends.

'Frank and Jeanie thought you might need some 'readies' along the way,' replied Joan as she handed another envelope and a heavy box up to Orla. 'And well... we also thought you might need this, too.'

When she opened the first envelope, she was lost for words. In her hand was a fortune — at least two hundred pounds!

She then opened the second envelope. It also contained money, but less than a pound. *Tylah's and Jesse's entire savings*, she guessed correctly. Orla was moved deeply.

'If my boy grows up to be just half as nice as your two, I'll be a very proud mum.'

The box contained ammunition for her pistols, at least one hundred rounds. A thoughtful gift indeed, for her supply was nearly exhausted.

'I suppose you remembered to pack those stupid damn pistols, then?' Joan asked resentfully, although with just a hint of humour.

Reaching inside her jacket, Orla removed an envelope of her own and handed it to Joan. 'Would you please see that Tom and Kate get this? I'll never forget them either, for what they've done for me and Niall.'

Orla then picked up the reins: Boss Boy needed little urging to stride away purposefully into the early morning mist. Fighting to control her emotions, Orla waved, but did not look back.

27

Barely three weeks passed and Orla started doubting her decision. Now in the colony of New South Wales, the weather had turned uncharitably cold. A persistent, penetrating wind painfully numbed her hands and face. The mornings were worst. Getting out of a warm bed to get dressed and then trying to light a fire to boil some water for tea and to warm Niall's food, in wet and near freezing conditions, made life an almost unbearable misery.

One particularly cold afternoon she almost abandoned her mission. In exasperation at the piercing cold, she stomped about, windmilling her arms and swearing on top note. That strange form of release somehow made her realise that going back would not relieve the cold... she'd just have to press on.

The following day the weather improved markedly, as did her temper and her resolve to continue. Regardless, there was a humorous touch to their morning routine. To be out of the wind, Boss Boy habitually stood on the lee side of the cart. At dawn he'd poke his head under the canvas and snuffle first into Niall's face and then Orla's as if to say, 'C'mon, the sun's up, you can't stay there all day.'

At first, Niall screamed and cried in fright. But with Orla's comforting words and reassuring cuddles, he soon learnt to tolerate those friendly greetings.

Boss Boy also proved to be better than a watchdog at night. When disturbed he would lean against the cart and make it rock; his signal that they had uninvited visitors, either stray dogs, or more likely, local aboriginals. And since Orla's colts were always near at hand, heaven help any intruder who either dared to steal anything, or menace them.

Thanks to Alf's thoughtful handiwork, when the additional canvas he'd fixed to the sides and ends of the cart's tray were unfurled to ground level, Orla then had an additional, relatively dry area underneath the cart. Here she temporarily stored cooking utensils, food tins, tools, and chaff bags, thus freeing up sleeping space within the cart. Although a bit confining, that under-space also provided somewhere to cook during inclement weather.

The cart's canvas top was unfailingly weatherproof, allowing Niall to amuse himself there while Orla either prepared meals or readied everything for a day's travel.

Orla's routine was simple: travel for three days, and then rest the next day. She always chose locations off the main track wherever shelter could be found either among trees or rock formations, away from prying eyes. By Orla's calculations, two hundred miles a month seemed realistic. She'd been assured that a farrier would not be required; nevertheless, at the end of each day, Orla always checked Boss Boy's hooves.

Riversides were Orla's favourite camping sites. At dusk, she enjoyed listening to the birds and watching the animals and reptiles as they went about quenching their thirst. She reflected upon Cocko's life as flocks of his free brethren flew screeching happily through the surrounding eucalypts seeking a suitable roost. The night threw out other sounds: the grumpy scuffles of possums and the monotonous calls of boobook owls as they talked up and down the river.

The riversides also occasionally revealed signs of aboriginals.

Though their proximity held no fear for Orla, none ever approached her campsites.

On other occasions, Orla sought high ground to camp. She loved the early mornings when mist poured over the mountain ridges, the kookaburras launched into their strange rounds of laughter, and the first updrafts of the day gently rustled the tree's canopies in the valleys below.

Niall turned one during such a camp. Orla prepared a special meal and fussed over presenting it to him. 'Pity your da isn't here to see this,' she said sadly as tears welled in her eyes. 'But life must go on, my big boyo.'

Not surprisingly that night, the grief that consumed much of her quiet time, continued to simmer in her soul. Ned's physical absence made her life hard. Being a single mother was difficult and she now felt desperately lonely. Her annoyance flared... but she now realised that being swept up by Ned's charm and aspirations had in fact been a huge indiscretion.

* * *

FEED AND WATER for Boss Boy was abundant. But so, too, were water-filled potholes and miles of slippery clay tracks that often made the going difficult and slow. Nevertheless, there were three constants: Niall's contentment, the stunning scenery, fresh and full of surprises, and Boss Boy's company.

The first time Orla saw aboriginals up close was in a small settlement. They were lethargic and unkempt, but worst, their faces reflected bewilderment and despair.

She recalled Ned saying that the white man was methodically and callously stripping them of their country and therefore depriving them of their cultural heritage and their dignity. She had also heard of the ruthless mass murders, the shootings and poisoning of so many blacks by white men. Newspapers referred to the black man's retaliations as *outrages and depredations*, but failed to provide equal, if any, condemnation of the white man's atrocities.

In her mind, Orla had previously rejected such atrocities actually occurred, or that such acts might still be happening. But the plight of these aborigines greatly saddened Orla, and sure enough, a not-unfamiliar frustration quickly surfaced as she now embraced reality. She was seething inwardly. *Bugger it, this is wrong! But what the hell can I do to help them?* A fair enough thought at that time.

About a mile north of the settlement Orla came upon a distressing scene. An untidy, bearded and fat middle-aged white man was wrestling with a thin and completely naked aboriginal girl who was perhaps sixteen. He was rewarding the girl's feeble attempts to escape with vicious whacks to the back of her head.

About a hundred yards off to the east, Orla noticed a small group of aboriginals huddled close together. It did not occur to her that they might be family, but they were looking intently in her direction.

A bay horse grazed nearby. A rifle lay on the side of the track. Spent cartridge shells lay scattered about. The attacker, red faced, sweating profusely and, obviously drunk, was now cruelly twisting the young girl's arm up behind her back. Again the girl tried to wriggle free. The man brutally twisted and then pushed her arm even further upwards. By now, Orla was close enough to hear a muffled *crack!* The girl screamed. Horrified, Orla assumed he'd just intentionally broken the girl's arm. In a flash, the man then released his trousers. As they fell, he hurriedly positioned himself behind the ill-fated girl and attempted to thrust his very large erection into her.

'Let the girl go, you useless piece of shite,' Orla yelled.

Understandably, the drunk was somewhat surprised by Orla's challenge. But he recovered quickly. 'Or what?' he slurred. Their eyes locked, but Orla looked through him as if he was made of air.

'Or the next time you look, fat boy, that *thing* will be at your feet,' Orla replied, her heart now pumping hard, her eyes blazing fiercely.

The man laughed raucously, contemptuously dismissing Orla's threat. He then roughly shoved the black girl aside. Despite being impeded by his trousers, he lurched towards Orla. However, before he'd taken two or three shuffling steps, the girl threw herself at him.

Unfortunately, he saw her coming and savagely deflected her onto her knees.

Obviously now infuriated, the man raised his fist. As he was about to viciously punch the girl in the face – Orla's colts coughed twice. The first shot tore three fingers from his fisted hand. The second shot saw him abruptly sitting on his backside, and now the recipient of a bloody groove scorched across his bald skull. He sat in stunned silence, staring in disbelief at his mangled hand as blood spurted unchecked.

Orla sprang from the cart and strode purposefully to the dazed man. Without hesitation she reached down, placed one of her colts between his legs and pulled the trigger. The man screamed in shock, then thrashed about wildly, obviously in dreadful agony. But worse was his anguish: the dual realisation of Orla's threat made good... and that he'd soon be dead!

He continued screaming like a stuck pig, but Orla ignored him and calmly walked over to the young black girl.

'Do you understand my language?' she asked the girl.

The girl was shivering in shock and trying to support her damaged arm, but looked wide-eyed into Orla's calm, attractive face.

'Yes, but why did you do that for me?' she replied tentatively.

'That drunken imbecile made me very, very angry! That's why. Nobody has the right to do such things to you, or to anyone for that matter. So what's your name, luv?'

'Call me, Lahni.'

'Right then, Lahni. Please call me, Orla. Now let me look at your arm.'

Orla examined Lahni's arm and realised it was dislocated, not broken as she'd first thought. Orla had once watched Tom Lloyd adjust Steve Hart's right shoulder after he'd fallen awkwardly during one of their mad races across the Oxley Flats. She remembered the excruciating pain Steve had endured. But she also knew that quick action was necessary to avoid permanent shoulder damage.

Orla surmised that Lahni, being aboriginal, would probably be refused attention in the nearby settlement, so it was up to her. She sat

Lahni down and explained what she was going to do... and that it would probably hurt.

'It be no worse than having my baby, I reckon.'

Orla saw the opportunity she needed to distract Lahni. 'You already *have* a baby? A boy, or a girl?'

Just as Lahni spoke, Orla pulled and simultaneously twisted Lahni's arm. There was a loud *'pop'*. Lahni gasped, her eyelids fluttered... then she slumped, unconscious, into Orla's arms.

As Orla cradled Lahni, she suddenly found herself surrounded by nine or ten very black people. She had neither heard nor sensed their approach, but upon reflection realised Boss Boy had been quietly whinnying, rattling his traces and bobbing his head in an attempt to get her attention.

The aborigines carefully carried Lahni to some nearby trees and covered her with kangaroo pelts. Orla then walked back to the cart, picked up Niall who was now crying, and retrieved one of her water bags. The woman to whom Orla handed the water bag nodded her thanks and then trickled some water into Lahni's mouth.

Nearby, the rapist's bawling could still be heard, though now only intermittently.

It wasn't long before Lahni regained consciousness. Members of her family immediately helped her to sit up; through clenched teeth, the girl winced in pain.

As Orla was about to examine Lahni's shoulder, some hands reached out to take Niall from her. At first Orla resisted, but when she looked into the non-threatening, friendly face of another black woman she relaxed and handed him over.

Lahni's shoulder joint seemed to be in place. Again Orla returned to her cart and retrieved some material from which she fashioned an arm splint. 'Listen, Lahni, it's going to hurt bad for many days,' Orla said firmly while positioning Lahni's arm in the splint. 'You must rest this arm for at least two weeks. You understand?' Lahni nodded.

During this entire episode, Orla totally ignored the white man she'd left dying on the side of the track. But now, she was *very* puzzled. There were splashes of blood in the centre of the track leading to a large, dark red pool of congealing blood on the verge, but there was no sign of the man's body... anywhere! The surrounding country was flat, desolate and basically devoid of trees and scrub, and no more than fifteen minutes had elapsed since the shooting. *I'd have noticed anyone removing his body. And he sure as hell hasn't walked away. So, what's going on?* Orla pondered as she picked up the dead man's rifle.

Later, Orla was to learn the ordeal started without warning, when the man charged up to the tribe and demanded at gunpoint that they hand Lahni over. When they resisted, he started shooting over their heads. Luckily none of them were hit, but they all ran for their lives, except Lahni. When the man seized Lahni, they saw him drop his rifle, but the tribe had no effective weapons with which to take action. Besides, they also had a sad history of being intimidated, and couldn't conceive of fighting back, knowing fully the probable consequences.

Lahni had reasoned that if she stayed behind, the others could escape and no harm would come to them or to her baby. Naively, she had expected to be herded off to provide free labour on the man's farm — from where she would eventually escape — not savagely raped in public, in broad daylight.

Next, Orla caught and hobbled the man's bay. She quickly realised it was in poor condition and without a brand or earmarks. Likewise she could find no distinguishing markings on the rifle, saddle or bridle. While packing these items into her cart, she resolved it was time to do a bit of her own wholesale and retail trading. After all, surely there wasn't much Orla didn't already know about that business — having learnt from arguably the country's best? She then hobbled Boss Boy so he too could browse nearby.

When Orla rejoined the aboriginal family group, they were sitting in a circle, watching two children play. She was delighted to see Niall and a beautiful black girl sharing some kind of crude toy. Orla joined their circle and soon learnt that the little girl was Lahni's daughter, Ruthie.

In turn, Orla deliberately looked into the face of each family member. She detected no sign of hatred, antagonism or distrust, just an openness and warmth. When Orla suddenly smiled, a few mouths creased in shared amusement. When she then chuckled, the entire family quietly chuckled with her. But then for no apparent reason, Orla started to roar with laughter — and in like spirit the whole mob joined in.

Boss Boy shook his head and whinnied as if to say, 'Silly buggers, what the hell's got into you lot?'

Lahni introduced each member of the family group to Orla, who tried hard to say each name correctly. During the next hour, Orla struggled to recall those names but with Lahni's patient help, the association of name and face soon became much easier. But Lahni's man was missing. Apparently, an enlightened farmer recognised the aboriginal man's natural talent with horses and employed him on his station about one hundred miles to the south. Her man would rejoin the tribe as soon as he could get some money together, but Lahni obviously missed him very much.

The other men lit a fire, so Orla produced her billycan and proceeded to make tea, which she sweetened with several large spoonfuls of sugar. She only possessed two mugs but the tribe had two of their own and soon each member had their cuppa. During this shared contentment, Orla quietly asked Lahni about the disappearance of the dead man's body.

'Oh, you not see eagle take him?' she laughed. 'Best you not know, for if white fella policeman he ever ask questions, you know nothing about nobody. He go where no spirit live. You not worry, Orla.'

And that was that. Orla was bemused by that unusual explanation, but felt a strange, compelling urge *not* to raise the matter again. Nonetheless, she spent an enjoyable afternoon with these shy but very friendly people.

With Lahni acting as interpreter, Orla soon shared the elder's experiences. But unbeknownst to her, she had now joined their repertoire of spirit stories to be talked and sung about for as long as this tribe existed: Orla's third 'adoption' since leaving Ireland.

The next morning, Lahni took Orla aside and again thanked her for her timely and brave intervention. She also solemnly promised that her spirit people would ensure Orla a safe journey, and see to it that one day they would meet again. Orla was secretly flattered but doubted if that could, or would, ever happen: her destination was many hundreds of miles to the north and surely far beyond the traditional lands of Lahni's tribe.

After courteous farewells to Lahni's family, Orla and Niall were soon on the move with the dead man's horse in tow. Surprisingly, however, the disdain Orla previously felt for the man she'd just killed was waning. Uninvited feelings of remorse were now seeping into her psyche.

28

They reached the outlying settlements of Sydney Town six weeks later, the going having been uneventful and relatively easy. However, Orla was understandably disappointed given that Christmas and 1882 arrived without her being able to celebrate either event. Although Boss Boy was handling his job with apparent ease and making good time, the opportunities of making camp off the main road diminished the closer they got to Sydney Town.

Niall was now increasingly more active. One evening as Orla was cooking, she proudly noticed him standing against one of the cart's wheels. Amazingly, Boss Boy was gently prodding him as if to persuade the child to take a step. And he did! But he fell over immediately on his well padded behind. Not deterred, he again hoisted himself up against the wheel, turned and beamed the broadest of happy smiles towards his mother.

The bay's physical condition was also steadily improving, and under Orla's firm control, adapting to being backed into the shafts of the cart. Orla figured that if the bay was broken to harness, he would significantly reduce Boss Boy's workload. Besides, a properly schooled working horse would eventually fetch a better price.

But her problems started on the day she decided to trial the bay's pulling ability. From the outset, Boss Boy took every opportunity to harass him. Orla put up with Boss Boy's behaviour for an hour or so, hoping things would settle down, but the bay was starting to retaliate, and their progress became erratic and unpleasant. Eventually she had enough; moreover, Niall's safety was to be considered.

Orla reined in, swung down from the cart, stormed up to Boss Boy and yelled her anger. After her tirade she put her arm around his neck and quietly led him to the rear of the cart. She then tethered him there, thus putting an end to his privilege to run free alongside. The next day, Boss Boy walked shoulder to shoulder with the bay as if challenging it to do better. All physical harassment stopped, thus giving Orla the opportunity to better appraise the bay. Regrettably however, the bay's behaviour in the increasing traffic was becoming unacceptably skittish. She therefore resolved to 'dispose' of him in accordance with her initial plans, sooner, rather than later. Besides, Boss Boy had made his point. He needed no help... *he* was boss.

By the time they'd reached the outskirts of Sydney Town, Niall could walk unaided for six steps. Orla flushed with pride at her little man's achievement. Ned, she knew, would have been equally proud.

Although it was no longer possible for Orla to camp away from other travellers, to her surprise and delight she easily befriended people who were, like herself, in transit seeking either a perceived better life, or gold, or love.

Many things were shared with those itinerants, from food to medicines, but more importantly to Orla, directions into and around Sydney Town were given freely. Many had travelled from the north and suggested the inland route to Brisbane Town. Although monotonous, it was apparently easy going provided it didn't rain, which then made travel impossible. Others suggested the coastal route. By all accounts it was better defined and had abundant grazing and clean water. But, it seemed, bushrangers were still a threat and, on occasion, the natives could be aggressive.

The choice was easy; she'd take the coast road. Good grazing and water were positives, and she held no fear of either bushrangers or aboriginals. Having made her decision, she refocused her questioning and soon had imperfect, but otherwise reliable details for her route northward.

By chance, Orla located a managed camping site about twenty miles southwest of Sydney Town. She'd already decided it was time to rest for an extended period, so the timing was perfect. A break also meant she could write to her family, the McIntyres, and the Stewarts: her letters would be delivered by the Royal Mail Service, whose stage-coaches regularly called at the camp site.

Early the next morning, Orla rode Boss Boy — with Niall perched in front of her — to investigate a lead from the camp manager that good quality but extravagantly priced horse feed could be obtained from a nearby farm.

When they arrived, Orla was met with suspicion... until she started talking.

'Orlagh O'Meara,' she said, while firmly shaking the farmer's hand and gazing directly at him. 'But please, call me Orla.'

'Bill Jones, and this is my son, Peter,' the farmer responded proudly. Orla then shook the boy's hand.

'I've heard you might have some chaff and oats for sale,' Orla continued confidently. 'If that's so, then I'd like to relieve you of a bag or two.'

'Yeah, we got both, but you'll have trouble carrying it on your horse, with the little bloke as well.'

'I'll pay you now and come back later with my cart to pick it up. By the way, my little bloke's name is Niall.'

Bill admired the easy, yet forthright manner in which Orla closed their deal. He was also surprised at how knowledgeable she was about farming in general and livestock in particular. Farmer and son were infatuated by her lilting Irish brogue and impressed by her somewhat derogatory opinion of police.

'What makes you think the police, or rather, 'our officialdom' might be any different here?' Bill responded sarcastically.

Orla soon learnt that Bill's father was dying. His wife had left to help care for him, but the latest news on his health was not good. Bill was understandably desperate to visit his father before he died, but he could neither abandon the farm, nor leave Peter alone to look after the farm.

In a flash, Orla saw her opportunity. She immediately offered to look after the farm in return for lodgings and agistment for her horses. She mentioned, though a little 'tongue in cheek', she'd spent most of her life running a family farm about the same size as this one... but failed to mention her four brothers who did their bit.

Orla and Bill struck an immediate rapport and talked for the next hour or so about the needs of his stock. He showed her around the property assessing in his own way, the skills of this apparent capable young woman. Peter happily took charge of Niall, which gave Orla the freedom to concentrate upon the rapidly unfolding outcome she was cleverly directing.

By noon Bill was satisfied with Orla's bona fides.

'Listen, Orla, I've got a deal to offer you. You know my situation here. Do you reckon you could look after the farm for a few weeks? I can't pay you much but you'll have the house to yourself and there's probably enough food to see you through that time. Can you help me out? I can't possibly impose upon my neighbours for that period of time.'

'I'd be honoured, Bill. And, I won't accept payment. I can move in this afternoon if that suits? I'll give you both a hand with your packing. It's important that Peter goes with you.'

'That'd be just great. Thanks, Orla,' said Bill, obviously very relieved at this most unexpected outcome. 'If we can get moving at dawn tomorrow, then God willing, we'll be with my dad by midday.'

The deal done, Orla rode back to the camp with Niall, to collect the cart and the bay. Had you been a passer-by as Boss Boy strode along, you would have heard the sound of a sweet Irish lullaby, interspersed with the occasional unladylike chuckle.

To her surprise, when Orla returned to the farm, Bill was visibly flustered. Peter's filly had developed a pronounced limp, which jeopardised the whole deal. Bill couldn't take Peter two-up on his horse and expect it to also carry their entire luggage.

Orla approached the stricken animal and expertly examined the mare's foreleg. Whilst there was nothing affecting its hoof, its fetlock was very hot and tender to the touch. Without hesitation, Orla untied the bay from the rear of her cart and walked with it to where Peter stood.

'Problem solved I believe,' she said and handed him the reins.

Peter's mouth was opening and closing, as he tried to say something... and he was almost in tears. Bill, too, was momentarily at a loss for words.

'God bless you, girl,' Bill eventually said. 'What have I done to deserve this?'

Orla just smiled.

That evening, with all outside jobs done and the packing finished, they shared a simple meal. As the daylight slipped away, Bill and Orla wandered around the farm talking companionably about their respective journeys ahead of them. It was clear to Orla that Bill was an honest bloke who loved his wife and son, and was on the verge of seeing some prosperity if the next winter rains didn't let him down.

'How long can you afford to stay in this caretaker role, Orla?'

'Don't worry about me, or your animals, for heaven's sake, Bill. Do what you must, and then return safely when you feel the time's right.'

Again Bill was lost for words; he simply offered his hand, which Orla firmly shook in acceptance of their mutual gratitude.

* * *

Neighbours soon visited, and again, as luck would have it, they had two children, both not much older than Niall. Curiosity satisfied, dinner invitations soon followed, together with offers of help in any emergency.

Time flew. Orla enjoyed every moment. The change from the monotony of the journey also gave her time to start planning a few solo activities after Bill and his family returned.

In the meantime, Niall's desire to constantly explore started to get him into strife. One morning, while watching his mother at work in the laundry, Niall overreached when attempting to grab one particularly tempting and lustrous bubble. He promptly slipped and fell headfirst into the washtub. Had Orla not been there, the outcome could have been disastrous. However, Niall's reaction to the dunking was not what Orla expected. No screaming, no crying — just some spluttering followed by determined wriggling as he again tried to capture those elusive, wobbling spheres.

It was cold outside, but within the laundry it was warm and steamy. So Orla filled an oversize bucket with warm soapy water and plonked Niall into it, clothes and all, to let him play. *That'll keep the little bugger amused for a while,* she thought, as she set about finishing her work.

But what she hadn't expected to see was Niall blowing bubbles through his chubby little fingers. This made him smile broadly and giggle each time he successfully created a new bubble.

Intrigued, Orla stopped what she was doing, knelt down beside him then plunged one of her hands into the soapy water. Through the fist she'd formed, she blew her own, much larger bubbles. As these orbs grew ever larger, Niall was soon in a fit of excitement as he tried to grab them before they burst.

The spontaneous joy of this moment soon had them both laughing madly. Niall thrashed his arms and legs in the bucket sending most of its contents flying. But there was soon a down side. Without warning, in a stream of volume Orla could hardly believe, Niall spewed the contents of his stomach onto the soapy, waterlogged laundry floor.

29

A fortnight later, Bill returned with his family. Orla immediately warmed to Bill's Irish born wife, Erin. Two very proud parents explained to Orla how their normally shy and quiet son strode to the podium and, with surprising confidence, delivered an emotional eulogy to his late grandfather. Peter acknowledged his grandfather's life, and then told stories of happy times, of fishing, riding or bushwalking with him. Real passion flowed as he related his grandfather's love and respect for all animals, in particular, horses.

It seemed their son grew up overnight. Orla had to agree. In just two weeks, Peter now exuded an open and confident bearing; very mature for a twelve year old.

As anticipated, Bill's father bequeathed his home and belongings to his only son, but his will included a surprise. A significant amount of money had been put into a trust to ensure his beloved grandson could receive the university education Peter already craved in the pursuit of equine husbandry.

When the euphoria of relating these events subsided, Orla and Bill strolled about the property stopping occasionally to inspect the pasture, or to dig small holes to gauge soil moisture.

'Everything's coming on nicely, Orla, but just a moment... is that what I think it is?'

'Yep, you're now the proud owner of a fine bull calf,' Orla replied nonchalantly. 'Mind you, when he arrived four days ago things were a bit *iffy* for a while. His stupid mother chose an awful place to deliver him, that's for sure. When he was born he undoubtedly tried to stand up, but must have toppled straight down the embankment of your dam over there and got stuck in the mud. It was bloody cold that morning, too, so I guess the poor little bugger was cold and wet — and frightened — so he started bellowing on top note. The mother started bellowing back; anyway, they were kicking up a hell of a racket while I was getting my breakfast.

'When I saw what was going on, I hitched Boss Boy into your dray and we manoeuvred it so that its rear end was up against the fence, and its body section along the top edge of the dam. Anyway, before the old girl realised what was going on, I waded into the dam, heaved the calf out of the mud and carried it up the embankment.

'She didn't seem too impressed. Showed no bloody gratitude at all, so I went home and finished my breakfast.'

Bill stood there, hat in hand, scratching the back of his head. He smiled in disbelief at Orla's casual account. Orla simply shrugged and returned his smile. She had in fact quickly summed up the situation, knowing that if she had simply waded into the dam to free the calf, she'd be between the cow and her calf... and that guaranteed an attack upon herself.

When Orla emerged from beneath Boss Boy's neck carrying the calf, the cow, having momentarily lost sight of its calf as it was hidden by the dray, was in a murderous state, bellowing, pawing the ground and scooping dirt over her lowered head. But as soon as Orla released the calf, despite a mock charge, the cow quickly shuffled up to its calf, licked it with parental recognition and then positioned herself to enable suckling to commence. *Too easy*, Orla reckoned, in a self-satisfied, though tongue-in-cheek manner.

Over dinner that night, Orla recounted for Erin and Peter the rescue of the bull calf, and then sadly reported the only bad news in an otherwise trouble-free fortnight.

'Unfortunately, Peter, your filly has shown no improvement. I've done all I can, but I think there's a break. That'll never heal properly, you know. I think it'd be best to end the filly's suffering, Bill. But get other opinions, I might be wrong.'

Bill nodded a few times and then said despondently, 'You're right, I'm sure. I'll attend to things first thing in the morning.'

Three weeks ago, that would have been the end of the subject, but to everyone's amazement and obvious pride of both parents, Peter firmly interrupted. 'No, dad, she's mine. I'll do it.'

After a minute or so had passed in mournful silence, Orla cheerfully changed the subject. 'By the way, Peter, how did my horse perform?'

'Best I've ever ridden. Seems eager to impress, but gets a bit spooked in the traffic.'

'Then he's yours, boyo, for two quid... and I'll throw in the saddle and bridle. What do yah reckon?' Peter nearly fell out of his chair: both parents gasped in surprise.

'You're joking surely,' Peter replied, shocked by the generosity and timing of this grand offer.

'Tell you what. Give me a quid as deposit. You keep the horse and saddle — and the bridle — and when I get to Gympie I'll write to you and send you my address. When you've saved up the balance, mail it to me. I'll give you six months to make the final payment. If you don't, then I'll be gunning for you, boyo. What do you reckon... a deal?'

'Done,' said Peter, who raced around the table and hugged Orla so hard that she wondered where her next breath would come from. He ran from the kitchen but returned in less than a minute to give Orla her deposit.

'I'll send you a receipt when I get settled,' said Orla. Bill and Erin caught Orla's subtle wink and smiled knowingly at her charade.

After Niall was put to bed, Orla casually broached her plans with Erin. They chatted for hours about things to see and nice places to visit in Sydney Town — and places definitely not to visit. Erin, she knew, would take good care of Niall.

* * *

ORLA GAVE Niall a long farewell hug and many kisses, and then Bill drove her to a pickup point where a stagecoach would transport her into the very centre of Sydney Town. For the first time in nearly two years, Orla would be on her own for three days of 'playing the tourist' in the largest and most rapidly developing city in the entire colony.

The journey was rough and swift but gave Orla the opportunity to adjust to an ever-increasing population and its associated pollution-haze. A confusion of streets, road signs, and rows of tents giving way to small houses and factories, now dominated the passing scenery. Everything was in stark contrast to the natural order of the mountains and open plains country she'd previously grown to love.

Cresting a rise, Orla gazed in awe at the grandeur of the harbour around which Sydney Town sprawled. An onshore breeze thankfully diluted the usual fetid odours of massed humanity with a strong hint of the ocean.

As if announcing Orla's arrival, the sun came out. Shafts of golden light penetrated the clouds and randomly highlighted features around the harbour, including a racetrack, which she correctly assumed was Randwick.

Orla easily found accommodation. Although expensive, it was also probably the best Sydney Town could offer and she was determined to have a relaxing time in the kind of luxury she'd not enjoyed since leaving London.

As Saturday dawned, hotel room service punctually delivered her pre-ordered and lavish breakfast. When finished, she bathed and dressed quickly, for she wanted to be on the streets to start a long overdue shopping spree as soon as the shops opened.

There was undeniable wealth in Sydney Town. Some shops screamed good taste in the form of the latest fashions from England and France, albeit displaying price tags that almost took her breath away. Tempted as she was, Orla settled upon more practical clothes for her journey ahead. But she did indulge in an elegant, tight fitting outfit best described as 'the riding outfit for the squatter's wife who has everything'. Her fabulous figure was accentuated by the skirt and the ruffles of her shirt only just hid the cleavage of her firm, well-rounded bosom. Next, she purchased some calf-height boots, the smooth soft leather perfectly highlighting her ankles.

Finally, she found a hairdresser. While she was having her hair washed, she simultaneously had her nails trimmed and manicured. Her hairstyle, short as she preferred, was expertly fashioned to compliment her large eyes and elfin features.

Even dressed in her old clothes as she returned to her hotel to offload her purchases, men stopped to either ogle or wolf-whistle her as she passed. This attention did her ego no harm, but she ignored them all; she was in town to enjoy herself... not to get involved.

Orla decided to have an early lunch at her hotel. While eating and enjoying the view of the harbour from her idyllically positioned table, she eavesdropped on the couple sitting at the table next to hers. They were arguing which horse was going to win the fifth race at Randwick that afternoon and for the first time in months, Orla over-heard the word 'bushranger'.

Instinctively, she concentrated on the couple's conversation. It seemed the morning's paper had reported that a bushranger up north was active, having recently relieved a property of many cattle. The couple finally agreed that the coincidence of that article was the clincher for their selection in the fifth; Bushranger Prince. *I'll make up my own mind on that,* thought Orla. But she was feeling alive, and shivered in anticipation of being trackside.

On the spur of the moment she caught the attention of the garru-lous couple. 'Excuse me,' she politely interrupted in her sweetest voice. 'Can you tell me how I get to the racecourse from here?'

'Why not come with us? We're being picked up in twenty minutes,' the man offered. 'Can you be ready in that time?'

'You bet, and thank you,' Orla replied without hesitation and jogged enthusiastically to her room.

She changed into her new outfit, grabbed her purse and rushed back to the lobby. Introductions followed, the wife purposefully placing herself between her husband and Orla. The man's expression said it all; Orla looked sensational.

They were an engaging couple, but overly pretentious and just a bit too nosy. So, when their coach arrived at the racetrack, Orla politely thanked them for the ride, wished them good luck and then quickly walked away and into the crowd.

Orla explored the trackside layout and soon located the best vantage point: she'd be in close proximity to the stables, the exercise paddock, and the betting ring.

Just prior to the first race, Orla wandered over to the stables for a closer scrutiny of the horseflesh on offer. All were good types, of sleek and well-muscled form that gave credit to their thoroughbred lines. Watching them being paraded, her experienced eyes soon noticed two horses were slightly lame and at least two others had a very bad rapport with their respective jockeys.

One animal, a mare, strolled in such a fashion that her head drooped and nearly touched the ground as the strapper commenced its pre-race exercise routine. *Is it tired, sick or just very relaxed?* Orla wondered. She didn't have long to wait, to find out. As the jockey was legged into the saddle, the mare lifted her head, obviously very alert, pivoting her ears as if either listening to her opposition or seeking encouragement from her rider.

'You'll do me, girl,' Orla whispered. To her surprise, when she arrived in the betting ring, the odds for her selection were twenty-five to one.

Orla conceded that the favourite looked like a tough campaigner, but it was even money and two points clear of the second favourite. In her mood of unexplained and carefree excitement, she boldly bet twenty pounds for a win on her selection. The bookmaker raised his eyebrows, but he gladly took her money while superciliously suggesting she would have been better off playing it safe on the favourite. Orla simply smiled, took the bookmaker's docket and returned to her vantage point.

The race was a cracker. Orla rode the mare all the way down the straight, shouting encouragement and advice, oblivious to the rest of the crowd who were urging on the favourite. And the favourite did everything right — except win. As if by magic about fifty yards out, the leading horses parted, leaving the mare a clear run to the finishing post. With the jockey's frantic urging, the mare accelerated through the opening and with only two or three strides to the line, edged past the favourite.

Orla screamed in excitement, punched the air, laughed and jumped about madly... announcing to anyone who wanted to listen, she'd just won a small fortune.

But when she approached the bookmaker to collect, he was in a very ugly mood. 'That's my day buggered... *yah bitch*! Why didn't yah stay home?'

'What, and miss a race like that? Call it luck of the Irish, boyo.' Orla replied in her sweetest, lilting brogue. 'Now just give me my five hundred quid and shut your foul, ugly mouth.' To add to the bookmaker's discomfort, Orla stared him down with a fierceness that clearly disturbed him.

With her winnings tucked into the deepest recesses of her outfit, she allowed the euphoria of the first race to pass while savouring some cold but expensive French champagne. Before each subsequent race she routinely visited the exercise paddock to conduct her appraisals, but refrained from placing any further bets until the competitors for the fifth race were paraded.

Now, what was the name of the horse that snobby couple was discussing? Orla pondered. *Ah yes, number 5. Bushranger Prince, how could I forget that?*

Orla was impressed, Bushranger Prince was a fine animal, but she thought there was a better prospect. She liked the look of the grey gelding with a high rounded rump, and a barrel chest. The animal seemed eager as he pranced around the parade yard.

When she returned to the betting ring, she noticed with some disappointment that the antagonistic bookmaker was gone, but she quickly chose another. The well-dressed punter in front of her who had just placed his bet, turned and brushed past her. Their eyes met briefly. The man, very handsome indeed, muttered his apology for making contact with her, and then continued to shoulder his way back through the crowd.

Orla was dumbstruck. *Those eyes, such a brilliant blue*, she thought. But what really disturbed her, were her next thoughts. *Shite... I think I know him! But that couldn't possibly be. Nah, surely not. Or could I? So who the hell is he?*

The people behind her were growing agitated and their voiced impatience broke her spell. She quickly placed her bet, collected her docket, and was about to return to her vantage point when a disturbance broke out nearby. The assailants moved quickly in her direction through the crowd, all the while shouting on top note at each other.

Momentarily distracted, Orla still felt the hand that brushed her hip as it deftly attempted to manoeuvre into her side pocket. In three bewilderingly movements, Orla grabbed the pickpocket's wrist with her left hand, took a step back, and with her right fist savagely punched the thief square in his startled face. As his head snapped back, broken front teeth flew into the air. The man staggered and almost fell.

Still holding his wrist, Orla jerked the dazed man upright. An equally fierce second blow crashed into his nose. Bone and cartilage exploded. Blood spattered across the man's distorted face, joining that already dribbling from his mouth. She released his wrist and he flopped to the ground.

Orla then turned nonchalantly and walked gracefully away through the crowd, chuckling to herself and massaging her right fist.

A bemused but appreciative audience started clapping.

Oddly, her buoyant mood evaporated completely when her selection lost by three and a half lengths. So, casually, she made her way to the coach bay intent on returning to her hotel.

Gradually, she felt a trickle of shame as she recalled the pitiless treatment she'd just handed out to the unlucky pickpocket. What confused her more was the hauntingly handsome face and incredible blue eyes of the other stranger.

* * *

THE FOLLOWING day Orla treated herself to a trip on the Manly ferry. She strolled from one end of Manly beach to the other and back, listening to the pounding surf and the seagulls. She pretended not to hear the occasional wolf-whistle.

Later, back at her hotel, she freshened up and then slept for about four hours. Upon awakening, she ordered a bottle of the finest white wine, it being her intent to get quietly drunk and watch the thunderstorm building in the northeast. As it grew darker, the atmosphere became warm and still. Alone on the balmy solitude of her hotel balcony, she watched the lightning as it flashed over the ocean. Suddenly, she felt very hungry.

And, inexplicably, for the first time in two days she felt anxious about Niall. He'd be missing her. She quickly discarded any feelings of guilt knowing he was in trusted hands. Nevertheless, her maternal instincts had surfaced, threatening to override her temporary contentment. Orla was also pragmatic and resolved to enjoy her remaining few hours in Sydney Town. Dreamily, she dressed in her new clothes then sauntered down to the hotel's opulent restaurant, the anticipation of indulgence exciting her.

She ordered a house specialty seafood platter and, just as the waiter was placing the meal on her table, she looked up as if expecting the other guests to be sharing in her surprise at the size and magnificent presentation of her meal. But instead, she was staring into those same incredible blue eyes of the day before. She hoped nobody noticed her reaction; she was stunned and slightly breathless. This most striking man was only twenty yards away and initially failed to notice her as he confidently approached the dining room entrance. Two women clung to him, contesting his undivided attention.

The man stopped to survey the seating accommodations, but

then froze. Orla immediately recognised his surprise as he in turn found himself looking directly at her. Orla nodded slightly and flashed a friendly, beguiling smile. Furiously she thought, *God, what's going on here? Who is this charming boyo? I don't know him... or do I, be Jeezus?*

The man simply raised an eyebrow and allowed a small but warm smile to crease his handsome face before returning his attention to his present company.

Biting her bottom lip in frustration, Orla studied the untouched meal before her. Her appetite had somehow deserted her and she was unfathomably embarrassed at the realisation she was actually jealous of those two women. She returned to her hotel room. Loneliness engulfed her. Although she went directly to bed, sleep evaded her. Intuitively, she knew there was more to that man than his eyes and good looks. But, try as she might, her earlier fleeting belief of recognition refused to return.

In the early hours of the morning, Orla eventually consoled herself believing that her frustration was the result of mistaken identity... or wishful thinking. With the remnants of the storm still rumbling in the distance, sleep finally claimed her.

30

———————

Orla rose early the next morning, and despite feeling a bit hung over, went on a leisurely walk along the nearby main streets. She stopped for a cup of tea, then sat and observed the bustling early morning tide of humanity for fifteen minutes before resuming her walk.

Orla suddenly remembered the letters she'd recently written and hoped the news of her progress would placate everyone's concerns, particularly about Niall's welfare. 'Niall, my little boyo,' Orla whispered to herself. 'Don't fret; I'll be with you soon.'

Realising the time was approaching for her to leave Sydney Town, she found a gunsmith's shop and purchased ten boxes of ammunition for her colts. While the shop owner packed her purchase, she admired the latest model '73 Winchester, a fifteen shot, lever action repeating rifle. Orla recognised the craftsmanship, balance and protection such a rifle could provide, so, on the spur of the moment, she bought not only the rifle, but five boxes of ammunition.

The shop owner noticed the expert, confident way his customer handled the rifle and was diplomatic enough not to query the purpose of her purchases. He gratefully took her money and carefully packed the rifle in a leather cover. No money changed hands for the cover, the girl's good looks, charming smile, and manner somehow clouded his commercial judgment.

Orla paid for her accommodation and made a point of tipping the hotel staff. Minutes later, she arrived at the staging area for her return journey to the Jones's farm. At the pre-arranged collection point, Bill, Niall, and Boss Boy were waiting for her. Niall was asleep on Bill's lap and obviously didn't notice Orla as she stepped down from the stage-coach, collected her luggage, and then walked over to the dray. She held Boss Boy's head and kissed him on his forehead and then patted his jaws and neck. The Waler responded by blowing his breath all over her face.

Bill mouthed a friendly 'hello,' smiled, and was in the process of handing Niall down to her when the boy woke to find himself looking directly at his mother. He struggled furiously to get to her, then threw his arms around her neck, and cuddled into her. After that, he smothered Orla's face with kisses and unmistakably said, 'mummy, miss mummy.'

'Listen to you, my little boyo... and barely sixteen months old,' an overjoyed and very proud Orla whispered into Niall's ear. 'If only your da could have heard you say that.'

As she said these words, Niall disengaged his arms, leant back, pivoted and pointed at Bill. 'Da, Da?'

Orla and Bill laughed gently, but the significance of this naive mistake was not lost on either of them. Bill had accepted without query that Orla's husband was killed in a building incident: in a building, yes, but no accident. Orla would have to deal with this iden-tity issue with Niall eventually, but for the time being he was too young to understand his unusual situation.

Orla quickly wiped away her tears of happiness, passed Niall back up to Bill then climbed onto the dray's driver's bench.

'Well, come on gang, let's get cracking,' Orla said cheerfully as she playfully nudged Bill in the ribs.

In a gruff little voice Niall suddenly yelled, 'Go, Bosh Bhoy.'

To Orla's surprise, Niall emulated her usual spirited command to Boss Boy. Delighted by her son's previously unheard repertoire, she gave him another hug as Boss Boy put his shoulders into the task. Then, in gratitude for Bill's thoughtfulness by bringing both Niall and Boss Boy to meet her, she leant across and kissed Bill softly on his cheek.

When they arrived back at the farm, Erin was keen to hear Orla's account of her brief holiday. Erin roared with laughter when she learnt about the luckless pickpocket, nevertheless, she winced when Orla showed her the cuts on her knuckles caused by the man's front teeth.

Orla also confided in Erin, explaining her most unexpected carnal interest in the handsome man she'd seen, admitting that her interest was heightened by her annoyance about his identity.

'Those emotions are natural for a woman so young and alone. Perhaps, those feelings will fade once your journey gets underway again. Time will tell, you'll see,' Erin reasoned with Orla. 'Mind you, there's no harm in keeping an eye out for a decent bloke, eh?'

After dinner, Orla announced she would be leaving the day after next. Bill and Erin weren't surprised and expressed their sincere thanks for her assistance and her company.

For most of the following day, Bill, Peter, and Orla carried out minor repairs and maintenance to the cart. Erin then helped repack it. But these jobs didn't prevent Orla from testing her new rifle. Late that afternoon, she handed her old rifle to Peter and together they walked to the end of the property. There she showed him how to hold the rifle correctly, load and aim, and how to hold his breath and not flinch when he squeezed the trigger. For his age, Peter proved to be a damn good shot. Then it was her turn to test her new rifle.

Orla fired fifteen shots in rapid order at targets she positioned at varying distances and elevations. The rifle's recoil was significant, but didn't unduly affect her balance. After each shot, she worked the rifle's lever action, and then smoothly swept the rifle tip from one target to the next. She scored thirteen hits and sent up a puff of dust alongside the other two targets. After reloading and making a slight adjustment to the sights, her next sweep produced a perfect score.

Next, she rigged a more challenging target — a block of wood the size of a brick hanging by a length of string from a tree branch. She set the target oscillating and then jogged back about fifty yards. Puffing slightly, Orla's first shot went wide. Her second attempt shaved a splinter from the block: her third and fourth shots demolished it.

'Good God, Orla, how'd you do that? Dad's a good shot, but where'd you learn to shoot like that? Quick, let me have a go, please,' Peter begged. 'I've got to see if I can do it.' It took him twenty shots before the next swinging target finally wobbled off its path.

Nightfall was upon them as they arrived back at the house.

'Hope you like rabbit stew,' Orla said to Peter's surprised parents as she threw three rabbits onto the kitchen sink. 'All head shots, compliments of your smart arse son.'

The following morning was cool but clear and after harnessing Boss Boy, Orla fed and watered him, filled the water bags, then joined the others for a hearty breakfast.

When Orla and Niall were almost ready to depart, Bill and Erin presented her with a package of homemade bread, some cheese and several cuts of salted meat. Orla warmly thanked them for their generosity.

'Hang on a minute, you'll be needing this, too, as I recall,' Bill said, as he pointed beyond Orla to where Peter was dragging two large bags from the feed shed. 'Boss Boy's chaff and oats. There's another two bags to come. Peter will load 'em for you. Don't say anything and don't even think of paying!'

When Peter had finished loading, Orla reached into the cart. 'I don't have much use for two rifles. You may as well keep this,' she said, handing him her old rifle and a package containing the remnants of her ammunition. In disbelief, Peter looked hopefully at his parents. Without hesitation, both nodded their consent. Peter then walked forward and offered his hand. Orla took it, but immediately pulled him into a warm embrace.

'Go kindly, young man. Take good care of yourself and the animals of this great country,' Orla whispered. 'And keep an eye on your folks, they're bloody good people.' With that she swung up onto her cart, waved both her and Niall's little hand goodbye and yelled, 'Go, Boss Boy! Gympie, here we come.'

31

The main coastal road north had many severe gradients. Rivers had to be crossed: punt services were sporadic and costly. Ford approaches were the worst, often deeply rutted and steep, which thoroughly tested Boss Boy. As a result, Orla walked beside him to lighten the load. On some days they barely covered five miles, so Orla changed their routine — each day of travel would now be followed by a rest day.

The number of people travelling south surprised Orla. But this allowed her to develop a good understanding of the conditions ahead, where to locate the best camping sites, and where she could reliably purchase food. In the meantime, rabbits were plentiful and easy targets. Although water and grass for Boss Boy were abundant, Orla continued to boil all her drinking water.

Weeks drifted by in a pleasant routine. Time lost its urgency: the journey's originally estimated travel time seemed irrelevant.

The terrain now varied considerably from fertile undulating grassy plains to dense vine-covered forest and, yes, even included the occasional passage close enough to the coast to hear the waves and to smell the crisp ozone of the ocean. But some things changed little, the seemingly never-ending blue-grey mountain ranges to the west, and Boss Boy's inexhaustible strength.

Orla spent hours teaching Niall the names of the creatures they sighted. It wasn't long before he'd point and call out their names even before Orla saw them. Hangarwoos, omhats, wizurds, o'annas, thnakes and fying fuxs were everywhere.

The many species, colours and calls of the bird life they encountered filled mother and child with fascination. There were chatty, multi-coloured rainbow lorikeets that made a relentless racket when congregating en masse; huge black cockatoos with bright yellow tails and mournful cries; families of kookaburras who never lost their penchant for boisterous laughter; and birds with gorgeous lyre-shaped tail displays and an incredible ability to mimic the calls of other birds.

But Orla's favourite bird was the pheasant-like coucal with a call that sounded like someone swallowing great gulps of liquid from a bottle. The clumsy manner in which it skulked away on short legs as if it had just been caught doing something wrong, often had her in fits of laughter.

The smells of the bush also intrigued Orla. In particular, there was a heady, hop-like fragrance, which often wafted from creek gullies. She searched extensively and inspected many different flowering plants and vines before finding the source of most of those smells. But one odour took no effort to identify — that of the fruit bats hanging clustered in huge colonies near the roadside.

The further north they travelled, a large tree species unfamiliar to her, now dominated. Undergrowth flourished. Long gone were the endless tracts of eucalypts.

* * *

LATE ONE AFTERNOON when Orla was looking for an overnight campsite, she heard a booming voice in the distance, followed by what sounded like a gunshot. Before long, a heaving, straining team of sixteen bullocks hove into view, their load appearing impossibly large despite the impressive size of each bullock. But move that load they did. With the bullock driver's urging and his long-handled stockwhip occasionally snaking across the rump of an unsuspecting beast to leave a painful sting, the timber jinker rolled on.

As the bullock team drew level with Orla's cart, the driver let fly with a volley of extremely colourful abuse directed at one particular bullock.

'Digger! Move yah big, fat, lazy arse or I'll skin yah where yah stand. Come on you horrible black bastard, make an effort or I'll sink my number twelve's so far up your arse I'll loosen every tooth in that brainless block head of yours.'

'Why don't you say what you really think?' Orla yelled to the driver, and then started laughing hysterically as she tried to picture the man actually delivering on his threats.

Orla's challenge surprised the driver. 'Oops, sorry missus. Didn't see yah there,' he called back cheerfully, as he emerged from behind the rig and politely raised his battered leather hat.

The bullocky wandered over to Orla. 'The name's Ken. Mind if I join yah here for the night?' he asked casually, yet courteously. 'The boys are about done and so am I.'

In spite of the ugly threats in the bullocky's earlier words, he now seemed remarkably calm although his eyes still sparkled from his exertions. Sweat lines on his dusty forehead and his cheeks gave his face a ghostly appearance, and sweat dripped from the tip of his nose and from his chin.

'Yep, that's all right with me. But hey, shouldn't you catch up to your team before they disappear?'

'No worries, missus, I'll turn 'em into the scrub and get 'em unhitched and hobbled before it gets dark. There's water in that gully up ahead and there's a good pick for my boyos around here I see. You got any tea, love?' he called over his shoulder as he set off after his team.

'Any amount,' Orla assured him, sensing an immediate rapport with this stranger who she guessed was 'fiftyish' and obviously shared her ancestry.

Just before dark, Ken returned to Orla's camp. 'By the way, my name's Orlagh,' she said in her best Irish drawl and then sat next to him, sharing the same fallen tree branch.

'Aye, it's good to meet yah, lass.'

He'd brought with him his billy, swag, and a small package containing some very old, dry cheese and equally stale-looking bread. Orla took one look at it then grabbed the package from him and threw the lot into the fire.

'Hey lassie, why'd yah do that?' Ken yelled angrily as he twisted to face Orla. 'What's a man gunna 'ave for his supper now, then?'

Orla smiled while holding up her hands as if surrendering. With a touch of ceremony, she hefted the lid from the fire-blackened pot suspended over the fire.

'This! What do yah reckon? Will stewed rabbit with potatoes, onions, carrot, and some rice do instead?'

'Aw, bloody hell, girlie, that'd be first rate. If it tastes as good as it smells I'll truly be in heaven. And with a nice hot cuppa... I wonder what the rich folk will be eatin' tonight? But hey, who's this, then?'

Niall's sleepy face peered down from the cart.

'Ah now, this is my son, Niall, my little helper,' Orla replied proudly.

Initially, Niall clung to Orla, but after ten minutes or so, Orla passed him to Ken. Niall immediately traced his tiny fingers down the sweat lines on the bullocky's weather-beaten face.

'Oohh, you've a champion boyo here then, Orla. Don't have any of me own, but I'll gladly take this one off yah hands,' Ken joked as Niall settled comfortably onto his lap.

After their meal and several cups of hot, sweetened black tea, Orla put Niall to bed then rejoined Ken by the fire. They soon started yarning, regularly feeding the campfire as the constellations continued their endless trek across the night sky.

Orla learnt much about Ken. He was born and spent his childhood and early adult life with his family, the Conricks, in the County of Tipperary, which adjoined her home county of Waterford. *Neighbours indeed,* they agreed.

'Gold was me undoin', Orla,' he confessed. 'Usually that what belonged to others. T'was healthy for me to depart Ireland in great haste, the police were on the right track in their suspicions of me involvement in a robbery under arms. This job'll do me for the time bein' though. I'm makin' good money and soon I'll be headin' for them goldfields down south in Victoria. Hopefully, I'll meet a good woman me own age, like, and then settle down and maybe buy a pub... and 'keep me nose clean', so to speak.'

Ken was one of a team of four bullock drivers working for a contractor based in Bellinger Heads (now Urunga). He explained that although most of the hard-won cedar from the nearby Don Dorrigo Scrub was hauled westward to timber mills in Armidale, some was hauled east to Bellingen where it was milled to order. The sized timber was then hauled to Bellinger Heads where it was either bought by local boat builders or shipped south to Sydney Town.

Ken's haulage job paid well but it was hard work. 'A lonely test of endurance for both man and beast,' he confided philosophically.

While they chatted, Ken was astute and gentlemanly enough not to probe too deeply into Orla's life. He also surprised Orla with his real affection for each and every one of his bullock team.

'Yah know, Orla, they're just so bloody brave and strong and unbelievably committed to their job,' he said proudly. 'I don't really mean what I say to them most times and would never do 'em any real harm, but they do need a tad of encouragement every now and then.' Ken paused to sip from his mug, and then continued. 'Take Digger, for example. He's by far the strongest animal I've ever worked with. He's a quality asset. A true leader, too, but he likes to knock off early. He seems to think he'll decide when the team's had enough. Like tonight, for instance. Mind you, he was spot on this time, eh?'

Another pause followed while Ken drained his mug. 'Anyway, I wanted 'em to get beyond that last climb by nightfall. Digger basically got 'em up, did yah know that? That next climb yonder though will take the starch out of 'em, to be sure. That's really why I let 'em stop early. I want 'em rested before tackling it.'

Orla listened intently, fascinated by the bullocky's stories. She learnt about the hardships endured by the cedar cutters in the Don Dorrigo Scrub region, which was about twenty-five miles northwest from their campsite. These men were obviously as tough as nails and displayed incredible stoicism with no outward evidence of their sufferings. Ken explained that some cutters were known to have worked on after accidentally lopping off a finger or a toe, knowing it was pointless to complain, since the nearest doctor lived in Armidale nearly one hundred miles and six days away — provided rain didn't make the bush tracks impassable.

Orla found it hard to believe that one hardy individual, who broke his leg, was carried out by stretcher, and then by horse and jinker, enduring the pain from the fracture for the best part of a week before a surgeon could be reached. Apparently there was not a whimper from him during the entire journey, at times through dense scrub and over very rough country. Amazingly, after only four weeks, he returned with a new axe and humping several bottles of Ainkum castor oil — the accepted bushman's cure-all.

Going hungry was an equally hard ordeal for the cedar gatherers, but Orla could relate to that. Although the forests surrounding the communities of places like Dorrigo, Tyringham, Rocky Creek, and Ebor were alive with bush turkeys, pigeons, and wallabies, staples like beef, bread, milk, flour, tea, sugar, and salt were always in extremely short supply. And so, many cedar cutters went to bed at night without having eaten anything, or very little of substance. They also denied themselves these essential commodities because of the high freight costs.

Ken re-assured her the pay was good, despite the risks and deprivations. Cedar was highly valued, particularly, red cedar. The current prices being obtained for it were high in comparison to those paid for other timbers, and there were hundreds of mature cedar trees which would continue to provide a rich bounty for many years.

Ken went on to relate the changing fortune of Dorrigo. 'Dorrigo's a flourishin' little settlement, to be sure, but it's a bit isolated. They'll be losing their schoolteacher soon. Apparently, she's found a sweetheart and now being knocked-up, wants to live in Armidale.'

For a while Ken went quiet but then produced an enlightened and surprisingly emotional philosophy. 'Orla, it's a damn shame she's leavin'. The poor buggers at Dorrigo are honest and hard working people and accept physical pain and starvation, but now they seem condemned to social deprivation. She'll be hard to replace. She's well liked and has done a great job with the kids.'

Orla immediately recognised his underlying concern — not unlike those living in far-away North East Victoria where good people often went unrecognised.

Late that night, they let the fire finally exhaust itself. Their conversation faded and the mood became one of quiet contemplation as the cool night air enveloped them. Ken eventually rose to his feet, wished Orla a good night, and was about to spread his swag when he paused.

'Just thought yah might like to know, you're headin' into bushranger country. There are two blokes to look out for. One's more than seventy years old and still claims to be a copper, even dresses like one, but he'll just as soon relieve yah of any money under the pretence of collecting road taxes, as give yah honest directions. He's known as Mad Mickey. They tell me he's a right nutcase and a dangerous bastard if he gets wind that yah might have money. He hasn't been seen for quite a while, but that doesn't mean he's not still active. Rumour has it, the miserable shit murdered more than two hundred blacks, so if he's not dead, I'd say he's living on borrowed time.

'The other bloke's less of a worry. He tends to borrow things without getting permission first, if yah know what I mean? Usually keeps to himself, but he likes good horses, like old Captain Thunderbolt. And it's also rumoured he's regularly relieving farmers of their cattle. Gets on really well with blacks, apparently — the complete opposite of Mad Mickey. He's a good lookin' young bloke, very persuasive with the women, so the story goes. No one's ever heard of him deliberately shootin' anyone. Anyway, Orla, just keep yah wits about yah, lassie, and where yah can, camp with other travellers.'

With those words still hanging in the air, Ken wriggled into his swag and then rolled onto his side, facing away from Orla.

Strange he assumed I knew who Captain Thunderbolt was, thought Orla. An eerie feeling of déjà vu crept over her, but she consoled herself she could handle anything any bushranger might dish out. Surprise would remain her greatest asset and her colts had the habit of ending dangerous or unwelcome confrontations. But from the recesses of her mind sprang Joan McIntyre's words. *Bloody guns! Worst things ever invented by man. God help those who live by guns, for they'll surely die by them!*

When Orla rose next morning, Ken was gone. However, she could clearly hear his bawdy expletives in the bush nearby as he ranted at one of his bullocks.

'*Stand!* Yah dopey bastard, or so help me I'll gut yah!'

Orla and Niall finished their breakfast and were preparing to leave when Ken wandered back, intent upon honouring his promise from the previous night.

'So young fella, you want to ride one of my boyos, eh?' Ken playfully swung Niall onto his shoulders and walked with Orla to where his team patiently waited for their first command of the day.

Ken then gently heaved Niall onto Digger's back. Niall was obviously in awe of the bullock's massive body and widespread horns, but although he gave the impression of being about to cry, his face suddenly broke into a beaming smile.

'Go, Digga, go.'

Digger twisted his huge head slightly and peered in Ken's direction. The look on Digger's face was comical, as if he were thinking, *who's this upstart trying to fool?*

Orla and Ken saw the funny side of this and shared their last laugh together. Ken retrieved Niall, handed him back to Orla, and thrust out his hand.

'It's been a lovely thing meeting yah, lassie. Look after that boy; he's a beauty lad. Good luck and God speed, though I'll probably not be seeing yah in heaven.'

'Good luck to you, too, Ken Conrick,' replied Orla as she smiled and returned his warm handshake. 'And may all your shamrocks grow in a row.'

As the team and its massive load crested the next steep rise and eased into the following descent, Ken stopped. Silhouetted against the early morning sky he turned around, held his hat high in the air, waved his arm from side to side... then trudged off after his team.

32

Early August 1882, was a glorious time on the mid-north coast of the colony of New South Wales: warm idyllic days followed by cool nights. When Orla passed through Bellinger Heads, she learnt that the next westbound sidetrack that headed into the blue-grey hinterland was the main road to Dorrigo. On impulse, she decided to visit the settlement, influenced, she knew, by Ken's words. *After all,* she reminded herself, *I'm not in a race to get to Gympie, despite my original timetable being shot to threads.*

That road was really hard work for Boss Boy. The surfaces were deeply rutted and the gradients were so steep in places that several timber jinkers had previously come to grief, the evidence to be seen in the deep gullies on either side of the track. Haulage jinkers lay contorted and smashed at the bottom of those gullies; their valuable loads a massive, irretrievable jumble.

Orla was deeply saddened by the hideous death that each brave bullock must have experienced. However, the brutality of those scenes was offset by the magnificent rainforest. Shafts of sunlight speared through the tree canopy to radiate a soft golden lustre over the profusion of underlying subtropical ferns and orchids.

Orla passed two more timber jinkers coming from Dorrigo, each loaded with three massive cedar logs. Both teams employed nine yoked pairs of bullocks, and all seemed to be receiving their share of the wicked sting of the driver's rawhide whip, even if they hadn't noticeably slackened their effort.

It took Orla five days to reach Dorrigo, which was on a high, cleared plateau. The approaching smell of humanity, masked by the pungent aroma of domestic cooking fires, reminded her of the first time she'd passed through The Junction on the Buckland River. *A lifetime ago,* she reflected.

Within half an hour of setting up her camp, a teenage boy boldly approached. Boss Boy saw him coming and shook his head, rattling his bridle to get Orla's attention. The intrusion only somewhat surprised Orla.

'What can I do for you, young fella?'

'Nothing, missus,' the boy replied politely. 'I'm on my way home from school and I saw your beaut horse, so I thought I'd say g'day. My name is Martin Ambrose. I live on the other side of this paddock. My dad owns this bit of land.'

'And g'day to you, Martin. My name's Orla and this is my son, Niall. I hope your dad won't mind us staying here for a few days.'

They chatted cordially for the next half hour. Despite their age difference, the boys got on well together. Martin handled Niall's attention seeking antics with good humour, and if he was irritated, it never showed. There wasn't much about this confident, forthright young man Orla could fault. From what he was telling Orla, it soon became evident that another opportunity was presenting itself... if she played her cards correctly. *Besides, damn it, I could do with a break,* Orla thought.

It seemed that Martin's teacher, having moved into her new husband's house, had no further use for the school cottage and that she was not handling her pregnancy at all well.

The next morning, Orla located the house where, Joyce, the schoolteacher and her husband lived. After introducing herself, Orla let slip her experience with the children on the steamer on the way to Melbourne and her role as nanny at the McIntyre's. Within an hour a deal was struck: in return for Orla's unpaid assistance, she could live in the teacher's cottage.

Orla easily found the cottage. The surrounding gardens were well tended. An added bonus was the fenced paddock neighbouring the cottage where Boss Boy could be safely accommodated.

The cottage was solidly built and raised about four feet above ground level. From the kitchen window she commanded a partial view of the main street and the view from the back veranda overlooked a heavily timbered valley. Niall could either have his own bedroom or share hers. Her own meagre belongings — bedding, blankets, and cooking utensils — were not necessary; everything she needed was already here. Orla was ecstatic, realising this was a very comfortable windfall no matter how temporary.

Although Orla also felt a strong sense of obligation to perform the job requested of her, she nevertheless decided to adopt a low-key approach.

A routine soon evolved. Her assistance at the school, although gradually increasing as Joyce spent less time teaching, still only occupied four or five hours a day. This gave Orla precious time with Niall and the opportunity to meet the residents of the town and to regularly exercise Boss Boy.

Their 'teaching team' was highly successful, but Orla knew it was due primarily to Joyce's energy, patience, firm discipline, and her sense of humour. It was easy to see why she'd be missed. Orla admired Joyce and enjoyed her company.

The children also impressed Orla, and they idolised her. Most of them seemed eager and excited about their education, and despite their isolation, they all aspired to doing something positive with their lives, either as a farmer, builder, governess or artist. There were a total of sixteen children whose ages ranged from five to eleven, and Martin, who was nearly fifteen.

Orla was equally impressed by the children's parents, all honest and forthright, and she sensed that their word was their bond.

Dorrigo was the first school for Martin. His parents wanted him to work on their farm for he'd shown a willingness to work and was proving to be capable and strong. But he possessed an insatiable appetite for learning, which his parents could not ignore. Academically Martin was advancing rapidly. He was also clearly becoming the schoolroom leader. Because of his size, he seldom participated in schoolyard activities; he just seemed to enjoy supervising. On one occasion, Joyce allowed Martin to run the school for a day; he performed beyond expectation.

Martin also took great care of Niall. Niall was generally tolerated and would wander around the classroom and join in most activities. He was never shunned, but at the first sign of him either being disruptive or showing signs of being tired, it was Martin who took him into Joyce's small office and put him to bed.

Eventually, Orla approached the boy's parents. 'Mr. and Mrs. Ambrose, your Martin is a very bright lad. You know that, so I urge you to consider allowing him to move to Sydney in the New Year to advance his education.'

Martin's parents looked at each other in obvious pride but that look quickly changed to dismay. 'We're simple folk, Orla, and what we've got saved ain't gonna pay for gettin' the boy educated in the big smoke,' said Martin's father.

'Hear me out. I know it's a big decision, but I might have an answer to your concerns. I know a wonderful family who live on the outskirts of Sydney Town. Their son is only a few years younger than Martin and he might welcome the company of a like-minded mate. But listen, first things first. Allow me to write to them, please.'

Martin's parents talked quietly to each other for a few minutes and then Mrs. Ambrose said, 'I'll tell you what, Orla. If these friends of yours agree, we'll allow Martin to leave home for a year only. If he does well, we'll consider allowing him to stay on. Regardless, we'll still need to watch our money situation closely.'

Three weeks later Orla received the reply she expected. Bill and Erin Jones were more than happy to look after Martin. She quickly passed this exciting news onto Martin and his parents, then, on their behalf, set about arranging a time for them to meet the Jones family, having already guaranteed Martin's parents that money, or rather the lack of it, would not prevent such a visit.

With the passage of another three weeks, an early December date was agreed. In anticipation of that visit, Bill and Erin sketched a map showing where their farm was located, itemized the likely costs of Martin's lodgings, and on Martin's behalf, even enrolled him in a suitable school. This outcome gave Orla great satisfaction as she focused upon preparing Martin for 'the big smoke'.

* * *

LIFE IN DORRIGO settled into a meaningful, pleasant existence for Orla. She enjoyed Niall's company enormously. He was becoming a chatterbox, ran everywhere... and would soon turn two. But time had flown by. So at the end of November, Orla floated the idea of 'an end of year dance'.

The response was immediate and overwhelming.

33

____

With the school year now over and the festive season rapidly approaching, arrangements were in full swing for the 'big night'. The school was to be the venue and the townsfolk worked enthusiastically to spruce it up. What had been the talk of the region was now a reality. Anticipation grew. Joyce's husband secured the services of a piano accordionist and a fiddler; they arrived at noon on the appointed day.

The evening was laced with excitement. A warm, gentle breeze wafted across the plateau and through the town. As the good folk of Dorrigo arrived at the school, they were greeted by the welcoming light of an array of oil and kerosene lamps. Huge floral arrangements adorned the interior walls, along with colourful paper decorations... compliments of the schoolchildren.

Niall was running free, tagging along with his schoolmates and having a great time in the dark — something he hadn't experienced before. But he was in good hands; Martin kept a close eye on him, guaranteeing his safety.

Trestle tables were set up along one wall and loaded with culinary delights, jugs of ginger beer, and flavoured water. Several dozen bottles of home-brewed beer were stacked under the trestles and a rotund, jolly man was liberally dispensing the dark foaming beverage. The band was waiting patiently at one end of the room and two men were moving through the crowd, methodically scattering lightly oiled sawdust over the polished floor.

By eight o'clock the schoolroom was packed and filled with tobacco smoke. The conversation was becoming louder and more animated as the band completed its final tune up. It was then that Orla stepped up onto the teacher's platform.

'Quiet please!' she yelled. 'Put a sock in it for a few minutes. Right, now that I've got your attention, I want to thank you all for coming tonight, and those who got this place into such good order.' Loud cheers and applause followed. 'You're all expected to have a good time tonight and I'm sure we will, but I want you all to reflect for a moment upon the achievements of your children. They all worked damned hard and you should all be very proud of your nippers.' More clapping and cheers thundered around the room.

'Now, for the program tonight. Our wonderful band will play beautifully for you, to be sure, but don't ply 'em with too many drinks – we want 'em playing properly beyond the first hour. I'll announce when you can get something to eat and recharge your ladies' glasses.'

Orla then turned to the band and yelled. 'Away you go lads! Give it your best shot and let's all have some *real* fun!'

As the band struck up, Orla grabbed the nearest man by the hand and dragged him into the middle of the dance floor. People moved to give them room and very quickly she had him stepping and swaying his way around the dance floor, albeit a bit clumsily at first. The man was a surprisingly good dancer and picked up the rhythm with little effort. However, they'd only circled the room three or four times before another man cut in and away went Orla again.

'Come on girls, grab yah man and get him doing upright what he thinks he does best lyin' down,' she shouted bawdily while erotically gyrating her hips. There was more riotous laughter and any remaining inhibitions vanished. Within minutes, the dance floor was a shuffling mass of smiling, happy people encouraged by the stirring mood set by Orla. Undeniably, the locals were witnessing a very different side to their assistant teacher.

The musicians had a surprisingly broad repertoire and played with great energy, but at nine thirty Orla called a halt. Everyone attacked the trestles devouring the food and scoffing the cool drinks. Boisterous adult conversation, much laughter and good-natured backslapping followed.

Ten minutes later a stranger appeared, casually surveying the room as he stood in the open front doors. For no particular reason, Orla glanced up. There stood the most handsome male she'd ever seen. Her body tensed in surprise.

'Well, I'll be buggered,' she whispered to herself, her heart suddenly pumping furiously; a yearning almost taking her breath away. 'God, those eyes! They're like blue opals, even in this light,' she murmured. 'But this time, my boyo, you *will* talk to me.'

As she was about to walk over to the stranger, he caught and held her gaze. Orla noted the vague look of recollection etched on his face. His head tilted slightly. He frowned; enquiring.

He then strolled nonchalantly across the room, stopped directly in front of Orla and said with just a hint of uncertainty. 'Well, how about this? We meet again. Why is such an enchanting city woman, here, of all places? My friends call me Stewie, by the way. And your name is...'

Orla was about to reply, but glanced over his shoulder towards the front doors. Three policemen now stood there... all carrying either a rifle or a shotgun. The stranger immediately saw the surprise and concern on Orla's face, swivelled to follow her line of sight, then immediately swung back to face her. He froze. Real fear gripped his face. She'd seen such an expression before — it was not unlike the look on Ned's face as he was being wheeled to oblivion. But this time, Orla did react.

Without warning, she kneed the handsome visitor in his groin. He gasped in sharp pain and doubled over to prevent any further damage being inflicted. This was exactly the reaction Orla expected. She grabbed him by his shoulders and quickly guided him, hunched over and unseen she hoped, behind the throng of merrymakers and into Joyce's office where Niall now slept.

'Damned effective but you could've been a bit gentler,' he protested as he struggled to recover.

'There's no time to thank me now,' Orla hissed in the darkened room as she opened the office window. 'I suspect your three uniformed friends will be looking for someone just like you to pick on. So get your arse outside and up to my place. It's the white cottage at the end of the main street, on the left-hand side. There's a horse paddock next door. Be there when I get home in about an hour or so. Now go!'

Without hesitation he slipped athletically from the window and found the shadows with well-practiced ease.

Orla then returned to the festivities and was surprised that only one person near to the office door commented upon the untimely departure of the stranger.

'Poor bugger was feeling crook. I caught him just in time before he spewed all over the dance floor. Sent him home,' she lied ambiguously. Orla then walked boldly up to the three uninvited policemen who were now at the trestles helping themselves to the food and quaffing beer.

'Hello, gentlemen. My name's Orla O'Meara. Can I help you?' she said cheerfully in her sweetest Irish voice. 'I'm a schoolteacher here and I organised this little bash. Not offending any souls are we? And why the need for guns, pray tell? No one here's done anything remotely close to breaking any law.'

'That's for me to decide, lady,' said the policeman in charge. 'We're lookin' for a stock thief. People we've spoken to reckon he's headin' this way. He's been knockin' orf cattle from 'round here. He's thirtyish, good lookin' fella they tells us, about six feet tall. And he's got blue eyes that can apparently strip a woman at fifty paces. Don't suppose you've seen him?'

'Officer, I'm recently widowed with a baby boy. Such a man certainly doesn't interest me,' replied a now superficially offended Orla. 'Nor would I associate with such a criminal. And, I dare say, neither would these good people of Dorrigo want to be associated with the likes of such a man.'

'Right, lassie, so you say,' the officer drawled sarcastically. 'But since we'll be stayin' in this 'ere town for the next day or so, I expect you — or any of the good people of Dorrigo — to let me know if yah sees this chap. He's got a reward of two hundred quid on his head. I'll make it worthwhile to any bugger who gives me info leadin' to us nabbin' 'im. You *will* let everyone know what we want, right lassie?' The senior policeman then turned, nodded to his companions and walked outside.

34

The arrival of the arrogant and armed policemen cast an unwelcome pall over the proceedings. By eleven o'clock, the musicians were nearly spent and the children over-tired. Most of the men were drunk and couples were leaving, so Orla took this opportunity to announce, albeit in a good-natured manner, that the event was over until next year.

Orla farewelled the last of the locals, some with arms around their mate's shoulders and all singing as they happily staggered off into the darkness. She then doused the lights, picked up Niall who had somehow slept through most of the music and festivities, closed the front doors and walked quickly back to her cottage. As she approached she was experiencing mixed emotions. On one hand she felt contentment from the obvious success of the evening, but plagued by *déjà vu* on the other.

'Who the hell *is* this bloke I've taken in?' Orla whispered to herself. But a smile then creased the corners of her mouth when she thought. *Could be a murderer and a bushranger to boot, but jeez a bloody handsome one, though. And a really nice body, too.*

Then it hit her. She stopped dead in her tracks.

'Not Stewie! Stewart! Oh, bugger me... he's Owen bloody Stewart!' she gasped.

In her mind's eye she could now clearly picture his self-confident pose and his handsome good looks. There he was staring inquisitively with those sparkling eyes from the sepia photograph on the mantel piece in the living room of the Stewarts' London residence.

Orla took a deep breath to compose herself and decided in that moment not to let on she knew who he was. That knowledge might prove invaluable. Besides it would be fun to tease out his past life and allow her to judge his true worth. It suddenly rocked Orla that she no longer felt any sense of betrayal to the memory of Ned, just a fleeting, matter-of-fact feeling of gratitude.

Cuddling Niall and still deep in thought she climbed the front steps to her cottage. From the dark and slightly behind her, a quiet, calm voice announced. 'I'll take him if you like.'

Startled but not shocked, Orla made an instinctive movement with one of her hands as if reaching for something at her side. But she froze when she felt a hard object being pushed into her back... *a pistol no doubt.*

'Take it easy lady, you invited me here remember?'

Orla accepted her hopeless position, realising she'd left her Colts at home. She reluctantly passed her sleeping child over to Owen, who carefully took the small boy in his arms and quickly followed her up the stairs. Orla opened the front door and stood aside.

'Go straight through to the kitchen and close the curtains.' She then followed him inside and after some fumbling, lit an oil lamp. As her eyes became accustomed to the low, flickering light, Owen handed her a stick, smiled cheekily, and then flipped open the fronts of his jacket to reveal his holstered pistol.

'Hang on lady, before you say anything, best you put this little bloke to bed.'

When Orla returned to the kitchen, she nodded towards the stick. 'Damned effective and thanks for not being too rough,' she said, sarcastically mimicking Owen's earlier remark. She then pushed back the fronts of her jacket revealing her twin colts. Before Owen could blink, one of the Colts was settled against his forehead.

'Don't *ever* pull a stunt on me like that again or you're dead,' she said, her tone measured and clearly menacing. 'It's time we cleared the air so we both know where the other stands. Right?'

Owen stared and nodded. His mouth opened and closed as if trying to say something. 'All right, all right, I meant no harm,' he eventually mumbled, but quickly added. 'Christ, is there anything else you need to show me? But if you keep threatening me, I'm leaving.'

Orla ignored him and slipped the Colt back under her jacket. 'My boy's name is Niall, by the way,' she said casually. 'Do you want a cuppa or something stronger to celebrate my saving your bacon?'

Obviously relieved, but amused, Owen replied, 'My name's Owen, Owen Stewart, Stewie to my mates. I'll try again. Your name is?'

'Orlagh Aileen O'Meara; my friends call me Orla.'

They shook hands, each looking the other squarely in the eyes. His grip was firm; hers equally firm in response. Their hands remained coupled for several heart-thumping seconds before Owen broke the silence.

'A cuppa would be nice, Orla.'

Over several cups of tea they talked comfortably, well into the early morning. The conversation ranged from Orla's home and family in Ireland, to her arrival in Dorrigo. She deliberately and skilfully excluded her more questionable past exploits, *and* that she knew Owen's parents. Although she mentioned that her objective was Gympie, it drew no response from Owen to indicate he might know his parents were now living there. Her reference to the death of her husband in a building accident drew genuine sympathy from Owen, and he was interested enough to ask and be told her husband's name was Edward.

Owen was similarly guarded in his commentary. He made very little reference to his family, why he was in Dorrigo or what his current occupation involved. *Poor Owen*, there really was no fooling her. She knew from what he was *not* saying that he was operating illegally, but didn't press him to elaborate; that would unfold later, along with a more credible explanation for the unexpected appearance by the police.

At the first signs of dawn, Orla said, 'It's been nice finally meeting you, Owen Stewart. But I need to sleep, I'm bushed. You can sleep on the couch, there's a blanket and a pillow in that cupboard behind you. But remember, keep away from the windows and if you need to go outside, keep out of sight and be quick about it. And keep away from my bedroom, boyo.'

When Orla gradually, painfully, surfaced from a deep sleep many hours later, she could hear Niall laughing and a strange voice urging him on in some unseen game. When she reached the kitchen, Niall was hanging from a roof rafter by his chubby fingers, laughing madly. On Owen's command Niall released his grip and Owen then made a big play of pretending to drop him — only to catch him just in time before he hit the floor.

'Enough!' yelled Orla, whereupon both boys spun around to see an enraged mother standing in the kitchen doorway. 'What the bloody hell do you think you're doing? Give him to me this instant.'

Niall was clearly disappointed with his mother's angry intervention and clung to Owen's legs, hoping their wonderful game would continue. It didn't.

'Awww, come on, Orla, I never would've let him fall and we were having such good fun. He's a game lad; I guess he gets that from you, eh?'

Orla relaxed somewhat, realising she may have overreacted. 'Maybe so, maybe not. But I don't want him getting hurt through your thoughtless games. Anyway, have you two had breakfast?'

'Oh yes, we had scrambled eggs, bacon, and some of those beautiful tomatoes you have growing in your veggie garden out the back. Niall helped me pick 'em. And we both had a cuppa,' Owen continued as he stooped to pick up Niall. 'But that was long before we had lunch. Do you have any idea what time it is? I'll make you something for your lunch if you like. Or would you rather wait another hour or so until I make tonight's dinner?'

Bewildered, Orla replied, 'Jesus, is it really that late? A cuppa would be fine. But Niall needs to have his afternoon sleep. Though I must admit, he doesn't look very tired.'

'Then he can stay up with us. I was showing him what it's like for a bird to live high up in a tree. And I promised him I'd finish my story about the butcher bird after he eats his dinner. He should be really tired by then... then *we* can decide what *we're* going to do,' replied Owen, his smile suggesting just a hint of mischief.

Through some welcome, powerful force of nature — but unbeknownst to Owen — Orla impulsively knew what she wanted from this man.

35

Orla did her best to persuade Joyce to remain in Dorrigo, but she could not be swayed. Joyce, in turn, attempted to persuade Orla to continue on as her successor. But, Orla had an overriding urge to resume her journey; the promise of further untold opportunity still beckoned in Gympie.

And furthermore, gratification had presented itself in the form of a very handsome, positive, and interesting bloke who possessed a refreshing sense of good humour. Owen was also apparently a shrewd man who had an eye for commercial opportunity, the contradiction being that this regrettably put him at odds with some graziers and, hence, the law. His attraction towards her was guarded so far, but intuitively Orla knew he was sexually attracted to her, judging by his furtive glances. And, he made her feel good; his thoughtfulness did her ego no harm at all. But most importantly to Orla, his affection for Niall was real.

Mid-Monday morning as Orla was washing the breakfast dishes and gazing from the kitchen window, she felt a sudden dread. The three visiting policemen were riding toward her cottage. She quickly told Owen and instructed him to keep quiet and out of sight. As the policemen drew rein, Orla opened the front door and walked down the first few front steps before feigning surprise at their appearance.

'Oh, good morning officers, got time for a cuppa before you leave?' she asked amicably, desperately hoping they wouldn't accept her offer.

'No, we've had breakfast,' the senior officer replied rudely and then continued in a supercilious tone. 'But yah can do something for me. Our earlier intelligence that our man was headed for Dorrigo was convincing. It seems your good town folk did in fact see a man who matched the description I gave yah. But we've been wonderin' 'ow he could possibly just disappear without further sightin'. You'd better tell me of his whereabouts, or yah gunna find yourself in the shit.'

Hands on her hips, an indignant Orla replied, 'I've already listened to your previous offensive threat and told you my situation. If you want public support, then act with some respect and refrain from intimidating people. Apologise, or bugger off.'

'Just trying to do our job, lady,' said the officer as he pushed his hat back on his head. 'Mark my words, though, any association with that man will be considered as harbourin' and I guarantee no leniency will be shown, regardless of gender.'

'I believe that's another unnecessary threat, sergeant!' Orla responded defiantly. Now fuming she added condescendingly. 'Be warned, you stroppy mouthed oaf... stop pestering me, and *piss off*!'

'Please yahself lady,' said the sergeant, who then smirked and said over his shoulder as he swung his horse away. 'But I'll take more than my share of pleasure if our paths ever cross again.'

You upstart bastard! Orla thought. *Not the most reassuring comment from someone supposedly committed to upholding the law.* Still furious, Orla watched the uniformed men ride south on the road to Bellingen. When they were finally out of sight she stormed inside.

'Owen, did you hear that little exchange?' she hissed. 'One thing's now certain, boyo. If I'm going to continue to save your bacon, then it's time you came clean and told me everything about yourself.'

'Fair enough,' Owen replied calmly. 'I must say, though, you handled that beautifully. I'll put the kettle on, but you look as if you could do with something stronger.'

For the rest of that morning Owen talked frankly and responded without hesitation whenever Orla sought further clarification. It was soon clear that he'd somehow spiralled into the depths of a life of crime. Real wealth had evaded him so far. As Orla knew, the irony of this situation was that he had very wealthy parents who loved him and, she suspected, he would still inherit a massive fortune one day. That knowledge must have been frustrating for Owen, but he was still lying to her about his reasons for leaving England.

'Look, Owen, you'd make a crappy card player,' Orla said impatiently. 'Every time you tell a lie, you either look down or smile as if expecting me to swallow what you're saying. Say it as it is. I mean it Owen, tell me the truth, or leave now!'

Somewhat taken aback by this blunt demand he slowly sat upright in his chair, took a very deep breath and looked directly into her determined face.

He gradually released his breath. 'Bloody hell, Orla, I do believe you're a mind reader. I killed a man in England... the result of a fight after I lost a lot of money. Yes, in a card game. His friends were gunning for me and swore retribution upon my family if I didn't pay up. I lost over two thousand pounds, but I didn't want to inflict my disgrace upon my parents or to see them harmed.'

'A misspent youth returned to bite your bum by the sound of things. Serves you right,' Orla interjected. 'And, obviously too much money at your disposal.'

Ignoring Orla's remarks, Owen continued. 'Stupidly, I stole the money from my parents, paid out my debt, then created a conflict with my father to give the appearance of disharmony and to give me justification, in other people's eyes, at least, that I was right to clear out. Which I did before my father discovered the theft, of course.'

'Another truly shitty act which you should never have foisted upon your folks.'

'Agreed, but that still left the death of my card-playing friend and how he'd be avenged by his mates. That torment was turning me into a nervous wreck. So I ran... here; to get as far away as possible from a wretched life I seemed powerless to fix.'

'You certainly are a long way from home, but I'm truly glad those boyos didn't nail you. You now seem in control of your life, so what put you at odds with those three coppers?'

'Not long after I settled near Ebor, I nicked the odd horse. But I soon got wind of a low risk earner involving the removal of stock from the valleys around the Bostobrick Station, which is northwest from here.

'Apparently the very earliest cedar cutters and gold prospectors knew of the cattle runs up that way. But because in those days it was almost impossible to get fresh meat up from Bellingen, those men struck a deal with the local blacks. They paid them to steal the cattle from those runs, kill and butcher them, and then carry the meat back to the cedar gatherers' and prospectors' huts.'

Owen drained his cup then continued. 'Because the blacks knew the shortcuts through the really difficult scrub and steep gullies, the meat arrived in good condition. And so the arrangement lasted, until about ten years ago.

'Apparently one of the station owners, a bloke named Clougher, or Mad Mickey to most, got tired of the continual loss of his stock. He suspected the blacks were not only responsible, but in collusion with white men, so he rounded up and murdered several hundred of them as retribution... an outrageous warning to everyone that the thefts had to stop. But the blacks kept at it, although on a smaller scale, despite other local squatters harassing them, too. Nevertheless, the cedar cutters still wanted good meat, so I stepped in and re-organised things. I could make *real* money.'

A horse whinnied nearby. Alarmed, Owen's eyes flew wide open. He then jumped up and reached for his pistol. 'It'll be them bloody coppers back, for sure.'

'Easy, boyo, it's only Boss Boy saying he's hungry,' said Orla, reassuringly placing her hand on his arm. Owen sat down again, exhaling heavily. He forced himself to relax and gathered his thoughts.

'Anyway, about three years ago, I rode into the Bellinger River valley and eventually found and befriended the leaders of the black tribes who were conducting the meat trade. I promised them more money if they did things my way and before long the money started flooding in. I had an insatiable market.

'I got efficient all right; the buyers came to me instead of the other way round. I provided meat in a couple of safe places on specific days. I chose defensible spots with secret escape tracks, and I had credible alibis all thought out.

'But therein lay my problems, Orla. I got greedy, I admit it. The property managers were starting to employ more cattlemen and arming them, not only with repeating rifles, but with strict orders to shoot any person, black or white, they caught on their land. They'd taken the law into their own hands, claiming the police had failed them miserably in eradicating bushranging. No more arrests, 'just shoot on sight and answer questions later' became their motto. Trespassing has become a serious health hazard, Orla. And, I've been shot at twice already! In fact, just a few weeks ago some idiot took a pot shot at me.'

Orla looked at the rueful expression on his face and felt like cuddling him. 'I'm glad they missed, but go on, finish your story.'

'The land owners, cunning bastards, had started their own little ploy to eliminate the blacks from these operations by rendering them brain-dead. It seems the station owners had discovered the black's shameless thirst for grog and were selling them large quantities of spirits.

'The irony, of course, is that the blacks have been paying for their grog using the money they'd received from the illegal sale of the stock they'd been pinching for me!

'At first, I ignored all that, but then learnt the blacks were starting to spill their guts whenever they'd had a skinful and talked freely about 'their white fella boss who pays real good'. I also learnt from a few of my bullock-driver mates that there was now talk of a reward on that white boss-fella's head, and that mounted police and bounty hunters were about to arrive in Dorrigo. And, somehow, they all had my bloody description! That sure put the wind up me.

'Before we met at the dance, I'd decided that the kitchen was getting far too hot to continue, and it was time to look for another vocation. In fact, I'd just paid my last dues to the blacks.'

'Ooohhoo, boyo, sounds like you've been really naughty,' Orla teased. However, she knew at last he was telling her the truth. 'But stop worrying, you can tag along with me. I've got just the stuff that'll change the colour of your hair and you can grow a beard. With luck it might improve your looks a bit. Anyway, we could complete your disguise by passing ourselves off as husband and wife travelling with our son to find our dream farm,' Orla proposed conspiratorially. 'But there'll be no further mention of the wholesale and retail stock business. Got that?'

By the look on Owen's face he was clearly heartened, even aroused by her proposal... and doubtless wondering where she'd learnt that expression.

'Right, into the bathroom and off with your shirt. After you've got your new head of hair, we start packing. And as soon as it's dark tonight, we're saying goodbye to Dorrigo and heading for Gympie. Right?'

'Gympie sounds good to me... it's nice to be invited,' said Owen cynically as Orla massaged the dye through his hair. 'But which way do you intend to travel?'

'Back the way Niall and I came here; through Bellingen. I must admit though, it worries me that those coppers were heading that way, too.'

'You know, Orla, since you're this far into the Dorrigo, you must see the Ebor Falls, particularly if there's been a bit of rain about. It's one of nature's gems. And hey, we just might see the ghost of Captain Thunderbolt. It's also your good fortune my previous services to this region means that I know the area intimately. In fact, I reckon I know every bend in the track from here to Ebor, to Tyringham and then on to Grafton where, as luck would have it, I own a humble cottage not too dissimilar to this one. Main thing for me, though, is to give the Bostobrick run a wide berth.'

'That sounds good to me, boyo. I'll ask Niall and Boss Boy what they want to do. In the meantime, please get dressed and start packing,' Orla urged, her eyes lingering on Owen's naked and well-muscled shoulders and back.

Early that night, Orla wrote a lengthy letter to Joyce, apologising for her spur-of-the-moment decision to continue her journey. She thanked Joyce for the teaching experience and wished her good luck for the future, leaving open the opportunity for future correspondence.

Her second letter was for the Stewarts informing them she was on the move again and that she should arrive in Gympie within the next two months. Joyce, she knew, would post this letter on her behalf.

There was a third envelope addressed to Martin. It contained a brief note wishing him good luck for the future... plus two hundred pounds.

At about ten thirty that night, Orla extinguished the oil lamps then closed the cottage. Owen and Niall were already sitting on the cart's driving platform but as Orla climbed aboard, Owen lifted Niall onto his lap to give room for his mother to take up her position.

Without warning and as clear as a bell, Niall yelled, 'Go Boss Boy!'

36

After they'd travelled about thirty minutes, Owen placed his hand on Orla's arm. 'Stop here please, Orla, I have to collect a few of my belongings. I'll only be twenty minutes, I promise. Don't go anywhere, eh?'

Orla covered his hand with one of hers. 'No way, boyo, Niall wouldn't let me.'

About twenty minutes later, Boss Boy snorted a warning. Orla heard hoof beats then caught the swift movement of a shadow weaving through the undergrowth. Owen must have heard Boss Boy for the shadow stopped, then changed direction and made directly towards the cart.

Owen drew rein alongside Orla and asked, 'Everything all right?'

'Yep. I've just put the master to bed and he's already sound asleep. How long do you reckon we should travel before calling it a night? Nice looking horse by the way.'

At first, Owen didn't reply. Instead, he dismounted and tied his horse to the rear of the cart. As he swung up onto the driver's platform he caught the faint scent of soap Orla used. Forcing himself to ignore it, he answered suddenly. 'Don't ask how I came by my horse. Listen, Orla, those traps worry me plenty. We really do need to get as far away as possible from Dorrigo, and as fast as possible. However, I happen to know a delightful hideaway on the Little Murray, about two hours from here.'

'So be it,' Orla agreed. 'Let's get a move on then.'

Sometime later Orla raised her concern. 'Owen, please don't be offended, but from tomorrow I want you to ride your horse. I don't want to knock Boss Boy around unnecessarily; we've got such a long way to go.'

'That's as it should be, Orla. Much of the country beyond Tyringham has long, steep pinches. Besides, if necessary, I want to be able to make a dash for it without having to stop to saddle up.'

Orla gave him a playful cuff to the back of his head then deliberately moved to sit so that they were touching from shoulder to hip.

Despite the darkness, Owen effortlessly found his suggested campsite.

Orla unhitched Boss Boy and gave him a quick rubdown while Owen hobbled both horses. She then climbed into bed, noticing with pleasure that Owen was rolling out his swag on the ground beneath the cart.

Although sleep overtook them quickly, their slumber was short lived. Niall was awake at first light, wriggling and needing to pee. When Boss Boy pushed his head into the cart, Orla admitted defeat. Barely awake, she started to climb down from the cart with Niall.

'I'll take him,' Owen said quietly. 'It seems we both need to go. You stay there; we'll be back in a few minutes.'

When Orla eventually awoke several hours later, Niall and Owen were gone. However, her anxiety quickly vanished. The men in her life were walking up from the river towards her, sharing the job of carrying a bucket of water.

She looked about, savouring the beauty of the land. The river gurgled and ran crystal clear, and the fog was lifting through an expansive tree canopy. Orla struggled to recall when she last felt this relaxed.

Owen good-naturedly thanked Niall for his help then demonstrated how to set the fire — and even allowed him to light it. After breakfast, Orla hitched Boss Boy into the cart, while Owen saddled his horse and then secured his swag.

'Can you hear 'em?' Owen asked.

'No. What exactly?'

'Cedar gatherers. They've been at it since dawn, about two miles upstream. We'll pass their haul-out track about four miles from here.'

Orla listened and then she heard it, the faint, rhythmic 'thunk,' 'thunk,' thunk' of axe falls. Those sounds were to become constant companions as they traversed the Dorrigo beyond the settlements of Ebor, Hernani, and Tyringham.

* * *

'WE'VE MADE GOOD PROGRESS, Orla, no doubt about it. But, by the look of those clouds brewing in the west, we're in for a decent storm. Let's push on and try and get settled before it hits.'

But their luck ran out. As they approached the tiny settlement of Ebor, the heavens opened. Rain fell in swamping sheets. Thunder exploded overhead. Forked lightning flashed disturbingly close by, and powerful, blustery wind tore at the surrounding bush and pummelled man and beast.

Shelter was scarce but Boss Boy instinctively headed towards a rock outcrop that gave some protection. Owen's horse was unnerved and difficult to control, particularly when the thunder and lightning crashed in unison. Orla stood with the frightened animal, soothing him, while Owen secured the canvas drop sheets around the cart. Boss Boy stood with his backside into the advancing wind and rain and remained amazingly calm, shaking his head occasionally to shed the rain from his face. Niall bawled in fear.

The storm passed as quickly as it descended upon them. They then fed the horses, changed into dry clothing and gratefully shared a hearty, hot dinner.

* * *

NOT LONG BEFORE DAWN, Orla was woken by a loud continuous rumble. To her surprise she found Owen standing beside the cart feeding Niall, comforting him with gentle, reassuring words, and trying to explain what was happening.

When Orla stepped down from the cart, Owen moved to her side. She didn't resist when he placed his free arm around her waist and drew her protectively to his side. Following Owen's gaze, she looked up. They were now beneath a mind-boggling explosion of millions of brilliant stars.

In that moment, Orla knew she was magnificently and hopelessly in love again.

In the false dawn Owen, now piggybacking Niall, led Orla towards the still unseen, but now roaring phantom. They could no longer hear each other talk. Abruptly, they arrived at the edge of a massive gorge filled with grey cottonwool clouds, and mist rising hundreds of feet into the air. The sun's first rays then burst across the western ranges, giving birth to a magnificent double rainbow, which looped above the gorge and then disappeared down and beyond a lower tier of rocks. At the head of the gorge, the sight of an enormous volume of brown frothing water descending the first tier was truly remarkable. The previous night's thunderstorm had obligingly released one of nature's most spectacular scenes, displaying a force few people, white or black, had ever seen.

They watched this spectacle in awe for about fifteen minutes before Owen indicated Orla should follow him. Still carrying Niall, he led her through the bush for about two hundred and fifty yards and then struck back to the edge of the gorge. Now spread before them was the lower tier of the falls, equally magnificent and just as boisterous. Again, they stood watching in amazement as the incredible spill of water continued unchecked downstream, destined for an uncharted wilderness.

Despite the huge puddles left by the storm, the water-filled ruts actually made it easier for Boss Boy to select his path along the track.

Late that day, they encountered the first bullock team since leaving Dorrigo. They stopped for a chat, boiled the billy and soon learned from the bullocky what they wanted to know. Three men purporting to be police had recently visited the nearby Bostobrick Station and were asking questions; they had not proceeded to Bellingen as Orla had thought. They wanted to know about trespassers, in particular, if any white men had been seen passing through. They also claimed they were on official business looking for some belligerent blacks for whom they had arrest warrants. Orla asked the bullocky to describe those men; there was no doubt in her mind they were the same three unwelcome uniforms who had disrupted life in Dorrigo.

That night, Owen's conversation shifted to Boss Boy. 'I must confess, Orla, I'm impressed with Boss Boy. He's confident and got a good ticker, that's for sure. He's devoted to you, you know. I'd be proud to own him.'

'You might not believe some of the things he's done. However, given your nefarious and questionable history, boyo, you can forget any designs you may have for him. He's mine. Besides, yours is a decent animal. You just concentrate on the road tomorrow, all right?'

Mid-afternoon, the following day, about two miles past the track leading from Bostobrick Station, Orla was first to see evidence of other horses.

'Judging by the hoof prints and the freshness of those droppings, there's definitely more than one rider... and not too far ahead either.'

'I'll bet even money it's those bastard coppers,' Owen suggested with a tinge of concern in his voice. 'They'll have taken the Bosto-brick track, back to this road, hoping to intercept me, or rather, us!'

The words were barely out of his mouth when Boss Boy threw up his head and whinnied, a certain sign other horses were close by. Before Orla or Owen could retreat, a lone rider broke from the scrub and drew rein in the centre of the road. A rifle rested across the top of his thighs. His finger looped on the trigger.

Orla calmly commanded Boss Boy to stop about thirty five yards from the rider. Owen followed suit on his mount. It was the same obnoxious individual Orla had encountered at Dorrigo, but he no longer wore a police uniform and his posture was unmistakably threatening.

'So, we do meet again, yah lyin' bitch,' the man said in a cold, yet triumphant tone. 'And you, pretty boy, despite the pussy beard and changin' yah hair, are about to make me rich. So walk-up and identify yourselves. Now!'

Orla didn't move, but immediately whispered to Owen. 'Stay put. Can you see the other two? One's in the scrub about thirty yards directly off to your right. He's elevated by twelve or so yards. And there's another one about the same distance away as the one in the middle of the road, but he's off to the left by ten yards. Can you see 'em?'

'Only the two up front, dammit,' Owen whispered back.

'Move your arses!' the armed man demanded aggressively. 'You're worth as much to me dead, as alive. Now, get 'ere and identify your-selves, or else.'

'Yep, looks like they mean business,' Orla said calmly, but then urgently whispered instructions. 'Don't move till I do. You'll have to deal with the bloke on your right. Sorry, boyo. The others are mine.'

Orla and Owen remained motionless. The pressure to make a decisive move was palpable. Suddenly, the man raised his free hand, an obvious pre-arranged signal. His rifle then sprang to his shoulder. He quickly balanced himself and took aim. Orla saw both movements and that of the second horseman off to her left as he also dutifully raised his weapon.

'Now!' Orla yelled. Her Colts magically appeared. Two shots rang out, followed instantly by two more shots. The clear mountain air was shattered. Birds screamed and sheered away in panicked flight. The nearby valleys echoed.

As focused as she was, Orla was aware of other shots being fired off to her right. Regardless, she sprang from the cart and ran towards the man in the middle of the road. The dust around the man's still twitching body was just settling. Given the bullet-hole in his forehead and the blood oozing through his shirt in the centre of his chest, his demise was certain.

She then ran to where the second man had been unceremoniously dislodged from his horse, and now laid moaning and writhing. Another shot rang out. The moaning stopped instantly... the writhing, a few seconds later.

Orla then ran quickly but cautiously back to the cart.

As she arrived, Owen walked from the bush. 'That bastard nearly shot me!' he stammered indignantly, while sucking in deep breaths. 'His first bullet hit the side of the cart, I think. Anyway, the bastard's dead.' Owen's third shot found the man's chest.

Neither of Orla's opponents got off a single shot before meeting their maker...

Niall was unhurt but crying from the unexpected noise and the violence he'd partially witnessed. Orla cuddled him until his sobbing stopped, then returned him to his bed. He soon drifted off to sleep. When Orla stepped down from the cart, Owen was sitting on the ground with his back against one of the cartwheels. His breathing was under control but he had a glazed look on his face and his hands were trembling.

'It was going to be either us, or them, you know,' Orla said quietly as she sat beside him. 'Come on, my boyo, we need to move them out of sight and round up their horses. With luck, their nags might fetch us a bob or two.'

'Jesus Christ, Orla, what the hell have we just done?' replied Owen as he dragged himself to his feet. 'And how did you do that? Where did you learn to shoot like that, for God's sake? If I hadn't bloody well seen it with my own eyes I'd never have believed it possible.'

'I'll tell you what we've just done. We've just shot three bounty hunters, or three property owner vigilantes — that's what! See how they're dressed? Not a police uniform anywhere,' Orla hissed her reply, but then nonchalantly added. 'Twas my darlin' Da who taught me to shoot. He insisted I should know how to look after myself... and a few friends taught me a trick or two along the way.

'Anyway, you did pretty damn well. Shooting at elevated targets can be a bit tricky. Or was it just good luck?' Orla teased, as she elbowed Owen in the ribs.

Now composed Owen replied, 'Yeah, right. Well, come on; give me a hand with these mongrels.'

After relieving the three dead men of what little money they had, their bodies were unceremoniously heaved over the edge of a nearby gully. With little emotion Orla and Owen watched each body crash through the canopy of the dense bush thirty yards below.

Next, they caught all three horses and inspected the contents of each saddle-bag. Not a stitch of police clothing was found, vindicating Orla's assessment. But what Owen found shocked him. His trembling returned as he read a poster informing the public that a reward of four hundred pounds would be paid to anyone who either killed, captured or could lead police to one particularly well described bushranger — him!

'No wonder the bastards were so keen to nail my hide to the nearest post,' Owen said with a serious look on his face as he handed the reward notice to Orla. 'It's well and truly time I made myself scarce, that's for sure. Gympie's sounding better and better. C'mon Orla, let's get moving.'

They agreed that selling the captured horses was too risky. Instead, they released them to roam free, and then threw the bounty hunters' guns, saddles, saddle-bags, and bridles into the same gully.

As they were about to leave the killing ground, Orla invited Owen to sit with her on the driver's platform. She slapped him on the knee, nudged him, and looked impishly into his face then started to chuckle, determined to raise his spirits. Before they'd travelled half a mile, both of them were roaring with laughter, their voices echoing along the mist filled gullies on either side of the track. But before day's end however, both were stricken by their consciences, and made a pact there would be no more killings.

38

That night when Niall was sound asleep, Orla joined Owen below the cart. A night of urgent, uninhibited sex followed, releasing feelings that had been building since their most unexpected first meeting in Sydney Town. However, both knew this consummation was more than lust; it bound soul mates whose future lives together held so much promise.

As Orla lay wrapped in Owen's arms, she was amazed at how she no longer saw the clear vision of Ned's striking and powerful features in her mind's eye. Ned's short life had run its course, but she knew intuitively he would have encouraged a new love once his own destiny had been determined.

* * *

THEIR JOURNEY to Grafton was unhindered, relaxing and full of fun. Often, Owen took Niall on his horse in search of kangaroos. Whenever they came upon a mob, he'd boot his horse into a full gallop and they'd charge after them. Niall's excitement soon overcame his initial fears: he whooped and kicked his legs, urging the horse to catch those elusive 'woos'. At first this annoyed Orla, but she realised Owen was a good horseman and knew he would never deliberately harm her boy.

For the first time in his life, Owen embraced real responsibility and admitted to himself it was not without its benefits... nor was it something he'd ever take for granted. For hadn't this stunning, courageous, loving, and highly intelligent woman now twice saved him from the certainty of either going to prison — or worse? *You're in love, mate,* Owen rapturously found himself thinking. *Go on, admit it!*

* * *

Four weeks after leaving Ebor, they arrived in Grafton. Owen's cottage was a further four miles northeast, on the eastern bank of a mighty river; the Clarence.

The cottage was a simple structure, raised about six feet above ground level. 'It gives me the edge over any uninvited coppers,' Owen confided. 'I can see for miles, which gives me a head start if necessary. And, I'll never get flooded-out.'

There were post and rail fenced paddocks at the rear, but the pasture and the property immediately surrounding the cottage were both overgrown. However, the cottage's interior, although a bit dusty, was in habitable order and airy.

After yarding their horses, they unpacked the cart and set about putting the cottage back into 'some resemblance of domestic order' as Orla called it. The following day, Owen rode back into Grafton under the pretext of buying food, but he failed to return until very late in the afternoon.

Orla waited on the front veranda ready to give him an earful, not only because he was so late, but because he was obviously quite drunk. Nevertheless, Owen was beaming jovially and waving papers in the air... and started speaking before Orla could pay out on him.

'Done it, me luv,' he said as he wobbled up the stairs. 'I've sold this 'ere cottage, sight unseen, too. Some silly bugger fisherman offered me twice what I said I'd paid for it!' Pausing to belch loudly, he then continued. 'He's even gunna pay cash on the knocker on the day we sign these. We got two weeks a'fore we hav ta leave. Agreed on that point, early on like… reckoned we needed a breather. So, what do yah reckon, Orla, me gorgeous princess?'

'Christ, we've only been here a day and you go and sell everything in one drunken piss up,' replied Orla in mock anger. Regardless, a crestfallen look appeared on Owen's face. 'I'm kidding, my charming boyo. You'd better come and have your supper and tell me all about it.'

An arm around each other's waist, Orla manoeuvred a very compliant Owen into the kitchen and sat him down. Instead of putting on the kettle she produced a bottle of brandy and poured two hefty measures.

'Here's to you, my beloved and favourite *retired* cattle thief,' Orla toasted Owen with a flourish. 'Here's to a grand sales job, done no doubt with grace and great cunning.'

'Yah could say that,' replied Owen who was looking slyly at Orla through drunken red-rimmed eyes. But his external state belied the clarity of his mind. 'I never paid a penny for this place yah know, so my askin' price seemed like a steal to that fisherman. By the way, I won this 'ere cottage in a card game, years ago. How d'yah like that? Thought yah said I'd make a lousy card player?'

'You're a cunning bastard, all right,' replied Orla with just the right mix of good-humour and sarcasm as she drained her glass. 'Where'd you learn to think like that anyway? From your livestock trading days, I presume?'

They both roared with laughter and then together drank the remaining brandy as darkness fell. Orla would have preferred a cuddle, but shortly after eating his dinner, Owen rose shakily from the table, excused himself and went straight to bed. He didn't surface until ten thirty the following day.

If Owen suffered from a hangover, he didn't show it. He checked the horses, and then spent the next few hours on overdue maintenance on the cart's wheels, canvas, and harness. And he had a helper. Niall chattered endlessly and practiced pronouncing words correctly whenever Owen gently pulled him up.

Three days later they rode into Grafton. Niall and Owen rode two up on Boss Boy and Orla rode Owen's horse. Grafton was a rapidly developing provincial country centre. It had a large and bustling riverside shipyard, which was the main loading point for transporting wool, timber, and a variety of other produce to Sydney Town. There was a grand church and a recently completed brick police station; in fact, the town generally radiated a feeling of progress and order. The climate was pleasantly warm and humid but any discomfort was tempered by a gentle breeze wafting from the Clarence.

After making several essential purchases they headed for the Real Estate Property offices where they met the fisherman and finalised the agreed sale.

'Now, *if* you were a bushranger,' Orla remarked casually when they stood on the footpath outside the office, 'where would your money be safest?'

'Next to the window, where you sleep with the Webley brothers.'

'Seriously, though,' Orla chuckled, his meaning not lost on her. 'If it's in a bank account, your money can be transferred with a guarantee that if it gets nicked, they'll repay it. If they don't, then we can always revert to bushranging and retrieve it.'

'Our money, Orla,' Owen replied immediately. 'It's our money, right?'

'Come on then, let's do it,' Orla commanded. 'We'll take only enough for the last part of our journey and put the rest into an account here in Grafton. That way, we'll have 'guaranteed readies' when we get to Gympie.'

Unfortunately, their stay in Grafton had to be cut short. Wanted posters were appearing in shop windows advising that three Law Enforcement Contractors were missing. Police were appealing for public assistance: it was assumed those gallant men met with foul play since their starving horses turned up, minus their owners. The notices implied that a bushranger known to be active in the Dorrigo area was responsible. An unnerving description of Owen followed, but no name. Orla and Owen had no intention of offering *their* public assistance.

Re-packing the cart was easy and routine. After closing the cottage, they again headed northeast on the main coast road, wanting to be long gone to avoid any possible linkage with those posters, or with the hasty sale of the cottage.

The going was easy so they travelled fast without unduly taxing Boss Boy. Orla marvelled at the increasing size of the Clarence River as they approached the timber shipping port of Maclean. Upon arrival, she arranged a ferry crossing but they had to wait until the late afternoon for their turn.

As the sun set, the river's surface, driven by a gentle coastal breeze, shimmered with gold-laced ripples. Occasionally, schools of small fish exploded along the surface either in pursuit of an evening meal or trying desperately to avoid becoming the meal of some larger predator.

Their crossing was uneventful and pleasant. Having disembarked, they quickly headed north for about a mile and then made camp. They decided not to rest Boss Boy the next day, but to press on, albeit, at a more leisurely pace. The going remained easy, the weather warm, food and water were abundant for their horses and they were not challenged by either police or bushrangers. They regularly socialised with travellers heading south, obtaining reliable northward directions at each stop.

But more importantly, they were deliberately developing a facade to deflect any suspicion they could possibly have been living outside the law — just a typical, happy and adventurous young family who were completely harmless.

39

As Orla and Owen moved further north, the temperature rose steadily; as did the humidity, which made Orla uncomfortable and irritable, a condition she loathed. Nevertheless, she was consoled by southbound travellers that she'd soon acclimatise.

However, it was Owen who offered the most sensible solution.

'Orla, for heaven's sake, you can't allow prudish feminine etiquette to override practicality. Strip off some of your clothes or shorten your trousers and remove the sleeves from your shirts. You can always cover up once the sun goes down.'

'I'll get sunburnt! You see how fair my skin is.'

'Not if I extend the roof of your cart's canopy. You've got spare canvas. Then you'll be in solid shade, and Niall can sit with you. He could even strip right off.'

'You're not here just for your good looks, eh?' Orla replied genially. 'Come on; let's get it done. But hang on, what about you, my clever boyo? I'll not have you stripping off in public.'

'I quite like this weather. Besides, I've got my hat, and my skin's darkish... like Niall's. Don't worry; I'll not be flaunting anything... in public anyway.'

* * *

THEY CROSSED two other huge northern rivers after saying farewell to the Clarence. The first of these was the Richmond. At one of their more reclusive campsites along its banks, they stumbled upon remnants of several long abandoned dwellings which were rectangular and which once had gabled roofs. Owen and Orla were even more surprised when told by locals that these buildings were constructed by aboriginals a long time before white men settled on this river. Given the European influence of those buildings, that possibility seemed bizarre since they were only familiar with the primitive, makeshift bark humpies the aboriginals seemed to prefer.

Ballina, on the northern bank at the mouth of the Richmond River, was surrounded by lush, subtropical growth and was a centre for the milling and shipping of the valuable red cedar cut from upstream forests and then rafted downstream. Shipbuilding here was again prevalent and obviously a flourishing industry, and like Grafton, Ballina was growing rapidly to accommodate the many families of cedar gatherers.

Their first sighting of the Tweed River was set against the dramatic backdrop of the McPherson Ranges and Mount Warning, to the west. They followed the Tweed along its eastern bank for nearly forty miles through a valley of dense rainforest, eventually emerging onto fertile lowlands and a broad estuary system. The town of Tweed Heads was located at the mouth of this river, also on its northern bank, and it, too, was a bustling timber-shipping port.

River crossings by punt were by now becoming mundane despite the ever-present risk of capsizing due to overloading. However, about three weeks after leaving Grafton they arrived unscathed in the Colony of Queensland.

'I say, Orla, tell me again why we're heading for Gympie?' Owen asked unexpectedly during a midday break.

'I've told you at *least* twice. I met some wonderful people in England on my way here remember? And remember I told you they were intending to establish a goldmining operation in Gympie?

When they offered me my own cottage if I ever decided to settle there, it sounded like a great opportunity. Besides, I promised never to lose contact with them. You'll love them, too, I reckon.' Orla sighed in relief; caught off-guard, somehow she'd avoided using names.

* * *

It was becoming a regular topic raised by southbound travellers that magnificent beaches were not far from their current location. So the next day they decided to investigate for themselves. That advice was a massive understatement. What they discovered were wide, pristine, yellow sand beaches that sloped gently to the ocean's edge. As the beaches receded into the distance they became shrouded in mist generated by the foaming white surf, which continuously rolled in from the sparkling blue Pacific Ocean. Orla was surprised at how closely Owen's eyes matched the colour of the ocean.

For the next three weeks Orla and Owen lounged about, made passionate love during the night when Niall was asleep, swam for hours or rode their horses for miles along the beach, occasionally racing. Owen and Niall collected deep suntans, and eventually Orla's skin turned a golden hue.

Niall enjoyed himself immensely playing with children from two aboriginal families who lived in the scrub just above the beach. However, he was seldom out of sight of either his mother, or Owen. The aboriginal parents were shy at first, but soon warmed to Orla's charm and to Owen's openness and interest in their activities. It was so easy to forget they were races apart.

By some mysterious means, however, Orla sensed the aboriginal elders seemed to know about her... as if she belonged in their culture. She regularly experienced a warm, comforting premonition that her defence of a young aboriginal girl was the cause for their curiosity. Consequently, she avoided answering most of their gently probing questions when Owen was within earshot. The right time to try and explain this to him would arrive soon enough.

Unfortunately, the constant sea spray began to rust the cart's steel rims, and it mercilessly attacked the harness leatherwork. Reluctantly, Orla announced that the next day would be their last on these magnificent beaches. With sadness they bade farewell to their aboriginal friends and turned north once again.

Considering it still far too risky, Orla and Owen unanimously agreed to bypass Brisbane Town. Well defined roads, easy terrain and plenty of water and feed for the horses allowed them to continue making good progress. At the Cobb & Co stopover at Mellum Creek (now Landsborough) they obtained clear directions for the route to the Gympie gold fields. Orla's grand journey was near its end.

Travelling had inexplicably become a chore for Orla rather than a daily pleasure. As if by stealth, it was becoming increasingly important to her to find some permanence in her life. She repeatedly thought, *God, I hope I haven't made a mistake.*

* * *

ALL DID NOT GO SMOOTHLY on that final run into Gympie. For the first time, the cart became a liability. A rim eventually worked loose and the wheel collapsed, shattering several spokes. In addition, the harness leatherwork was disintegrating.

'I can't repair anything, Orla, I'm sorry,' Owen announced. 'We haven't got the right tools. We'll take only the most important stuff and dump the rest.'

Boss Boy carried a huge load... and never once protested. By necessity Orla and Owen rode Owen's horse three up with Niall. This significantly limited the distance they could travel each day, which added to their impatience to arrive at their destination.

40

───────────

The threesome arrived in Gympie accompanied by a rainstorm that saturated their belongings and dampened their spirits. The rain also threatened to make short work of the map the Stewarts sent to Orla, but fortunately, a local pointed them in the right direction before the map became illegible.

Eventually, about two miles out of town they found the cottage. To their surprise, a light was shining from within. With rain still pelting down, Orla dismounted, leaving Owen sheltering Niall under his oilskin coat. She opened the fence gate, carefully ascended the wet steps, crossed the veranda and knocked firmly on the front door. To her surprise another hauntingly familiar but somewhat frightened woman's face appeared behind the partially opened door. The woman was about her own age and attractive. She too was holding a small child.

'Don't be frightened, my name's Orla. I understood this cottage was left vacant for me by the Stewarts, but I must have the wrong place or else they've had a change of heart.'

Before Orla could say anything further, the door flew fully open. The woman gently lowered her child to the floor and placed one hand over her heart.

'Oh, my God. Is it really you? Orla! Please, please come in, come in! We've heard so much about you.' The young woman threw her arms around Orla and hugged her tightly. During the embrace she peered over Orla's shoulder, out into the darkness and rain. Suddenly she pushed away from Orla, stumbled a few steps backwards and then froze. For the second time in a minute there was a look of total disbelief on her face.

Orla quickly glanced back over her shoulder to see Owen standing forlornly at the top of the steps under the veranda, still holding Niall closely to him, protecting them both from the rain with his coat.

'It ca-can't possibly be?' the woman stammered. 'Can it? Oh, my God! Owen!' She then ran across the veranda and threw her arms around him.

'James! James! Come quickly, see who's here,' she shouted excitedly. 'I can hardly believe this. Come out of the rain you two and get inside quick. And hey, I'll bet this is Niall. I'm so pleased to meet you at last, young man.'

For Orla the mystery was over. *It was Anne!* The face that confronted her was that in the photograph, which stood alongside her brother's on the mantelpiece of their parent's London home.

Anne took a very sleepy Niall from Owen then ushered Owen and Orla into the cottage. As they walked into the kitchen, a man walked in from an adjoining room pushing braces over his shoulder with one hand, while carrying an oil lamp in the other.

'G'day, pleased to meet you,' Orla said immediately. 'My name's Orla and you must be James. And this is my son Niall. Oh, and by the way, I don't believe you've met your wife's brother. This is Owen.'

Owen cast a shocked, quizzical look at Orla, and then dutifully shook hands with James. 'It's fantastic to meet you, James, and to find you both here. But I thought you lived in Adelaide. What are you doing here? What's going on?'

Then it hit him. 'Hang on a minute. I don't suppose, Orla, that my sister and brother-in-law are here visiting your friends also? And, on the off-chance, I don't suppose those *friends* just might happen to be *my parents!*'

'Yeeess, yes,' Orla yelled excitedly, while jumping around and pumping her arms in the air.

'You bloody vixen! All this time you actually knew my parents... *and* who I was!' he protested. Then with a mock expression of murderous intent on his face, he put his hands around Orla's throat, pretending he was about to strangle her.

'Take it easy, boyo. I didn't know Anne and James would be here, honest. But it's a fantastic surprise all 'round, you have to agree. But hey, your parents don't know we've arrived in Gympie and that's going to be another one hell of a surprise for them,' Orla suggested as she removed Owen's hands from her throat and cuddled into him.

'Good gracious, what's going on here?' asked a very excited Anne. 'Are you two a couple as well?'

'Oh yes,' Orla replied casually. 'He's tolerable just so long as he keeps his pants up and puts food on the table.' Laughter filled the room.

While Anne made cups of tea, everyone excitedly fired questions back and forth. It was soon established that Frank and Jeanie were at home and in good health. Unanimously, they agreed to call on them immediately after breakfast the next day.

'But first, the horses,' Owen suddenly interrupted. 'Have you got somewhere I can yard them in case a bushranger takes a fancy to them?'

'No self-respecting bushranger would be out on a night like this, you dill,' Orla responded in a flash.

'No problem,' James announced eagerly. 'Got just the thing. Come with me, mate. I'll give you a hand, seems like the rain's eased a bit.'

They tethered the horses in a lean-to at the rear of the cottage, unloaded Boss Boy, removed the saddle from Owen's horse, and then wiped both horses down with dry bags. What oats remained was fed out equally. Next, they hung Orla and Owen's wet belongings under the veranda in the hope everything would dry out before mildew set in.

When the men returned inside, the children were in bed and the visitors' beds were made up. Anne was busy brewing more tea and toasting sandwiches over the kitchen fireplace. They happily chattered and talked non-stop until midnight. The only disappointment was learning of the timetable to which Anne and James were committed. James promised his bank he'd be back in Adelaide before the end of the month, which meant at best, they had only three days remaining before they had to leave Gympie. Understandably, James was anxious about whether he'd left himself sufficient stagecoach and sailing time for the return trip. The prospect of forfeiting his new senior appointment by further extending his leave of absence held little appeal for him.

As Owen told his story, Orla occasionally frowned at him or very gently shook her head, those subtle gestures being his cue to limit what he was saying. In turn, his slight look of alarm as Orla seemed about to reveal too much, were enough for Orla to deftly change the subject. Owen and Orla nonchalantly worked off one another's almost invisible but intimate signals to avoid relating any of their more questionable activities.

Orla was confident this couple knew nothing about Niall's real father. If they did, neither raised the matter. Nevertheless, Orla felt it was important she quickly determine just how much Jeanie and Frank *had* confided in them.

James suddenly remembered something — a letter the Stewart's left on the kitchen mantelpiece. He retrieved it and handed to Orla. It was from her mother, Kathleen. It seemed her brothers were interested in visiting her, but were all extremely busy. And Kathleen bluntly said she was now too old for such a journey, thus dashing Orla's anticipated hopes for her own family reunion. Her mother's words hurt and saddened Orla, but she did not allow them to dampen the excitement of the evening.

'James is a really nice bloke,' Owen confided to Orla, just before sleep swept them up. 'It'd be nice to get to know him better. And just think, Orla, this splendid cottage will soon be ours. It's hard to believe, eh?'

Orla cuddled into Owen and resolved to tell him in the morning about the disappointing news in her mother's letter. But deep down Orla knew only two things really mattered now, regardless of what else might unfold in her life. She'd found the most likeable and loving man she'd ever known, and she had the most adorable son.

41

They hid their horses behind some scrub growing about one hundred yards from the Stewarts' homestead. Owen followed the line of bush until he was within thirty yards of their house. He could hear someone chopping wood, so he jogged across the remaining clear ground, anticipating he would not be noticed. When he reached the back of the house, he paused, and then slowly poked his head around the corner of the building. There was an old man, tall and thin; the energy with which he attacked the block of wood in front of him belied his real age. Owen stepped around the corner and took two steps forward.

'Can I give you a hand with that, Dad?'

On his backswing, Frank froze. He then slowly rotated his suntanned head, repositioned his spectacles and then gazed wide-eyed upon his son. He leant the axe against the partially cut block of wood, and stood to his full height.

'Thought you'd never ask. How are you, son?'

In two more strides Owen reached his father and they threw their arms around one another. Owen was surprised by the strength of his father's return hug. He could feel Frank's rapidly beating heart and the gentle shuddering of his father's body as he wept.

Between sobs, Frank whispered into Owen's ear. 'Oh son, thank God you're alive. We've missed you so much, boy. We thought we'd lost you. But you've grown into a strong and handsome bloke, that's for sure.'

Owen, too, was sobbing. Unfortunately, his father had changed considerably in the past six, *or was it seven years?* Frank was an old man now, not frail, but much thinner than he could remember, and what hair remained was now white. Owen felt a sting of guilt, suspecting his actions had needlessly contributed to his father's aging.

They remained in an embrace for another minute then Frank gently pushed himself away. 'Hey, Jeanie... Jeanie! Come outside and see what the cat's dragged in,' he yelled excitedly.

When Jeanie emerged from the back door, there were father and son, arms around each other's shoulders, grinning like drunken imbeciles, with tears of joy still streaming down their cheeks. Jeanie almost fainted but managed to compose herself as she ran to her son.

Owen threw his arms around her and easily picked her up, hugging her tightly. He then lowered her, and placed his hands on her shoulders.

'Why would such a beautiful woman continue to live with such an old bastard?' he asked, while smiling and gazing mischievously into his mother's eyes. 'God though, Mum, it's great to see you.' Arms now around both of his parents' shoulders, Owen said, 'C'mon, how about a cuppa?'

As they entered the kitchen, there was a knock on the front door. Jeanie tentatively opened it... There stood a small boy about three years old, his arms cradling a huge bunch of flowering shrubs. As he handed them to her, he said in a quiet, confident, but well rehearsed voice, 'G'day nanny Stewart, these are for you. I'm Niall.'

For the second time in only minutes Jeanie nearly lost her breath in surprise and delight. 'Niall, it's so *lovely* to see you! Thank you so much for visiting us. And your flowers are lovely, too. Thank you.

'You know, Niall, we already know each other,' Jeanie continued as she squatted down so her eyes could be level with his, and so that she could more easily put her arms around him. 'But I reckon you were too young to remember me and your pappa. Welcome anyway young fella, but where's mum?'

Niall walked to the side of the house and reached out. As he did so, an arm appeared and a woman's hand gently clasped Niall's little hand. As Orla stepped into view, Jeanie gasped and gazed in wonder at her truly gorgeous friend. This time the excitement did get the better of her. She not only lost her breath, but also wobbled and almost fell. Orla moved quickly to steady her and held her in a strong embrace.

'Hey, it's all right, Jeanie,' Orla whispered. 'We're here to stay, so please don't conk out on us now. Let me have your word on that, eh?'

'I'm fine really, it's just that, well, good God, Orla, this is the most fabulous day in my life, I think. You and Niall arrive at my front door just after my son walks in the back door! Quick, come and meet, Owen, he's... hang on! Don't tell me you already know him?'

Jeanie quickly ushered her visitors into the kitchen where Owen and Frank were chatting happily. Abruptly, the men stopped talking and looked at each other. Owen raised his eyebrows and shrugged as if to enquire, 'Who's this then?'

'Good God Almighty! It's Orla and Niall!' Frank yelled, then rushed to Orla and gave her an affectionate fatherly hug and a kiss on her forehead. 'Orla, this is just bloody marvellous. We thought we'd lost you, too.'

More kisses, hugs and handshakes followed, as Niall was re-introduced to his pappa. Frank then slowly stood, looking at first baffled, then bemused... for Orla was nestled into Owen, his son's arms wrapped lovingly about her waist.

Frank walked over to Jeanie and placed his arm around her shoulder. 'Where and how, pray tell, did you two meet?'

And standing just inside the kitchen doorway and beaming huge smiles of approval was Anne nursing her infant daughter, and James holding the hand of their son, Michael.

42

The balance of that day was memorable on many fronts.

Owen spent a few hours talking with his father while they cut wood, Owen doing the lion's share. He vigorously attacked the wood but knew there was more than just sweat running down his cheeks and his uncontrollable sobs were not just from his physical effort. But this reaction seemed to be cleansing his soul. Gasping, and having almost worked himself to exhaustion, he stopped and handed the axe to Frank.

'A bloke can be a bloody fool, eh, Dad?' Owen said quietly in-between puffs. 'I was really worried for my life back in London, I'll admit, but I should've been able to solve my problems honourably without stealing from you and Mum.' After a pause to gather his breath, he continued. 'To clear out without giving either of you a decent explanation and lying to your friends must have hurt you both. I'm so sorry, Dad. What I did was shameful. Can you forgive me, knowing that I also killed that bloke?'

Frank picked up the axe. After a few half-hearted strokes, he stopped. 'I admit that I initially responded badly to your situation. But what you did *was* reprehensible. I wanted to disown you. I was angry and very disappointed. And your mother was badly affected, too. She believed we'd lost you to God knows what, killed in some backstreet probably, and your body dumped. The frustrating thing was that I could've helped you, son.

'Anyway, I was inclined to agree with, Jeanie, but after we received your first letter, that changed everything. It gave us real hope and your absence became bearable. Since then, we've never doubted we'd get back together one day. And yes, we forgive you for taking that man's life. I eventually discovered what you did was an act of self-defence... but your maker may see that differently.

'Right, I reckon that's enough wood for the next three years, my boy,' Frank joked, but then added. 'Let's make a pact, son... no more secrets, eh? Life's too damn short.'

Looking squarely at each other, they firmly shook hands. 'That's a deal, Dad. You've my word on that. And thanks, I feel so bloody relieved.'

'Tell me, though, son, how do you *really* feel about, Orla? Do you intend to make an honest woman of her, or what? And what about the boy? Owen, he's very special you know. How do you feel about him being in your life?'

Owen thought for a moment. 'What say we talk about this tonight after the kids have gone to bed?'

* * *

AFTER A BRIEF INSPECTION of the interior of the Stewarts' magnificent, brand-new double storey homestead and its wide wrap-around verandas, Orla and Jeanie wandered arm in arm through the rather grand outdoor surroundings. Many varieties of native trees and shrubs were at different stages of establishment and thoughtfully placed throughout lush manicured lawns. Formed gravel pathways wound through those plantings and there was even a fishpond, fed from a nearby permanent spring. In one corner of the large, wonderful backyard, a four foot high rabbit-proof fence enclosed a flourishing vegetable and herb garden. The boundary fencing was of post and rail construction and painted white, which enhanced the sense of wealth generated by the impressive homestead building and the fledgling botanical setting.

Orla was impressed by the modern stables where Boss Boy and Owen's horse clearly made themselves at home and were contentedly working their way through nosebags of oats. Jeanie proudly introduced Orla to her new black mare - a magnificent thoroughbred.

Orla told Jeanie much about her marathon journey... and the circumstances under which she'd met her son. Jeanie chuckled happily at Orla's description of the look on Owen's face when he finally discovered that Orla already knew his parents.

Of Owen's prior livelihood, Orla said nothing, and there were two encounters, which she steadfastly did not raise — her murder of the drunk and the multiple killings after leaving Dorrigo. In response to Jeanie's question if Orla could still use her pistols 'to good effect', Orla vaguely replied, 'I really wouldn't know... I haven't needed them for ages.'

'The climate's wonderful here, Orla. I don't think either of us has felt this good for years,' Jeanie remarked, but continued in a matter-of-fact manner. 'But I'm concerned about how hard Frank's been working. I've been trying to convince him he should retire. He could easily hand everything over to Robert D'Angelese. That amazing man has organised our entire mining operations to guarantee us prosperity for at least the next decade. You'll meet Robert soon enough. He's not only a brilliant engineer; he's a close and dear friend.

'Apart from that, we've got wonderful neighbours, too. Gympie's growing, and it's nice to know our mining venture has created jobs.'

* * *

WITH THE CHILDREN TAGGING ALONG, Jeanie and Frank returned inside to make lunch. That gave the opportunity for Owen to spend more time with James and for Orla to get to know Anne. James liked Owen and the feeling was mutual.

'Mate, I love your sister and our children, but I also love this great country,' James confessed enthusiastically. 'It's a land of enormous opportunity. We'll soon see nationhood if our economy continues to grow, and hopefully injustices by our earlier 'guiding authorities' will be corrected. And, you know, we might soon be thrashing the English at cricket.

'One really good thing, though, we'll soon be rid of bushrangers. I suppose you had to fight your way through those bastards to get here?' James innocently jested.

'They're not all bad bastards, you know.' Owen laughed. 'If you were seriously down on your luck and had no idea where your next meal was coming from, then things'd be different. I can see why desperate men might knock off the odd beast just to survive and hope like hell they didn't get caught. But some blokes who didn't get caught often found it habit-forming and easier to steal than work. That's when a bloke's *really* off the rails. But they're thieves, not really bushrangers, eh?

'Actually, I did meet one unusual bushranger,' Owen said conspiratorially. 'Killed some blokes who'd become bounty hunters. They reckoned they could earn a fortune capturing cattle thieves that the traps couldn't. But they hadn't counted on this particular person being smarter and much faster on the draw, or so she said.'

'*She!* You just said 'she',' responded a very surprised James.

'Did I? Well I meant 'he',' said Owen, instantly realising his mistake, and then added. 'The last known woman bushranger was probably Captain Thunderbolt's woman, but she died many long years ago if I recall correctly.' Then, to change the subject, he quickly asked, 'So how long did you say it'll take you to travel back to Adelaide?'

* * *

NIALL HAD a whale of a time playing with his 'cousin' Michael. They particularly liked climbing trees to see if the nests they'd located contained eggs, and if so, would put one into their mouths, thus enabling them to use both hands to climb down safely. However, during his last descent Niall learnt that it was unwise to talk whilst so occupied… the contents of the broken egg made him gag and he damn nearly fell.

* * *

DESPITE DIFFERENCES IN THEIR UPBRINGING, current life styles, and outlooks, Orla tolerated Anne; just.

'Orla, I'd never do what you did,' she said condescendingly. 'The heat, the spiders and snakes, and going to the toilet in the bush, or in the rain… for heaven's sake! That must've been awful. And as for Niall… well, I'd never consider such a trip for my children. I'd leave James if he tried to foist something like that on me. Travelling first class to Gympie was bad enough.'

She means well, and has been kind to me, thought Orla. *But, she's nothing like her mother, and how does poor James handle such self-centredness?*

However, Anne loved horses and generously praised Boss Boy for his achievement. Boss Boy nonchalantly returned her attention with an occasional nudge of his head into her midriff or shoulder.

'How on earth do you measure the worth of such an animal? You must be very proud of him, Orla. Do you think I could ride him before we leave?' Orla happily agreed.

After a memorable lunch, all the three women went riding. The outgoing leg was leisurely, but the return leg inexplicably became a serious contest. Over the uneven ground, Boss Boy overhauled the other horses within a hundred yards of the homestead. As Orla knew, he was, after all, the master of such races.

* * *

NOT SURPRISINGLY, the three men formed a strong camaraderie. Perhaps, the bottle and a half of rum helped. Nevertheless, their conversation was wide-ranging, candid, and driven by a common theme: they were all free colonials, no longer English or wanting to be referred to as English-born colonials, just 'free colonials'.

'Thanks to Robert's efforts, our mining venture has become an incredible success. But now Jeanie's at me to retire... and she's right,' Frank confessed. 'But beforehand, I need to sort out an equitable transfer of ownership to my children... and to my loyal friend, Robert.'

Owen was dumbstruck; he couldn't imagine his father *ever* retiring.

'Listen, Frank,' said James. 'I've already inherited an immense fortune from my parents. I'm well entrenched in the banking system and I'm soon to be handsomely remunerated as a senior bank manager. I'm sure that'll see my family comfortably through this life. Anne and I have already spoken about this kind of situation, and our decision was made years ago, before you initiated your mining venture in Gympie. Thanks, but respectfully Frank, Anne doesn't need any consideration. No arguments, right?'

Frank was surprised by James' firm, unpretentious announcement, but grateful, too, for it simplified his task. But before he could say anything, James continued.

'Keep the mining business in your family's name, Frank. But appoint Owen as an equal partner with your Mr. D'Angelese. You retain the equity but all future profits can be shared equally between the two of them. And then Frank, well, you can just sit back with Jeanie and smell the roses, eh? What do you think? When you eventually sell the mine, then you can decide how you want to divvy it up. I'd be more than happy to arrange all necessary paperwork and settle any legal fees.'

It seemed bizarre to Owen — that it was being suggested he and Orla, and a 'stranger', the mine manager — would inherit almost everything. Things were moving too rapidly, his head was spinning.

'Sounds about right, James, if you're genuinely happy,' Frank acknowledged. 'But what if Owen doesn't want to become involved? And what if Owen and Robert don't get along? In fairness, my son knows nothing about mining and any involvement, no matter how well intended, may put Robert's nose out of joint.'

'Think about it, Frank. You know your son and you obviously trust, Robert. Do *you* think they could work together?' James replied pragmatically. 'Even if they don't get along, the business will continue to flourish under Robert's management... and to his ongoing financial benefit. But, if that's the case, then we'll just have to find something else for Owen. Though personally, I don't think you have too much to worry about.'

'So, what do you reckon, son. Are you interested, or not? Do you and Orla have any other plans?'

'Bloody hell, this scares me a bit, to be truthful,' Owen replied, feeling self-conscious. 'No, we've got no other immediate plans and your proposal's extremely generous. In fact, it's almost beyond my comprehension. Dad's right, I bring no expertise. I've never worked in a mine or ever been remotely interested in mining, except perhaps when I did a bit of prospecting near Dorrigo. Mind you, the offers appealing. What's this D'Angelese fella like?'

'I'm certain Frank will teach you everything you'll need to know before he retires,' the ever-practical James interjected. 'And that'll give you and Robert time to measure each other up. He seems like a damned decent bloke to me. If you're square with the man, Owen, in my opinion, there's no reason you won't pull together and maybe even double the mine's current output.'

'Righto, righto, you've convinced me. If this is acceptable with you and Mum, then I guess it's time I met this bloke and have a sticky nose over the operations. I must say though, if Orla has any reservations, you need to know that she and Niall come first in my considerations, no matter what.'

43

———————

As the shadows lengthened and the first chill of the evening approached, Orla felt a wave of gratitude when Anne and James rounded up the children and took them back to the cottage for their dinner and to get them into bed. She suspected they both realised she and Owen needed to spend some quality, peaceful time with the Stewarts, to catch up on the past few years of their lives.

After dinner, they sat around the open fireplace in the Stewarts' exquisitely furnished and carpeted lounge room and gazed contentedly into the flames. It was Owen who spoke first.

'You know, Orla, I've got to know you reasonably well but I'm still curious. You've been traipsing all over this country as if you're looking for something, but I sometimes get the impression that you're actually running from something? Look, if I'm speaking out of order then please tell me.'

'You're right, my dear boyo, and you're not speaking out of order,' said Orla, looking him square in the eye. 'I most certainly do owe you an explanation and it's time for that, but first there are some things *I* need to know, so please be patient a wee bit longer.' Turning to face Jeanie and Frank, Orla asked, 'Have either of you ever told Anne or James about Niall? Do they know who his father is?'

Jeanie shook her head. Frank spoke. 'They've no idea, Orla. We've not denied his existence, of course, and if friends ask us about our grandchildren we include Niall, but only ever as an O'Meara. We never talk about what happened back then, unless we're either out in the paddocks, or certain we're alone.'

'What about Joan and Alf?' Orla continued. 'Do you know if they've ever...'

'You shouldn't concern yourself, girl,' Jeanie interrupted. 'They've written to us and we've shared whatever news either of our families learnt about you and Niall on your travels. But, we've only ever used his first name and we've burnt those letters anyway.'

'Thanks,' Orla replied, genuinely relieved. 'I knew you'd keep your word.'

Orla turned to a now very intrigued Owen.

'There are some things you need to know about me, but before I tell you, you must promise me you'll never, ever, disclose what I am about to tell you about Niall; promise?'

'I've no idea why you'd want to tell me your secret, whatever it may be. But regardless, I give you my word, Orla. And I'm positive that Mum and Dad would give me hell if I ever broke such a promise.'

For the next two hours, Orla explained her past — all of it. She felt no regret for any of her actions. But she failed to disguise the occasional catching of her breath and her involuntary tears when she recalled her brief love affair with Ned, their friendship with the two old Chinamen, the wonderful McIntyres and their children, and her stalwart friends, Kate and Tom Lloyd. Orla could tell by the incredulous looks on Jeanie's and Frank's faces — their lip biting and their hand wringing — that her unrepentant account of her killing of the drunk was another example of her unsettling impetuousness... and clearly unacceptable.

But, Owen nodded knowingly. He said nothing as Orla recalled the strange disappearance of that man's body, and raised his eyebrows at the equally bizarre reverence, which Lahni conferred upon her. At that point, Orla introduced their meeting with the coastal aboriginal family south of Brisbane, and did her best to explain the inexplicable bond she felt so strongly with them. It was when Orla started to talk about her day at the races in Sydney Town that Owen finally joined in.

'I noticed Orla from a distance as she walked into the betting ring, and liked what I saw. You'd done some serious damage to one of the bookies, as I soon found out.' At this point Owen was smiling in delight at his recollection of what followed. 'Now, I've seen some things in my life, and seen this girl here do some pretty incredible things, but this takes the cake.

'When a pickpocket friend of mine tried to relieve Orla of her winnings, she grabbed him and proceeded to belt the be-Jesus out of the poor bugger. She then just dropped him and walked away with a great big smile on her face.'

Orla was flabbergasted. 'So *what* became of *your friend*?'

Owen replied, while trying to keep a straight face, 'I suggested he either visit the on-course doctor for some treatment, or go straight back after you and give you a hiding; just to square the ledger like. He didn't fancy doing either as I recall. Never saw him again.'

Orla suddenly launched herself across the room and put Owen in a headlock. Owen pretended to defend himself against her onslaught but soon wrestled her onto his lap and put his arms around her waist.

'You're a bugger, Owen Stewart,' she chuckled at his most unexpected revelation. 'If that little shite had got away with my money, and I'd found out he was in cahoots with you, those front teeth of yours would also be missing by now. And who were those floosies you had in tow that night, Owen, my dearest? Pickpockets of a sort I suppose, or long-lost cousin's maybe?' Orla goaded him.

'Oh no, definitely not pickpockets,' a blushing Owen replied. 'And they certainly weren't my cousins. Nothing happened, really! Yes, I paid for their dinner, but when I refused to pay the ridiculous prices for their drinks, they got all shirty and dumped me. That's all, honest.'

Still sitting in Owen's lap, Orla continued her dissertation, talking at length about her teaching stint in Dorrigo, the tough life of the cedar gatherers, the unexpected astuteness of the bullock team drivers and their brave, loyal bullocks. When Orla tried to describe the beauty and ferocity of the Ebor Falls, she called upon Owen's support in case Jeanie and Frank thought she was exaggerating.

And, predictably, the unconventional way Orla had treated Owen on the night they first met at the Dorrigo dance made Jeanie and Frank chuckle. But their mirth quickly changed to shock and disappointment when Owen felt obliged to explain the unlawful reasons for the tight spot he found himself in that night. That revelation hurt Jeanie and Frank. But, they were desperately troubled when Orla took it upon herself to explain her 'middle of the road stance', and the subsequent shooting and disposal of the three bounty hunters.

'Please don't judge us. We were worth many hundreds of pounds to them... alive, *or dead!* We had no option. They levelled their guns on us first. Regardless, Owen's worth a lot more than that to me and Niall and, I dare say, to both of you. Please, try not to worry. There's no way the police can link us to those deaths, let alone find us. And there were definitely no witnesses.'

'Those blokes meant business, all right,' Owen interrupted. 'Without Orla's timely help, I'd probably be dead now, or in prison. But I give you all my word that I'll never return to a life outside the law. Mind you, I still don't agree with many of this colony's laws.'

After giving his parents a few moments to accept this, he asked Orla to continue her narration of the balance of the journey to Gympie. She certainly had the 'gift of the gab'. It was well after midnight when Orla and Owen finished the account of their experiences. A further fifteen minutes elapsed before anyone spoke.

'Oh, by the way Orla, Dad has made me an extremely generous offer. Are you interested in hearing it?'

'Yes, of course, please do tell.'

She listened intently as Owen explained the offer. 'I'll not be going anywhere for some time, my boyo. My travelling days are over, I reckon. And you'll not be repeating any of your past antics, either. Right?'

Owen then concentrated his full attention upon Orla. 'Not likely,' he said seriously. 'So, would you do me the honour of becoming my wife? It's not just you I love, Orla, I already think of Niall as my own son and being Niall Stewart removes any chance of him being recognised as another man's son. Besides, in some ways, I can relate to Ned, and believe I can help bring up his son the way he would have wanted it.'

'Oh, my darling boyo,' replied Orla with tears of pure joy streaming down her face. 'Of course, I'll marry you and I'll live with you to my dying day. But let's get properly settled first, eh?'

'Thought as much,' Owen replied mischievously. 'Then that's it, Mrs. O'Meara Kelly-Stewart... come here.' They hugged and kissed passionately.

The old couple's faces belied the suffering they were experiencing.

* * *

AS SHE CLIMBED INTO BED, Jeanie was sobbing, desperate to share her feelings with Frank.

'I feel sick and my head aches with worry. It's wonderful that we've got Owen back, and that he's met and fallen in love with Orla. But, oh God, Frank... they're both outlaws *and* murderers. How on earth do we handle this?'

Frank put his arm around her. 'I'm not sure, my love. But we're duty bound to protect our kin, regardless that God may disapprove.'

Jeanie stopped sobbing after a minute. 'As parents, I suppose we must begrudgingly accept the circumstances into which Orla and our son put themselves... and ultimately forgive them. But in truth, everyone's future happiness lays in our continued shielding of Niall. He deserves the chance to live a life free of either public accusation or family reprisal.'

Frank turned off the lamp, then leaned across and gently kissed Jeanie. 'You're right as usual, my dearest. Life must go on, eh?'

* * *

Departure day for Anne and James and their children arrived. Orla knew that the vast distance which separated these families, was frustrating, but it could easily be overcome. Wealth had its advantages even though time might be running out for Jeanie and Frank.

Orla joined everyone at the woodpile where they sat and drank ginger beer, taking it in turns to tell the odd story, stretching the truth for effect, extracting bouts of boisterous, happy laughter. But Orla sensed an undertow of sadness; each person, for their own reasons, would genuinely miss the company of the others.

Under the pretext of checking on the kids, Owen took his leave so that Frank and James could talk privately about company business. Orla and Jeanie joined Owen and they wandered about the homestead gardens chatting about the future. Anne volunteered to prepare a light lunch for everyone. Orla noticed that Niall and Michael had only half-heartedly continued their exploration of the creek and were now sitting, intermittently chatting and listlessly throwing the occasional stone.

The Cobb and Co stagecoach arrived at about two o'clock in the afternoon. The coach driver guaranteed James they would arrive safely in Brisbane Town late the following day, and in plenty of time for his family to catch the designated steamer to Adelaide. But from then on, they would be at the mercy of the weather and the ship's crew to minimise any delays at the ports the steamship company had scheduled for stopovers along the way.

Firm handshakes, hugs, kisses, and tears preceded the stagecoach's departure: wild waving and final shouts of farewell followed as it disappeared into the heat-haze.

STEPFATHER

& SON

44

―――――

The following day Frank introduced Owen to Robert D'Angelese, then left them to get acquainted. Robert took Owen on a tour of the entire mining operation, starting at the ore body face and finishing at a secured underground bunker where their precious gold ingots were stored.

'Because the bushrangers are so damned unpredictable, every consignment to Brisbane leaves under armed police escort,' Robert explained. 'Anyway, before the gold goes into the Treasury vaults of the Colony of Queensland, each ingot is again weighed, stamped and recorded. Only then do we get paid.'

'The tour was a bit daunting at first, nevertheless, it *was* bloody interesting,' Owen declared as they left the bunker. 'Mate, you've got all those processes and machinery and the men working brilliantly. And you've obviously gone to a lot of trouble with the cage grab systems and the ventilation to make things safe. There's so bloody much to keep an eye on and then there's all that maintenance. Good God, Robert, how do you it?'

'Thanks for the compliment, Owen, but remember, I've been doing this sort of thing most of my life.'

When Frank, Robert, and Owen met for lunch, Frank solicited his son's impressions. Half an hour lapsed before Owen eventually sat back and took a breath.

Frank took the opportunity to speak. 'Well, mining seems to have triggered your interest after all, son. I'm really glad, but regardless, I've decided to call it quits in six months time.'

Robert felt his mouth open involuntarily. His shoulders slumped. 'I must confess I'm disappointed that you're snatching it, Frank,' said Robert. 'But, your decision *is* overdue... you know that, eh?'

'Yes, we've been a damn good team, Robert, but now listen carefully. I want to explain my succession plans.' Robert and Owen hung on Frank's every word.

'If I understand your very generous considerations, you've just made me a very rich man, for which I'm humbled and extremely grateful,' Robert responded. 'But, Frank, you'll have to clarify Owen's role for me. Respectfully, he knows nowt about controlling ore quantity, balancing resources and manpower or maintaining equipment reliability. His inexperience *is* a problem and that's inconsistent with him being an equal contributor and beneficiary. He just can't be expected to make correct decisions overnight.' Robert knew that if things didn't work out, he could rely on Frank to put them right. But Robert respected Frank's judgment. 'I've got to say, though, Owen's interest seems genuine, and he's bloody quick on the uptake, I'll give him that.'

'Look, Rob, there's no way I'll ever overrule or question your decisions,' said Owen, who'd remained quiet until that point. 'You're running the show magnificently. And there's no way I'd feel comfortable assuming Dad's role unless I've first lived and breathed the entire mining operation.

'Starting tomorrow, how about you get me working at the ore face, and then decide the best progression of jobs that I should take on, and for how long. There's to be no favours and no special considerations. Only when you reckon I'm up to the mark, let Dad have his turn at teaching me the ropes. Can we do all that in six months? I'd really like to have a go at it, Rob, but for heaven's sake, if I don't measure up, tell me and I'll move on. No recriminations, no arguing, right?'

'Sounds straightforward enough to me,' Robert answered, much relieved by Owen's upfront and pragmatic declaration. 'I can see that Frank's happy with that arrangement, so it's welcome aboard, mate.

'Report to my office at six thirty tomorrow morning and I'll introduce you to the boys. They'll get you started soon enough, but may I suggest you get a good night's sleep.' The three men shook hands on their pact.

45

Owen threw himself into each new role. Initially, his thighs, back, and shoulders ached fiercely, his hands developed huge blisters and he struck his head several times before adjusting to the height in the tunnels. He also openly admitted his fears of close confinement but the miners taught him how to overcome claustrophobia. And he made mistakes, nothing lethal, but potentially so. Veiled threats not to repeat his mistakes had to be taken seriously. Lessons were learnt.

From the mine management perspective, Owen's formal education in England made his progression to that responsible role much easier than expected. But Owen still worked damned hard, though, now with his mind.

Orla and Niall were eventually given a grand tour of the mining facility. The oppressive heat, the incessant noise from the ore stamper batteries, and the pungent fumes from the retort operations left them both glad to be leaving.

Happily, Owen and Robert were to get on extremely well together as the next four years slipped by.

* * *

DURING THE EARLY months of Owen's apprenticeship, Robert introduced him to his friend, Andrew Fisher, simply Andy to his family and friends.

Owen liked Andy from day one. He was an imposing Scot, who Owen guessed was roughly his own age. After arriving in Australia he briefly worked in various coalfields before moving to the Gympie goldfields. Andy was a political activist, genuinely interested in the welfare and fair treatment of workers. It seemed only natural that the paths of Andy, Robert, and Owen would cross: their shared concerns translated into fewer accidents, increased output, and even a miner's share in the company's prosperity.

* * *

BUT ORLA WAS RESTLESS. Whilst she loved her one-on-one time with Niall, her participation in the mining operations was minimal. And so, she confronted Owen.

'I've been thinking, my love. Correct me if I'm wrong, but there are three realities facing our life here. The first is that our gold keeps Gympie growing. Second, our gold is keeping the Colony of Queensland from bankruptcy, and third, the gold will inevitably run out. Right? And,' she paused, 'if we don't diversify, and soon, Gympie will become a ghost town.'

'Agreed,' replied Owen. 'So, what have you got in mind?'

'Gympie will soon be connected to the main north-south rail line and we're surrounded by vast forests of cedar. That's our future... I'm convinced!'

'There's more, right? Well, go on, spit it out.'

'The rail link to Brisbane's the key,' Orla continued excitedly. 'And it's likely to be completed within the next five years. The timing's perfect. I reckon it'll take all of four years to complete what I've got in mind, at which stage we'll be able to scale up our operations to take advantage of an ever increasing demand for what we'll be offering.'

'For God's sake, Orla, what exactly are you proposing?' replied

Owen, feeling exasperated and genuinely excited in equal measure. 'Go on, I'm listening.'

'Bear with me, boyo. The first step is to apply for a twenty-year agreement with the Forestry Department. If we're successful, we'd be entitled to clear-fell cedar in places allocated only to us. But we'll have to finance the felling and removing of the timber. We won't own the land, and we'll be expected to replant native trees suitable for Queensland's Rail Authority.'

'Bloody hell, girl, you've certainly been doing your homework,' quipped Owen. 'But you haven't finished, have you?'

'No. Now, the centrepiece of my plans,' replied Orla, fidgeting in her excitement to reveal the details. 'The Rail Authority is happy for anyone to develop the land adjacent to their proposed freight handling yards here in Gympie. So... I reckon we should build a huge timber mill right there. And that, my dear boyo, will enable us to load our sized and finished timber straight onto their flat-deck carriages. No double handling, and fast delivery to Brisbane.

'We'll use traditional harvesting and haul-out techniques,' Orla ploughed on. 'But the handling and feeding of logs into the mill will be done using the best and most modern steam driven winches and cranage systems. And steam will power the latest high speed circular saws.'

'You're bloody amazing, Orla,' Owen replied, finally able to get in a word. 'The magnitude of this'll test our finances for sure. But, we're not exactly destitute, eh?

'It's a marvellous and grand plan, indeed, and definitely possible. Look, I'll be honest, Orla, I'm getting tired of the monotony and predictability of the mining operations. I want to spend more time with you and Niall, and I crave to work outdoors again. Damn it! Let's do it! I'm sure we can persuade Dad to back us.'

Orla threw her arms around Owen. 'Thank you, my darling boyo. But, we'll need someone to set up and run the whole shebang. No prizes for guessing who I've got in mind.'

The next day, Orla invited Frank and Jeanie, and Rob and his wife to their cottage for dinner. Following a magnificent meal, Orla and

Owen enthusiastically laid out their plans. Cost estimates, timing, and the likely return on their investment were tabled for all to analyse and criticise. The job of Chief Engineer was offered to Rob, and the proposition of financial backing, if they needed it, was put to Frank.

Frank was the first to respond. 'My God, you've got a bloody good head on your shoulders, girl, and you've certainly been busy. What you're proposing is a truly awe-inspiring opportunity; bloody exciting, actually. I'm confident you'll not squander it, so my finances are at your disposal.'

'I acknowledge the honour inherent in your offer,' said Rob, in a more measured and reserved tone. 'But I need more time to think about the plan and to go over the figures again. I'll give you my decision within the next three days. I'm not ruling anything in, or out, at this stage.'

Two days later when Orla joined Rob and Owen for lunch, Rob suggested they all go for a walk. They strolled in silence for ten minutes before Rob finally spoke.

'I'm in! But first, we need to sort out a few things.'

'Yes!' Orla and Owen yelled in jubilation. Orla felt incredibly relieved that Rob was on board, and equally determined that any of his demands would be met.

'My first condition is that we sell the mine. In my estimation, the mine has a life of no more than four years at peak production. I believe we should convince Frank to put it up for sale in about two years' time. It could take another year or two to find a suitable buyer, by which time we'll be close to completing the mill.

'We won't necessarily be selling a dud mine,' Robert suggested, but then added with a tongue-in-cheek expression. 'Just one with *untold* potential.

'My second condition is that I want to retire in about six or seven year's time. That'll limit how long I'll continue to work for you after we dispose of the mine. But, I suggest we continue to fulfil our present jobs as normal as possible for the next two years. Then during the third and fourth years, we promote the most deserving individuals and train them to succeed us. That'll be a sure sweetener for any prospective new owner.'

Owen interrupted. 'Strewth, this bloke's as cunning as you, Orla.'

'From today, if we're in agreement, I'll begin the engineering design,' Robert continued enthusiastically. 'You and Orla can start thinking about recruitment, establishing our markets, and getting agreements in place for railing out our finished timber.

'It won't be easy sailing, you know. Starting from scratch, we'll encounter problems you could never envisage. But, I agree, this *is* an exciting venture. The potential for it to be highly profitable over many years is great, and the operation will undoubtedly benefit Gympie.

'I've got to emphasise, though, we all need to work fast. And *don't* broadcast what we're doing. By my calculations, if we can be at or near to full capacity in four years time, it'll take our present opposition roughly the same time to scale up their mills to match our operation — that's *if* they can arrange the financing! By which time, my dear friends, I'll have my feet well and truly up.

'I've got just one other condition. I want a guarantee that my financial position is never compromised. So Owen, get on to your brother-in-law, James, in Adelaide, straight away. I'd feel better knowing this whole operation is underwritten by a bank. That burden shouldn't be on Frank and Jeanie alone. We also need to get into Andy Fisher's ear. He'll be an invaluable ally.'

Smiling happily, Owen enthusiastically shook Rob's hand. Orla hugged Robert and kissed him on the cheek.

'Consider it all done, and thanks, Rob. We could never have tackled this without you.'

That night Owen and Orla lay exhausted, sharing the glorious aftermath of orgasm and the euphoria of the bold, exciting changes about to unfold in their lives.

46

Now six years old, Niall was determined to learn. His speech was well advanced, enabling him to question things, which he often did — and which tested Orla's patience. Plus, he could be quite cheeky, never missing an opportunity to mimic something learnt from his school friends, like farting loudly when Orla or another adult was talking.

His reading ability and comprehension were equal to that of children several years older and his numeracy skills were so advanced he won prizes in competitions against much older children. Although he didn't generally show off, he tended to talk quite loudly and too fast, which infuriated his friends. His normal manner, however, was usually relaxed, polite, and cooperative and he joined his friends in most activities in the innocent pursuit of having fun.

When he was nearly eight that sense of fun also gave him his first taste of real punishment. Several older boys coerced him into experimenting with smoking. Eyes stinging and gagging on the hot smoke from his first cigarette, he threw the butt away in disgust, not caring where it landed. It was only after he staggered from the scrub, spluttering and wearing the jeers of his worldly mates, that they all saw billowing smoke and then flames shoot up through the undergrowth.

Luckily, the fire was quickly extinguished, but Niall knew he was in for it.

'Bloody hell, Niall, I thought you had a bit more sense than that,' Orla growled when she learnt of his complicity. 'You should be ashamed of yourself and I should tan your backside, boyo.' But after a few moments of reflection she sent Niall to his room, and then rode into Gympie.

When Orla returned, she sat in the kitchen and rolled ten fat cigarettes. Niall was then ordered to smoke them all... one after the other. Cheekily accepting his punishment, Niall commenced smoking with a bemused look on his face. But, his whole world changed at cigarette number four. His head was spinning and he now felt truly unwell. He never made it to number six, throwing up all over the kitchen floor before Orla could usher him outside. Niall staggered to his room and failed to reappear until mid-morning the following day.

He later confided to Orla he'd been stupid to be so easily led and apologised for throwing up in the kitchen. His vow never to smoke again followed shortly afterwards.

Whilst Niall was growing rapidly and enjoying the rough and tumble of the schoolyard, on the day of his tenth birthday he had his first serious fight.

Niall had a competitive nature and, being athletic, tended to play with older children. On this occasion, he doggedly, but fairly, challenged a boy called Allan in the quest to win a race to catch a ball. Niall won the race, but as he was about to turn to throw the ball back, Allan, still running at full speed, plunged his shoulder squarely into Niall's unprotected back. The force of the contact felled Niall, momentarily stunning him and almost winding him.

With hands firmly clenched into fists and his face contorted in a menacing grin, Allan towered threateningly over Niall. Niall sprang to his feet, staring in bewilderment. But again, Allan vigorously shoved Niall backwards onto the ground. Niall recovered quickly, leapt to his feet and stepped forward — this time *really* eyeballing the older boy — and with his own hands now firmly made into fists.

At that moment there was an odd change in Allan's demeanour.

What he'd seen in Niall's eyes frightened the hell out of him: they had an intense reddish hue that he correctly guessed meant one thing. He stepped back, dropping his hands. A ghost of fear flittered across his face. He was no longer certain, despite being bigger and older, whether he now really wanted to continue the fight.

Niall was on the verge of throwing his first punch, when two other boys attacked him from behind. One put him in a headlock while the other helped toss him onto the ground. All three then set upon Niall, kicking and punching. Luckily a teacher noticed the commotion and soon broke up the fight, but not before Allan spat in Niall's face.

That night, a somewhat disillusioned Niall, explained why his clothes were ripped and why he had skinned knees, a cut lip, sore ribs, a sore nose, and a black eye. At first, Orla wanted to confront the parents of all three boys but Owen believed he had a better idea. Niall received his first boxing lessons.

Owen also taught him wrestling manoeuvres guaranteed to inflict really hurtful and debilitating results. They practiced these moves and tactics every night for the next three weeks and Owen was genuinely impressed with Niall's speed, strength, and natural boxing ability. Owen reminded himself, *I shouldn't really be too surprised, after all his old man's been immortalized as one of the best bare-knuckle fighters this colony's ever seen.*

Owen talked to Niall about using these new-found skills only for self defence — unless, of course, a one-on-one confrontation was unavoidable. Owen didn't have to wait long for his words to bear fruit.

After dinner, about a week later, Niall quietly confided in Owen. 'Sorry I was late home tonight, Dad, but you remember that boy who got his mates to give me a hiding? Well, we sort of met up on the way home and I invited him to throw a punch at me before his mates arrived. I explained it should be easy for him, being so much bigger and stronger than me, but he sort of got all fidgety and looked around a lot. S'pose he was lookin' for his mates.

'Well, he wouldn't start anything. All he did was walk backwards so that I couldn't hang one on him. Finally, he just ran away. But before he did, I reminded him that I knew where he lived, and if he wanted, I'd come over on Saturday and get him to show his parents how tough he *isn't.*'

'That's my boy!' said Owen proudly and gave him a quick but gentle punch on the shoulder. He then roared with laughter but eventually offered Niall some more advice. 'A coward's life is hell on earth. Hope the boy realises that and grows up real soon. But listen, if he and his mates ever try anything again, let me know first... not your Mum. I'll then sort things out, once and for all.'

But Owen's intervention was never called upon. Allan initially gave Niall a wide berth but about a month later he approached Niall and offered his hand in apology. They never became close mates.

* * *

BY THE END OF 1891, Orla's plans were progressing well. Their cedar forest allotments were secured. In readiness for the arrival of her felling and haulage crews and their families, a small base camp comprising fourteen huts, a general store, a blacksmithing business, and a bakery was nearing completion.

Orla shrewdly and quickly found suitable workers through Joyce, the teacher, in Dorrigo. Orla offered significantly higher wages, a one-off relocation bonus, free accommodation for three years, and a guaranteed place for their children in one of the two schools in Gympie.

To her delight, Ken the bullocky, plus six local axemen she'd met and befriended in Dorrigo, soon arrived. Other axemen, sawyers, bullockies, and mill hands came from Bellingen. Everyone settled in quickly and happily, all keen for felling to commence, for this was their gold... red cedar.

Boundaries were soon defined, cut lines pegged, and haulage trails surveyed and cleared. Bullocks that Orla and Owen purchased during the previous two years were placed into training and soon the valleys were echoing to the sound of whips and the colourful urgings of the teamsters.

Although he denied any involvement in either the rapid and highly profitable sale of the mine, or in the purchase of the land close to the proposed railhead, Frank had clearly exerted his influence in some way. Rather than question his intervention, Orla and Owen gladly accepted the outcome. And so, preparatory to harvesting and arrival of the first cedar logs, Rob forged ahead with building the timber mill, and clearing and levelling the surrounding area for the log stacks.

It was an exciting time as the steam generating plant, the power winches, cranes, and massive circular saws arrived and were installed. On the day the last of the saw drive-belts were fitted, news reached them that the rail-link from Brisbane was now only ten miles from Gympie.

* * *

NIALL WAS interested in the developments going on around him and was often privy to decisions taken by his parents. He enjoyed the jobs Rob found for him, often working with tradesmen. He eagerly demonstrated his willingness to attempt anything, and finished every task he was given.

Niall was also aware his parents were encouraging his involvement, but they ensured he was only paid in keeping with his effort. That was a deliberate character forming decision and their 'reward for effort' principle was not lost on him. Money wasn't what motivated him though; he simply wanted to help.

* * *

NIALL ALWAYS ACCOMPANIED his parents when they visited the cedar gatherers' camp. Everyone there liked him and he knew them all, even their nicknames. And, like most, he loved watching the giant cedar trees being felled.

But what Niall loved most were Sundays and religious holidays when he rode with his parents into the coastal wilderness. They hiked through rainforest and woodlands of Banksia and scribbly gum, and swam in the lakes and waterways.

Camping overnight gave them more time to relax, to inhale the bush fragrances and just listen to the birds. Owen occasionally shot a kangaroo for meat, and together they robbed native beehives for honey to sweeten their tea.

On one particularly memorable trip, when exploring further east than ever before, they came upon tall coastal sand cliffs. These cliffs ran north and south, apparently unbroken, but Owen soon found a path, which led them down onto a pristine beach. Viewed from the beach, the cliffs formed a giant easel with vertical coloured layers, from black to pastel pinks and orange. Set against an azure cloudless sky, the cliffs were a truly magnificent sight.

They set up camp on the beach, raced their horses flat out along the waterline and swam in the gentle, cooling surf. Orla then organised a shooting competition, starting with fixed targets. Niall was confident and a surprisingly good shot with his mother's pistols. He was also uncannily accurate with her rifle. Next, Orla hung a can from a tree and set it oscillating, a seemingly impossible target. However, with her patient instruction, Niall hit the can with his tenth shot. Owen needed twelve shots; Orla just one!

Dinner that evening was their favourite; grilled kangaroo and potatoes cooked in the ashes of the fire. As night fell they were lulled to sleep by the soft rattling sound as each wave flooded up onto the beach, and the gentle hissing as it collapsed and then retreated back to the ocean.

In the false dawn of the next morning, Orla and Niall walked north along the beach for several miles, often holding hands and sometimes racing each other along the leading edge of a wave to be the first to reach the point where it completed its frothing ascent up the sloping beach.

As the sun peeked over the rim of the Pacific Ocean, they sat shoulder to shoulder and watched the dark cloak of night as it was replaced by a soft mauve, and then a golden blush that heralded the new day. They quietly discussed thoughts about the future and of

happy events in the past, and then suddenly, somehow it surfaced —
bushrangers!

Orla turned slowly to gaze proudly upon her son. He was
approaching twelve, tall and well built for his age, not yet a man, but
resourceful, strong-willed and caring. The moment Orla dreaded was
upon her. She was certain Niall was now old enough to learn the
truth about his father, but nevertheless, she thought, *this will really
test his true feelings for me and Owen*. With equal certainty Orla knew it
would be cruel to continue withholding that news... to continue
denying him the opportunity to also love his real father.

Orla quietly related the story of her arrival in England, where she
had first met the Stewarts, and how subsequently she had met and
lived with some wonderful friends on a farm near Wangaratta, in the
Colony of Victoria.

'You mean the McIntyres,' Niall said. 'You've mentioned them
often, Mum, and their kids.' But he suddenly became alert and very
curious when Orla started relating a story about another young
woman who apparently lived on that farm.

Tears streamed down his mother's cheeks as she talked about
how, twelve or so years ago, that girl met and fell hopelessly in love
with a tall handsome man who also loved her deeply.

'Niall, that man was strong willed — just like you — and a leader.
He was also generous and caring, and he somehow retained his good
humour despite persecution of his family and his friends by the
authorities. His name was Edward, Ned to his friends, and his family
name was Kelly,' Orla sobbed.

Niall sat in stunned silence. The girl his mother spoke of... was, in
fact, *his mother*! And the man in her story was Ned Kelly, the
armoured bushranger he'd been taught about at school... the bloke
who'd been captured in a shootout with police at Glenrowan, and
later hanged in Melbourne. The sudden reality of his mother's story
struck Niall... *hard*.

'I know this'll be difficult for you Niall, but please listen to me,'
Orla continued before Niall could say anything. 'You've nothing to
fear. I'm not ashamed of my love for your father, nor should you be

ashamed of him. Very few people know about your birthright to the Kelly name, but those who do have given me their oath never to betray that knowledge and are sworn to silence. There's so much I need to tell you. Do you want me to continue?'

Niall nodded, smiled, and then put his arm firmly around his mother's waist. In relief, Orla placed her head on his shoulder. As the sun rose steadily Orla told her story without embellishment, answering Niall's questions as she proceeded; from her unexpected meeting and falling in love with Ned, to meeting and living with the other Kelly gang boys, and about the unquestioning friendship of Tom Lloyd and the poignant sacrifice made by the lovely, Kate.

She spoke emotionally of other dear friends; Charlie and Ong, the old Chinese gold-prospecting brothers who lived in a fortress-like shack cut into the side of a mountain; two incredible men who shared Ned's dreams for political freedom.

Niall listened attentively as Orla described the Buckland Valley where the brothers lived. He thought it funny the way that the brothers kept their beer cold — by suspending their bottles on strings into the depths of a deep pool in the river that ran right past the front door of their fortress.

Niall also learnt of his father's dream for a country free from the injustices of overzealous British rule, why Ned responded with such a deadly plan, and why people would subsequently find it difficult to accept the legitimacy of such a response without having lived through his father's torment.

'Niall, there are some other things you need to know about me,' said Orla taking a deep breath. 'But first, you must give me your word you'll never tell anyone what I am about to say. Only the McIntyre's, Owen, and Jeanie and Frank know about these things. Perhaps, long after the six of us leave this earth, then you *can* tell my story, but choose wisely who you tell, promise?'

As Orla explained her predicament, Niall looked at her, his expression not displaying disgust, but rather, one of love and trust. Niall sensed his mother's relief as she unburdened her secrets. He knew her well enough to know she was passionate about fair play despite her past tough times. He also understood her innate need to defend herself and property. Owen had taught him that, too. Niall smiled knowingly, understanding the risk any person took if they underestimated his beautiful mother. Nevertheless, the revelation she'd killed four times was a shock to him.

By mid-morning, Orla was spent.

'Thanks, Mum, I'm not ashamed of you,' said Niall. 'I'm so proud you're my mum, and I'll never speak about what you've done. I want you to promise me something, though. If I ever want to hear more about my real dad, you'll tell me. And don't worry, I promise I'm not planning on becoming a bushranger.'

In relief, as much as delight at Niall's sense of humour, Orla laughed until more tears ran down her cheeks. As they headed back to their camp, they could see Owen in the distance riding to meet them.

As mother and son strolled along the beach, Orla said, 'I'll tell you more about Boss Boy, later on. He did more than just get us to Gympie, you know. He's a once in a lifetime horse, that boyo.'

'Bloody hell, you two, I thought you'd done a runner on me,' Owen yelled in feigned annoyance as he dismounted from Boss Boy. 'Are you both all right?'

'Yeah, Dad, we're fine,' Niall replied as he stepped forward and put his arm around Owen's waist. 'You never had anything to worry about. Besides, Mum's got her Colts with her. Bushrangers beware, eh?'

Orla smiled and winked at Owen.

Just how lucky can a bloke get? Owen contentedly thought to himself as he walked alongside his son, and gorgeous wife.

47

———————

'Friends of yours, luv?' Owen asked as he gestured with his chin towards the cliff tops as they approached their beach camp. 'They've been up there since first light, and there's about eight or ten of 'em.' Sure enough, there stood a group of aboriginals dressed in traditional possum and kangaroo skins. All were holding spears, though not in a threatening way.

Orla stared in disbelief. 'Sweet Jesus, I think I *do* know these people. Surely that can't be, we're hundreds of miles from where we met. Remember, I told you about a drunken good-for-nothing who was about to rape a young native girl? Well, it's that girl's mob, I'm bloody certain of it!'

'That defenceless bloke you shot?' Owen replied sarcastically. 'Yes, I remember, but why are they *here*?'

'There's only one way to find out, boyo. Come on you two, let's go and have a yarn with 'em. If it's who I think it is, we're in no danger. They're good people.'

The horses worked hard to ascend the collapsing, unforgiving sandy track leading to the ridge. Turning north, they followed an animal track that headed in the direction where the mob had been standing. At a clearing, which extended to the cliff edge they saw many human footprints, but there wasn't a soul in sight. They dismounted and draped their horse's reins over nearby scrub. Following Orla's example, they all then sat in the centre of the clearing.

They waited in silence. A few minutes later, Boss Boy whinnied. As if by magic, and no more than twenty yards away, ten dark figures appeared in the scrub. While placing a restraining hand on Owen's shoulder, Orla stood. She then strode confidently over to the mob.

'Lahni, is that you?'

An attractive, semi-naked woman a few years younger than Orla stepped forward. She was accompanied by a tall black man about fifty-five, of confident, proud bearing. A skinny, pubescent girl followed.

They walked up to Orla. 'It really good we meet again, Orla. But no surprise really, the *Cooloola* spirits guide Lahni to you.'

The women embraced warmly. 'This my husband, Jimmie. He good man. I tell 'im 'bout Orla, the woman who make us all laugh after killing that one terrible man... and fix Lahni's arm. You remember who is this beautiful girl then, Orla?'

Sinking onto one knee, Orla looked into the young girl's bright brown eyes then hugged her warmly and replied. 'Oh yes, I know this girl. She will one day be even lovelier than her mother. How are you, Ruthie? My word, you've grown.

'You're a lucky man, Jimmie,' Orla then said, offering her hand to the black man. 'No wonder Lahni thinks you're a bit of all right. You're more handsome than my bloke.'

Jimmie chuckled and beamed a warm smile. 'I'm spoken for Orla, but it's real good to meet you,' he replied in near perfect English. 'Lahni, she often talk 'bout you, you know. And thanks for helping my Lahni.'

'That's in the past, Jimmie, but I'm glad I stopped and met your family.' Orla then called to Owen and Niall. 'Well, don't sit around all day. Come and meet my friends.'

Orla first introduced Owen to Lahni. She was initially a bit bashful but with Owen's welcoming words, she was soon at ease.

There was no such reservedness between Owen and Jimmie. They shook hands warmly.

'It's really good to meet you, Jimmie. Orla tells me you worked down on the Murray River in Victoria. That's a bloody long way from here, mate. I've never been there. You must tell me all about it.'

When Orla introduced Niall to Lahni, he politely shook her hand. 'G'day Lahni, it's nice to see you again, but to be honest, I don't remember you that well.' He then turned and shook hands with Jimmie. 'It's nice to meet you, Jimmie. Gee you're tall. I think you're even taller than my dad.'

Jimmie laughed. 'And it's beaut meeting you, young fella. By the look of you, you'll end up being tallest of all.'

Niall then turned to face Ruthie.

'Niall, do you remember, Ruthie?' Orla asked quickly, realising she'd neglected to introduce the two children. 'You played with her a long time ago.'

'To be honest, no, not really,' replied Niall as he looked carefully at the black girl. 'Ruthie, do you remember me?'

Ruthie had averted her gaze and seemed shy. However, she suddenly raised her head proudly. 'Don't you be silly bugger with me,' she said defiantly. 'I'm much younger than you. But it's good to meet your mum again... and you, I suppose.'

After more introductions, the adults sat in a circle and talked happily. However, Niall and Ruthie climbed onto Boss Boy and rode back to the beach. Niall gave Boss Boy his head and they galloped at full speed along the firm sand near the water's edge, their shrieks of laughter rising faintly above the rumble of the surf. After about a mile, Niall reined in Boss Boy, dismounted, helped Ruthie down and then took off his boots.

With Boss Boy tagging along behind, they headed back to the campsite, chatting animatedly. They examined shells and dead marine creatures that had washed up onto the beach, and occasionally ventured up to their thighs into the foaming surf.

When they arrived back at the beach camp, they were met by a near exhausted and very angry Jimmie. 'First you nick off not telling us where you goin', and then you damn near get killed!' Jimmie yelled furiously while pointing and jabbing his finger at the surf. 'Look! This side them waves, right there. You didn't see them bastards?'

Startled, the two children spun around and looked in the direction Jimmie was pointing. There, cruising along a shore-break channel were four sinister shapes, each about twelve or thirteen feet long. Ruthie gasped in shock, and then spun to look at Niall.

'Shiiite, was that bloody lucky, or what?' gasped an equally shocked Niall. 'But how did *you* know they were there, Jimmie?'

'I was up there stretching my legs and talking with your father, when I noticed 'em,' Jimmie replied. 'I reckoned you hadn't seen 'em, so I bolt down here to stop you going back in the water.'

'You made it just in time,' Niall replied sheepishly. 'We *were* just about to go swimming. If we'd been another fifty yards up the beach, we would've been dead ducks. Thanks, Jimmie.'

Just then, Owen arrived on the beach, puffing heavily.

'Jimmie saved us for sure, Dad,' Niall announced quickly, while pointing to the now almost stationary sharks.

'He's a good man, all right,' Owen replied between deep breaths. 'There's much about Jimmie you'll like, son.' First, Owen, then Niall, shook Jimmie's hand in gratitude.

The families camped together on the beach for another two days. The men and children went fishing in a nearby freshwater lake, caught several plump eels and found dozens of mussels. They also shot two kangaroos. More importantly, their absence provided the two young women some most welcome privacy and gave Orla the opportunity to solve some mysteries.

The most intriguing of these was how the tribe knew where to find Orla. Lahni's comment about the *Cooloola* *spirits* when they met two days ago was said earnestly and with such natural conviction.

'I thought you were from the south son walkabout in that land. So how come you're here?'

'No, Orla, you misunderstand. We were not on traditional walkabout. We were forced from our homeland. That be here! All matters between unfriendly tribe up north, and the much increase number of whites in our land, cause many fights. All caused by that same tribe stealing a white woman many years ago. That woman she be rescued, but deaths on both sides happen. Our homeland it become much dangerous.'

'Yes, I read about that somewhere. But go on, Lahni, I'm listening.'

'We peaceful mob, Orla, but the whites they real angry. They reckon we part of that other mob, but they wrong. They not listen to reason or want trust us. Anyway, they keep chasing and shoot at us. All very sad.

'We much value life, so we move far away, 'bout fifteen years ago. That nearly kill us. Our land very special to us. Other places just not the same. We were dying inside. Not long after we meet you, we finally decide it be time to return to our traditional land. Far better we die here than in some strange place not belong us. Luckily, it seems people here getting along better now.'

That explained how the small family group knew this region. It was their home, but it didn't explain how their 'spirits' could know where to find Orla.

Orla probed... and Lahni replied fervently. '*Cooloola*, it be our wind spirit. It being our word for sound the wind makes when it blow through special trees in our land. Wind spirit it talks to us about many things. White people not understand these things. It tell Lahni many months ago you nearby. It tell me only three days ago you living amongst us and right here in this place. You much honour us Orla by visiting our land, and those two men of yours be always welcome here.'

Orla nodded politely, not with understanding but in acceptance and awe, at how this could be. To press Lahni further would only offend, so Orla changed the subject.

'Hey Lahni, that white-fella I killed. You never did tell me what your men did with him. You told me that an eagle took the body, but I doubt that. You also said he would go where no spirit will take him.'

'Oh, him? No, I joke 'bout eagle, you should know that, Orla. But I not make joke 'bout spirits. That white-fella, he one bad person. Had nothing in his heart for us black people. Our spirit people never take him. In your religion, you would say he can go rot in hell,' Lahni continued, all rather matter-of-factly, but then added with a mischievous look on her face. 'For sure, he go to hell... but did rot in chimney first.'

'Righto, I give up,' asked a perplexed Orla. 'What's this about a chimney?'

Lahni was now chuckling to herself at Orla's bewilderment. Staring straight into her friend's eyes, Lahni replied, 'You not remember the surrounding country where it happen? It were flat, few trees, and many rocks. But one old farmhouse it be nearby, all falling down 'cept for stone chimney. You remember now?'

Vaguely the image created by Lahni impressed itself upon Orla's memory... then all of a sudden, yes; there it was, clear as a bell. Obviously the tribesmen, unable to find anywhere to hide the dead man's body, had struck upon the novel idea of dropping him down the old farmhouse chimney.

'Well I'll be buggered; you're a cunning lot. But it's actually very funny you know. What if the next people who occupy that house clean the chimney and find his body. I bet they'll be hoping it wasn't Father Christmas!'

Both women laughed riotously, but Lahni less so. She understood the intended humour well enough, but she also knew there was no such farmhouse on that windswept landscape.

* * *

As Orla, Owen, and Niall prepared to head for home the following day, Lahni took Orla aside and said again with conviction. 'We take your family into our tribe. You all now connected with our long history, so be proud of your beginning with us. And remember, if you need help in this short life, or in your dreamtime, you know you can always call upon me.

'Beware though, Orla, the *Cooloola* calls to me when I sleep... you must take great care. It be good having you all with us, but now I count the days before we meet again. Return to us soon, Orla.'

* * *

ORLA KNEW NOTHING OF TELEPATHY. But she did sometimes have dreams, which seemed to either contain information, or direction for her life; the type of dreams which she knew she'd never experienced prior to meeting Lahni and her family. And blissfully, like Orla, neither Owen nor Niall knew anything about hypnotism either. More enlightened persons — particularly many of those who had pioneered the opening of Australia's outback — never doubted these dual powers or the ability of most aboriginal tribes to pass those powers down from one generation to the next.

48

The heavens opened when they returned to Gympie. Orla watched in dismay as the rain pelted down, non-stop, for days. The Mary River was soon in full-flood and the countryside surrounding Gympie was inundated. Despite desperate efforts to deflect torrents from the gold mines, many were soon abandoned, a disaster for the community's economy. Large stock losses were also reported. Fortunately, the flood was likely to have only minimal impact upon the timber mill's scheduled completion.

'Do you remember I was reasonably certain this flood would hit us sooner rather than later?' Rob philosophically reminded Orla and Owen. 'The local blacks reckon flooding occurs every five or six years and brings new life to the 'gimpi gimpi' stinging grass that grows along the banks of the Mary. That flood threat was one of the reasons why I wanted Frank to sell off the mine. And Orla's idea to buy land near to the proposed rail head, and not be tempted to buy cheaper land on the river flats, was absolutely spot on.'

'Yes, you're both undeniable smart arses,' Owen joked.

But the water did have an impact on the cedar gathering operations. Haulage from the forest was curtailed, it being simply too muddy to expect even the strongest and bravest bullock team to work. Logs ready to be hauled across the river to the mill were swept downstream. Luckily, none were lost, but it took weeks after the floodwaters subsided before they could be retrieved. Logs brought to the mill several weeks previously were unaffected by the rain. They had already been stacked several levels high and chained together, a practice intended to minimize wood rot. Accordingly, the decision was taken to commence milling those logs and start assembly of their first orders before the new rail link to Brisbane was completed.

* * *

BY THE END of February 1892, the entire timber gathering, milling, and loading operation was functioning smoothly and near to full capacity. Payments for their first delivered orders were honoured promptly, and every worker received a bonus in recognition of their hard work and commitment to the mill's success.

Niall was now working full time at the mill, but arrangements were in place for him to attend a private school in Brisbane the following year. He'd be going on fourteen by then and was looking forward to the experience, even though he knew he would miss his parents and their camping breaks. Whilst Niall was already capable of fending for himself, Orla and Niall wanted him to complete this year at the mill by which time he'd have valuable skills — and some hard-earned money of his own to spend as he chose, when in Brisbane.

Niall visited the timber gatherer's base camp twice a week to distribute items previously ordered by the villagers, and to hand deliver their mail. Inevitably, he returned home with a new purchase list and outgoing mail to post.

The men at the timber mill became reliant upon his news of log tallies ready to be hauled to the mill. Any other useful news such as equipment faults, bullock illnesses or injuries — in fact, anything that might have an impact on the flow of cedar to the mill — Niall passed onto his parents.

Despite a busy routine, Niall and his parents planned several more camping trips. A trip to Brisbane was also looming; Niall needed to visit his chosen private school and make boarding arrangements. They were all looking forward to seeing 'the big smoke', and, if time permitted, which Orla insisted it would, they'd return to the fabulous beaches to the south and hopefully again meet the local aboriginal families with whom they'd previously spent such a memorable time.

* * *

ALTHOUGH THE MILL foreman had no means of checking the integrity of every link on every securing chain in the yard, it's unlikely he'd have acted to replace a suspect chain: chains just didn't break. Hidden deep within one of those trusted iron links lurked an imperfection. With the chain under tension, a fissure resulting from that flaw migrated to expose itself to the outside world.

The amount of water needed to penetrate that fissure, and thereby guarantee the triggering of the rusting process, was infinitesimally small. And that tiny amount of moisture — possibly even the very first drop of rain, which fell with the recent flooding rains — would eventually guarantee the destruction of that link.

* * *

LATE IN THE afternoon of March 9th 1894, Orla rode Boss Boy back to the mill after witnessing the loading of their largest consignment so far onto the train. She elected to tell Owen about the success of the loading first, rather than go directly home and relay the details to him later during dinner. Besides, she had some other exciting news: without doubt, at last, she was now pregnant.

Lost in those thoughts, she urged Boss Boy through the gates to the mill yards and headed towards the manager's office. Her chosen path took them behind the huge stack of cedar logs waiting to be fed onto the saw benches.

The sound made by the link as it shattered, was a short, energy packed 'clung'! As it flew apart, enormous tension was placed on the two remaining securing chains. Microseconds later, both of those chains flew apart. Their now loose ends thrashed viciously.

Orla, initially, heard nothing. Boss Boy did. But not recognizing its origin above the noise of the hungry saws, he didn't react. Orla glimpsed a movement. High up to her right the huge cedar stack collapsed. Massive logs headed towards her; coming with great speed...

'Move! Boss Boy! Move!' she screamed. Boss Boy jinked power-fully to the left.

It was too late. Realisation struck. Orla knew she was going to die. She screamed again: inexplicably, she heard nothing. She would have only heard the deadly collisions of logs as they charged over her. Her last memory of life before everything went blank, were beautiful smiling... then, gradually, fading faces. And, one last, poignant, almost silly thought flashed through her mind: *you were wrong, Joan... no guns!*

It is most unlikely that either Orla or Boss Boy lived through the initial impact. But, had they survived it, the trailing logs, which subse-quently rolled and bounced and ground their way over their unpro-tected bodies, would have guaranteed their deaths. No blame could be levelled at Boss Boy. He had still been strong, but he'd aged and his quick reflexes had regrettably deserted him years ago.

When the last log had spent its energy and come to rest, there was no sign of either Orla or Boss Boy. From the demise of the iron link to their hideous deaths, the entire event took no more than twenty seconds. The only sound, then, was the scream of circular saws.

Shocked, and powerless to act, Owen witnessed everything. He was standing on the office balcony waiting to greet Orla. A strange cold feeling grabbed his heart as the reality of those deadly few seconds took root. Disbelief quickly followed shock, his intended warning yell, a ragged hiss. Despair engulfed him. He sank to his knees and began shaking uncontrollably.

Faintly at first, a groan rumbled from deep within Owen's soul. It steadily grew in intensity. The scream that followed was one of hopeless, utter distress. 'Aaaahhh... God. Pleeease... no! Not Orla!'

Even above the ear-piercing racket made by the saws, most of the workers heard both the collapsing log stack — then shortly after, Owen's agonizing scream. They all ran into the yard to investigate and found Owen staring pitifully at the jumbled mass of logs.

Rob was quickly at Owen's side, realising immediately what just occurred. He put his arm around his mate's shoulders in an attempt to give some comfort, but Owen impatiently shrugged him away.

'Oh, dear God. How could something like this possibly happen? And why now... just as everything she planned is now a reality? How will I live without her, Rob? And Niall... how do I tell Niall?' Owen whispered. 'Please, get her out, mate... and spare no effort.'

Owen staggered away, a totally shattered man. Tears flowed unashamedly down his ashen face. The pain of his grief threatened to overwhelm him — a pain like none other he had ever experienced.

* * *

OWEN FOUND Niall at home but collapsed onto the kitchen floor before he could say anything. Niall helped his distraught father into a chair, but knew there was obviously something very, very wrong. As Owen stuttered a brief explanation of events, the anguish impaling him, found another victim. Niall looked disbelievingly into Owen's face.

'It can't be! She can't be dead. Please, Dad... tell me Mum's not dead!'

Owen sighed deeply expecting the look on his face would remove any doubt. Owen then took Niall in his arms. With great difficulty he explained in detail what he'd seen. Stepfather and son sobbed; their shared grief doing little to appease their broken hearts. They stayed in that embrace until Niall gently pulled away.

'But why Mum?' he whispered.

'I can't answer that question, son,' Owen replied. 'Wish I could, but I can't. It's just so bloody unfair. I've misjudged our God. Your mother sometimes did unexpected things, but she rid this earth of some very evil men. What she did wasn't evil in my book; she didn't deserve this as punishment.'

* * *

WORD of the accident travelled quickly. The Stewarts rushed to be with their son and grandson. During the following hours, people called by to convey their commiserations and to make genuine pledges of assistance if needed. Rob's wife stayed to help pacify the Stewarts and do what she could to comfort Owen and Niall. Jeanie, however, was devastated — and would probably never totally recover from the shock of losing her beautiful, dear friend.

Much later that night, Orla's body was eventually located. The mill workers worked tirelessly with ropes and chains and crowbars, and in so doing, took huge personal risk to secure chains and ropes around each unstable log.

By lantern light, Orla's mutilated body was grotesque. Rob quickly had her wrapped in a tarpaulin to save the workers any further distress. Those men who'd retrieved her body were sent home and told not to report to work for the next two days. Given the extreme lateness, Rob had little choice but to leave the gruesome task of preparing Orla for interment until first light.

* * *

BEYOND THE CIRCLE of light formed by the workers' lanterns, a group of dark figures stood motionless for two hours. That nobody knew they arrived was understandable, but why these people turned up was a fact known only to them.

* * *

INSTEAD OF GOING HOME, Rob decided to drive his cart into Gympie to notify both the doctor and the undertaker of the accident. Whilst the doctor was annoyed at the interruption to his sleep, Rob's no-nonsense demeanour made it obvious it would be useless to protest further. Besides, he'd known Orla professionally and was shocked by the terrible news. He explained to Rob it was necessary for him to examine her body and to formally record the cause, time, and date of her death. He assured Rob he would attend the scene at seven o'clock that morning.

'That's all right, I suppose,' agreed Rob. 'But believe me, doc, you don't want to see her,' he added, looking back over his shoulder as he walked into the night.

Rob called on the undertaker next. When shaken from his drunken sleep, the man was totally unforgiving of Rob's request for help. 'Piss off and call back in the morning,' he demanded.

By then Rob had enough. Unable to contain his rage, he grabbed the undertaker by the front of his jacket and slammed him up against the wall of his living room. A semblance of sobriety returned when the undertaker suddenly realised his tenuous position.

'Select a casket from the shed at the side of the house. I'll attend to matters as soon as I can in the morning.'

'Be at the mill by seven, or so help me God, I'll come back here and kick the be-Jeezus out of you,' Rob yelled.

Rob loaded a coffin onto his cart and then drove to Owen's cottage. Not surprisingly, Owen was awake and still in a tortured state. Rob explained what he'd done since Owen had left the mill, and tried to comfort his mate.

'Hold onto the image of her beautiful smiling face and her cheeky grin,' Rob said as compassionately as he could, knowing it would do neither Owen nor Niall any good to view Orla's broken body. Rob made no effort to control his own tears. 'Think of her achievements and, above all mate, think of her love for you and Niall.'

They agreed Rob should leave his horse harnessed on the cart and tethered in the cottage's accommodation paddock, and meet again at six o'clock. Finally, they shook hands and embraced vigorously. Owen then walked dejectedly up the front steps of his cottage and disappeared inside. Rob walked briskly back to his own home, oblivious to the night's chill.

Sleep eluded Owen. He dressed and went outside, determined to fulfil an urgent need to hold his woman one last time and to say his farewell, fearing his own death from heartbreak if he didn't. As if in a dream, he then drove Rob's cart to the now very quiet timber mill, his arrival coinciding with the first rays of daylight sprawling across the mist-filled paddocks. At the place where Rob said he would find Orla's tarpaulin-wrapped body, the tarpaulin was there... but no sign of her body.

Once his bewilderment and disappointment subsided, Owen sat quietly, head in hands, thinking furiously, rapidly posing questions to himself. Finally the realisation struck. *Someone believed they had greater custodial rights than me. Lahni!* He vividly recalled having discussed with Orla the reverence with which Lahni's tribe held her. *But to interfere with white-man's business is altogether another matter!*

Then other thoughts jolted him. *I can understand and accept Lahni's motives are honourable, but bloody hell, how did she know, and how do I explain Orla's missing body? Shit! I can't allow Lahni to be implicated. That could lead to the coppers asking too many questions and unwittingly lead them to wondering how I met Orla, and...*

Without further deliberations, Owen selected several large off-cuts of timber, wrapped them in the tarpaulin, placed the bundle in the coffin then quickly nailed the coffin lid closed. No sooner had he finished this task, than Rob and the doctor rode into the timber yard closely followed by a badly hung-over undertaker on his hearse.

'Jesus mate, you didn't need to do that on your own,' said Rob with dismay when he dismounted. 'You should've waited until we got here. Are you all right?'

'I'm feeling bloody awful,' Owen mumbled. 'But glad it's done.'

'Listen, doc,' Rob said firmly. 'Let's not get carried away with procedure and paperwork. There's no way I'll allow you to reopen that coffin. It must've been bloody awful for Owen to do what he's just done. Obviously, it meant something dear to him, but I won't stand by and see him subjected to further grief so that you can put your signature to something that was patently obvious.'

The doctor thought for a moment. 'Under the circumstances, and given your status as a witness to this tragic event, I'll sign the papers now. In your own time, ensure Owen signs the death certificate as the person identifying the poor woman, but I want you to also sign the document as witness to him having done that. Then deliver the document to me. Understood?'

After offering his condolences the undertaker drove away with the coffin, the arrangement being that Orla was to be buried in the glorious gardens of the Stewart homestead where she'd spent many happy and memorable times with her adopted family.

A second much larger grave was also to be prepared, adjoining Orla's plot... Boss Boy's final resting place.

The doctor returned to his practice in Gympie. Rob rode home to be with his wife. Owen chose to walk home to a very distraught son.

49

Those who knew Orla were still in a state of disbelief at the graveside funeral. The service was deliberately brief, but it cloaked them in a common, sad reality. Frank's eulogy moved everyone to tears, but what amazed most, was Niall's tribute to Boss Boy. Just as the celebration of Orla's life was short on detail, so too did Niall astutely sidestep Boss Boy's history-making deeds.

When the last mourner departed after the service, those who bore the coffin — Owen, Rob, Frank, Andy, Ken the bullocky, and Niall – sat around the woodheap drinking large tots of rum. Even Niall was permitted to taste the fiery liquid given the sombre occasion. They toasted Orla and discussed how incredibly lucky they were to have had her in their lives. No one asked 'what now', for none of them knew. They did know their lives had changed forever.

Frank explained he'd already written to Orla's mother and the McIntyres, notifying them of her death. He also assured Niall he'd inform the good people of Dorrigo. Later, when the others were out of earshot, Frank promised Niall he'd also somehow get the horrible news to Tom and Kate Lloyd.

There was another reality to face; the timber mill's continued operation. Owen and Niall were free to either remain involved, or sell off their interests... but that decision could wait for a few weeks.

Eventually, Owen rose unsteadily to his feet. 'I can't take much more. I've got to get some sleep. Thanks again for your support. See you all soon, eh?'

Niall followed his stepfather, but didn't look back. Tears were streaming down his cheeks; he found it hard to breathe and his chest ached. Gripped in that dreadful moment of finality, he wondered how on earth he'd ever forget this day.

It was nearly dark when Owen and Niall released their horses into the accommodation paddock. Lost in their thoughts, as they stepped onto the cottage's veranda, a voice startled them.

'Mate, we need to talk.'

'Jimmie! Yeah, of course,' replied Owen. 'I've been expecting you.'

Niall lit the veranda lamp as Jimmie, Lahni, and Ruthie stepped from the side of the house and hesitantly walked up the steps to the veranda.

'Wish it were under better conditions we meet,' said Jimmie. 'Lahni she has something to tell you, though we reckon you might already know what it's about. We mean no disrespect, quite the opposite. Your loss is ours, too. We're all very, very sad.'

They sat on the veranda bench seats in easy company. Jimmie and Lahni were on either side of Owen, though not invading his space. Ruthie sat next to Niall, their shoulders touching.

Lahni spoke first. 'We take Orla. She be safe in woman's sacred place. Now with dreamtime spirit people and forever be legend in our dreaming. *Cooloola* it now talks of good and many different things... for all of us. It say your lives be long. That be good. It also say Orla and our spirit people watch over you both... forever.'

Lahni again explained for Niall's benefit the circumstances under which she met his mother and why Orla's actions were considered so important. Lahni's forebears had been brutalised and pointlessly killed over several decades by ruthless, uncaring white men: Lahni's family was now few. Orla had restored their belief that not all white people were bad. Her intervention to preserve just one black person's life was seen by Lahni's dreamtime spirits as the act of a saviour, not only for Lahni's remaining small family group, but for all black people.

'Thank you, Lahni. Your story is powerful,' Owen responded. 'You've done us a great service actually. Let me explain'. And so he revisited the conclusions he'd reached in those pivotal moments before placing the timber off-cuts and the tarpaulin impersonating Orla's body into the coffin.

Niall relaxed, accepting Lahni and Owen's explanations, after all, their actions were clever and definitely not offensive. Ruthie's body radiated strange warmth; he also suddenly felt very tired, but his mind was now at peace.

Before either Owen or Niall could ask the obvious question, Lahni spoke again. 'In six days, you must meet us at place of coloured cliffs. If you need help, Jimmie he show you the way.'

'We'll be there; we know the way. And thanks again, Lahni,' Owen replied. 'Now, go safely my friends, we need to get some sleep.'

Unforeseen events two days later sent the Gympie doctor hurrying off to places unknown, a scandal involving a pregnant schoolgirl precipitating his hasty retreat. Unaware of this, Rob, on that same day, signed Orla's death certificate and then delivered it to Owen. He witnessed Owen's signature, and left Owen to return the certificate to the doctor.

Upon learning of the doctor's humiliating departure, Owen started thinking. *The last thing he's going to be interested in right now is this damn death certificate. Niall's secret will be safe.* Owen promptly destroyed the document, knowing Orla's death would never be recorded even though everyone, including Niall, would assume it was. And Orla's real grave was unlikely to ever be the subject of investigation, officially, or otherwise.

* * *

OWEN AND NIALL met Lahni at her appointed meeting place. Together, with her small family group, she led them through coastal banksia and then into dense scribbly gum. The terrain began sloping downwards, the trees thinned and the litter filled topsoil turned to scree. Descending further, it was obvious they were now in an ancient watercourse. This led them inland for at least another four hundred yards where they found themselves at the bottom of a steep-walled chasm, at least fifty, perhaps sixty feet deep.

The chasm ended abruptly. Incredibly, the surrounding sedimentary rock had been fashioned over eons of time into massive blocks and, in so doing, created the impression they had somehow been deliberately heaped one upon the other. The steep walls supported small shrubs and the occasional larger tree, living in this barren place by some miracle. Some of those blocks were undermined by water; their collapse and subsequent disintegration partially blocked the chasm.

'In the Dreamtime, our ancestral Water Spirit, a huge snake, it burrowed into the earth at this place,' Lahni explained. 'In many other places it come back up through the earth, creating all lakes and rivers nearby. That land be traditional home of my family.'

At the end of the chasm, the dislodged blocks left behind large openings like dark sightless eyes gazing forever over the surrounding landscape.

Lahni led Owen and Niall through the rocky jumble and then started climbing. They soon entered one of the openings. Lahni made them sit while she sang to her spirit people to let them know the mortal members of Orla's family were amongst them. After a few minutes she led them deeper into the cave, then suddenly stopped, turned and pointed towards the opening. On a head-height rock shelf, Owen and Niall could see a bundle that appeared to be animal pelts.

'That be Orla's sacred burial place,' Lahni said quietly, but added bluntly. 'Spirits only allow you to see because you both important to us. But never in future will any white man again visit here.'

In a surge of despair at again confronting his mother's death, Niall cried, his grief heightened by Owen's inconsolable sobs.

* * *

ON THEIR RETURN journey to Gympie, the images that flooded their minds were that of the marvellous stick figures freshly etched upon the walls of the cave. They depicted a woman and a small boy sitting in a strange horse-drawn cart, and that of a man riding beside them.

And strangely, try as they did, then — and in subsequent years — neither Owen nor Niall could ever recall *exactly* how they got to that magical gallery!

Apart from the few letters Orla had written to her mother, the McIntyres, and the Stewarts, that wall-art was the only written record that Orla trod the earth of this vast land.

* * *

THE TIMBER MILL was managed by Owen and Robert in the same spirit of cooperation as when the gold mine was the focus of life. And Andy never lost the opportunity to promote the success of these two ventures to anyone who would listen to him on his many visits to Brisbane and other industrial regions and towns throughout the Colony of Queensland. Andy's passionate meetings with leaders of industry, using these two operations as shining examples, heralded the arrival of previously unheard of workers rights.

Those business owners who, in due course, embraced that intangible but very real culture were rewarded with increased wealth. Andy was also rewarded, though personal wealth was not his principal objective. He was not only a champion of the working man but a genuine leader of men. In 1893, Andy became the Labour Party Representative and Member of the Legislative Assembly for Gympie.

Andy had spent a lot of time with Orla, Owen, Rob, and Niall. They loved nothing better than to debate the colony's emerging strength within the British Empire. Although Andy had strong

306

loyalist views, he was 'left breathless', as he would say, by the enormous commercial and rural opportunities which lay ahead given the right people to lead the country. He privately conceded to his friends that in his opinion the separate colonies would one day emerge as a great federated nation that would eventually free itself of British domination. That time was approaching and gaining momentum quicker than most people realised.

But the drive behind the success of the timber mill was now severed. Both Owen and Niall completely dropped their bundles and wanted never to return to the mill. Orla's aim to build a sustainable timber milling business and then grow it into a highly profitable enterprise was on target, but unless Owen and Niall returned to inject their enthusiasm and energy, the future of the mill was uncertain.

Undaunted, Andy played a major role in getting Owen and Niall back to work. In his own caring and positive way, he counselled and gently challenged both of them. With well chosen words he'd typically say, 'Grieve until you ache, but please, move on and honour Orla's ambition.'

And grieve they did. Even Owen's beautiful ocean-blue eyes seemed to fade.

Andy and Rob also worked tirelessly to rescue Owen from the booze. They cajoled him into staying involved in every new and important decision, forcing him to make the casting vote, to think about matters other than his grief, or alcohol.

'Mate, you've got many loyal, paying customers and they're relying on you to address their orders, or they'll take their business elsewhere,' Andy reminded Owen, and then pressed on doggedly. 'Everyone in your employ — and their families — look up to you, mate. They understand your distress, but unless you show some interest soon, they too are likely to move on. And you have to give away the piss!'

Owen listened, but still felt detached. Gradually he started thinking. *What about, Rob? I'm letting him down when he needs me most? Then what'll become of the operation if he packs it in? Listen to yourself. You once gave him your word that you'd drive this business together. I can't break my word. And, boyo, Orla would never have wanted me to do that!*

Overnight, Owen stopped drinking: his mind cleared and his anguish retreated.

Niall liked both Rob and Andy and appreciated their understanding. But only Ruthie gave him real comfort. They went on long walks in the bush and talked for hours about many things. Occasionally, a hurt and bewildered child would cry uncontrollably, but there were also signs of a strong man emerging. Ruthie maternally comforted one and audaciously encouraged the other.

'I'll always miss Mum. But your family has suffered far worse, eh?'

Ruthie smiled knowingly at Niall. 'True, but we'll both get over it. You simply must get on with your life, Niall.'

* * *

AFTER NEARLY FOUR weeks of idleness since Orla's death, Owen and Niall sat watching a magnificent sunset from the veranda of their cottage. Long overdue, they discussed their innermost feelings and ambitions until well after dark. Owen realised in amazement that Niall, though still only a youth in years, was now a young man and his most loyal friend.

'Regardless that you've lost your mother, you're still my son,' he said reassuringly. 'And she'd want me to always keep an eye on you.'

'And me, you! Thanks, Dad, you're the best. But hey, don't you reckon it's time we got back to work?'

* * *

THEIR RETURN to the timber mill the following day was greeted with genuine warmth and amazing enthusiasm — and Rob and Andy's tremendous relief.

50

The timber mill prospered, but it wasn't until late 1898, that Rob retired and with his wife, relocated to Brisbane Town. That event followed Rob conceding that he'd taught Niall all he could in problem solving and equipment maintenance. Owen likewise taught Niall how to monitor expenditure, control costs and maximise their profit without disadvantaging their workers.

Niall's enthusiasm to receive a formal education gradually faded: the idea was deferred and finally abandoned. Salesmanship came naturally to Niall and he was encouraged to take responsibility for preparing quotations and negotiating contracts. By nineteen, his apparent easy-going manner masked a naturally astute business mind. Typically, when payment was an issue, he'd negotiate and approve favourable payment terms, but not without first having obtained from that customer a commitment to purchase their timber only from his mill. He also understood the limitations of the entire cedar gathering and milling operations and when a delivery commitment was made, Niall made certain every promise was met: late delivery penalties would not only impact their profit, but would also undermine their hard earned reputation for reliability.

But he could also sense when a customer was simply 'trying it on'.

Late payment of progress payments, without his approval, resulted in subsequent deliveries being suspended. Beyond that, they were then delayed indefinitely until the customer understood that Niall's word was based upon mutual trust.

But life was not all work. There were three pastimes Niall loved — riding through the hinterland forests with Owen, going bush with Ruthie and her family, and playing cricket.

His passion for cricket obsessed him and, like most of his team-mates, he lived by the creed that 'the English may have given us the game, but we'll teach the bastards how it should be played'. He had the reflexes of a cat and the eye of a hawk. Catches he took sometimes seemed impossible and he bewildered the opposition batsman with his extremely fast bowling. But, most of all, he loved batting. He could either totally dominate the opposition bowlers or, in his enthusiasm to score quickly, impulsively get himself out without scoring. He played the game hard but fair and always socialised with the opposition players and the umpires, 'partaking in the odd cold one' as they euphemistically called their after-match gatherings. As often as not, these drinking sessions resulted in much laughter, good-natured teasing, and exaggerated stories of past exploits.

But during the summer of 1899, another topic crept into those fun-filled hours of youthful exuberance. It seemed the British Empire, then at its zenith in power and prestige, had its High Commissioner for the Cape Colony in South Africa, Alfred Milner, wanting more. He wanted the Empire to gain ownership of the gold mines in the Dutch Boer Republics of the Transvaal and the Orange Free State. He also wanted to create a Cape-to-Cairo confederation of British colonies and thereby dominate the African continent. And, of course, he wanted to rule over it.

To achieve this end, Milner started a war with the Boers. Ever confident, British generals and politicians predicted 'the war would be over by Christmas'. Word of the initial successes of the Boers in Natal and Cape Province, followed by the retaking of the towns of Ladysmith, Mafeking, and Kimberley by the British in June 1900, came to the attention of all British colonies. Despite a massive build-up of men and materials prior to those engagements, the British suffered huge losses.

Irrationally, the British considered the war over. But the Boers were not about to give up so easily. They escaped into the thick bush and mountains, which bordered the vast veldt country, formed commando units and became a fast and highly mobile guerrilla force, blowing up trains and ambushing British troops and garrisons. Their unexpected hit-and-run tactics thoroughly frustrated the British and caused further huge losses they couldn't afford. The British Army tried unsuccessfully to adopt the Boers tactics, and the war degenerated into a devastating and cruel struggle between British righteous might and Boer nationalist desperation.

And so, with the British losses remaining high, calls for reinforcements soon spread throughout Britain's colonies. The colonies of Queensland, New South Wales, and Victoria rallied first. Those who owned their own horses were the first volunteers to be recruited. Believing it their duty to support their Queen in her hour of need, they soon found themselves bound for South Africa for basic set piece military training... yet another British folly given the altered combat circumstances.

Surprisingly, it was Owen who first raised the recruitment drive with Niall. 'Between you and me son, I have to admit I'm bored with the daily grind at the mill. I've been seriously considering volunteering. Besides, I've always wanted to see Africa, having heard so much about it from Rob.'

Niall also wanted action, after all, he considered himself invincible. And he, too, wanted to see the world: the African conflict was the perfect excuse. 'If you're serious, you're not going without me, Dad,' he announced firmly.

At first, Owen tried to dissuade Niall, confident that Orla would never have wanted her son to do anything to support the British. However, he knew with equal certainty that Niall's mind was made up, and so relented.

Their announcement at the mill shocked their workers.

'Listen you lot! You're more than capable of running things without us for a short time,' Owen told them with conviction.

Jeanie and Frank were angry and saddened by their decision and only reluctantly gave them their blessings. Frank said vehemently, 'You're both free colonists for God's sake — not English! Let the fools get themselves out of this mess; they created it!'

Not a bad speech for a retired Londoner, but he does have a point, thought Owen with humour, and a measure of self-doubt.

Ruthie was deeply hurt but she tried to inject some humour into Niall's sudden announcement. 'If you get yourself killed, Niall O'Meara, I promise I'll never speak to you again.' On a more serious note she continued. 'Take good care of yourself, Niall. We've got so much to do when you return.'

* * *

NIALL HAD SPENT a lot of time with Ruthie over the years and often wondered why she hadn't married in accordance with aboriginal custom. Unbeknownst to Niall, she'd flatly rejected her arranged betrothal. He was also unaware of the torment and offence that decision caused within her family group.

But, eventually, the *Cooloola* spirit spoke to Lahni... and acceptance finally settled upon Ruthie's family.

51

Owen, because of his seniority, was given the responsibility of recruiting at least fifty men and acquiring seventy-five horses. He achieved that within a week. However, these men were not the first Queenslanders to leave the colony.

In the absence of a birth certificate, Owen vouched that Niall was his son. In Niall's mind, being a 'Stewart' was as natural as being either an 'O'Meara' or a 'Kelly'.

All volunteers had to be good riders and, preferably, marksmen. The task of selecting suitable volunteers was easy; all were tough, hardened Bushmen — the most desirable attribute to counter the highly mobile Boers. Getting them to Brisbane was another matter. Most of the men behaved, most of the time. But there were a few who continually drank to excess or repeatedly initiated fights. Eventually, Owen had enough. The two men who next chose to ignore him found themselves incapable of travelling the following morning, not from the effects of grog, but from having been '*gently* persuaded to toe the line'. One caught up and apologised. The other was not seen again.

Whilst such action was extreme, it had the desired effect. Order followed, as did a keen spirit of camaraderie. Owen's leadership style was never again questioned and as the men got to know him better they all enjoyed his company. Niall received no special consideration, but his confident, positive, and friendly outlook also gained respect.

Upon arrival in Brisbane, they were met by a British Sergeant who promptly explained where their horses were to be yarded, and then directed them to their temporary tent accommodation. After storing their belongings, the men were assembled to receive their initiation into military life.

The British officer was likeable and pragmatic. He outlined the Boer's guerrilla tactics, which were delaying the end to the war... much to the enormous embarrassment of British generals and politicians. The role of Owen's men was clear: match the techniques adopted by the Boers — to harass their commandos, their farms and food supply lines — and so relieve the relentless pressure on fatigued British held positions.

He then explained that over the following days he expected more volunteers would arrive, whereafter everyone would be placed into platoons of ten men. They would be known as non-commissioned volunteers, but referred to as troopers. Each platoon would then be an integral part of a company of one hundred men, and be generally known as the Queensland Imperial Bushmen.

Owen was chosen for overall command of a company and became a Lieutenant. Upon his insistence the men from Gympie were retained in his company; their excitement grew as they were outfitted with uniforms, slouch hats, and riding boots.

An unknown, likable university educated man of about thirty years of age was appointed second in command and given the rank of Sergeant. Also upon Owen's insistence, Niall was given the rank of Sergeant; his justification being that Niall already had the men's confidence, and was therefore the best man to assume a leadership role if anything happened to either himself or the other Sergeant. Initially however, Niall was assigned to oversee the loading, feeding, and subsequent care of the horses during their impending voyage.

Whilst under overall British command, Owen and his men would be expected to follow orders. But the real surprise was that whilst objectives would be stated in all orders, exactly how those objectives might be met would be at Owen's discretion and without British interference in the field — an amazing departure from the normal inflexible, and clearly failed, British set piece mentality.

'Just beat the Boer at his own game, *regardless,*' the British Sergeant emphasised.

Rifles, ammunition, bayonets, and water bottles would be issued by the British upon arrival in South Africa. In the meantime, parade ground drills were commenced as a merchant steamship was readied for their transportation.

Under Owen's urgings, he soon had his men riding in line formation, two abreast. He joined with them to practice a recommended manoeuvre involving separation at speed into a single, shoulder-to-shoulder line. This involved fast dismounts at a designated location, followed by rapid-fire target practice using their own rifles. Upon Owen's pre-arranged command, they'd quickly remount — still spitting dirt and trying to blink dust from their eyes — then charge off at breakneck speed to repeat the manoeuvre.

In the heat and humidity, dehydrated and close to exhaustion, the men and their horses persevered; their initial lack of coordination soon gave way to acceptable organization. The accuracy of their shooting was consistently high, despite their ragged breathing, for they knew the basic tricks: to determinedly hold their breath just before firing... and to ignore the incessant flies as they explored lips and the corner of eyes.

Most of the horses were sound and in good health and, predominantly, Walers. Niall was adamant that each trooper scrupulously care for his own horse. Those who ignored his intolerance of 'half-arsed attention to detail' soon wished they hadn't also ignored the menacing, strange reddish colour of Niall's eyes and his slowly opening and closing fists when he challenged their laziness.

In the days leading up to their departure, men were assigned specific tasks. Some became farriers, others repaired bridles and saddles. The loading went surprisingly well. Most of the horses allowed themselves to be led from the jetty and up the gangplanks to their assigned stall. Those that rebelled were blindfolded and then slung on board.

Just before casting-off, a last-minute arrival was ushered on board: a veterinary surgeon, not quite thirty years old. Apparently, he'd been sent for by Owen's second in command, who insisted upon the need for his specialist skills. This younger man, because of his professional qualifications, was assigned as the company's Warrant Officer.

Upon arrival in Melbourne, the horses were taken ashore, grass fed, and lightly exercised. Ample hay, chaff, oats, and fresh water were then loaded; sufficient they hoped for the duration of their journey almost halfway around the world. While that work proceeded, all troopers were given leave to explore the town.

As the transport ship met the swell of the Southern Ocean, the horses became restless. The decks were reasonably well ventilated but there was the constant smell of horse manure and urine. There was also the constant clatter of hooves as nervous horses shifted to compensate for the ship's erratic motion. And there was the occasional totally unexpected '*bang*' as one the horses released its frustration with a well-aimed kick to the backboards of its stall. Niall spent many hours checking and comforting those beasts struggling with motion sickness. Some lay down in their distress; most, however, suffered in silence.

Late one afternoon, during a period of relatively calm weather, Niall was sitting on some bags of grain, quietly humming a simple tune in between sips from a mug of tea. The vet casually walked onto the stalls deck and greeted him. The two men had grown to like each other and Niall cheerfully returned his greeting. They walked companionably along the rows of stalls, and in-between inspections and general conversation, Niall continued to hum his song.

As the vet was about to bid farewell to Niall before going topside, he stopped dead in his tracks. His head tilted slightly, listening. He then slowly turned.

'Hey, mate, where'd you learn that tune?'

'Oh, I think it's an Irish nursery rhyme my Mum used to sing. Why?'

'Well, it's just that, well, years ago I met a remarkable Irish woman who used to hum that same tune. She stayed with our family for a short time and looked after our farm when my folks and I attended my grandfather's funeral in Sydney Town. Do you know something? She even gave me one of her horses when mine had to be put down. And she taught me to shoot and later gave me her old rifle. And... and she had a small boy with her and a covered cart. And a fabulous horse, a Waler. Now what was his name?'

'Boss Boy', gasped Niall, stunned, the exchange sending goose bumps creeping up his back.

'That's it! This is bloody unbelievable, mate,' said the vet before Niall could speak. 'Good God, that boy was, *you*! And that lady was, Orla... *your mum*, right?'

'Certainly looks like it. Well, I'll be buggered,' said Niall, now very excited. 'It's hard to believe, eh? Mum told me about you and your family. But when we were introduced the other day, I didn't connect you with the Peter Jones who she talked about.'

Peter fixed Niall with a quizzical look. 'I don't think your mum ever told us her surname. Hang on, yes, she did; it was O'Meara. But your name's Stewart, right?'

'No, my name *is* O'Meara. Stewart is my stepfather's surname. He's also our Company's Lieutenant.'

'Get out of it,' Peter replied, equally excited. 'Now just listen to this, mate, it gets even better. Your mum encouraged me to go to boarding school in Sydney Town. She also did the same for someone else who came to live with us. Even gave him money to get him started. And that bloke's right here on this ship, too! He came from a small timber town called Dorrigo where your mum was his teacher for a while. As I recall Martin telling me, apparently she ran off with a stranger and was never seen again.'

'Now hang about!' exclaimed Niall. 'I remember an older lad whose name was Martin. Martin, Martin.... now what the hell was his surname?'

'Does the name Ambrose ring a bell?' asked Peter.

Niall jumped to his feet. 'Yes, Christ almighty, that's him! You mean... ahh, come on, it can't be. He was kind to us little kids and really looked after me.' Barely containing himself, Niall continued. 'Martin Ambrose, well I'll be buggered. I can't wait to see Martin and Owen's faces when we tell 'em what we've just uncovered.'

'No doubt about it, it's Martin all right and he's my best mate. We've done everything together. School, then university, sailing, even travelled to Adelaide once... and now we're going off to war together.'

Niall and Peter burst into Owen's office both trying to talk at once, and as luck would have it, Martin was with him. Owen quickly took control and suggested they both calm down and explain what was going on.

'Niall... God, you've grown,' said Martin, as he vigorously shook Niall's hand, clearly impressed by the man now facing him. 'It's great to meet you again. And how's that *wonderful* mother of yours?'

Silence! All the happiness and excitement drained from Niall; Owen's face contorted in sadness.

Realising that something was badly amiss, Martin recovered first. 'I venture to say that my question is out of order. No hurt or disrespect was intended. Please, forgive me if I've said something tactless.'

Owen spoke for himself and Niall. 'Mate, you weren't to know. Orla was killed in an accident at our timber mill in Gympie, March '92... as was Boss Boy. Listen, let's call for another brew and I'll tell you what happened and how it was that I ran away with Orla, not the other way round as I believe it's been claimed.'

* * *

THREE HOURS and many cups of black tea later, the four men became more than just mates who'd volunteered to go off to war — they'd become the staunchest of life's allies.

Their lives had all been touched by a most amazing and courageous Irish girl who had, in her own thoughtful way, set them all onto differing paths of success and happiness and had somehow, mystically, ordained this re-union. Others might speculate — and possibly convince themselves — that this meeting was through a common circumstance and, hence, pure chance.

52

There was another short stopover in Perth before taking on the vastness of the Indian Ocean. The horses were in good shape, but they would need exercise on the last leg of their voyage. With some ingenuity, Niall and Peter refashioned the stall decks so that each horse could be walked the ship's perimeter before being returned to its stall.

The weather was generous, almost benign, until they were within a day's steaming of Cape Town. Overnight, a gale threw itself at them. Freezing rain preceded a raging, howling wind. Unsecured objects were ripped into the night. The ship's hull shuddered as its bow crashed into the wave's troughs. Seawater exploded over the decks. Then the ship developed a corkscrewing motion. Horses and soldiers became understandably alarmed.

The skipper chose to heave to on the ship's sea anchors and ride out the storm rather than continue to try and make headway.

Niall and Peter, and a few concerned troopers, had their hands full trying to soothe the horses. Regrettably, two terrified horses broke free: in their panic, they fell heavily on the slippery decks, both breaking a leg. Peter humanely silenced the thrashing, screaming animals.

Not long before dawn, the wind dropped as quickly as it had arrived, but a huge swell still ran. Eventually, the ocean began to flatten and the sea anchors were retrieved. Within an hour of making way again, land was sighted and the dead horses were hastily thrown overboard. Many of the troopers secretly wished they too could be thrown overboard, reasoning that death by drowning, or to be eaten by sharks was surely more acceptable than dying from their chronic seasickness.

Eventually, a berth was found for their ship. Almost immediately, orders were given to commence offloading the horses. Neither man nor beast needed encouragement to once again feel the earth beneath their feet.

When the last of the men and their supplies were offloaded, two British Warrant Officers introduced themselves to Owen. They instructed him to have his men saddle their horses, collect their belongings, and then follow them in orderly columns, two abreast, to their new quarters.

They made their way through bustling waterside streets, much of the activity obviously in support of the war effort. The column travelled northeast for about twelve miles until arriving at a gently sloping valley at the bottom of which was a large and orderly military base surrounded by fenced paddocks containing hundreds of horses. A small clear creek wound its way through their well grassed paddocks. Every horse appeared to be in top condition.

They rode by sandbagged fortifications from which armed guards waved cheerfully to Owen's men. Given they were so far south from the war zones, it surprised Owen that the British had gone to so much trouble to defend a training centre. The place felt safe, but Owen had been assured by the Warrant Officers, that every British establishment still remained a Boer target.

Having descended to the bottom of the broad valley, they were promptly directed to an area where rows of tents bordered the horse paddocks. After releasing their horses, the men were assigned to four-man tents where they could store their equipment and, hopefully, sleep in peace. Each man received a basic hygiene kit: shaving was not optional, unless deployed in active field service.

They were then called onto parade and told in very certain terms what was expected during a typical military training day. There were specific times allotted for ablutions, meal times, feeding and grooming of their horses. Bayonets, sabres, and .303 Lee-Enfield eight shot carbines were issued to every man. British drill Sergeants instructed them in the care and proper handling of those vital items. Hand-to-hand self-defence training followed, as did hours of rifle practice, both from the prone position and from horseback.

In addition to the British regulars and their own volunteers, there were volunteers from other non-British countries, principally those from Canada, India, and the Colony of New Zealand. Niall made friends with many of the men and invitations to visit each other after the war were freely exchanged.

Someone produced a cricket bat and ball, whereupon fiercely contested 'knock up games' ensued at the end of each days training.

'Seems we're living in luxury compared with the Boer,' Owen told Niall and Martin after returning from an officer's briefing meeting. 'Supplies are not our problem, but apparently the Boers are desperate. They've sacrificed a lot, so they'll continue to inflict as much grief as possible — not just on the Brits — but on us, too. Impress upon your men that there's nothing glamorous about this war. And, by the way, we'll soon be off to the northern regions of Transvaal.'

* * *

AFTER THREE WEEKS of demanding training, Owen was instructed to have his men assemble with their horses. Ammunition was issued. Objectives conveyed.

* * *

TRAVELLING NORTH, the Company changed trains three times before reaching Pretoria. Each leg of their journey was uncomfortable and painfully slow. Thankfully, exercise stop-overs were taken at De Aar and Bloemfontein.

Each train had dedicated open-sided carriages fitted with back-to-back Maxim-Nordenfeldt automatic machine guns. Regardless, all troopers were told to keep their rifles within easy reach.

The men often remarked how much the veldt lands, distant mountain ranges, and rivers reminded them of home. However, three things struck them all as sinister. First, was the almost complete absence of wildlife. Second, particularly north of Bloemfontein, was the ever increasing evidence of war — an intrusive smell of death, derailed trains, smashed communication lines, burnt farm houses and crops and fencing, abandoned military field pieces, and ammunition carts. Third, was the number of black people; not the occasional small aboriginal family, which one would see at home, but literally thousands of displaced, destitute individuals.

Approaching Pretoria, word was passed to remain vigilant since they were now in a 'hot zone', where Boer commandos were recently active. Upon arrival Owen, Niall, and Martin were briefed on the current situation and were left in no doubt as to the dangers now surrounding them.

A sentry roster was drawn up to guard their position and their horses. Tents were provided, each accommodating six men. Owen ordered that at least one box of ammunition per tent had to be open at all times.

After they'd settled in, Owen and Martin rallied their men, outlining for them the nature of their own earlier briefing. Fear, if it was present, never revealed itself, masked perhaps by respectful alertness. Nevertheless, the excitement was palpable. These proud 'Queenslanders' had received their first assignment, a twenty-mile patrol sweeping a particularly hot region.

The British Captain who detailed their objective for the day provided two experienced Sergeants to help Owen interpret their military maps and to identify the geographical limits of their patrol. However, those boundaries were flexible if in pursuit of the enemy.

Owen gave his direct order of the day. 'Harass and engage the

Boer forces, other than in set piece combat. Take as many prisoners as possible. At all times, a wounded enemy taken prisoner is to be given due consideration and are not to be refused medical aid. However, any prisoner who subsequently attempts escape is to be shot. That just about covers everything.' Owen chuckled sarcastically.

* * *

AT DAY'S END, the enemy remained elusive, though signs of other horse movements were everywhere.

'This is ridiculous. We're too cumbersome as a company,' declared Owen, clearly as frustrated as Niall and Martin. 'The Boers can see us coming miles away. From tomorrow, we'll form into three platoons. We'll each lead a platoon, but I'll stay in overall command. One of us will always be on patrol, the others either resting or standing by as reinforcement. I'll square it away with the Brit Captain.'

Niall nodded in agreement. 'We'll move much faster and cover more territory, that's for sure.'

'Sounds about right to me,' Martin added. 'We'd better let the boys know straight away, they're getting a bit pissed-off.'

On the tenth day of no action, Niall led his platoon out of their current camp. Fighting off boredom, heat and flies, he thought he heard thunder, but the sky was clear. It quickly dawned on him that it was volleys of nearby gunfire. They proceeded cautiously and soon discovered six British supply wagons under attack. The wagons were on open ground and about three hundred yards away.

From their elevated and concealed positions, the Boers' repeating rifles were wreaking havoc amongst the hapless British soldiers who were offering only a token defence of their supply wagons. And because the Boers' Mauser rifles were using smokeless cartridges, the task of the remaining British soldiers to hone in on the enemy was made extremely difficult.

Being above and behind the enemy, Niall's patrol had the advantage of position and surprise. He led his troopers unnoticed to within eighty yards of the Boer lines. He then gave a quick arm signal. No hesitation. Horses advanced quickly at a fast walk. Now, only forty yards of open ground. Niall flashed another arm signal. His troopers opened fire; one round each, then into a full charge. Murderous yells of engagement joined the sound of thundering hooves.

Most of the Boers dropped their rifles and threw up their arms. Some bravely returned a few rounds before they, too, recognised the hopelessness of their situation and chose to surrender. All were quickly relieved of their weapons.

Niall's men were unscathed. However, two of the Boers were killed and four wounded. Eleven others were taken prisoner. All of their horses were found tethered within a depression, about fifty yards up the hill behind their ambush position... but no sentry.

Niall then rode down to the wagons to see if his troops could be of further assistance. He was appalled that only four British soldiers had survived the ambush.

'You have my sympathies, but come on, pull yourselves together,' said Niall, easily taking command. 'The mob who bushwhacked you won't be giving you any more grief. I'll be back with those boyos and my men in fifteen minutes to escort you. Now, get yourselves sorted and be ready to pull out.'

As he rode back to his men, an unexpected chuckle formed deep in his chest. By the time he reached his men and the prisoners, Niall was roaring with laughter. To his men, this behaviour seemed incongruous given what they'd just done. But, nevertheless, it had the effect of releasing the tension in his men and they, too, were soon smiling and chuckling to themselves, glad to be alive and exulted by their first success. Failing to see any humour in their position whatsoever, the prisoners gave their captors filthy looks.

Back at the base camp, Niall reported the events of the day to Owen and Martin. The surviving four British soldiers corroborated his report and thanked Niall for his intervention. It was soon learnt that had the Boers been successful, their prize, apart from the wagons and horses, would have been sufficient food to feed one hundred men for a month! A detail was ordered for the next morning to bury the thirteen British soldiers killed in the attack.

After their evening meal, Niall quietly commented, 'Hey Dad, have you seen how skinny those poor bastards are? And their clothes are just rags and their boots are completely buggered, too. But that doesn't stop 'em from being bloody good shots with those Mausers. Surely their mates who remain can't keep going forever, particularly if they're not covering their rear? That seems odd, eh? Their horses, too; they're as poor as all get out.'

* * *

BUT THEIR MATES did fight on, massively outnumbered in manpower, in arms and in every other resource, except courage. For another twelve months, despite some harrowing defeats, ever dwindling numbers, being half starved and trying to tend to their equally starving horses, those heroic men refused to capitulate.

During that time, Owen and Niall learnt much about the Boer psyche and realised their plight was not dissimilar to some underlying problems encountered and previously acted out in their country. These people really hated the British, their wealth grabbing intentions and their domineering, insensitive enforcement of justice.

53

Ironically, Owen owed much of his military successes to his years of being the 'bushranger-butcher'. On many occasions throughout their two-year campaign he called upon his mastery of the tough Dorrigo terrain while conducting his cattle rustling and meat distribution operation. That knowledge enabled him to predict the locations of the Boer's safe havens… and thus set many successful ambushes. His company were ultimately engaged in thirty-nine actions against an elusive, stubborn enemy, accounting for two hundred and seventy Boer soldiers; mostly captured.

Owen was also blessed: his son, Martin, and Peter were left unscathed and had formed great bonds of mateship. All three provided amazing support to Owen throughout the campaign and proved to be first-rate soldiers. And like Owen — and contrary to Orders issued by the British — all of them refused to burn farmer's houses or their sheds, or to kill their livestock, certain, however, that many of those farmers remained sympathetic to the Boer cause. The regular British forces were not so benevolent.

But Owen was not without his own losses: eighteen troopers killed in action and thirty-one injured so badly they had to be evacuated to Cape Town for treatment. Seven of those men died from infections. He also lost over seventy horses, either shot by sniper fire or victim to some flu-like virus, which Peter was unable to treat.

Each loss burned into Owen's soul. The war could not end soon enough for him. He even confided to Niall that he sometimes rued his decision to volunteer, having seen enough death and misery perpetrated against both man and beast to last him a lifetime.

Niall also had some firm views. 'I'll tell you what, Dad. If the chiefs orchestrating this stupid war don't broker some sort of peace soon, then I'm going to desert. Bugger the consequences!'

* * *

A SURRENDER DOCUMENT – known as The Treaty of Vereeniging, was signed by the Boers on the last day of May in 1902. Everyone could go home to their beloved Queensland... now part of the Federation of Australia!

* * *

TRAGICALLY, the order was given for all of the remaining Australian horses to be put down regardless of their condition. It was said that Australia's breeding program of high quality horses would be at risk of infection if any of these horses were to return home. All requests for these brave and loyal horses to be donated to the farmers of The Orange Free State, Transvaal, and Natal also fell upon deaf ears and were refused. No logical reason was given for such a heartless decision.

And so this gruesome task became Peter's problem. To him it was an appalling act of betrayal to mounts that had so gallantly swept their countrymen into battle, and who had directly saved the lives of so many of them. It became too much for him to endure: with his last bullet Peter took his own life in protest.

Peter's suicide shocked everyone, no one more so than Martin who had shared so much of his life with him. The entire company mourned the passing of their intelligent, caring, easy-going friend.

But that noble act of principle seemed to precipitate an unexpected urgency for everyone to get on with their lives.

* * *

To most, their futures seemed clear-cut and they freely discussed their plans and aspirations during their preparations to leave Africa.

Owen was determined to return to Australia as soon as possible and made official enquiries regarding how to achieve that. The best advice indicated he should catch the first available train to Port Elizabeth and then board a steamer to Perth. Many of those from his Company were of like mind and quickly confirmed they would join him.

Martin, on the other hand, had it firmly fixed in his mind he was going to England to study law. He planned to catch a military train to Cape Town and then sail to England when the opportunity seemed right.

However, Niall had another duty on his mind. Recalling how Orla had spoken so fondly of her mother and four brothers, it seemed like a great opportunity to continue onto Ireland and hopefully meet his relatives. Owen wholeheartedly agreed.

* * *

The morning of Owen's departure was cold and overcast. But those conditions neither quenched the excitement that hung in the air nor undermined the warm farewells as mates firmly shook hands, exchanged friendly shoulder punches, and happily endured much backslapping.

'Hey Dad, you did a really great job out here, you know,' Niall said as the train was about to depart. 'Take good care of yourself getting home and please give my love to Ruthie and, of course, to Jeanie and Frank.'

'Couldn't have done it without you, son,' Owen replied. 'Give my regards to Orla's family. Let 'em know I'll try and catch up with 'em one day. Don't forget to write... and keep your wits about you, too. And hey, good luck, boyo.'

They embraced in a quick parting hug, and then shook hands firmly while looking one another squarely in the eye. From the top step of the train carriage, Owen turned and waved. He was grinning broadly and his brilliant blue eyes sparkled in his weather-beaten but still handsome face.

Niall's cheerful return wave went unseen; Owen had already stepped into the carriage.

54

Niall and Martin travelled together to Cape Town and spent a few weeks in relative luxury, drinking and eating excessively, sightseeing and falling victim to the seduction of some local girls.

Normality had not returned to Cape Town. The aftermath of Britain's massive war effort left the capital in physical and moral shambles, which led to theft, fights, and even murder amongst the locals and the returning British soldiers.

Niall and Martin quickly tired of this anarchy and soon found themselves England bound, their steamer heading for Portsmouth.

A strong, unspoken bond continued between Niall and Martin. Just as Martin had naturally assumed a guardian role with Niall when they first met as young boys in Dorrigo so, too, had he adopted a similar role then... still even-handed and uncompromisingly loyal. Though Niall could look after himself, he greatly respected Martin's pragmatic approach to life.

Martin never flaunted his considerable intellect, but Niall was amazed by his friend's appreciation and knowledge of the arts. So it was no surprise to Niall having arrived in London that Martin sought out libraries, museums, art galleries, and concert halls where they indulged themselves for days and many nights. Martin introduced Niall to paintings of amazingly beautiful landscapes by the French artist Paul Cézanne. And, for the first time, Niall attended live classical music performances. He heard works by the French composer Claude Debussy but it was Beethoven who totally enthralled him. He even jumped to his feet at the end of the Beethoven performance clapping as loud as he could, and madly shouting 'bravo' along with the appreciative audience.

He also found himself drawn to an exhibition of Chinese artwork; a priceless collection. There were intricate solid gold, ivory and jade sculptures of fish, pigs, and monkeys, but he was most intrigued by the incredible porcelain equine figurines, each of remarkable lifelike form and proportion. And then there were the exquisitely carved buildings, masterpieces that stood about three feet tall. Martin explained that each structure may have taken the sculptor several years to complete and each miniature replicated a cherished holy place.

'Mate, I've got to get started with my studies,' Martin eventually announced. 'Trouble is, I don't have much money left. I need to find somewhere to live and I've got to find a job.'

'No problem. I've heard it's possible to send telegrams that enable you to transfer money from Australia to England. I've got quite a few quid tucked away back home... so, how much do you need?'

'Fifty quid should be plenty. I'll pay you back as soon as I can. Maybe you'll need a good lawyer one day.'

The money was available four days later, but Martin was somewhat frustrated. 'Don't suppose you want some company if you're heading for Ireland? I've been accepted at Oxford, but it turns out, I can't bloody well start for another three weeks!'

'Congratulations,' said Niall as he shook Martin's hand. 'You're more than welcome to join me, mate. Let's book straight away, eh?'

The following week they made their way to Swansea, then boarded a merchant ship bound for Cork. Still resplendent in their Queensland Imperial Bushmen uniforms and their distinctive slouch hats adorned with plumes of ostrich feathers, they booked into a pub for the night before moving on to Dungarvan.

The pub they selected was busy and their evening meal excellent, but some of the customers seemed annoyed by their presence. Odd comments, better suited to the sympathies of Northern Ireland, were muttered loud enough for Niall and Martin to hear.

'I say, Martin, those four boyos seem to have it in for us. Think I'll wander over and ask 'em what their problem is.' Before Martin could dissuade him, Niall stood up and walked casually over to the noisy punters.

'Don't get up, lads,' he said cheerfully. 'I was wondering if you'd like join us you for a drink? My shout of course.'

'Ahh, get fucked, yah dopey prick. Why don't you piss off back to your English shit hole,' said the largest of the four.

'Nice to meet you, too. No offence taken,' Niall replied sarcastically. 'A case of mistaken identity, mate... we're Australian, not English.'

'A smart arse, for sure,' added the most rotund of the antagonists. 'The only thing worse than an English prick are you lackey colonials. And just look at that stupid fuckin' hat,'

'Now look what you've done,' replied Niall indignantly as he removed his hat and carefully placed it on a nearby table. 'You've gone and insulted me and my country, boyo. Do you and your fat mates want to apologise in here, or outside?'

Chairs scraped on the floor as the men stood. Charged with alcohol induced bravado they approached Niall — and Martin — who had casually arrived to stand at Niall's right shoulder. Suddenly, the louts realised just how big Niall and Martin were. They hesitated. But they were four... unbeatable!

Niall focused totally on his immediate adversary and thought, *the stupid bugger's pissed. He can hardly stand but he's going to regret what he's just said.* As Niall's rage grew, he opened and closed his fists ready for the onslaught he was about to unleash.

Martin noticed Niall's eyes were now an eerie red; he'd seen that look before. He quickly moved to stand back-to-back with Niall and muttered, 'Seems they're not thirsty, mate. Fancy refusing a free beer.'

The leader of the gang raised his fists. There was a blur of movement. Niall's right fist crashed into the man's unprotected face. The blow felt satisfying; perfect timing. As if shot, the man's head jolted backwards, his nose hideously rearranged. Teeth rattled across the wooden floor. The unconscious man's legs then went into spasms, his feet darting about in little jabbing steps.

'I believe that's what's called an Irish jig,' Niall goaded.

When Niall spun to confront his next attacker, the other three almost had Martin at their mercy. One had him in a head-lock while another was trying to pin his arms. Martin was doing his best to avoid the third man who was skipping about, impatient to launch a punch as soon as Martin was held still. Just as that third man was about to release his first punch, Niall struck again. It was a short ripping blow. Ribs cracked. There was a loud gasp in disbelief at the sudden pain. The man sagged to the floor. Eyes bulging, he tried to speak... but instead, fainted.

Their numbers were even. The remaining two Irishmen released Martin and backed off. Martin immediately grabbed a nearby chair, smashed it to pieces across a table, and then quickly grabbed one of the legs. Instead of raising it to use as a club, Martin pointed it down and slightly forward. One of the men, thinking he had an opening, foolishly threw a punch at Martin's head. In one fluid movement, Martin sidestepped and viciously jabbed the end of the chair leg into the man's unprotected midriff. The man doubled over and vomited copiously.

Niall watched in awe as Martin spun around and using his momentum he pitilessly clubbed his sick opponent, hard, right behind his left ear.

'Jeez mate, that was a bit unfair,' Niall said mockingly. 'We had him two on one and you went and did that. Mind you, I'm bloody impressed. Where'd you learn that?'

They roared with laughter as the fourth assailant scarpered from the pub. But they hadn't impressed everyone. The pub owner was now pointing a double-barrelled shotgun squarely at them. Niall picked up his hat, threw a few pound notes onto the counter, and then placed his arm around Martin's shoulders.

'That's for the chair from my bad-tempered mate here.' Their laughing continued as they walked out onto the street.

Rather than risk provoking a repeat, they decided to purchase new 'civilian' clothes in the hope of blending in. When they explained the reason for their purchases to the shop owner, he laughed.

'Bloody good show. Those bastards aren't from around here. They've been annoying the hell out of everyone and even have the local police bluffed.'

'Well, you'd better go on down to the pub and let those boyos know we're thinking of staying here for a few weeks,' said Martin. 'We're not in fact, but it might give them something to think about.'

Niall and Martin returned to the pub two hours later. The troublemakers had departed. The publican accepted Niall's apology, then slid two large glasses of stout across the counter.

* * *

EARLY THE NEXT morning they found their way to Dungarvan and were given directions to the O'Meara farm. Martin waited at the front gate while Niall walked onto the property.

As Niall was about to step onto the front veranda of the farmhouse, a voice called out. 'What is it ye'd be wantin, young fella?' Niall turned and was confronted by a man dressed in typical farmer's clothes. He was of medium build, in his mid to late fifties... and casually hefting a shotgun.

Without warning, a large white dog, barking furiously, raced towards Niall. Hackles raised, it stopped about three feet away, snarling and displaying its fangs behind a quivering top lip.

'Ignore him, 'e just wants to play,' the farmer suggested with just a hint of a warning. 'So, what brings you here?'

'Well, I'm looking for my mother's four brothers actually,' Niall replied calmly. The farmer's jaw dropped noticeably and he stared in amazement. Niall quickly glanced at the dog now sniffing his boots, hackles down, lips no longer aquiver... but still growling softly.

'Good God, man, is that really you? Niall?' Before Niall could respond he added, 'Well, I'll be buggered. To t'ink we'd given up on ever meetin' yeh. What an unbelievable day this is.' He stepped forward, offering his hand. 'I'm Colm, by the way, and welcome to my humble farm.'

'Yep, it's me all right and it's great to meet you, Colm. We've got a lot to talk about, eh? But first I want you to meet my mate Martin.' Niall gestured for Martin to join them. The dog wandered off content that his duty was done.

After introducing Martin they went inside.

'Niall, it's really marvellous that yeh've put yourself out to visit us, but there's some sad t'ings yeh must know. Yeh grandmother, bless her, passed away nigh ten years ago. She's buried next to your grand-da in our family plot. At least, yeh'll get to see their graves. I'll show yeh about soon.

'We all loved our little Orla so very much and we've all missed her dreadfully,' said Colm with tears streaming down his face. 'But, my God, she could be a hothead. Ah, to be sure though, yeh'd always want her on yeh side.'

'Yes, I think I know exactly how you feel, but you can be extremely proud of her,' replied Niall. 'She lived her life to the full and often talked about Dan and Kathleen and you boys. She loved you all heaps, too, you should know, Colm. And she was the best mum!'

'I can vouch for that,' Martin quietly added.

At these remarks another look of anguish creased Colm's face. 'Niall, it hurts me to be the bearer of further bad news,' he said softly. 'My oldest brother Sean drowned at sea in '89 somewhere in Indonesia, and my youngest brother, Clive, left home wit' a big political chip on his shoulder. Haven't seen or heard from him for years. I t'ink that was what finally sent Mum to her grave not knowing why he held such strong beliefs.

'But there's some good news,' Colm added happily. 'My other brother Liam is living in England. He teaches law at Oxford. I know that sounds remarkable in this time of discrimination, but he's always been so impartial. That used to really annoy Orla, yeh know?'

Niall and Martin instantly looked at each other, mouths gaping in disbelief. Martin recovered first. 'You're not going to believe this, Colm, but when I leave here, I'm heading to England to start a law course at Oxford.'

The three men talked for hours and became firm friends. The dog also befriended Niall and Martin, taking it in turns to allow them to fondle his ears.

* * *

It surprised Niall how accurately his mother had described the home of her childhood. At the graveside of his grandparents, he paid his respects but experienced an unexpected wave of frustration. *If only I could've met you both*, he thought.

Still lost in those thoughts he wandered down to a nearby stream. He stood alongside a small scattering of glistening white stones watching the water glide by, unaware of the immense significance those stones once held for his mother.

After the evening meal, Martin retired early, leaving Niall and Colm alone to talk freely. And talk they did. Niall hid nothing from Colm, revealing his mother's short adult life — as she had once confided in him.

In the early hours of the morning as they were about to retire, to Niall's surprise, Colm said, 'Orla wrote to us and told us about yeh, but she never revealed the identity of yeh father. We knew his name was Edward, but *Ned Kelly*, never. It would've been grand to have met the great man. Oh yes, Niall, we learnt all about Ned Kelly here in Ireland... well, almost everything. And yeh should never be ashamed of yeh father, or the name Kelly. Ned fought for freedom and a better way of life, his own way, just as we've been doing for a long, long time.'

* * *

NIALL AND MARTIN spent the next week together enjoying the beautiful countryside on foot and on horseback. They met many interesting and genial neighbours and drank far too much.

'Mate, it's time for me to get back to England,' Martin announced reluctantly, breaking their shared mood of euphoria. 'What are you going to do?'

'I'd like to stay here and see more of this beautiful country. But I'll be returning to London and then travel to Oxford with you, if that's all right? I'd like to meet Liam. Then I'll make tracks back to Gympie. Mate, I really do miss home.'

55

Niall was determined to visit his Aunt Anne and her family in Adelaide en route to Queensland — another opportunity too good to pass up. Many years had passed since he'd last seen his cousins and he was keen to rekindle the friendships he only vaguely recalled from his childhood.

But as joyous as that occasion was, Anne was obviously struggling with grief. Her husband, James, and son, Michael, had also both volunteered to serve in the Boer War. James was repatriated after receiving an ear injury only weeks into his active service. However, it seemed Michael had just disappeared.

Their grief could have been prevented had Michael's letters explaining his intentions found their way into a letter box, but selfish preoccupation with his new life in post-war London distracted him from completing that simple duty. Several months would pass after the war ended before Anne and James were to learn of his safety. In the meantime both parents understandably mourned as if they had lost their son. As they later learned, Michael had opted to live in England... to study at Cambridge.

Regrettably, Niall only just missed catching up with Owen, who had also leapt at the opportunity to stay with his sister and James. He departed for Gympie during the week prior to Niall's arrival.

During the second week of Niall's stay in Adelaide, James and Niall went on a long walk.

'Niall, there are a couple things you need to know,' James announced when they stopped for lunch and were downing their third pot of beer. 'Neither is bad, it's just that you'll probably detect a change in Owen when you get home. Seems he's reassessed what he wants from life. He'll no doubt explain things to you, but he wants to sell his share in the timber mill and he wants me to oversee the sale and transfer of ownership, and so forth. The second matter's one of the heart... and most likely that's my fault.'

James purposefully pushed aside his beer glass then looked Niall squarely in the face. Having successfully captured his full attention, James continued. 'You see, when Owen was here, I introduced him to one of my bank staff, Margaret. She's a lovely woman in her mid-forties with a ribald sense of humour, a loyal but lonely lady who loves nothing better than to spend hours in the bush either painting or just exploring. Seems they hit it off straight away. Your stepfather was fawning over her constantly. It's not for me to judge, but Owen's a lonely man, too, and he needs a new life. Margaret really likes him and if they were to hitch up, I'm sure it'd add much to both of their lives.'

Niall took some time to recover from his surprise. 'You know, James, war changes a bloke's outlook on a lot of things. I've also felt for some time that I've run my race at the mill and I'll certainly not stop Dad from selling up. I'll probably do likewise come to think of it. This woman Margaret; she's not just trying to trap Owen, knowing he's vulnerable and bloody rich to boot?'

'I understand your concern, Niall, but in my opinion you've nothing to worry about. She's an honest woman,' James replied frankly. 'She can be forceful at times, mind you, but she's a considerate person. You would like her, I reckon.'

'Well, I'd better get back to Gympie and sort things out then,'

Niall said matter-of-factly. 'Thanks for your hospitality and for filling me in, Uncle. I'll get cracking tomorrow.'

* * *

WHEN NIALL ARRIVED IN GYMPIE, his cottage was empty. Clearly it had recently been lived in… but Owen was gone. The lengthy letter on the kitchen table detailed the reasons for his decision to sell his share in the timber milling operations and return to Adelaide, just as James had predicted. Initially, it annoyed Niall that he couldn't sit down with Owen and discuss everything, but he soon realised their now joint decision unleashed an unexpected feeling of freedom. He could visit Owen at any time. And in his letter, Owen was encouraging Niall to do just that.

'Perhaps I could convince Jeanie and Frank to come with me,' Niall said quietly to himself. 'Anyway, the best of good luck, Dad… and you too, Margaret.'

* * *

AFTER A BRIEF INSPECTION of the timber mill, Niall called a stop-work.

'It's great being back in Gympie and thanks for your welcome. You've worked wonders. Orders are up. Profits are soaring. Bloody well done.' Clapping and cheers followed.

'But listen, there's something you need to know. I'll also be quitting the mill.' The announcement was greeted with gasps and moans of disappointment.

'Please, hear me out. As you know, Owen has moved to Adelaide to start a new life. Anyway, we've agreed on everything. For instance, very shortly, *you'll all own this mill.*' More gasps, but this time in utter surprise.

Niall continued, holding up his hands to stop interjections. 'My Uncle James will take care of all legal matters and manage the ownership transfer. That won't cost you anything. So, at some time in the future, you can divvy-up the assets if you ever decide to sell up. As you know, Owen and I are entitled to a share of this operation. But listen. This is what we've got in mind. We'll each take forty percent of what money's in the company's bank account, leaving you with twenty percent for on-going working capital. That's a lot of money, by the way. And yes, all future profits will become yours to share. So, what do you reckon?'

Niall watched with pleasure as looks of disbelief on the faces of his loyal workers quickly changed to understanding. Slow hand clapping rippled around the building but quickly surged, to be replaced by deafening cheers of joy and much hand shaking and back slapping.

Niall quit the mill that day, his conscience clear, knowing he could handle any bittersweet memories. *I'll write to Dad and James tomorrow,* he thought. *I'm certain they'll be relieved and happy our succession plan's been accepted.*

* * *

TOGETHER WITH THE money Orla had left him — essentially a third of the accumulated profits from the earlier success of Frank's gold mining company — and his payout entitlement from the timber mill, Niall suddenly became a man of *considerable* means.

Jeanie and Frank were thrilled at Niall's safe return. They were now looking old but were still alert and enjoying their lives. They talked for hours about the happenings of the past two years and accepted the decisions he and Owen had made. They also readily agreed to accompany Niall whenever he decided to visit Adelaide.

After dinner, Frank confronted Niall. 'You've done well in your short life, Niall. You've earned your wealth. However, my boy, did James explain *our* wills?'

* * *

WHEN NIALL RETURNED to his cottage, he still struggled to get his head around Frank's announcement. He would also now inherit part of the Stewart's fortune, not just a vast sum of money, but properties in Australia and England. He would not simply be a man of considerable means, but rich beyond his wildest dreams. *God Almighty,* he kept thinking while shaking his head in disbelief.

Although the time was late, Niall was too wound up to consider going to bed. Suddenly, his thoughts were broken by a soft tapping on the front door. When he threw open the door there stood Ruthie. She was dressed in European women's clothes not unlike the riding outfits Orla once wore. Her silky black hair was pulled back, exposing her exquisite facial features and a slightly shy, but bewitching smile. Niall just stared, stunned by her beauty.

They stepped forward and threw their arms around each other. Ruthie gently pushed herself away and gazed deeply into his eyes. She then took his head in her hands and kissed him fully and longingly on his lips. Niall responded in like passion. In that wonderful moment their platonic friendship crossed many barriers to become a true and enduring love.

When they finally broke their embrace, Niall escorted Ruthie inside. 'It's so... so fantastic to see you, Ruthie,' stammered Niall. 'And, and, I've got so much to tell you. *But hang on,* how on earth did you know I was back?'

Before he could say anything further, she grabbed his hand and led him into his bedroom. 'Not now, Niall. That can wait. You're going to listen to me and learn something. You're such a dope. Why you never see how much I love you?' she whispered into his ear as she pulled him down onto the bed. 'Tonight you'll see how much. Anyway, welcome back.'

They were soon lost in lustful, uninhibited sex. Periods of deep, exhausted sleep followed. Their outpourings of love, infatuation, and commitment filled their senses, summoning mutual ambitions of starting their own family.

When Niall eventually climbed out of bed at midday, Ruthie was still fast asleep. He gazed upon her, realising she meant so much more to him than all the wealth he either currently possessed or he would soon inherit.

That evening they visited Jeannie and Frank and announced their plans to live together. Jeanie was not surprised for she had seen for years, as perhaps only women could, that Ruthie was madly in love with Niall.

'At last,' she said with admiration. 'But it took a bloody war to open your eyes. Take this lovely girl and do what's right by her. She's really *very* fond of you, Niall.'

Frank, too, was delighted for he had often seen Ruthie staring longingly at Niall. He had talked with Ruthie about many things, of his world and of hers, and learnt much.

'Good on you, boy,' he later said in confidence to Niall. 'Look after her; she's a beaut girl all right... and smart.'

To that old but gracious couple it was irrelevant whether Niall and Ruthie could marry legally or not; it was obvious to them their commitment was sincere and complete. Nevertheless, they discussed Ruthie's rejection of the customs of her culture.

'I've known for years that our way of life it nearly over,' Ruthie explained. 'And I could not honour traditional marriage anyway, even if I wanted to. Which I don't. There be simply too few of us left. Too many shot and raped. By white-man, you know? But still, I love *this* white man. Always have, always will.'

Niall and Ruthie were painfully aware that most whites would not respect their relationship, and most likely mistreat them. In frustration, Niall also realised his wealth would never change the obscenely misplaced intolerance of such people.

As if reading his mind, Jeanie asked quietly, 'Niall, can you handle the bigotry that *will* regrettably come?'

'Yep, like water off a duck's back. We could leave Australia, but this is our country. We belong *here,* for God's sake. We'll make our own way in this great land.'

'What do you feel about leaving this region, Ruthie?'

'*Cooloola* guide me, so Lahni says. But I nothing like our elders. I been told our people die if they leave ancestral places. But I not believe that. Will see many beautiful places, I reckon. Anyway, I always be with Niall. Never afraid then.' She paused then continued. 'Why you two stick up for me and my mob all this time?'

'That's simple, my dear,' Jeanie replied. 'You were always Orla's friends... and, therefore, you'll always be our friend.'

* * *

THE FOLLOWING WEEK, a very proud and contented couple departed Gympie, heading south to places unknown.

56

———————

Eighteen months later, Niall and Ruthie received word from their good friend Rob D'Angelese that Jeanie had suffered a stroke. Niall raced back to Gympie only to find that Frank had mothballed their lovely property and moved to Brisbane to guarantee Jeanie would get the best possible care and treatment.

When Niall finally visited Jeanie she had no idea who he was. She just stared straight ahead, unresponsive to anything Niall said, his questions unheard. Only once did she shift her gaze and look into his face. Niall saw only bewilderment in her eyes and not so much as a flicker to indicate this wonderful woman was once one of his staunchest allies.

Frank, ever the pragmatist but feeling desolate, tried to keep his life together by keeping busy. In Niall's company he broke down, irrationally blaming himself for Jeanie's condition.

Things quickly deteriorated. Just two weeks later Frank became considerably more unhinged and joined Jeanie in a hospice for the mentally ill. Niall visited them both regularly over the weeks that followed, but had to finally accept the doctor's advice that neither was likely to recover. Their predicament deeply saddened Niall.

Anne and Owen were likewise shattered to learn of the rapid, unfair decline in their parents' health and vowed to visit them within the next three weeks.

But time was now pressing on Niall. He had to return south... Ruthie would soon be giving birth to their first child. Rob assured Niall he'd keep him posted of the Stewarts' condition, and that if either Frank or Jeanie, or both, died while he was away, he would see to it that they were buried alongside Orla and Boss Boy's graves on their property at Gympie.

* * *

RUTHIE WAS LISTLESS. She had no appetite and the child's movements were becoming weaker. Niall accompanied his wife as they sought medical help at Coffs Harbour, but to no avail. The cruel power of nature — or fate — intervened yet again; both Ruthie and their son died during childbirth.

Lahni knew her Ruthie was in danger and knew where to find her. But she had neither the means of stopping Ruthie's uterus from haemorrhaging, nor the ability to breathe life into her grandson's tiny lungs.

Losing Orla had been traumatic, but to lose Ruthie shook Niall's soul. He now knew how difficult and profound Owen's grief must have been when Orla died. That knowledge did nothing to abate another overwhelming anguish, for he was now experiencing the same grief his real father must have felt — Ned never saw his son, either!

Local aboriginals took control of Niall and Lahni's plight and ceremonially buried Ruthie and the child near the Ellenborough River Falls. According to that Aboriginal family, this was a most fitting place for such a burial: from here the spirits of mother and son would soar and then unite with others in the eternity of their dreamtime.

However, Niall remained inconsolable. His expectations of a

happy family life were cruelly dashed. Loneliness and confusion were constant, uninvited companions. He started drinking— heavily — hoping it would dull the pain. It did, but not for very long.

* * *

IN THE MONTH leading up to the commencement of World War I, Niall received another shattering piece of news via a letter from James in Adelaide. Owen had drowned! He'd been fishing alone where the Murray River disgorges into Lake Alexandrina. The majority believed it was an unexpected storm that flipped his small boat. And, given the relentless waves generated by the storm and the soft clinging entrapment of the lake's silt bottom, he had little chance of survival.

As this information gradually seeped through Niall's alcohol-soaked brain, a heart shattering shock impaled him. His body went into a spasm. When the shaking stopped, he spewed violently. Although still in disbelief he re-read the fateful letter, and then cried hysterically. Tears stung his eyes and poured down his cheeks. His chest ached.

James also wrote that an Aboriginal family had found Owen's body and buried him in the vastness of the Coorong sand dunes. One of them reported the death to the police who then searched for the burial place, but they failed to find Owen's body. The letter did not state that although the police later searched widely for the Aboriginal family to further question them, no sign was found of them, either.

* * *

THE GROG THREATENED to end Niall's life. He could find no solace after that latest crushing loss. All of his riches could not bring back the people he loved and respected so much. Those riches neither gave him the incentive to start a new life, nor any desire to invest in or start a new enterprise. So overpowering were his bouts of drinking that he'd invariable spew until he dry retched. He would then black out. When he awoke he sweated profusely, or shivered and sobbed uncontrollably. He often contemplated suicide.

Wallowing in self-pity, he was drunk more often than sober and his physical condition deteriorated rapidly. Food was a vague afterthought. Gambling became his only distraction, his addled mind making a sucker of him, a bookmaker's dream. Consequently, his fortune began to erode. People avoided him because of his strange behaviour and for his appalling appearance... and, even worse, body odour.

'Poor bugger. Obviously couldn't handle the war,' was the popular, though uninformed, refrain of many.

Now living a completely itinerant life throughout Queensland, Niall one morning found himself at a railway station, watching indifferently as a train approached from the south. The train shuddered to a stop and several men climbed down to the ground. All were elegantly suited, carrying briefcases, and engrossed in very businesslike conversation.

Niall idly watched them as they bustled by. Most of them did their best to ignore the tall, heavily bearded, dishevelled, and obviously hung-over man leaning against a wall of the station office. But the man attracting the most attention from his colleagues did glance at him. The man slowed... then stopped dead. He turned swiftly and retraced his steps.

'Jesus, Christ Almighty! Is that you, Niall?' the man said, glaring at Niall in shock and disapproval.

Through an alcohol-induced haze, Niall tried to focus, cursing in his frustration that whilst he thought he recognised the man's voice, he couldn't properly see the man's face. He blinked rapidly and then furiously rubbed his eyes. Then it hit him.

'Yes... it is,' Niall sobbed. 'But I wish you hadn't seen me like this, mate.'

'Get that man into accommodation immediately,' the businessman ordered. 'Get him cleaned up and fed. And I want him in my office by noon — sober and dressed in some half-decent clothes.' He then pivoted and briskly walked away.

'Yes, Mister Fisher, straight away,' chorused several of the men who then grabbed Niall by his elbows and frog-marched him from the station.

* * *

AT THEIR REUNION, Niall spoke first. 'Bloody hell, Andy, I feel so embarrassed.'

Andy initially said nothing, but smiled broadly and casually thrust out his hand. Andy's handshake and the look on his face were firm and reassuring in equal measure.

'Don't be, mate. Relax, you're with friends. Those other blokes you met are all good men and I've explained your situation to them. If you need anything, just ask them, all right?'

They talked into the late afternoon and by dinnertime, Niall felt as if a massive weight had been lifted from his heart. His head no longer throbbed and for the first time in months he felt good – without being under the weather.

During their meal, Andy spoke quietly but firmly. 'It's not for me to judge you, mate. I know you've been through a rough trot and I'm really sorry to hear what's happened. But listen to me, Niall. Life must go on, so pick up your act. Surround yourself with things you like and start planning for the future. Recall all the good times you spent with your wonderful mum, the Stewarts, Ruthie, and of course, Owen.

'But don't dwell on their deaths!' Andy almost shouted. 'Find yourself again and for God's sake, stop blaming yourself for things over which you had no control.' Rising from his chair, Andy concluded their meeting. 'I'm here to talk at a local council meeting, so I must bid you goodnight and good luck. But remember, mate, you're always welcome on my doorstep. And keep off the grog!'

With that they warmly shook hands and Niall said in parting, 'I reckon I'd have been dead within a few weeks if you hadn't recognised me. You're right, mate, it's time to pull me head in. Thanks Andy, I'll be forever grateful. One thing though... I never doubted that one day you'd become our Prime Minister.'

57

Niall had no intention of serving in World War I, which, in his view, represented no direct threat to Australia. He was still of an age to serve, fit enough and experienced in warfare, but he'd simply had enough of dealing with death. It was not a matter of cowardice; he simply objected to the futility of war and so chose to live by the dictates of his conscience.

For the duration of World War I and beyond, Niall satisfied a persistent craving to see the grandeur of his great country. He also experienced an amazing sense of freedom. He now saw reason in everything he chose to do and accepted that if his individuality did not offend or upset other people, then his life was as it should be.

During his travels throughout those years, he helped farmers with fencing, assisted in repairing steam engine drive systems, and carried out repairs and routine maintenance on motor vehicles. He also cut sugar cane. For an extended period he visited the Kimberley region of Western Australia, mustering, marking, and branding cattle. Generally, he would not accept any pay, but when it was forced upon him, he usually donated it anonymously to either an outback mission or to a city orphanage.

The terrible thirst he had for grog had almost relented but he acquired another thirst; reading now dominated his time. His reading interests also meant he became aware of upcoming art exhibitions. Niall attended many of those events in the capital cities and marvelled at the artistic talent emerging in Australia. Niall was also privileged to visit other magnificent galleries — those of Arnhem Land.

At every opportunity Niall attended country race meetings, immersing himself in the rough companionship of the punters, owners, breeders, jockeys, and bookmakers. He never placed a bet, but his 'tips' were now seldom off the money.

The most positive thing about this period was that Niall found direction and purpose. His physical strength returned. His mind was again sharp and he had his emotions under control. *Time will cure all*, he kept reminding himself. Regrettably, Niall had one significant folly... women. Of some he was very fond; though, to none would he commit.

Determined now to settle down and not waste his money, he purchased two cattle grazing properties in New South Wales, one in the foothills of the Mograni Ranges near Gloucester, and the other near Tumut, in the fertile lead-up country to the foothills of the Snowy Mountains.

Niall paid for his Tumut holding to be managed, but chose to live a solitary life on his Gloucester property. He enjoyed driving his new car between his properties. His arrival at Tumut was always met with pleasure by the manager's family.

For years Niall profited handsomely from the sale of his consistently high quality cattle. He also kept horses at Gloucester and regularly explored the magnificent Gloucester and Barrington Tops. Twice he rode all the way to Scone on the western side of the Great Dividing Range. On both occasions, he observed several magnificent native wild dogs.

It upset him to learn that the western plains graziers were persisting with trapping, shooting or poisoning those proud dogs in retribution for raids on their sheep. On the other hand, he was heartened by some enlightened farmers who were planning to reconstruct a fence – one that had first been built in the 1870s to keep the native dogs in the high-plains country. Perhaps, without an anonymous donation, that fence may never have been twice rebuilt.

* * *

IN EARLY JUNE 1923, Niall was inspired by a locally produced newspaper. It featured an article recalling the life and times of a local bushranger, Captain Thunderbolt. That article got him thinking about the story his mother told him of the friendship between his father and Tom Lloyd. This led to some enquiries: a message soon arrived assuring him that Tom was indeed alive and still living near Glenrowan.

Encouraged by this news, Niall drove to Glenrowan. Whilst nothing about the terrain was familiar to Niall, he suspected that the modern country road over which he travelled, probably took the same route along which Boss Boy had so faithfully laboured all those years ago.

Following the directions he'd been given, Niall easily located the right house. The front door was open so Niall called out through the flyscreen as he knocked on the doorframe.

'Hello. Anybody home? Niall Kelly's the name. I'm looking for Tom Lloyd.'

Tom, in his mid-sixties was not a well man, but strong enough not to have a heart attack as that call reverberated through his home. At first he appeared tentative, almost shy, but then abruptly threw open the flyscreen and eagerly shook Niall's hand.

'Bloody hell, no mistakin' who you might be, boy,' Tom said pleasantly, though in a matter-of-fact manner.

Tom easily engaged with Niall. They chatted for hours, tears unashamedly running down Tom's weather-beaten cheeks when he recounted aspects of his life with Ned, Dan, Joe, Steve, and of course, Orla and Kate.

Kate, he explained, had moved on and married a bloke named Cleave with whom she subsequently had seven children.

'Three of her kids died real young. Damn shame, that. Anyway, I don't get to see much of her now, even though she lives not far from 'ere,' Tom lamented. 'But perhaps you already knew all that? Orla and Kate wrote to each other for years, you know. Kept me posted, too.'

'Well, I'll be buggered,' replied Niall. 'No, Tom, I had absolutely *no* idea about that.'

Tom also spoke of two small, very clever old Chinamen who worked tirelessly to help Ned's cause. 'Totally devoted to Ned and Orla, they were,' Tom mused.

'I remember Mum telling me about those men. Brothers weren't they?'

'Yes, they were, and really likeable old buggers, too,' Tom replied. 'But tell me, young fella, by what name do you go? You sure as hell look a lot like Ned with that beard, though I think you're a bit taller than he was.'

'Mostly, it's Stewart, but sometimes O'Meara. Depends on the company I keep. Never Kelly when I go into a bank, though; some people have incredibly long memories.' The men erupted into boisterous laughter.

Having settled down, Tom continued. 'Not too many people know that I rode with Ned and the boys to Jerilderie to rob that bank. While they did the business, I looked after their horses. By jeez those boys rode hard. Music and their other Walers never once let 'em down. That Music was a true beauty, yah know.

'Your dad was special to me, son. When I accidentally killed my cousin John, I felt lousy for a long time, but Ned got into me ear. He got me doin' all kinds of things. I probably would've killed meself if your dad hadn't sorted me out.'

They continued talking until it was almost dark. When Niall rose to say farewell, Tom became wistful.

'Yah know son, it was a night just like this when the boys headed for Glenrowan. Wish the hell yah dad had listened to me and your mum. Perhaps, he might still be alive. Mind you, Ned and Joe were both bright lads. Had their ideas panned out as they wanted, it would've changed many, many things I reckon. Looking back, I'm glad I didn't ride with Ned and the boys that time. I could've, but I discovered pretty quick after putting on that damn armour that I suffered from claustrophobia. Ah well, what's done is done, I suppose. Call by any time, young man.'

As Tom was about to step inside his old house, he paused. 'And I'll tell you something else. I reckon you've both topped Ned's achievements. Just imagine how it'll be if the world ever finds out about your dear mum... and you!'

Chuckling to himself as he went indoors, Tom called out, 'Anyway, I'm sure your dad would 'ave been rightly proud of yah, son.'

* * *

NIALL STAYED in Glenrowan that night. After his evening meal he walked in the moonlight to the place where his father had finally been captured, then close to death and in great pain and mental torment. And it was only fifty or so yards from this place where Orla saw Ned for the last time. Niall controlled a surge of emotion and walked purposefully back to his lodgings.

A cold, gusty wind whispered mournfully through the nearby she-oaks as Niall retreated. But nothing registered with him. It might have been a different matter had either Lahni or Ruthie been in that place with him. To them, to hear that message on the breeze would have revealed Orla was trying to tell him something — wanting to guide him.

* * *

NIALL'S long drive back to Gloucester gave him plenty of opportunity to think of the time his mother and Ned lived together. Tom's perspective had been honest and insightful, for which Niall felt extremely grateful.

Sadly, when he stopped at Wangaratta he learnt that the McIntyres had sold their property and retired to the coastal town of Port

Campbell in the Western District of Victoria. The new owners were only too happy to give Niall the McIntyres' new address. Although disappointed, Niall made a solemn pledge that one day soon he'd visit those marvellous people who so many years before had befriended and cared for his mother.

Alas, two years later, when Niall attempted to fulfil that commitment, only a demented Cocko had survived long enough to greet Niall.

* * *

COINCIDING with the end of World War 2, Niall decided to sell one of his properties. Although now in his mid-sixties, still strong, mentally alert, and not suffering any major ailment, the reality of owning two properties was too demanding. Niall sold his Gloucester interests and relocated to Tumut.

The surrounding countryside was picturesque. The Snowy Mountains formed a challenging backdrop, which inexplicably beckoned him. Niall frequented those lofty, mostly uncharted ranges for weeks at a time. He loved the solitude of those unspoiled mountains, never tiring of the beauty brought by each season.

He also hiked for many miles, witnessed breathtaking gorges, crossed many glittering mountain streams, and slept under the stars. On the highest plains he discovered massive clusters of moths hidden in rocky crevasses. Niall learnt later that according to the Aboriginals, those hairy, fat moths were considered nutritious and tasty... however, he never put that taste to the test.

When, in a region north of the settlement of Buchan in Victoria, he came upon a particularly wild gorge of the Snowy River where he found caves with examples of ancient rock-art. These images depicted annual moth gathering forays made by the various Aboriginal tribes as they traversed the gorge on their way to the high plains.

It was also during one of these trips that Niall learned the Australian Commonwealth Government was about to finance the building of The Snowy Mountains Scheme, the largest engineering feat the world had ever seen. That scheme would involve capturing the vast volume of water flowing from the spring snow melt, redirecting it through tunnels under the mountains to the dry western hinterlands and, in so doing, generate hydro-electricity for Melbourne, Canberra, and Sydney.

The benefits of such a scheme were not lost on Niall, but he resented the possibility that the landscape of the Alps, as he knew it, might be recklessly changed forever. It saddened him he was utterly powerless to do anything to alter the momentum of that project.

58

On a fishing trip near Corryong in December 1951, Niall camped beside the Murray River where one afternoon he landed two yellow-belly, a favourite eating fish. On the spur of the moment, he decided to give his catch to his camping neighbours. They were delighted and invited him to join them for dinner. It wasn't long before the beer and stories were flowing in equal quantity. After all, it was a warm night.

When Niall returned to his camp, for some curious reason, he kept thinking about what his new friends just told him. They'd recently camped in the Buckland Valley and the trout fishing there was outstanding... but it wasn't just that.

Before he fell into a now rare, beer-induced sleep, Niall thought, *Yeah, of course, that's where those bloody Chinamen lived.* He could even vaguely recall the mud maps his mother drew to show him where they had lived.

* * *

When Niall returned to his Tumut property, he made another life-changing decision. It made more sense to be living where he could be guaranteed prompt medical attention; not that he had any major illness to worry about... apart from perhaps the occasional giddy spell when he stood up too quickly. And so, in 1954, he moved to a property near Bright in North-East Victoria.

Now going on seventy-five, Niall still carried himself proudly. He suffered few ill effects from his advancing years and continued to indulge in his favourite pastimes — making his own bread, fishing, taking long bushwalks, shooting the occasional rabbit, and enjoying 'an occasional cleansing lager'.

In December 1956, he purchased a brand new DeSoto utility, only the second of its type in the area according to the police when he registered it at the Bright police station. The other vehicle was owned by the Beveridge brothers, Jack and Syd, who were well-known cattlemen and pioneering identities who still lived in the Buckland Valley.

Soon after, Niall introduced himself to these men, who were roughly his own age. They quickly became good friends, swapping many stories; some real, others unashamedly stretching the truth.

Eventually, Niall asked them the questions that had been plaguing him for years. After all, these two old blokes had been around a long time and probably knew the Buckland Valley and its history as well as anyone. Of Ned Kelly they, surprisingly, only knew of rumours and what they'd read in the papers.

'Hey Syd, ever see any Chinese gold workings in the valley, or hear stories about what the Chinese got up to?'

'Nope. Never saw them actually at work, but they were an industrious lot apparently,' Syd explained. 'Most of them were treated shabbily. A lot of the poor buggers were shot or given terrible hidings to get 'em to move on, like.

'They'd all moved from around here before we took up our lease. Mind you, there was a grocery and butcher shop, a bank, hotels, and joss houses still standing up at The Junction back then. From our place here, it's about twelve miles upstream. But these days, there's nowt to see. Everything's since collapsed and rotted away, or is covered in damn blackberries. They left a lot of deep mine shafts, too. Bloody dangerous, they are. They've claimed more than a few of our cattle over the years.'

'Listen, how about we take you up there tomorrow so you can poke about? You just never know what you might find,' Jack offered. 'We'll take our rods and a few beers and make a day of it. What do you reckon?'

* * *

As they drove up the Buckland Valley on the narrow, winding dirt road, there was evidence of many cattle in the area judging by their droppings on the road, but no actual sightings, not even that of a single beast.

Syd stopped his utility unexpectedly. He got out, grabbed a bucket from the rear tray and walked about twenty yards, depositing several mounds of a white substance as he went. To Niall's astonishment, Syd suddenly released a strange series of booming guttural calls. He then returned and leant against the utility, peering into the surrounding timber. He continued to call intermittently.

'Here they come, look!' Jack announced excitedly, pointing to a brindle bull as it crashed through the undergrowth about forty yards away. 'I haven't seen that old bastard for at least two years. They love their salt, eh? They've probably jogged a mile, more maybe, just to get at Syd's little treat. It's our way to gauge their numbers and their condition. And, believe me, mate, this is a damn sight easier than doing it on horseback.'

Niall nodded, recalling his stepfather's account of his days as a cattle thief, and how then, even in the prime of his life, just how hard he said it had been penetrating the scrub on his horse, to locate and muster ill-disposed cattle.

In admiration, Niall watched as fifty or sixty cattle ghosted into view. Most were Herefords, though a few multi-coloureds mingled amongst them. With their heads held low and sniffing loudly, they ran to the mounds of salt and started to greedily devour it. But this group was only the experienced vanguard of a much greater mob. Within fifteen minutes, their numbers had grown to over two hundred head, all jostling to get at least one lick before the salt disappeared. Before long that jostling gave way to fights, their bellows of frustration echoing along the valley.

'By geez, they're in good nick,' Syd proudly announced. 'Reckon we should take a few off during autumn, though. How many do you suggest, Jack?'

With a thoughtful expression on his face, Jack replied. 'At least four hundred, I'd say.'

Niall was impressed.

The three men drove on to The Junction. With word pictures, much arm waving and pointing by Jack and Syd, plus a bit of imagination, Niall eventually visualised the general layout of that early settlement.

Later, they all caught several pan-sized trout and, at the day's end, cleaned and gutted their catch. As shadows lengthened and crept across the valley floor, they feasted on butter-fried trout. Several bottles of cool beer helped to wash down their succulent meal.

It intrigued Niall how cold the beer remained despite the temperature of the day — until it was his turn to retrieve another bottle from the creek where Syd had 'planted' their beer earlier in the day. Niall then remembered that immediately downstream from where the creek joined the Buckland River, the river's temperature suddenly dropped. And so he should have remembered, for he'd landed two feisty rainbow trout at that very confluence.

At home that night, Niall reflected upon his day's outing, but for some annoying reason, also kept trying to recall details of the story Orla had told him of his father's first meeting with Charlie and Ong.

But what's that got to do with today? Niall pondered. Out of the blue, he felt compelled do some serious exploring. Orla had definitely said the Chinese brothers lived just a few miles *upstream* from The Junction. That detail he did remember.

* * *

INSTEAD OF STOPPING at The Junction, Niall drove on for about two and a half miles and eventually came upon a reasonably well defined, but little used track on the left side of the road. He parked and walked contentedly down the shale-covered track to the western bank of the Buckland River.

The day was warming up quickly. He squatted and splashed water over his face and, with his cupped hands, scooped up some water and drank deeply. He casually examined the underside of several rocks to determine whether this site held a mudeye population just in case he came that way again for a spot of fishing. There had to be, he reckoned, given the number of jousting dragon flies whose gossamer wings crashed noisily, their bright blue bodies iridescent in the sunlight.

When he stood he realised the location was used as a crossing point, albeit infrequently, probably by the Beveridge brothers when moving their cattle onto the high plains. He waded across the river and turned downstream, following another barely discernible track. After walking three hundred yards or so, he came to an abrupt bend in the river where he took a breather to soak up the peace and beauty of his surrounds.

As he looked about, images tumbled into his consciousness. Suddenly alert, he suspected he'd been intuitively following Orla's mud map, the coincidence of his surroundings being uncannily familiar. The bend in the river. The huge logs and rocks piled in an overgrown jumble right up to the river's edge giving the impression of a land slip many winters ago. Beyond that jumble; yes, there were remnants of manmade channels, only just visible under decaying branches and thick overgrown grass.

In his mind's eye, Niall compared this scene with his recollections of Orla's descriptions. *Bloody hell! There it is... the hut and its veranda protruding from the mountain, the vegetable gardens; even the pig sties.* He felt the hairs rising on the back of his neck as the reality struck... he had undeniably found the home of Charlie and Ong, just where Orla said it would be: tangible evidence of the truth of his mother's sketchy maps and her stories.

Without prior knowledge to the history of the place it would have been impossible to appreciate what lay before him, just as, no doubt, many fishermen never previously recognised what they were looking at.

It was now hot, but Niall shivered. He forced himself to control his excitement while looking about for further evidence of past habitation. There was something else Orla told him about, something either novel or comical. Gazing into the scrub and then at the massive eucalypts surrounding him, a thought imposed itself. *I bet a few of you grand old stringy-barks could tell me a story or two, eh?*

In his mind another image gradually became clearer. *Stringy bark... stringy. Yes, strings!* Niall thought furiously. *To keep their home-made beer cold, those Chinamen suspended their beer bottles into the river... on strings! Good God, it was right there in my face just a few bloody days ago. Those Beveridge brothers knew the same trick. I saw it, but I still didn't tumble to it. Christ, I must be getting old.*

Despite feeling a bit light-headed at this revelation, Niall wandered over to the pool formed by the bend in the river. It was obviously at its deepest there, and probably the coldest. *And most likely the place where the Chinamen had suspended their beer bottles,* Niall reasoned.

As he peered into the depths of the pool, a weird bright spot on the riverbed grabbed his attention. He walked a few steps upstream to alter his viewing angle. The bright spot changed shape slightly, but remained motionless. He realised that if he drew an imaginary line from where he now stood through the centre of the light, the extension of that line would pass through the dead centre of the jumble of timber and rocks.

Niall stood thinking about this for a few minutes. It then dawned on him. *Good God! There's gotta be a tunnel leading from the middle of that mess to the bottom of the pool.*

'Well, there's only one way to find out,' he whispered as he started removing his boots. He then stripped to his underpants.

'Here goes.' Niall slid into the pool directly over the light. Holding onto the rock-face of the pool, he allowed himself to be swept low into the water while exploring with his feet for the expected opening. Something slippery glanced off one of his legs; a good-sized trout retreating from its lair. Taking a deep breath he shoved himself completely below the surface, and then deeper, until he peered into the entrance of a tunnel.

On the spur of the moment, he kicked furiously and pulled himself inside the tunnel. It was wider than his shoulders and had plenty of clearance above and below his body. Another confused and frightened trout charged past, brushing against his naked back. With a few more kicks he broke the surface.

He was now within what appeared to be a chamber. Overhead, two massive logs separated allowing a shaft of sunlight to penetrate. As Niall's eyes became accustomed to the gloom, he looked about and then hauled himself out of the water, up onto some rotting wooden planks — an ancient floor!

There was a cloying, pungent odour. Bats flittered around his head emitting sharp squeaking noises in protest at his intrusion. There was also a strong earthy smell of mould, and the trickling sound of gently cascading water.

Niall located where the water ran into the chamber, no doubt a permanent spring judging by its extreme coldness. As he moved about on the slippery planks, they groaned in protest under his weight and threatened to send him arse-over-head if he misplaced his footing. Otherwise, the structure seemed sound and unlikely to collapse.

Although the light was poor, Niall could see a table upon which stood an oriental temple. Occupying the centre of the chamber was a collapsed bed covered with rotting, heavily mildewed bedding. In a corner, partially covered by rocks and debris, was an uninteresting heap of what looked like domestic paraphernalia.

Niall was now very cold. Keen to return to the sun's warmth he cut short any further inspection, but vowed to return with suitable lighting... just in case there was anything of perceived value worth removing.

Wet from exiting the tunnel, Niall slowly wended his way back up the shale-covered track to his DeSoto utility. Still in disbelief at his amazing discovery, he thought, *not a bad effort for an old bastard.*

59

Ten days later, Niall returned to the Chinamen's old home, armed with battery-operated torches, a kerosene lamp, an assortment of different sized screw top containers, several pieces of fabric for wiping objects clean — plus two kerosene drums modified so that one end of each drum was removable and watertight.

The buoyant drums were difficult to manhandle inside the tunnel, but Niall persevered and eventually heaved them onto the slippery floor of the chamber. The drums had done their job; everything inside was dry. Within minutes, the chamber was flooded with light from the kerosene lamp, much to the annoyance of the resident bats.

Although the lamplight was even, Niall still needed a torch to conduct his detailed inspection. He started with the old bed. As he peeled back the rotting blankets he made a gruesome discovery... a small skeleton wrapped in its desiccated and blackened skin.

This discovery momentarily took Niall's breath away, not from the smell — there was none — but from the sheer unexpectedness of his finding. He noticed there were two holes in this skeleton's head: the offending pistol still clasped in the person's right hand.

Niall recalled Orla's story of how Ong had sadly passed away while in Ned's service; Charlie bravely hid his terrible grief from Ned. Orla had also assumed Charlie buried his brother somewhere nearby. Niall concluded that Charlie's grief, probably exacerbated by later learning of Ned's capture, presumably led him to say whatever prayers he believed were important to him, and then lit the fuses to demolish his home. Niall winced as he visualized the old man blowing his tortured brains out shortly after he climbed into the bed.

Niall knew from recollection of his mother's words that this place had once been a gold mine, a fortress, and a home: it was now a simple but special tomb. Long before, Orla correctly guessed the reason for its destruction. 'A monument to the nicest Chinamen anyone would ever want to meet', she had philosophically convinced herself.

It suddenly flashed through Niall's mind what Orla had told him several times... 'When the brothers died, she and Ned were expected to take what they wanted of their belongings as a reminder of their friendship'. *Treasure perhaps?* Niall immediately thought. *Whatever it might be, it's of no damn use to them now!*

He needn't look too hard to satisfy his curiosity. Out of interest he picked up the miniature temple. It was surprisingly heavy. He then carefully dusted a section of its exterior. He stared, astounded. The temple was an exquisite work of art, of beauty equal to that he'd seen in a museum in London. It had been meticulously hand carved from a solid billet of what looked like red gum. Instinctively, Niall recognised it was also of great value.

However, removing it to the outside world posed a major problem. The temple's structure now appeared brittle: to risk manhandling it through the water tunnel would have been foolhardy. *I'll come back for it later,* he reasoned.

He then noticed an unremarkable rawhide tray about the size of a child's schoolbag lying behind the temple. Its contents blazed brilliantly under Niall's torch beam. *Gold!* The tray was full of it! Excitedly, Niall sifted his fingers through the valuable metal, the bulk of it comprised of small, uniformly sized specks; randomly throughout the mass were several pea sized nuggets. One nugget was the size of a walnut!

'Good God Almighty, there's a bloody fortune here,' Niall whispered incredulously. 'Wonder how long it took those boys to win this lot?'

He excitedly transferred the gold into six of his largest screw top containers then placed them into one of his watertight drums.

While still pondering on how to safely remove the temple, he casually focused his attention upon the dusty statue of a horse he'd overlooked on his initial visit. He gently picked it up from the floor and began to carefully wipe it clean. It stood approximately fifteen inches tall and was eighteen inches or so from head to tail. In the fading light of his torch, he recognised it as another piece of exquisite beauty. It was of fine porcelain, skilfully configured in the motion of walking. Head held high. True in form and exact in proportion. And it was expertly glazed. *Priceless!* Though exulting in finding such a fine piece, something was frustrating Niall's senses. Then it came to him!

'Oh, Jesus! That's Boss Boy!' Niall whispered loudly in equal measure of recognition, disbelief, and pleasure. 'It's bloody perfect; even his exact colour! In the right circles this is probably worth triple the value of the gold.'

Apart from Niall, no one alive who could appreciate either the significance of this statue or the utterly determined effort Charlie must have made to complete this legacy before choosing to take his life. Niall carefully wrapped the statue within several layers of fabric and meticulously packed the bundle into the other watertight drum.

Next, Niall turned his attention to an old wallet he noticed lying on the table. He carefully parted the layers of ancient leather to reveal a faded but still quite clear studio photograph of five poker-faced young men. Four of those men he recognised from newspaper photographs; regrettably, he knew only one of them personally — Tom Lloyd. Niall had to sit: he was overwhelmed by a giddy spell and gut-wrenching emotion now making it difficult for him to breathe.

He was about to place the photograph back into the wallet when he realised there was a second one stuck behind it. It was just as well he was still sitting, because there, in their best studio poses and staring back at Niall, was a very young and beautiful Orla, his handsome father, Ned, and two gap-toothed old Chinamen.

Hot tears tumbled down Niall's face. He cried shamelessly, his body shuddering with each great sob. At least twenty minutes passed before he controlled his emotions. He stood shakily, realising he was again feeling cold... but he still had work to do. He returned the photographs to the old wallet and then placed it, suitably wrapped, into the drum with the gold.

As Niall made preparations to leave, he cast the beam of his torch about one last time. Eventually, it fell upon the assorted hotchpotch of objects he'd previously rejected as unworthy of interest, let alone of any value.

He casually kicked at what appeared to be the largest object in the heap. To his surprise it was solid and didn't budge. He stooped and pulled. Out slid a large, strangely curved steel plate.

The hairs instantly shot up on the back of Niall's neck. 'Shiiite, what the hell have we got here?' Niall had seen enough photographs of the famous Kelly Gang's armour to know what the object was. At his feet lay either a breast or back-plate from one of those suits!

He then proceeded to drag into the light another breast or back-plate, front and back aprons, and last, but not least, a tall cylindrical helmet with the hallmark horizontal eye slot — and still clearly visible through the rust on the helmet, were the unmistakable letters: *TOM L.*

* * *

Getting the metal drums out through the water tunnel was awkward; their buoyancy still posed a major challenge.

Niall carefully carried the drums back to his utility but had to take several 'breathers' along the way, for the day was again warming rapidly. By the time he'd cushioned and secured the drums and found a safe location to turn his vehicle around, he was sweating profusely and extremely hot.

Twice before he arrived back at his home, he had to stop for a drink of water. It was at the second stop when he was sitting in the shade thinking about how he might go about removing the Chinamen's temple and Tom's armour, he knew something wasn't right.

The day was bloody hot, and he'd exerted a reasonable amount of energy getting into and out of the water tunnel. And yes, he'd just experienced a most unexpected emotional hour or so. But he now felt tired, as tired as he'd ever felt in his life... and seldom had he sweated as he was right then.

He also knew if he stood up at that moment, he risked getting another giddy spell. Since that prospect held no appeal whatsoever, he sat quietly in the shade for another fifteen minutes, breathing steadily.

Having recovered sufficiently, he walked back to his utility, muttering to himself, 'Niall old boy, it's time you took it a bit easy, mate. Looks like you've found your limits. But still, not a bad day's work for the seventy-six year old bastard son of a bushranger, eh?'

* * *

THE BOSS BOY statue held pride of place on the mantelpiece in his lounge at Bright, but he eventually gave it to a teenage girl for a Christmas present. The two photographs he always kept in his wallet.

He converted the gold into cash, which joined his considerable personal wealth, though that transaction garnered many questions as to the gold's origins. Those whose inquisitiveness eventually became intrusive were told, 'Get off your arse and find your own bloody fortune.'

Of the temple and the armour he told only one person. In the interim, Niall remained confident he would eventually find a way of possessing both items, 'provided his perch didn't stop swinging in the meantime'. However, infirmity and the forces of nature conspired to frustrate his ambition.

Sadly, during the evening of the 17th of January 1961, Niall died.

PART IV

THE MEETING

60

In early January 1958, three years before Niall's passing, a freak thunderstorm blasted along the lower Buckland Valley, raising the river's water level and flattening surrounding vegetation. Nobody anticipated a second rise: a huge surge generated thirty-five miles upstream, the result of an earlier massive deluge dumped over the Barry Mountains. These events profoundly affected me, the son of a happy, down to earth, working class Melbourne family.

At the first break in the rain, I set off for the river. The clouds were brooding and low. Thunder still rolled through the valleys and the deliciously cool air was filled with the heady smells of washed pasture. At our favourite swimming hole, half of the rocky outcrops I used as diving platforms the previous day were submerged. Muddy water now rushed boisterously between the walls of the small gorge forming the swimming hole. Regardless, I was impatient to try out my new fly rod. As I began working the bend in the river leading into the pool, I became vaguely aware of a noise now rising above that of the swirling river: a crashing and deep grinding sound which I subconsciously dismissed as receding thunder.

In a well-practiced routine I completed a forward cast concentrating upon the location where I anticipated my lightly weighted nymph would gently settle. I froze in disbelief. A huge, tsunami-like wave was charging around the bend in the river — and only twenty or so yards away!

That churning monster was destroying everything in its path, dragging with it stumps, up-rooted trees, fence posts, wire, and a mash of bush scrub. Rocks 'pinged' as they collided with each other in their headlong drive towards me.

I was terrified. It felt like an eternity before I could move. I had two or three seconds to escape — *but to where?* I dropped my rod and in desperation lunged upward seeking the highest diving ledge of the swimming hole.

The flood surge smashed into me. *Oh God, the pain!* It's strange how the mind works when you believe you're about to look into God's eyes. *Well, that's me buggered,* I recall thinking to myself. *No hope of playing cricket for Australia now!*

In a flash, the surge's momentum pulled me under. I was only seconds from surrendering to a deadly pummelling. But, incredibly, I was somehow being hauled free.

Trying to rid your lungs of water is another excruciating pain — surely dying is not as bad, though I have no compulsion to ever test it. As something resembling full consciousness surfaced, I realised what happened. I was also certain at that point my dad would give me my first thrashing. But the eyes into which I looked for compassion were neither those of God nor my dad. *So, who the hell was this old bloke talking quietly to me, reassuring me that I was not yet due for heaven?*

Acutely embarrassed, bruised and still shaken, I allowed my bearded lifesaver to half-drag, half-carry me out of further harm's way. We sat mute for several minutes, catching our breath, and watching in awe as the leading edge of the surge charged forward and then collapsed as it ran onto flat farming lands bordering the river downstream.

We occasionally glanced at each other, silently acknowledging what we had just averted. This bloke was without a doubt the oldest person I'd met so far. What hair he still had was almost white but intermingled with dark streaks; his mid-length beard was the reverse.

Due to his exertion, sweat ran down his suntanned, deeply lined face and into his beard. At first glance, his eyes appeared black, but they were actually dark green.

After we'd both recovered, I muttered my gratitude. It's fair to say we were both relieved the ordeal was over. As we stood, I realised he was probably over six feet tall and looked remarkably healthy for his age. We walked side by side in silence back towards my campsite at nearby Devil's Creek.

We were soon intercepted by my understandably anxious family, who had come to look for me. They had heard the deep rumble of the raging flood and Mum, in particular, was convinced I was a goner.

'G'day mate, the name's Frank Tucker,' my dad said in friendly greeting as he offered his hand to the stranger. 'And this is my usually calm wife, Marion, and this is our daughter, Jill. It looks like you've already met the boy.' Turning his attention upon me, Dad continued. 'What the bloody hell's happened? And where's your new rod?'

'It's OK, Frank, there's nothing to worry about,' replied the stranger. 'My name's Niall Kelly, by the way. Pleased to meet you all. Unfortunately, I couldn't save your son's rod when I plucked him out of the drink.'

The significance of those few words did little to calm my mother, but Dad was obviously relieved, grateful, and impressed. 'Bloody hell, thanks, mate,' he said. 'But listen. Before we all get too excited, how about joining us for a beer? You can then both tell us what happened. And you'll stay for dinner, OK?'

That evening we shared a memorable feast of rabbit casserole followed by stewed plums and, understandably, our conversation centred upon a detailed account of that afternoon's event.

Niall had been appraising my casting technique from a nearby ridge and heard and seen the approaching danger long before I had. He instinctively knew that yelling to alert me was pointless, so he ran to where he hoped to catch my attention to warn me to get away from the river. But he, too, didn't realise the speed of the surge and only just made it to the rock platform above and about ten yards downstream from me. He'd watched in dismay as I went under, but threw himself flat onto the rocks and reached forward in-the-nick-of-time to grab my right wrist as I swept by. Had I slipped and fallen in just before the crest of that surge hit me... I would definitely have drowned.

This old man's bravery was awe-inspiring. Niall politely down-played the fact he'd risked his life to save me. He proved adept at deflecting our appreciation and, from that point on, the event faded and seldom ever re-surfaced. I was left with a feeling of enormous gratitude, yet Niall patiently emphasised I should not forever feel obligated to him.

The kitchen tent was warm despite the unseasonable coolness. The smell of smouldering mosquito coils and the occasional waft of smoke from our outdoor fire eventually replaced the aromas from Mum's cooking.

For another two hours or so we enjoyed Niall's convivial company. He was obviously relaxed and delighted in 'pulling our legs' and told his share of jokes. We covered many subjects that night: test cricket, horse racing, and the progress of the Snowy Mountains Scheme, which would eventually supply water and hydroelectricity for much of eastern Australia. When the stupidity of both World Wars was raised, Niall briefly mentioned that he'd served in the Boer War. At about 11:00 pm, Mum excused herself and went to bed and my sister and I followed shortly after. However, Dad stayed up with Niall for at least another hour.

Mid next morning, when Dad finally dragged himself from the camper trailer, he was in a reflective mood, albeit slightly hung-over. 'Bloody nice bloke that,' he muttered. 'Really interesting, too, but lonely poor bugger. Said he was going to sleep in his car but it looks like he's changed his mind and cleared off home. Ah, he should be OK. I'm pretty sure he said he lived near Bright, so he didn't have too far to go.'

Had I decided not to go fishing that particular day and those incredible few seconds of my life not occurred, an unexpected part of Australia's history would have gone untold. Regardless, that fluke encounter was the starting point of a wonderful few years for the de-facto family who 'adopted Niall Kelly'.

* * *

HISTORICAL NOTE: In the summer of 2003, DSE Project Fire Fighter Mrs. Cheryl Barber-Fankhauser drowned when on duty. She was swept to her death from the rear of a 4-wheel drive vehicle when it failed to cross the Buckland River, which was experiencing an unexpected flash flood. That incident occurred at a place known as The Junction, about 20 km from Porepunkah, where two tributaries flow into the Buckland. Ironically, that flash flood occurred during the immediate aftermath of the 2003 bushfire season, but, as with the 1958 flood, the intensity of the storm conditions, which triggered both floods, had not been forecast by the Weather Bureau.

* * *

WE SPENT most days in Niall's company during those 1957-58 Christmas holidays and every Easter and Christmas holidays over the following three years. As soon as we set up camp, Niall would invariably arrive and we happily resumed our companionable routine.

Niall was a keen punter and loved cribbage. He also had a shameless sense of humour, delighting in exaggeratedly mimicking Dad's frantic dashes to our long drop — the result of Dad having developed a 'belly wog'.

Despite Niall's age and failing vision, he was still a fantastic shot, often dropping a rabbit on-the-hop. When asked how he had become so good with his .22 rifle, he said, 'My dear mother taught me... as did a stupid bloody war.'

Fishing trips to the head of the Buckland Valley to the Beveridge pastoral lease were my favourite times with Niall. When presenting live baits we both caught many trout but, try as he might, Niall never mastered fly-casting.

But the best time of each day was twilight, after the flies had retired and before the mosquitoes attacked. During these tranquil times, Niall responded patiently and without any trace of annoyance when Jill and I innocently probed him about his life.

Long after the rest of us went to bed, Niall and Dad often sat around the campfire chatting until the early hours. Dad reckoned he always got the best from Niall when the scotch was produced. And to limit the boredom of our four-hour return drive to Melbourne, Dad often raised those talks, revealing snippets of Niall's intriguing reminiscences.

61

(THE SUMMER OF 1960/61)

We set up camp in our usual place beside Devil's Creek, eagerly awaiting our old friend. On cue, Niall arrived in his faithful DeSoto ute mid-morning the following day. With obvious effort he levered himself from the cabin and, uncharacteristically, shuffled slowly towards our tents. Sadly, he also by then had a pronounced stoop.

But his spirit was unchanged. After handshakes, hugs, and much good natured leg-pulling, Niall produced some unexpected Christmas presents. He gave several boxes of .22 rifle bullets to Jill, and I received his entire collection of wet and dry flies.

'Me eyes are buggered,' he explained dejectedly. 'None of those things are any good to me anymore.' Under protest, Dad accepted Niall's rifle. For Mum he produced a bottle of her favourite liqueur.

Despite the heat and the torment of the relentless bush flies, we spent a fabulous Christmas dinner together. But this holiday season was to be different. Niall's physical condition sadly ended our shooting and fishing trips in his company, but nevertheless he shared in our spoils. He was now in his eighty-second year and his loss of weight made him appear feeble. His eyes became rheumy and they gave the appearance he was crying for no reason. And although his personal hygiene was also slipping, he never took offence at Mum's quiet jibes about his body odour. Without hesitation, he headed for the creek and washed. Thankfully, neither his hearing nor his good humour ever abandoned him.

As the hot summer days rolled by, we regularly found Niall and Dad deep in conversation. They sat for hours in the shade on canvas camp chairs, dangling their feet in the cool water of Devil's Creek, from time to time listening to the races and drinking the occasional beer or whisky. The contrast between them was comical. There was Niall, the country bloke in his faded long green trousers and buttoned down long sleeve shirt; and Dad, the city bloke, naked except for his rolled-up shorts.

I remember overhearing my dad saying excitedly things like: 'Well I'll be buggered, what a find' or, 'Christ, that'll put the cat amongst the pigeons' or 'are you certain that's them?' Or, 'I don't give a bugger what others may think, mate; I believe you, go on, keep talking. And don't worry, mate, I'll find a way to get that stuff out in one piece.' Unbeknownst to me, it was during this time Niall confided his entire life story to my dad: Niall chose wisely.

Early in the New Year, Niall produced a paper-wrapped bundle. With great care he unwrapped a magnificent statuette of a horse. Ceremoniously, he offered that fragile form to my sister, his eyes glistening with real tears.

'I've got no use for it anymore. You like horses, eh, Jill? Believe me girl; there's been no better horse than this one. Get your dad to tell you and your brother all about this bloke one day. His name was Boss Boy.'

Although Niall was now weak and in obvious ill health, a few days later he insisted my dad accompany him on a drive up the Buckland Valley to a place known as The Junction. He wanted to show Dad where an amazing Chinaman's fortress and home once stood. Regrettably, the flood surge three years ago — the one that had nearly killed me — swept away most of what was left of the dwelling. But because Niall knew where to look, some of the handiwork of those skilful and mysterious Chinamen was still barely visible. To anyone else, the site would, at best, resemble either a failed or worked out gold mine.

During that trip my father obviously learnt something else. When he returned to our camp he started to describe what Niall had shown him, but then, for some reason, cut short his explanation and changed the subject. No matter how much we begged and cajoled Dad to tell us more, he steadfastly deflected our inquisitiveness. Years later, however, all was revealed to me.

On the 17th of January in 1961, just two days before our planned return to Melbourne, the afternoon was oppressively hot. Impressive cumulus clouds were rapidly building over the Barry Mountains, heralding some relief, but also announcing the threat of another storm. Just before dark it started raining heavily, driven along by strong, gusty winds sweeping down the Buckland valley. Undaunted by the wind and rain, Niall cheerfully volunteered to retrieve some ropes from his ute to help Dad tie down our tents. We all knew how strong and sustained these winds could be.

When Niall had not returned after ten minutes Dad began to worry. He draped a plastic raincoat over his head and shoulders and dashed from the tent to find out what delayed our friend.

As Dad disappeared into the rain he yelled back to us. 'He's probably had one of his giddy spells.'

Dad returned ten minutes later, wringing wet. Appearing dazed, he lowered himself into a canvas chair. 'The poor bugger's dead,' he quietly announced, his voice catching in distress as he spoke. 'Heart attack, I reckon. He's not breathing and there's no pulse. I... I was too late to help him.' Trying, but failing to totally control his emotions, Dad continued. 'I've covered him with a tarpaulin and left him in the tray of his ute. Only thing I could think of doing for the time being.'

I'd never seen my dad cry before, or since, but he broke down and wept unashamedly that night.

'I reckon he knew something was up,' he lamented quietly, while brushing away his tears. 'That's why he was so keen to offload his stuff and tell me so much about himself. God, I'm going to miss the old bugger.'

Mum tried her best to comfort all of us, and when Dad had his emotions under control he continued. 'We can't do anything for him now, so in the morning I'll take him into Bright and make a report to the cops. After that, we're going straight home.'

That was a dreadful night. The wind and rain lashed our tents, adding to our collective sadness and unease. Even our dog, Paddy, seemed to sense my dad's distress, sitting for hours with his head resting upon Dad's knees, just gazing into his face.

The storm departed as quickly as it arrived. At first light, Dad dressed then squelched his way to where Niall had relocated his ute earlier the previous evening. That relocation, to avoid possible tree damage resulting from the wind, meant walking about fifty yards up a rise and along the scrub-lined track leading into our campsite. This effectively, albeit unintentionally, put Niall's ute out of sight from our tents.

When Dad reached the end of that track, he froze. The old DeSoto was gone! In disbelief, he walked to the exact place where the ute had been parked. There were many human footprints in the surrounding soft mud — and muddy tyre tracks leading onto the bitumen surface of the Buckland road... but otherwise, nothing!

When Dad returned to our camp he threw himself into one of the camp chairs. He was totally rattled. After he'd animatedly explained what he had just found — or rather, not found — he yelled out in frustration. 'How the bloody hell can that happen? It's nineteen-sixty-bloody-one for Christ sake. Nobody steals dead people... surely?'

'Perhaps they do, love,' said Mum handing him a folded piece of paper. 'I found this on the table in the kitchen tent.' Despite Paddy's well earned guard dog reputation he had not challenged anything or anyone throughout the previous, wild, moonless night.

Dad unfolded the sheet of paper and read the badly formed but clear message. *Orla tell Cooloola to guide us here. Son soon be nearby Orla in special place of dreaming.* The note was signed 'Jimmie'. Dad relaxed at last. At least, *he* now fully understood Niall's disappearance.

Our family lost a dear friend that night, but still, several years elapsed before my father chose to enlighten me about Niall: the man who claimed to be the illegitimate son of Australia's most notorious bushranger, Ned Kelly.

$$* * *$$

WHEN I THINK BACK, I can recall a particularly warm day during the week before Niall's death. My parents finished shopping and decided to stop at the Porepunkah pub for a cold beer before returning to our campsite. Rather than go inside I sat outside in the shade and read the paper. I soon noticed several old aboriginals just across the road from the pub. Their strange presence haunted me that day and continued to haunt me for many years afterwards. I often wondered why they were there — about thirty yards away, motionless, and all staring straight at me — and why I was feeling as if I was being inter-rogated.

Eventually, I too, understood why they were there.

$$* * *$$

THE SAGA *you have just read is the telling of a missing piece of Australian history, which spanned approximately one hundred years. It records my first-hand recollections of events as they occurred: essentially the recollections of a dying man, as retold to me by my father.*

If this were a work of fiction you would not be able to invent its historical coincidences. I, therefore, believe this story closely reflects the reality. Let the sceptics and historians raise an eyebrow in disbelief if they so wish.

AN AFTERWORD

A friend, given the opportunity to read my finished manuscript, innocently commented: *'The veracity of your story seems to fit between possible and probable. But, by its very nature, will always be highly controversial.'*

It's up to you to decide.

Regardless, by now, you will realise this is a work of *faction* and that it is not about Ned Kelly but, rather, his one true love; an amazing Irish girl who likewise loved Ned dearly — their son, Niall Kelly — and the man who subsequently helped to raise Niall. This story is also a tribute to those whose altruism kept this story a secret for so long.

* * *

As luck would have it, after I had completed this story, I stumbled upon the following passage in Ian Jones's book, *Ned Kelly: a Short Life:*

"As a youth, Ned understood that the black man's sense of freedom acknowledged no bondage imposed by an alien race. He also learnt from them the ways of the bush and of its creatures, which he used for survival during his outlaw days. But Ned genuinely feared the black-trackers for

their skills and felt that inevitably they would track him down. It was Ned's respect for their race, which earned him the black man's ultimate tribute, an honour unrivalled by any other man, white or black."

That passage is not correct, though it was doubtless thought to be true at the time of its writing. *Despite* the decades of ill-will and persecution focussed upon Australian Aborigines by many white settlers and colonists, I fervently believe Ned Kelly would not have been the only recipient of such a tribute. Clearly, Aboriginals bestowed dreamtime status upon Orla, but did she ever learn of Ned's place in their mythology... I wonder? What's more, the unusual disappearances of Orla, Owen, and Niall's bodies also challenge that passage.

I also remain convinced that Aboriginals still possessed telepathic and hypnotic powers until at least 1961; they may still do so today. Regrettably, though, their ancient ritual of passing those skills down from one generation to the next has been significantly diminished due to the calculated and disgraceful killing of so many of their forebears.

My research revealed a reoccurring, shameful theme in Australia's history about which the early British settlers and some colonists of this country should forever be condemned. For example, their treatment of the Chinese on the Buckland Valley goldfields, and elsewhere, can at best be described as disgraceful.

But worse was the cruel, systematic slaughter (by either shooting, poisoning whipping, decapitation, being run through with a sword, or starvation) of so many of this country's native people. Those heinous, deliberate actions deprived subsequent generations of their land (their very life!), and almost eliminated a very special race of people. The ability of their descendants to maintain traditional skills such as telepathy and hypnotism (a variant of an ancient custom of 'pointing the bone') has regrettably all but disappeared.

Incredibly, monuments have been built to celebrate the life of some of those early settlers and colonists who thought nothing of rounding up essentially defenceless Aborigines and shooting them for 'a bit of Sunday afternoon sport'. Sickening, but true.

When researching this story I had the pleasure of meeting, Mr.

Barry Sinclair, a dedicated and highly regarded historian who lives in Uralla, NSW. That's when I learnt of a man named Michael (Micky) Clogher, (my character called Mad Mickey). This fellow held the Bostobrick Station N, N-W of Dorrigo and his atrocities are recorded in Mr. Sinclair's research notes, repeated in part below. Although not immortalised by a national monument, Mad Mickey is a perfect example of such inhumane action.

(Information source: NSW Death Register re Michael Clogher. Ref. 1912/5872.)

"Michael came from Rosscommon in Ireland. He was sentenced on the 4th July in 1837, for stealing sheep. He was given seven years and transported to Australia in November 1837, on the ship 'The Diamond'.

"After his parole, he was employed as a special military policeman and posted to the New England area. Mickey, as he was called, was an excellent tracker and greatly feared by the local aboriginal people. There were many stories of his harsh treatment of them, particularly after the Meldrum Massacre, where the farmer's wife, two of his workers, and three of his four children were killed by a local tribe. The act was retaliation by the aboriginals when they discovered the farmer had been lacing their flour with strychnine and killing many tribal members. As a result of those murders, Clogher is said to have rounded up over two hundred members of the tribe and driven them to their death over a cliff on the property."

The Meldrum Massacre was reported as 'an outrage and depredation inflicted by the blacks,' but the abhorrent, real massacre was essentially overlooked... and went unpunished.

Fortunately, not all settlers and colonists were of like disposition. The following is part of an article in the Readers Digest, Australian Places.

"Myall Creek Station, between Bingara and Delungra, symbolised a turning point in Australian race relations.

"The cold-blooded massacre of Aborigines there in 1838 was far from unusual. More than thirty Aborigines — mostly women and children and old men — were shot or decapitated and their bodies then burnt.

"But for the first time, after half a century of mounting strife, white men were punished for a crime against blacks. At the insistence of a newly appointed governor, Sir George Gipps, legal force was given to an unfashionable proposition that the native people were as much human beings as the colonists.

"Though the offending colonists were arrested, they were then released on the grounds of self-defence. Subsequently, a new trial was ordered where self-defence was no longer a justification... and those white men <u>were</u> hanged!

* * *

I suspect history readers will assert that my story is 'a highly idiosyncratic approach to accepted evidence'. One likely problem for historians, however, is that my story relates in part to an era when very little is either recorded or is indeed known about Ned's whereabouts and his activities. Conjecture probably ran rife during that period, but I have nevertheless relied heavily upon the spoken word of my late father as evidence of a brief but amazing romance during this little known 'grey period in Ned's otherwise robust life'. However, any such undeserving criticism of my account should not be advanced too hastily, certainly not without first disproving Orla's existence.

In fact, the majority of my source information comes from my father's recollections; detailed information was entrusted to him when it became obvious Niall's death was imminent.

Some may say my father simply made up a story to amuse us kids. Others may think Niall was just some old bloke either suffering from an overblown ego or simply a bloody good liar who loved spinning a good yarn. Those assertions do not fit either my father or Niall's character. In fact, I find both assertions offensive. My dad deliberately kept the truth of certain family matters from me when I was young, or delayed those truths, but he never lied to me. And I doubt very much Niall could have pulled the wool over the eyes of my father. It was also obvious to me that Niall unquestioningly trusted my dad.

Nobody is compelled to accept this story. However, whilst physical proof is probably long gone and the word of my father is second hand, I am not prepared to undermine his story by contradicting its genuineness. Over the years, my dad's recollections never varied; the same point he made in relation to Niall's personal account.

Our family held tangible evidence regarding Boss Boy: the loss of his statue is an embarrassment, however. Having been charged with the safe keeping of potentially a priceless artwork, we somehow managed to smash it. Regardless, Boss Boy's legacy should live on; as should the Waler breed of horses of which he was undoubtedly one of that breed's finest examples.

And perhaps one day, a lucky fisherman might still stumble upon Tom Lloyd's armour before time returns it to the earth forever. However, in the fifty or so years since that summer of '60/61, I have fished the Buckland River many times in the water upstream from The Junction... I've never found anything, which even vaguely resembled a fifth suit of Kelly armour.

Of those photographs Niall kept in his wallet, it's my guess they are still with him in his resting place, near Orla and Owen, somewhere in the Cooloola National Park, in Queensland. Regrettably, also, I only vaguely recall seeing those photographs of Ned and those dear to him.

* * *

Sceptics are also entitled to ask, 'Why did I leave it until February of 2007 to start recording this passage of our history?' They can be assured there was no hidden agenda in that delay, I simply placed more importance upon raising a family and running a business. Nevertheless, the events of Part 4 are, notwithstanding trivial issues long forgotten, substantially as they occurred.

However, I did exercise license in naming some people, those known to have been historically involved — whose names my father could not always 'swear as being correct'. Consequently, names such as Rupert Golding, Peter Jones, Martin Ambrose, Tylah and Jesse, Robert D'Angelese, Ken, James, Michael, etc. are all fictitious.

To protect the 'Stewart' and 'McIntyre' families, their Christian and surnames are also fictitious. However, Jeanie, Frank, Owen, Anne, Joan and Alf were real people. Similarly, Charlie and Ong were real people. The name Ong, however, whilst often used by Chinese settlers as a Christian name, was probably the brother's surname.

Cocko and Boss Boy were also real; my father insisted their names were factual.

Andrew Fisher, of course, was a leading statesman and former Australian Prime Minister.

The Beveridge brothers are still remembered by many families in North Eastern Victoria as 'gentlemen pioneers'. In fact, a brass plaque commemorating these men is fixed to a rock on the northern end of their 'top' grazing lease in the Buckland Valley.

Lahni, Ruthie, and Jimmie were interesting people to discover. Of their existence I have no doubt; however, their names are 'borrowed'.

And of Orla and Niall? They were very real people — their Christian names are unchanged. Orla's family name is deliberately fictitious.

None of the characters in this book reflect the true persona or character of any known person sharing my 'borrowed names'. All other characters are essentially creations of my imagination. I believe 'like people' would no doubt have lived and experienced some contact with Orla and Niall, at some time.

* * *

In part, this story can only be fiction, for which I make no apology. But, nevertheless, I am here today to tell you I firmly believe Ned Kelly's son saved my life in January 1958.

Also, by necessity, verifiable historical events accompany this story. Needless to say, elements of this story have been embellished to provide the most likely continuity of events.

Probably the most important period is when Orla met Ned; a

period recorded by historians 'when Ned was like a wandering wind in the night'. In fact, *very little* is known of Ned's whereabouts for most of 1879 up to, and including, May of 1880. And although much conjecture to the contrary seems to have prevailed amongst 'the locals', and in police records of that time, even less of what people were saying had any substance whatsoever.

Place names are as correct as possible, although there were periods where Niall's whereabouts are somewhat vague; for example, *precisely* where he went after he lost Ruthie, and later when he learnt that Owen had drowned.

* * *

Niall was, arguably, a hero. He died a very wealthy person; although in his old age he gave the appearance of 'not having two bob to rub together'. His life experience was unique, eventually coming to terms with who his parents were, and never doubted the love they shared, albeit, so briefly.

He was also blessed: Orla's quasi-family, the Stewarts and, of course, her amazing friends Tom Lloyd, Ned's cousin Kate Lloyd, and Joan and Alf McIntyre all prevented Niall from being psychologically savaged by the dubious history created by Ned.

However, Niall confided to my father that he often wondered what it would have been like to grow up alongside Ned, to have talked with him, or to have hugged him, or to have simply shaken his hand. I found that breathtakingly sad.

Losing his good mate, Peter Jones, the vet who committed suicide under such baffling circumstances at the end of the Boer War, undoubtedly, rattled Niall.

* * *

What puzzled me for a long time, however, is why my dad never reported Niall's death, and the missing DeSoto ute. I suspect it was because he doubted the police would have given his story any credibility. Perhaps, Dad was simply honouring a dying man's wishes, that Niall remain anonymous.

And what of the timber mill in Gympie? Well, in March of 2008, I visited Gympie but could find no tangible evidence of its existence; though several mills ceased operation in the mid 1930s. Perhaps some of the exhibits at the Gympie Historical Society came from that mill?

Also, have you wondered what became of Orla's pistols? I certainly have. Unfortunately, I cannot recall my father mentioning their final resting place, but I have two theories. First, the Stewarts may have taken it upon themselves to collect and dispose of Orla's clothing and belongings after her death. It would have been consistent with their stage in life to have gladly disposed of the pistols. To have sold them is nonsense; they certainly did not need the money. Second, Lahni knew how those pistols had shaped Orla's life, but it's my understanding all aboriginal gravesites are special, personal and sacred, and not the place where artefacts are assembled. Perhaps, she made an exception.

By the way, are you wondering what became of Niall's fortune — well, some of it anyway? It wasn't long after Niall's death that my parents purchased the house they had been renting in Kew and undertook extensive renovations. They also purchased a residential block of land on the Mornington Peninsula in Victoria and, about a year later, bought a brand new Chevrolet sedan, plus a thirty-foot caravan.

ACKNOWLEDGMENTS

• Dr. Bob Rich: Thanks, mate, for your patient guidance. At times apparently ruthless, but always on the money.

•Peter Watt: One of Australia's greatest writers. If you don't believe me, read his marvellous work. Thanks Pete, for encouraging me to tell this story and to maintain the belief that I could do it. Now I know exactly what you meant by 'others can never really see what it takes to write a story. Only you and I know that as we ply our craft'.

•Brian Cook's team at the Manuscript Appraisal Agency: for their frank, measured and unbiased considerations of my work; thank you all.

• The late Clive Baum: A greatly valued friend, yet often the devil's advocate. Without his eye for history, and his clinical opinions, this story may well have ended up like Tom's suit of armour — collecting dust.

•The Readers Digest Illustrated Guide to Australian Places: thanks to all those who had a hand in putting together such rich snapshots of Australia's beauty and amazing history.

•Barry and Morna Sinclair: An unexpected source of historical information; i.e. accurate background material relating to life in the early days of the Dorrigo scrub country and of questionable characters ranging the bush during that time.

•Daphne Yarram: who is not only the Manager of the Yoowinna Wurnalung Healing Service in Lakes Entrance, but also a respected leader and role model in many aboriginal communities throughout Victoria. Daphne is very proud of her heritage and continues to maintain cultural practices, beliefs, traditions, and values reflected in her daily life. Thanks for allowing me to bounce my 'Aboriginal themes' off you and for giving credibility to those themes.

•My sister, Jill: thanks for introducing me to Daphne Yarram. Thank you also for calling my attention to the overuse of certain words and for your suggestions in the use of impact words and phrases.

•My dear friend, Kaye Lincoln: Thank you for your 'wake up calls' that there is one gender who just might take offence at some of my more macho extravagances.

•My son, Callum: Thanks for allowing me to use you as a sounding board. Your bemused facial expressions, rather than your benevolent words of praise, gave it away for me: looks that said, 'The old bugger might be onto something!'

•My first wife, Yvonne: thank you for your encouragement, typically, 'Bloody hell Tucks! This is really good.' (And for your 'eagle eye' in spotting overlooked grammatical errors.)

•Mary Steepe, Ray Garland, Graham Randle, and historian Robin Budge: Thank you all, for your unexpected and enthusiastic assistance in providing me with incredible historical information about the dingo fence that meanders across the Barrington Tops and environs. Hopefully, someone will more completely document the heritage of this fence and encapsulate the many marvellous stories associated with its existence.

•Liz and Trevor Watt, former booksellers, in Sale, who alerted me to potential publishing pitfalls and encouraged me to complete my writing journey... thank you.

•If only I could acknowledge in person, my late mum and dad, Marion and Frank Tucker. What amazing parents. I reckon they would have approved of, and enjoyed reading this story.

• Last but not least, my friend, Tony Park. Not only is he recognised as one of the very best authors on the international stage, but at every opportunity advances the need for preservation of all wildlife. Thanks too, for sharing your knowledge enabling me to enhance this novel.

BIBLIOGRAPHY

- *The Readers Digest Illustrated Guide to Australian Places*
- *The Norman Tindale Tribal Boundaries in Aboriginal Australia*
- *Ned Kelly: a Short Life* by Ian Jones
- *The Fatal Friendship* by Ian Jones
- *The Ned Kelly Encyclopaedia* by Justin Corfield
- *Matthew Brady & Ned Kelly* by Paul Williams
- *The Secret River* by Kate Grenville
- *Our Sunshine* by Robert Drewe
- *The Dreaming* by Barbara Wood
- *A Ghost called Thunderbolt* by Stephan Williams
- *The Boer War* by Denis Judd & Keith Surridge
- *Snowy. The making of modern Australia* by Brad Collis
- *True History of the Kelly Gang* by Peter Carey
- *Ben Hall* by Frank Clune
- *History of Australian Bushranging* — Volumes 1 & 2 by Charles White
- *Sources of Australian History* by Professor M. Clark
- (www.siezethemagic.com) 'Interview with An Aboriginal Woman' by Loraine Mafi Williams — 'a traditional teacher and custodian of aboriginal customs and wisdom; who tells it as it is'.

TREVOR TUCKER

Trevor Tucker retired in 2005 from the oil and gas industry and although his first interest in writing was from a technical perspective, it soon evolved to 'faction'. The author adds: *Though having been bitten by the writing bug, I sometimes wonder if I have retired.'* A chance meeting with a man who saved his life, soon revealed a history that needed to be rewritten; Trevor took it as his responsibility to share a story related to his father.

Ned Kelly's Son is the author's first novel and his interests in Australian history, bushwalking, and exploring his homeland, reflect with passion throughout the book. With believable characters and a reliance on recorded history, he implants a strong probability of something neglected or overlooked in previous records about Australia's most notorious bushranger, Ned Kelly.

Trevor's other interests include spending time with his kids and grandkids, writing, fishing, reading, bike riding, Test cricket, AFL football, and power flow yoga. Future works include another novel of Australian history and an anecdotal short story collection.